Passion and
the ni

# HER
## *Billionaire*
# BOSS

Complete your collection with
all four books!

# The professional is about to get very, very personal!

Four fabulous collections of stories from your favourite authors

**Her Mediterranean Boss**
Helen Brooks
Barbara McMahon
Trish Morey

*March 2009: Hot-blooded Latin passion in the boardroom – and the bedroom!*

**Her Billionaire Boss**
Cathy Williams
Jessica Hart
Kathryn Ross

*April 2009: Experience wealth and glamour in the boardroom – and the bedroom!*

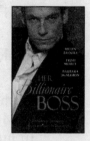

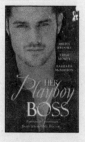

**Her Outback Boss**
Sharon Kendrick
Barbara Hannay
Lindsay Armstrong

*May 2009: Journey to Australia and fall in 'ove with these commanding tycoons!*

**Her Playboy Boss**
Penny Jordan
Jennie Adams
Chantelle Shaw

*June 2009: He works hard, he plays harder – can he be tamed?*

# HER
## *Billionaire*
# BOSS

**CATHY WILLIAMS**
**JESSICA HART**
**KATHRYN ROSS**

M&B™ and M&B™ with the Rose Device
are trademarks of the publisher.
Harlequin Mills & Boon Limited, Eton House,
18-24 Paradise Road, Richmond, Surrey TW9 1SR

HER BILLIONAIRE BOSS © by Harlequin Books S.A. 2009

The Billionaire Boss's Bride © Cathy Williams 2004
Contracted: Corporate Wife © Jessica Hart 2005
The Boss's Mistress © Kathryn Ross 1998

ISBN: 978 0 263 86896 8

010-0409

Printed and bound in Spain
by Litografia Rosés S.A., Barcelona

# THE BILLIONAIRE
# BOSS'S BRIDE

**CATHY WILLIAMS**

**Cathy Williams** is originally from Trinidad, but has lived in England for a number of years. She currently has a house in Warwickshire, which she shares with her husband Richard, her three daughters Charlotte, Olivia and Emma, and their pet cat Salem. She adores writing romantic fiction and would love one of her girls to become a writer – although at the moment she is happy enough if they do their homework and agree not to bicker with one another.

# CHAPTER ONE

THIS, the first day of Tessa Wilson's new job, was not proving to be a very good day. She stood at the reception desk in the foyer of the avant-garde glasshouse that housed the computer software group for whom she was now working on a super, quite unbelievably bumper salary, and frowned at the chap smiling at her. His badge said that he was called George Grafton and he looked like a George. Plump, balding, comfortable. Tessa's first job had been with a George. They could have been brothers.

'What do you mean you saw them all leaving the building this morning?' Tessa looked at her watch. It was a sensible Casio watch. No frills, no calendar indicating day, month and year, no option to see what time it was in all major cities across the world or to time herself should she spontaneously decide to do a spot of exercise. It was as practical as she was. Practical, diligent and *punctual*.

'And it's eight-thirty in the morning! Surely...'

'You'd think so.' The man at Reception nodded sagely, reading her mind. 'Most people are buzzing in to start the week, but...' He raised his shoulders in an expressive gesture of incomprehension.

Tessa glanced around. Yes, people were pouring into the squat five-storeyed building, which was cunningly designed like Lego bricks surrounding an inner courtyard with benches and eating areas on most of the ground floor. Busy, industrious people who worked for the other companies there. Meanwhile, she was to believe that everyone working for the Diaz Hiscock group had mysteriously decided to take a day off for no apparent reason. It didn't make sense. She wondered nervously whether this was some sort of test, some kind of trick initiation procedure that she was required to get through.

'I'm sorry. This is my first day here. Look. See for yourself.' She pulled out her letter of employment and pointed to the date she was supposed to commence work.

'Yep. You've come on the right day, all right.' Now the man was looking sympathetic, as though she were the recipient of some brutally bad news. 'Can't explain it. I mean, you can go up to the floor and have a look for yourself, but I was here at six and they were streaming out of the building.'

'Maybe they all went out for breakfast,' Tessa said hopefully. That, in itself, was a ludicrous notion. What sort of company operated along the lines of mass desertion at the start of a busy working day, by employees who needed to have breakfast when they surely would have only just arrived?

'Third floor.' He nodded over to where three lifts were furiously trying to deliver employees to their various destinations and reached to answer the telephone.

Tessa dubiously looked at the suited crowd and wiped her sweaty palms on her skirt. She had been full of enthusiasm when she had got out of bed at seven. A little nervous, sure, but she was an experienced PA and confident that she could handle whatever was thrown at her.

Now she wasn't too sure. Now, it occurred to her that the whole interviewing process had been a little on the odd side.

Yes, Diaz Hiscock was a family company, a small but successful and powerful family company, but hadn't it been a little strange that her interview for the job had been with the boss's *mother*? And conducted in the elegant sitting room of a house, over scones and tea? Six weeks ago, Tessa had found it very charming and such a blessed relief from the frantic pace of her old firm. Now she just wondered whether she was dealing with lunatics and had made a fatal error in jacking in her ordinary but perfectly secure job working for an accountancy firm.

'I suppose I'd better... Well!' She neatly folded up her letter and stuffed it back into her handbag. 'Thanks for your help!' She extended one polite hand and smiled. 'And I guess I'll be seeing you around!'

'If not in ten minutes!' He grinned with his hand over the receiver and she smiled weakly back.

'Ha, ha.' If that was meant to sound reassuring then she sincerely hoped that George never decided to go into counselling.

Her face was burning as she waited by the lift, sneaking in when the doors opened and maintaining zero eye contact with anyone else in it, focusing one hundred per cent on the gradual ascent of the lift to the third floor. She wondered whether there would be a roar of laughter behind her when she stepped out onto the third floor, whether they all knew that floor three was vacant.

Roar of laughter, no. Vacant floor, yes. Just as George had predicted. It wasn't a huge office. Reception desk, empty. Tastefully arranged desks with occasional partitions filled the space behind the reception desk. All empty. And as Tessa made her way along the corridor, her feet making no sound as they sunk into the thick pile coffee-coloured carpet, she could feel her heart sinking. Offices to the left and the right, empty. Spacious offices, some with several plasma-screen computer terminals, offices that emanated financial well being, all deserted. The lighting wasn't on and the bleak winter sunshine struggled to make its way through the glass and into the uninhabited office.

She felt like an intruder, but she switched the lights on and they buzzed into fluorescent life. Why the outer door hadn't been locked, she had no idea. Anyone could enter, provided they could get past George. She cleared her throat, meaningfully and noisily, and ventured a tentative, 'Hello.'

The silence that greeted this was deafening.

'You'll find my son a very interesting man to work for,' Mrs Diaz had assured her, sitting back in her high-backed chair and folding her hands elegantly on her lap.

By *interesting* Tessa had assumed willing to give her responsibility. That had been one of the downsides of her last job. She'd done a lot and she'd been respected for what she'd done, but the chances to broaden her horizons hadn't been there. She had heard the adjective *interesting* and been immediately captivated by the prospects it had promised.

Well, day one was proving to be very interesting indeed, if you could call walking around in a ghost office, wearing a suit, interesting.

'Poor Curtis hasn't had much luck with secretaries ever since Nancy quit to live in Australia with her husband.' Mrs Diaz had shaken her head sorrowfully while Tessa had waited for her to expand. Somehow Mrs Diaz was not the sort of lady to interrupt with a barrage of questions. 'He's had a series of doodle heads, little glamour pusses fluttering around and batting their eyelashes. Quite, quite unsuitable for the job of working for my son.'

From the looks of it, anyone would have been quite, quite unsuitable for working for a man who shut up shop at six on a Monday morning, when his new secretary was supposed to arrive that day.

Tessa reluctantly proceeded down the corridor, glancing into the various rooms, increasingly aware that she wasn't going to find any signs of life. It left her in the awkward position of either leaving and risking not being around if everyone in the office reappeared as mysteriously as they seemed to have vanished, or else sitting around in ghost town central twiddling her thumbs until her official going home time of five-thirty.

She was frantically trying to rack up the pros and cons afforded by going or staying when she heard it. A sound. Coming from the office at the very end of the corridor. She picked up speed and walked towards the noise, making sure to check all offices *en route* just in case.

The plaque on the door indicated Curtis Diaz's office. It was slightly ajar. She pushed it open, stepped through into a smaller outside room, through which was a much bigger office, and this time the winter sun was making no headway because thick cream velvet curtains were resolutely closed across the sprawling bank of windows.

Tessa's eyes adjusted to the gloom and she immediately saw the reason for the closed curtains.

Stretched out on a sofa against one side of the wall was a man, lying flat on his back, one arm flung behind him, the other resting contentedly on his stomach. The soft noise that had drawn her attention was simply the sound of his intermittent snoring. In the middle of her appalled inspection, the man cleared his throat and turned onto his side, scaring her witless in the process.

He was wearing a pair of jeans and a long-sleeved rugby-style shirt. Tessa tiptoed towards him and the view expanded into a swarthy face with a hint of stubble darkening his chin. Rumpled black hair completed the picture. Tessa stared, heart thumping, calming herself with the knowledge that at least she wasn't in the building alone. She might have stepped into the twilight zone on the third floor, but all the other floors were teeming with people and good old George was only a phone call away.

She stepped briskly past the inert figure on the couch, reached for the cord by the wall and pulled.

'Okay, buster! Who are you and what are you doing in this office?'

The man struggled awake, groaning, and then subsided back, this time with one of the cushions covering his face.

Tessa walked towards him, gazed at the rumpled sight with distaste, and yanked the cushion straight out from beneath his arm, and this time it worked. Gratified, she watched as the bum blearily hoisted himself into a semi-sitting position and focused on where she was standing with her hands pinned to her hips and her mouth narrowed into a line of uncompromising severity.

'I don't know how you got into this office, buddy...' Of course she knew! Hadn't it been wide open to whoever might choose to enter? Hadn't she herself wondered at the utter lack of basic security? 'But you can get right out! This isn't a doss house for any passing vagrant who decides to come in for a quick kip!'

'Wha...?'

'Oh, yes, you heard me!' Tessa could feel herself well and truly on a roll now. First, she had showed up, *on time* and dressed in a spanking new suit, ready to make a good impression on day one, only to find herself wandering through an empty office like a fool, and as if that wasn't enough here she was, confronted by a supine figure snoring away merrily, probably sleeping off a hangover from whatever bottle of methylated spirits he had downed the night before outside the building.

'Look at you!' she snapped, leaning forward and wrinkling her nose as the apparition pushed himself into a more upright sitting position so that he could look at her in perplexed astonishment. 'You should be ashamed of yourself!'

'I should?'

'You most certainly should! An able-bodied young man like yourself, sneaking into an unoccupied office and just *going to sleep*! Don't tell me you can't get out there and find yourself a job!' The able-bodied young man was staring at her in a way that was beginning to make her feel very self-conscious. He was also, now that she could see him properly, an extremely good looking specimen, underneath the scruffy demeanour. His face was darkly handsome, in a tough, rugged sort of way, a compelling face that made her breath catch in her throat for a second or two. Tessa got a grip of herself and glared.

'I'm afraid I'm going to have to report you,' she said quietly, while narrowed blue eyes began to gleam with amusement. 'And you won't find that very funny! Have your fun and grin away, but when the police come and you're thrown into some cell *downtown*, you *won't be grinning*!'

'*Cell downtown?*' He couldn't help himself. His lips twitched and he grinned with wicked amusement. 'This isn't New York, this is London. I think you've been watching too many American police shows.' He raked his fingers through his hair and reluctantly stood up.

Disconcerted, Tessa took a couple of steps backwards. The man, who was now massaging the back of his neck with his hand and glancing round the office in an offhand way, was very tall. Very tall, with a solid muscularity that was a bit alarming.

'Maybe I have,' she said placatingly. She watched warily as the man ambled over to the window and peered out.

'What time is it, anyway?'

'A little after half past eight.'

That met with a grunt. 'No wonder I feel like something the cat brought in,' he muttered, swinging round to face her.

'I'm going to have to call George...' Tessa began. He had made her feel like a melodramatic idiot for having mentioned police and cells. George would have to deal with this. It wasn't part of her job—secretary and makeshift security guard for premises that should have been locked in the first place.

'Who are you, anyway?'

'Who am *I*?' Tessa regarded the man with amazement. 'Let's just say that I'm the person who found you comatose on a sofa, *trespassing, from all accounts*.'

'Yes, but do you have a name?' He plonked himself down on the leather swivel chair at the desk and she gaped incredulously at the sheer nerve. 'Oh, God. No. Skip that question. It's coming to me now. I know who you are.' He pushed the chair back just far enough to enable him to stretch his legs out onto the desk, then he folded his hands behind his head and proceeded to look at her with a highly amused, alert expression.

'Do you? You mean you're a trespasser *as well as* being a clairvoyant? I'm impressed! I'm not too sure whether George will be—'

'You're Miss Wilson.' He grinned but with the ground rapidly shifting underneath her feet, grinning back was the last thing Tessa felt inclined to do. 'Have a seat. Really. You look as though you might just fall down if you don't.'

'I think I need to call George...' she said uncertainly, sitting down.

'You don't. Well, you *can* if you really feel you need to, but believe me, that'll just lead to embarrassment. Yours. Look, let me put you out of your misery and introduce myself...' He stood up, all formality now, even though the impression was hijacked by the casualness of his clothes. 'I'm Curtis Diaz.' He stretched out his hand and smiled with sickening kindness.

'You...you can't be...' Tessa ignored the outstretched hand and grasped the handbag on her lap tightly.

Well, she *had* been bored with the monotonous tedium of her last job! What better antidote than to be thrust into a surreal world where she didn't have a clue as to what was going on?

'Why not?'

'Because...'

'I know.' He looked ruefully down at himself and shook his head. 'Code of dress, right? Powerful men who run powerful companies dress in pinstriped suits and ties, always carefully knotted at the neck.'

Tongue-tied and mortified, Tessa stared back at him, her mouth half open and a delicate bloom of colour rising up her cheeks. She wasn't fashioned to deal with situations like these. Above all things, Tessa Wilson liked to be in control. Time and time again she had seen people passively and helplessly steamrollered by events. It happened in their jobs, it happened with their love lives. She often wondered what would have happened to her and Lucy if she had been like all those people who never seemed to cater for the unforeseen.

The unforeseen had happened with her and she had dealt with it, and had continued dealing with life by reining it in. She liked to know where she was going and how she was going to get there because working things out, knowing where she stood, made her feel safe.

She also resented the fact that he was laughing at her.

'I don't know what's going on,' she said stiffly. Her body was ramrod straight in the chair.

'And I apologise. Profusely.' He levered himself back into his chair and reclined back. 'Allow me to explain. My team and I have just completed a weekend of virtual solid work, thrashing a deal out with one of our suppliers and then finalising the nitty-gritty with the lawyers. We didn't finish until the early hours of the morning at which point I decided to let them all go home and catch up on some well-deserved rest.'

So this was what his mother had meant by interesting, Tessa thought dazedly. When she had used that word, Tessa had tied it up in her head with the job and not the man. The man, she was slowly realising, was nothing like she had expected. She had expected someone a bit like Mrs Diaz. Sophisticated, very English and probably fair haired. The man staring at her, waiting for her to digest his information, couldn't have been further from her expectations. Restless, passionate energy vibrated out of him in waves and the only bit of him that resembled his mother were his eyes, which were as blue and as piercing, except a lot more dramatic against his olive colouring and dark, springy hair.

'Right. Well, I wish you had telephoned me to explain that my services wouldn't be required today...'

'Never occurred to me,' Curtis informed her truthfully. He idly switched on one of the two computer terminals on his desk and it buzzed into life with a faint humming sound.

Poor woman, he thought, glancing across at the rigid pink-faced figure sitting opposite him. He really should have stood firm and recruited his own secretary, but he loved his mother dearly and giving in had eventually seemed preferable to staging a protracted war. Mothers liked to think they knew best and his mother was no exception to the rule. She had stared at him gimlet-eyed and told him in no uncertain terms that hiring floozies, as she had called them, was a waste of company money.

'But they look good,' he had protested, thinking back to the last one, a red-haired, buxom wench who had worn delightful handkerchiefs, which she had loosely claimed were miniskirts.

'Which is hardly a satisfactory recommendation when it comes to being a secretary.'

The tirade had gone on and on until he had thrown up his hands in resignation and left it to her to sort out.

Unfortunately, looking at the Tessa character now, he could immediately see the downsides of his mother's well-intentioned but misguided rationale.

The poor girl looked as though she had suddenly found herself wandering in the vicinity of hell without any map giving her the quickest route back to normality. He sighed under his breath and raked his fingers through his hair.

'Look, Miss Wilson...now that you're here, maybe we should go and grab some breakfast, have a bit of a chat...'

'Some breakfast...?'

'That's right,' Curtis said, curbing his irritation, 'I haven't eaten since yesterday...some time...' He stood up and stretched, eyeing her out of the corner of his eye, which only confirmed his opinion that she was not going to be suitable for the job.

'I'm hungry,' he told her bluntly, throwing on his over-coat. 'I need something to eat and dried-up slices of pizza in the bin just isn't going to do it for me. And we need to have a little talk.'

Tessa scrambled to her feet and hurried after him as he headed out of his office. It took quite some running. High-heeled shoes might look the part but when it came to scurrying after someone who walked at a pace that most people ran, they weren't exactly practical. She nearly careered into him when he finally came to a dead stop by the lift.

'So,' he began conversationally, noticing the way she had edged away from him in the confines of the lift, back pressed against the side as though her life depended on it, 'it must have been a bit of a shock when you came to work this morning and found the offices empty...?'

'I was a little surprised.'

'Hmm. A little surprised. Diplomatic choice of words.'

'George at Reception had warned me that he had witnessed a mass exodus earlier in the morning, but, naturally, I thought that he might have exaggerated a bit. I...well, I wasn't prepared for...'

'A scene from a late-night horror movie?' The lift doors disgorged them back into the expansive waiting area where George was still in attendance. He winked at her and exchanged a large grin with Curtis.

'So you managed to find one still alive and kicking, then?'

'Don't tease her, George. She's had a very stressful day so far.'

The banter made Tessa feel suddenly foolish and sidelined and the unfortunate butt of some ongoing joke at her expense. 'I wouldn't say *stressful*,' she retorted, 'just a little *disorienting*.'

She felt the warm pressure of his fingers on her elbow as he led her towards the revolving door and heard the deep throb of his laughter, which brought on an attack of unwarranted confusion.

'Okay. Disorienting. Are you going to be warm enough out here with just a suit? The café's not far but it's still a walk...'

'I'm fine.' She resisted the temptation to add that she would have brought her coat if she had foreseen a day that involved walking. But, on day one, she had decided to treat herself to a taxi both ways and had not envisaged needing anything heavier than her cream-and-black-flecked woollen suit.

'I don't suppose your last job involved too many episodes of *disorientation*?'

'Most jobs don't.' Their destination was within sight.

Literally a good, old-fashioned café with no trimmings. It was heaving, with an eclectic mix of suited businessmen, rough-and-ready workmen, taxi drivers and women who looked as though they had spent the night on the tiles and were on their way home. Most, though, were taking their breakfasts away with them and it was a relief to be out of the cold and in the warmth.

'Do you come here often?' Tessa heard herself ask inanely.

'Does a good breakfast. Now, what will you have?' He positioned her at one of the tables and narrowed his eyes to read the blackboard with the specials, which was behind her.

'Coffee.'

'Right. Wait here.' Within ten minutes he was back carrying a tray on which were two steaming mugs of coffee and a plate mountainously piled with bacon, egg, black pudding and what looked suspiciously like fried bread.

Oh, your arteries are really going to thank you for that injection of cholesterol, she was tempted to say.

'Don't even think of saying what's going through your head.'

'I wasn't thinking anything!'

'Tell me about your last job,' was all he replied, leaving her to wonder uncomfortably how he had managed to read her mind.

'I told your mother...well, it's all there on my CV.' Comprehension filtered through. 'But I guess you didn't read my CV.'

'I left the finer details of your employment to my mother. Your last job?'

Tessa sipped her coffee, which was surprisingly aromatic. 'I worked for a firm of accountants. Not one of the top three, but one of the bigger ones, doing all the usual stuff. I'm fully computer literate and can handle pretty much anything from spreadsheets to invoicing.' Silence followed that, interrupted only by his eating. 'I've also arranged training courses, overseen meetings, in short done everything a PA is trained to do.'

Curtis washed down the last of his breakfast with a generous mouthful of coffee, then sat back in his chair and looked at her assessingly.

'And you enjoyed it, did you?'

'Well, yes, of course. I was there for a number of years—'

'Why the change of job, in that case?'

Gone was the light-hearted, unconventional man who had confronted her at eight-thirty that morning. In its place was someone shrewd and forthright and very focused.

'It wasn't going anywhere.' Tessa flinched away from that disconcerting blue gaze. 'I felt that I needed to expand my horizons and, in a company like that, it's only possible if you're one of the professionals.'

'But you liked working there, aside from the obvious limitations, am I right?' He watched as she nodded and could hear her wondering where this was going. 'You liked the order, the environment, the routine.'

'Those things are very important, I think, in the successful running of a company,' Tessa said defensively.

Order. Routine. Yes, she did like those things. They formed the perimeter of her life and always had. How else would she have been able to cope with bringing up her unruly ten-year-old sister when she had only been going on eighteen herself? In fact, compared to Lucy, or maybe because of her, she, Tessa, had always had her head firmly screwed on. Her parents had always praised her for that. Lucy might be the beauty with the ebullience, but Tessa was the responsible one, the one on whom they relied. The one on whom they had still been relying when their car had swerved into a tree on a rainy night back home. Tessa had mourned and grieved and picked up the pieces the best she could and, yes, had fallen back on order and routine to help her through.

She blinked away the sudden intrusion of her past and, when she looked at him, she found him staring at her, his bright blue eyes narrowed on her face.

'Don't you agree with me?' The way he looked at her made her feel hot and bothered, even though he didn't seem to be looking at her in a critical way. Perhaps it was the level of containment, at odds with the aggressively confident and outgoing exterior. Here was a man, she suspected, who did precisely as he liked and yet remained a closed book. It was nerve-racking. 'I mean, you run a successful company. Surely you don't just jump in a haphazard manner from one day to the next, hoping for the best and keeping your fingers crossed?'

Curtis threw back his head and laughed. 'No. Not quite. That approach doesn't often work, although it sounds as though it could be quite a lot of fun.'

Tessa shuddered. *Fun?* Never knowing from one minute to the next what life was going to throw at you? Not a chance.

'You don't agree? Well, never mind. So you've worked in your last job for...how many years?'

'Nine, give or take a few months,' she said uncomfortably.

Curtis gave a low whistle under his breath.

'And you are...? Age...?'

'Twenty-eight.'

'At work at nineteen and then staying put with the same company...'

'Which should tell you how experienced I am.' Why did

she have the sinking feeling that this was the interview that should have been conducted from the start? 'I'm sorry. I thought I *had* the job. I thought your mother was in a position to offer it to me.' She could feel herself perspiring under her armpits and she wished she had removed her jacket when she had first sat down, just as he had done with his overcoat. He looked as comfortable as a cat on a feather quilt while she felt rattled, uneasy and hot.

'Oh, of course she was.' He shrugged. 'It's a family firm. I run it completely, take full responsibility for all profits and losses, but my brother and my mother are naturally still interested in what's going on, and occasionally my mother will offer her input. In the matter of my hiring someone to work for me, she insisted, and I expect she told you why.'

'She mentioned that some of your secretaries in the past had been a bit…unsuitable.'

'Except I don't imagine she was quite so restrained in her description.'

Tessa frowned and tucked her hair neatly behind her ears. She had fine, slippery, very smooth shoulder-length auburn hair that had a tendency to slide forward and brush her face if she wasn't careful about tying it back. Today, on Lucy's advice, she had decided to wear it loose so that she wouldn't look like a schoolmarm on her first day out. Now, she was regretting the impulse because for some reason she felt as though she needed the protection of her normally very restrained look.

'I'll bet she referred to them as *bimbos*,' Curtis added helpfully as Tessa was struggling to come up with a diplomatic way of paraphrasing what had been said to her.

'The thing is…' He leaned forward and rested his arms on the table. He had pushed up the sleeves of his jumper and she noticed that he had very strong forearms, dusted with black hair. He, too, wore a simple watch although his looked crashingly expensive, unlike hers. 'Bimbos suited me. How can I explain this?'

Tessa's heart went into freefall at that rhetorical question.

'I don't work in an environment that's anything like the one you have spent the last nine years, give or take a month or so, enjoying. The world of computers and computer software is far more about creativity and vibrancy and foresight than the world of accountants. The bimbos might have been a little lax when it came to typing and shorthand but they knew how to work around me.'

'Your mother said the last one was only there for a matter of six weeks.'

'Ah. Fifi *did* have a spot of bother now and again with some of the basics...'

'*Fifi?*' Two spots of angry colour blazed on her cheeks and she leaned forward into him, clutching the mug with both her hands. 'Are you telling me that I'm too dull to work for you because I'm good at what I do and don't fill all the physical attributes you think are necessary to a good secretary?'

'I'm telling you that what I don't want is someone addicted to schedules who is incapable of going with the flow. That would be unfair on me and even more unfair on you. Obviously, I would give you healthy compensation for the inconvenience caused.'

'*Inconvenience?*' Calm and control flew out of the window at the speed of light. Tessa inhaled deeply in an attempt to retrieve some of it. 'I have thrown in a perfectly good job in order to take up this one. I simply cannot afford to be tossed out onto the streets like a...a *beggar* gatecrashing a private party to scour the employment agencies looking for something else!'

'A beggar gatecrashing a private party...?' Curtis sat back and gave her his full attention. The peak breakfast-hour rush was over and the café was now relatively quiet, with only one other table occupied and stragglers coming in for their daily tea and bacon butties.

'This isn't funny!'

'No, it's not. And, like I said, you won't walk away empty-handed. A highly qualified girl like you should have no difficulty finding another position in a company that would suit your talents a lot more.'

'And how do you know what would suit my talents when you aren't even prepared to give me a chance?' The horrendous unfairness of it sent a streak of molten fire racing through her. 'I have bills to settle, Mr Diaz! Food to buy, rent to pay and a sister to finish supporting!'

'You support your sister?'

'At art college. She has one more year there.'

Curtis sighed and made his mind up. Three months' probation. He owed it to his mother, after all, and if the girl didn't work out, then at least he had given it a go. He would give her vital but background jobs to do and would just have to make sure that she didn't compromise the vibrancy of his company, which had gone some way to catapulting it from obscure newcomer to innovative front runner.

'Okay. Three months' probation, then we can take it from there…'

Tessa breathed a sigh of relief. Three months would give her a bit of time to look for something else and the pay was so fabulous that she would be able to put aside a healthy amount of money in that space of time. Because the bottom line was that the man was right. She needed to work for someone organised, someone more *grounded*, someone less flamboyant who didn't make her stammer like a schoolgirl every time he fixed those vivid blue eyes on her. And, whatever his mother had said, he needed someone to look good and to slot in. He needed another Fifi.

# CHAPTER TWO

'OKAY! Where the hell have you put that file?'

Curtis stormed out of his office and proceeded to circle her desk until he was standing squarely in front of her, and, as if that weren't enough, he then leaned forward, planting both hands on her desk until Tessa was reluctantly forced to acknowledge him.

The past two weeks had been a learning curve. Curtis Diaz was brilliant, forceful, outspoken, alarming and utterly unpredictable. He obeyed none of the rules most bosses observed. The first in-house meeting she had gone to had been an experience that had left her feeling dazed for hours afterwards. Ideas had bounced around the room like bullets, voices had been raised and anything suggested that had failed to take into account probable loopholes had been loudly shouted down without any attempt made to soothe nerves or compromise.

Interestingly, none of the staff had seemed disconcerted by their boss's unconventional approach to company management.

'Well?' Curtis roared. 'Have you gone deaf? Is there life in there?'

'There's no need to shout,' Tessa said quietly, but she was adjusting fast to his displays of temper. Rule one, she had learned, was not to automatically cringe back. To start with, she had wondered how his Fifis had coped with his overpowering personality. Then it occurred to her that he had probably never raised his voice in their presence. They were there for his visual satisfaction and, as she had discovered, most of the intricate work had been done by one of the other secretaries out of loyalty to their charismatic leader. The various strings of Fifis had filed, brought cups of coffee and brightened up his office. She, on the other hand, not having the glamour looks to fall back on, was treated like everyone else.

'I am not shouting,' he growled now, thrusting his dark face further forward. 'I'm asking a perfectly reasonable question.'

'Oh, right. Well, thanks for pointing that out. My mistake.' Tessa said that with such understated calm that he made an unintelligible sound under his breath and drew back.

'I gave the file to Richard yesterday before I left. He wanted to go over some of the costings again.'

'Well, you'd better go and fetch it.' He prowled off to stand by the window, hands stuffed into his pockets.

'Anything else while I'm there?' Tessa stood up and looked at him. She might be getting used to the way he operated, but she doubted in the three-month target she had set herself that she would ever become used to the way he looked. He was quite simply overwhelming. When he banged around the office or called her in so that he could dictate something to her in that rapid-fire manner of his, she was fine, but every time he focused his attention fully on her, as he was doing now, she could feel every nerve in her body begin to quiver with clammy, restless awareness.

'No.' Blue eyes did a frowning, absent-minded inspection of her and returned to her face, which had pinkened. 'Just get the file and come into my office with it. There are one or two things I want to discuss with you. Oh, you might as well grab us both a cup of coffee while you're about it, even though you're not much use on the coffee-making front.' That little jab seemed to do the trick of snapping him out of his mood because he grinned at her. 'Now, I bet you're going to tell me that a highly qualified PA isn't responsible for making decent coffee for her boss.'

Tessa took a deep breath and counted to ten. He didn't often tease her and, when he did, it always sent a tingle of unwanted emotion racing through her. The only way she knew how to handle that was to be as bland and literal as possible, so she gave him a perplexed look as though considering his criticism fully at face value.

'You haven't complained about my coffee-making skills before.'

'Too weak. Weak coffee is for weak men.'

This time her finely arched eyebrows flew up in an expression of amused disbelief.

'Oh, really? I never realised that before.'

'Didn't think so. Aren't you glad that you're learning such amazing things every day, thanks to me?'

'Oh, absolutely,' she murmured, looking down and sliding away from her desk. 'I really don't know how I survived in my last job before.'

She could almost *hear* him grinning as she swept out of the room and headed to Richard's office.

Three days after she had started, his mother had telephoned her at the office to find out how she was enjoying working for her son.

'It's a unique experience,' Tessa had confided truthfully. 'I've never worked for anyone like your son before.'

'I hope you're managing to keep him in order,' Mrs Diaz had said. 'He can be a little intimidating to the uninitiated. Runs rings around people.'

'Well, he doesn't intimidate me,' she had replied without pausing for breath.

Well, he did, though not in the way his mother had implied. She was confident in her abilities to do her job to the highest standard, thereby giving him no chance to slam into her for inefficiency, but on the personal level it was a different question altogether. He had a certain magnetism that made her quail inside and it was a source of abundant relief to her that she could school her expressions so that that particular weakness was never exposed.

He was waiting for her in his office when she returned ten minutes later with the file and a cup of coffee that was so strong that she could almost have stood the teaspoon upright in it.

He had pushed his chair back and pulled out the bottom drawer of the desk, which he was using as an impromptu footrest.

'Pull up a chair,' he said, 'and close the door behind you.'

'Close the door?'

'That's right. No need to repeat everything I say parrot-style.'

Tessa didn't say anything. She shut his door, handed him the file and then sat down with her notepad on her lap and her hand poised to take down whatever he was about to dictate.

'So,' he began, 'how are you enjoying it here?'

Tessa looked up at him in surprise. 'Fine, thank you.'

'Fine. Hmm.' What he *had* intended to discuss, amongst other things, were the costings of extending IT operations somewhere in the Far East. She might not, he had realised, be the eye candy he had previously employed, but she hadn't been kidding when she had told him that she was good at what she did. Not only were his thoughts channelled into expert documentation, but she could involve herself in more complex debates, which he had discovered was quite a useful talent.

Her persona, though, was a more difficult nut to crack. She greeted everything he said with the same unshakeable composure, which was beginning to prick his curiosity. His method of management was an open-door policy, whereby all his employees were free to voice whatever was on their minds, and they did. Moreover, he had become accustomed to a fast turnover of secretaries who wore their feelings on their sleeves. He liked the people who worked for him to be three-dimensional; he enjoyed the fact that he knew about their personal lives as well as their professional ones. It made for a tightly knit team of people who were secure enough in their abilities to take criticism and felt valued enough to dish it out should they see fit.

Tessa, thrown into this volatile, verbal bunch, was an enigma and it was beginning to bother him.

'I'm concerned that you might be finding the pace of this industry a little too swift for you.'

'Would you mind explaining that?' She looked at him with unreadable brown eyes.

Curtis watched her, irritated by the fact that he couldn't get underneath that smooth face of hers to the workings of her mind. He began to tap his propelling pencil softly on the protective leather mat in front of his computer.

'I feel I'm keeping up with the pace of work here,' she interjected, trying and failing to think back of any time over the past fortnight when she had been unable to cope with the lightning speed of his thoughts.

'Oh, I don't deny that.'

'What, then?'

'Being successful at a job is only partly to do with an ability to cope with the workload. Coping doesn't necessarily equate to happiness and happiness goes hand in hand with motivation.'

'There's no need for you to be concerned with my happiness,' Tessa told him. 'If I was unhappy, I would quit.'

Having not meant to bring this topic up at all, Curtis now found himself uncomfortably aware that he wanted to prolong it until she said something personal rather than simply showing him the same face of complete composure that she had shown ever since she had first started.

'Why? Have other people been complaining about me?'

'Oh, no. On the contrary. I've been told in no uncertain terms that it was high time I hired someone a little more down-to-earth than my usual brand of secretary.'

What woman in her right mind would like being described as *down-to-earth*? Tessa wondered. Especially when the description came from someone who looked the way this man did? Today, in deference to a board meeting that had been held with some particularly crusty clients, he had toned his dress code down a notch. Even so, the pink-and-white-striped shirt failed to give the impression of a conservative traditionalist, especially as it was twinned with an outrageously patterned, very slender tie, the likes of which she had personally never seen before, leading her to assume that it must be handmade.

'But you don't agree.' The criticism, packaged up like a compliment, hurt more than she liked.

'My theory is that for an employee to really enjoy his or her job, they've got to feel as though they fit in.' He wondered why he was labouring this point and whether it was so important to get to the bottom of her when she was doing her job perfectly well. Better than well, in actual fact.

There was no answer to that. She spoke to everybody, sometimes she even went to lunch with a couple of them, although the workload was so intense that she was happy to eat a sandwich at her desk, a half-hour break before she carried on with what she was doing.

'We're like a family here,' he broke into her thoughts, his voice piously ruminative, 'and, call me old-fashioned, but I like to know what happens in my employees' lives. It makes them feel wanted and it's very important to me that they feel wanted.' He looked at her from under his long, dark lashes and noticed the very slight shift in her position.

'I don't think anyone could call you old-fashioned,' Tessa said, dodging the net he was trying to throw around her.

'No? Why would that be, do you think?'

'Because...because you really don't...you're quite unconventional compared to the other people I've worked for.' That was the understatement of the year, she thought. He was like a peacock amongst sparrows compared to her previous employers, for she had circulated within the firm in which she had worked on a fairly regular basis over the years.

'Hence my unconventional approach to my employees...'

'And you don't mind if they have an unconventional approach to you in return?' Tessa felt quite proud of this neat sleight of hand that had managed to toss the question right back at him.

'Not in the slightest. My personal life is an open book.'

'I'm...I don't believe in bringing my private life to work,' Tessa said, staring down at her fingers. She wondered what he would make of her private life. It was an open book as well, except hers had very little writing in it, at least on the men front, which she was now sure was what was niggling him. 'Perhaps we could discuss these costings?' she prompted tentatively. 'I really need to leave on time tonight and it's almost five-thirty.'

That sparked his curiosity again. What exactly did she

get up to when she left this office? Nothing that relied on her leaving her work promptly, he knew, because over the past two weeks her hours had been anything but regular and not once had she complained.

'Why's that?' he asked idly. 'Hot date?'

Tessa flushed. She could feel herself reddening and it made her more defensive than usual. 'Actually, tonight's hot date is taking place in the supermarket and involves cooking spaghetti Bolognese for four of my friends from my last job as well as Lucy and two of *her* friends.'

'Lucy?'

'My sister.' Blonde, blue-eyed and beautiful. Just the sort of woman that Curtis Diaz would make a beeline for. If she could have yanked back her words, she would have.

'Oh, the one you're putting through college. By the way, how is it that you're responsible for paying for her education?'

'That's just the way it is and it has been that way since I was a teenager.' She shrugged, dismissing his interest and looking down at the redundant pad sitting on her lap.

'Must be a burden on your finances,' he remarked thoughtfully. 'Is that why you took this job? Because of the salary?' His thoughts were already moving along, though, playing with other possibilities and enjoying the probing process while being fully aware that he was prying into areas of her life in which he was unwanted.

'Amongst other things.'

'Oh, sure, job satisfaction.' He linked his fingers behind his head and surveyed her with open curiosity. 'Of course, more money would be reason enough. After all, there's only so much of those free pleasures you can have, especially in winter when it's freezing cold outside. Walks in the park just aren't quite the same, I find... Oh, I forgot. All your money's going to help your little sister through college. You should tell her to take on some evening work so she can put herself through.'

'Lucy isn't into evening work,' Tessa said without thinking. She could have kicked herself. She could almost hear his ears pricking up at that admission. The truth was that she *had* mentioned evening work to Lucy and had hit a brick wall. Her sister liked to party. The small legacy from their parents, which had been shared between them, had been put into storage, on the advice of their very shrewd solicitor who had foreseen a time when it might be needed to buy property. Tessa had had no difficulty in concurring with this as far as her half went. Lucy, after much nagging when she had hit her landmark eighteenth birthday, had agreed to have a small allowance paid into her bank account every month to fund her lifestyle. Tessa should have stood firm, but as always she had caved in. Most people did when faced with Lucy's optimistic, winning smile.

'Not into evening work? You mean she's happy for you to pay for her so that she can enjoy herself?'

'I don't mind.'

'Tut-tut. There's nothing worse than a martyr.'

That did it. Tessa snapped shut her notepad and gave him her steeliest glare. 'I can think of lots of things worse, actually, and I am *not* a martyr. Lucy is much younger than me and she's always been the baby of the family. We all indulged her, including me, and I don't mind at all paying for her fees. She deserves to have a good time while she's young!'

'Because you never did?' he asked quickly, hitting the mark with such effortless ease that Tessa's mouth dropped open and she was momentarily lost for words. 'I mean,' he continued to expand in a lazy, musing voice, 'you were forced into the role of surrogate mother when you were just a teenager and since then you haven't really stopped. Who knows? Maybe you get a personal vicarious thrill from your sister's fun-loving lifestyle because you were denied it.'

'I thought we were going to go through these costings.'

'We are. In a minute. It's just so rewarding finding out more about one of my employees, knowing what makes them tick.'

'You're not *finding out more about me*,' Tessa said coolly, sitting back in her chair. 'You're second-guessing my life.'

'You're not denying any of what I've said.'

'I don't have to. I'm here to do a job. I don't have to defend myself in the process.'

'True.' He sat forward abruptly and gave her a dazzling smile loaded with a mixture of charm and apology. 'And it's outrageous of me to start prying and probing into what's none of my business! I'm glad you spoke your mind and told me to back off!' He absent-mindedly flicked his tie between his fingers and continued to look at her contritely. 'That's the problem, you know. I rush in where I'm not wanted and make a nuisance of myself.'

'It's good you recognise the problem, in that case,' Tessa said weakly. The warmth and sincerity in his voice had punctured all traces of indignation. Now she felt as though *she* should be the one apologising, for what she had no idea!

'Oh, I do!' He shot her a crooked smile that would have had any little old lady buckling at the knees. He was also an incurable flirt. She had seen him in action, taking time to chat with the cleaner who came in after hours, even though she was a happily married lady in her mid fifties. He did it almost without thinking. She wondered how many of his young, pretty secretaries had lost their heads over him. Whatever, she assumed that he was as charming when he dispatched them as he was when he hired them, because in the space of two weeks she had transferred no less than three separate calls from women who said that they had worked for him in the past and were just phoning to touch base.

It was to her credit, she thought now, that she could withstand his personality as successfully as she did. She did so now by sending him a dry look that warned him not to overplay his card and he laughed, reading the message in her brown eyes.

As always, though, when it came to work, he was all concentrated brilliance. She barely noticed the time flying by when, after an hour, his office was occupied by four of the computer whizkids sprawled on the sofa, one perched on his desk, all animatedly discussing ideas for some new software while she sat rapidly making notes and working out in her head their order of priority for when she came to transcribe them the following morning.

She realised the time when Robert Harding, a brilliant computer mind behind thick spectacles and the classic nerd look, stretched and stood up to leave. Then she looked at her watch and gave a little shriek of dismay.

'I have to go!' She stood up, feeling like a traitor because she was leaving work ahead of everyone else, even though five-thirty had come and gone a full forty-five minutes ago.

'Oh, yes, the spaghetti Bolognese!' Curtis grinned and stood up as well, putting an end to the impromptu meeting which, uncharacteristically, met with groans of reluctance.

'Now, now!' he chided them, sauntering over to unhook his bomber jacket from the sleek walnut-fronted cupboard that stored several essential items of clothing just in case he happened to sleep in the office one night. Through the dividing door, he could see Tessa scuttling around her desk, frantically tidying things away. Strands of hair were escaping from her neatly coiffured coil, as if even *they* were in a state of agitation about the lateness of the hour.

'I think we ought to stay on for, let's say, another hour or so, Curtis!' Adam Beesley's youthful face was bright with enthusiasm.

'Remember what they say about all work and no play! You don't want to end up a dullard, do you?' He moved towards his office door, keeping Tessa within his line of vision while he continued to address the assorted crew now reluctantly rising to their feet. 'Fine line, team, between hard-working and sad!' He exited his office to hoots of laughter and followed Tessa to the lift, insinuating himself in front of her just as she was about to press the button.

'I want to apologise for keeping you here so late,' he murmured.

Tessa pressed the button and stared in front of her. 'Normally, I wouldn't mind. I don't like clock-watching but tonight—'

'Yes, the friends, the cooking. Here's where I come in.' At that moment the lift arrived and the doors parted. As soon as they were in the lift, he turned to her and smiled. Maybe it was her imagination, but that full wattage smile in the confines of a lift seemed to be a lot more potent. She felt her skin heat up and the hand she had thrust into her coat pocket curled into a little, nervous fist.

Curtis at work was her boss, even when the man intruded. Curtis out of work was something she didn't think about although unconsciously she must have found the thought disturbing because she had not once taken up any offers to go anywhere for a quick drink with the gang before heading home.

'Since it's my fault your meal's going to be ruined, let me take all of you out to dinner...'

'What?' Her head swung round sharply and for a few

nightmarish seconds she actually struggled for breath while she tried to cope with the horror of his suggestion.

'I said—'

'Yes, I heard what you said! And it's…very…well, considerate of you, but out of the question. Thank you all the same!'

'But you won't have time to prepare your meal…'

'I can whip something else up. No need for you to worry about it.' Panic licked through her and she tried to see his suggestion for what it was, an offbeat but instinctively gracious offer from someone who had kept her working later than intended. Curtis was not a man who was stingy with his gestures. He would think nothing of taking her out along with seven other people for a slap-up meal at some expensive restaurant somewhere.

She realised that her reaction was out of proportion because *she* didn't want him to invade her private life at all, not in any way.

The lift had reached the ground floor and she scooted out, planning to escape into the dark cold outside, thereby putting an end to their conversation.

'So I take it you won't accept my offer…' He reached out and swung her around, leaving his arm curled on her wrist. 'I'm cut to the quick.'

'No, you're not!' Tessa said sharply. His hand was burning through the layers of clothing. She could feel it like a hot brand stamping down into her flesh, making her want to squirm.

'You're right. I'm not. But that's only because I expected you to refuse my offer.'

'You did?'

He nodded gravely and the pressure of his hand lessened, although he didn't remove it and didn't appear to notice her surreptitious attempts to ease it away.

'I did.' He shot her a smug look. 'Isn't it nice the way I can tune in to you after only two weeks?'

Tessa ignored that. 'Well, why did you bother to offer if you knew I was going to refuse?'

'Because I still intend to help you out, whether you like it or not.' Instead of heading towards the revolving door at the front, he swivelled her back round to the lift and pressed the down button. 'I'm going to drive you to your house and, on the way, I'm going to stop off and get a take-away and, before you open your mouth to gently turn my magnanimous offer down, there's no debate.'

She was ushered back into the lift, this time down to the basement, where a handful of people were given the privilege of secured parking. In central London that in itself was worth its weight in gold.

'Slightly selfish reasons here,' he continued, leaning back against the mirrored side of the lift.

'What?' Tessa's voice was apprehensive. Trying to predict this man's moves was like trying to predict the weather from a sealed box underground. Utterly impossible.

'I need you to do me a small favour.'

'Favour? What favour?'

He didn't answer immediately. Instead, as the lift disgorged them into the compact underground car park he led her towards his sleek, low-slung sports car, a shiny black Mercedes that was the last word in breathtaking extravagance and just the sort of car she would have imagined him driving. Not for him the big, safe cars with practical boot space and generous passenger-toting potential!

'One of my babies,' he said, grinning at her and sweeping a loving hand across the gleaming bonnet.

'One of them? You mean you have a fleet of cars lurking away somewhere?' Yes, she could imagine that too. A dozen racy little numbers tucked away somewhere, ready and waiting for when they might be put to use driving his racy female numbers to racy little nightclubs. She scowled in the darkness and wondered how such creative genius could be simultaneously shallow and superficial.

'You snorted.'

'I beg your pardon?' Had she?

'You snorted just then. A very disapproving snort. What's wrong about having a fleet of sports cars? I thought you women liked that sort of thing.'

'Some might.' His amusement was very irritating. She tilted her chin up and stared frostily out of the window.

'But not you.' He slotted a card into the machine at the side and the exit barrier went up.

'That's right,' Tessa said crisply. 'I happen to think that men who feel the need to buy small, fast cars are just subscribing to the truth of toys for boys.'

*'Toys for boys?'* Curtis chuckled. 'I can assure you that I'm no boy! Haven't I already proved that by the kind of coffee I drink?'

'Yes, of course you have. Silly me. You're all man!' She slanted an ironic, sideways glance at him and just for a fraction of a second their eyes met and she felt a rush of unsteadiness. The glint in his eyes was wickedly, darkly teasing and for one heart-stopping moment it spiked into the very core of her, sending every pulse in her body shooting off into overdrive. 'You might want directions to my house,' she said in a very steady voice. 'I live out towards Swiss Cottage. If you—'

'I know where Swiss Cottage is.' He paused. 'Now to the original point of my conversation.'

Curiosity overcame apprehension at the oddly serious note in his voice and Tessa shifted to look at him. 'Yes. The favour you wanted to ask of me. What is it? If it's to do with working overtime, then I'm sure it won't be a problem, just so long as you let me know in advance what days you require of me.'

'Oh, well, some overtime might be needed but it's to do with my baby, actually.'

'Your *car*?' Wasn't this *baby* thing going a little too far? Boys with toys was bad enough but boys obsessed with toys was beyond the pale!

'No, of course not,' Curtis said impatiently. 'I'm talking about Anna!'

'Anna?'

'My mother *did* tell you about Anna, didn't she?'

Tessa thought back. She was certain she would have remembered the name. 'No,' she said slowly and thinking hard. 'Who is she?'

Curtis swore softly under his breath and pulled the car over to the side of the kerb, then he turned to face her. 'Anna is my daughter.'

*'Your daughter?'*

He swore again and shook his head, scowling. 'I take it my mother forgot to mention that little detail. Or rather chose not to.'

'But…I don't get any of this. *You have a daughter?* Are you *married*?' He didn't *act* like a married man. He didn't wear a wedding ring. And did married men have strings of sexy secretaries because they decorated their offices, with practical skills not of prime importance? Would his wife approve of that? Did she *even know*? Maybe, Tessa thought with a sickening jolt, they had one of those modern open marriages.

In the middle of her freewheeling thoughts, he interrupted with, 'A daughter, no wife. And I'm surprised this wasn't mentioned when my mother saw you.' The cunning fox, he thought indulgently. Had his mother thought that bringing up the question of his daughter and the spot of coverage that might be occasionally needed would have put off the perfect candidate? One of the reasons he had succumbed to her insistence on choosing his next secretary had been the little technicality that Anna was going to be on half-term for two weeks and his mother would be out of the country on a gadabout cruise with her circle of friends. Someone would be needed to help out with coverage should it become necessary and, in his mother's words, a flighty bit of fluff would not do.

'Anna is going to be home for a fortnight from her boarding-school tomorrow. Next week she's going to be coming into the office and I want you to take her under your wing. The following week should be fine. I intend to have the week off, but next week's a bit trickier with this trip to the Far East to source potential computer bases.'

'Boarding-school.'

'Hence the fact that she has to come into the office. None of her friends live locally and my mother left the country a couple of days ago.'

Tessa couldn't take her eyes off his face. She could picture him as just about anything apart from a father. He had too much *personality* to be a father! Then she thought what a ridiculous idea that was.

'Are you following a word I'm saying?'

Tessa blinked. 'I just find it a bit difficult to comprehend...how old is...Anna?'

'Fourteen.'

'Fourteen. But you never talk about her...have pictures...' Was he *ashamed* of being a father? Was that why she was at boarding-school? Because she cramped his eligible-bachelor lifestyle?

'I have pictures in my wallet. Care to see them just to verify that I'm telling the truth and that she looks like a

normal kid, no nasty side effects from my being her father?'
He raised his eyebrows and Tessa blushed.

'No, of course not!'

'Can I ask you something?'

She nodded, still furiously examining the scenario that
had unfolded in front of her.

'Did my mother know that you had raised a kid sister
virtually on your own?'

'Completely on my own,' Tessa absent-mindedly
amended. 'Yes. Why?'

'"A most suitable woman for the job."' He quoted his
mother with a grin. 'Not only did you come with a sackful
of references, but you were single, with a sensible head on
sensible shoulders, and you had firsthand experience of
communicating with a teenager. No wonder she failed to
mention the little technicality of my daughter. You were so
ideal for the job that she probably didn't want to jeopardise
the chances of your accepting the offer.'

'I feel manipulated.'

'You'll have to mention that to my darling mother the
next time you see her.' He pulled out slowly from the kerb,
leaving her to her riotous thoughts for a while.

'But what exactly am I supposed to *do* with your daughter?' Tessa eventually ventured. If she had just one drop of
his volatile blood in her, then she would be more than a
handful cooped up in an office when she would rather be
hanging out with teenagers. Tessa shuddered at the prospect
lurking ahead of her.

'Supervise her. Give her little jobs to do. I'll be around
for most of the week. When I'm not...'

'She can't possibly stay with me...!'

'Her old babysitter will take over. Don't worry. I have
every faith in your abilities...'

# CHAPTER THREE

ANNA was nothing like Tessa had expected. In her head, she had imagined her own sister at fourteen, but with Curtis's dark good looks. Gregarious, smilingly wilful and utterly boy crazy. Thrown into this mental picture was the added bonus of being the only child of a millionaire father. The equation was terrifying, not least because she knew from firsthand experience that she would spend the week tearing her hair out just to make sure that her beady eyes never ceased their constant supervision.

She had arrived on the Monday a full hour and a half before she should have just to make sure that she did as much of her own workload as possible. Just in case.

Curtis and Anna had finally come in some time about ten, Curtis flamboyantly explaining that he had made an essential detour to take his daughter out for breakfast, while in his shadow a tall, awkward teenager with her hair pulled back into a pony tail had hovered with her eyes lowered, staring down at her curiously old-fashioned shoes.

That had been three days ago. The boy-crazy handful of hormone-driven teenager had turned out to be a studiously polite and excruciatingly shy girl who seemed to enjoy working in the office more than she did leaving it and who only really smiled when her father was around. Then, she lit up like a Christmas tree.

'Anna?' Tessa looked at her now, head bent over the mighty stack of files that she had been allocated to go through, making sure that the paperwork corresponded to

41

what was on the computer. 'Fancy you and I going out to lunch somewhere?'

Anna looked at her and smiled.

She had the prettiest face, Tessa thought, but the look was ruined by the hairdo and the clothes and the way she walked, slightly hunched as though ashamed of her height. Having gone through the wringer with Lucy, who had never believed in concealing her assets and who had been able to wield an eyeliner pencil at the age of fourteen like any professional make-up artist, Tessa knew that she should be vigorously counting her blessings that this one week was not turning out to be the nightmare she had expected.

However, it just didn't seem natural that Anna should be fourteen going on middle-aged.

'I've still got quite a few files to get done...' she said apologetically. 'I mean, I know it's only a pretend job but I'd still like to do it as well as I can.'

'It's not a pretend job!'

Anna gave her one of those shrewd, mature looks and Tessa laughed. 'It seriously is not! Those files are in a disastrous state! I don't think your father's last secretary was that bothered by something as mundane as filing.'

'No. I don't suppose she was.'

'Anyway, your dad's not back from the Far East until tomorrow.' Tessa stood up, switched off her computer and firmly began putting on her thick jacket. 'We can play truant for an hour or two.'

'Truant?' She giggled. 'Are you sure? I mean, won't you get into trouble?' The anxiousness was back. Teenagers shouldn't be anxious, Tessa thought with a pang, amused to catch herself wondering if she had been the same at that age. No, she hadn't. Her anxieties had come later. At fourteen, she hadn't been wild like Lucy, but she had been carefree and unburdened.

'Oh, I'll chance it. Now, come on. If we carry on debating this any longer, we'll talk ourselves out of it.' She waited as Anna stuck on her coat and quickly neatened her pony tail.

'How are you finding it?' Tessa asked as they settled themselves into the back seat of a black cab, heading towards the King's Road.

Anna shrugged. 'It's nice. I mean, I knew Grandma wasn't going to be around for the half-term and I'd be in the office with Dad, but I'm relieved that...' She chewed her lip sheepishly and hazarded a smile at Tessa.

'That what?'

'Well, I know what some of Dad's secretaries have been like. I mean, it's not that I've ever come in to the office to actually work or anything. This is the first time, actually. But sometimes I've come there to meet him for lunch or something, and well...'

'Gorgeous women in very short skirts can be a bit daunting,' Tessa agreed, astutely reading behind the hesitation. 'I know. I find that as well.'

'I could always see the way some of them looked at me, as if they couldn't really believe that I was his daughter or something.'

'You're beautiful, Anna,' Tessa said truthfully and Anna burst out laughing, a high, girlish tinkle that was all the prettier because it was so rarely heard.

'No, I'm not! My mum...now my mum was beautiful. I've seen pictures of her. She could have been a model, actually.'

Curtis's wife and Anna's mother had died when she was only a young girl in her early twenties. A freak skiing accident. This piece of information had been relayed to Tessa by Curtis, part of his explanation as to why his daughter would be working at the office for a fortnight in the absence of her grandmother. There had been no embroidering of details and he had shown no emotion, nothing whatsoever to indicate how the premature death of his young wife had hit him. Tessa had had no idea what the woman had looked like but she wasn't surprised to learn now that she had been beautiful.

'Dad likes beautiful women,' Anna was saying, her eyes glowing as they always did at the mention of her father. 'Grandma always says it's the Spanish blood in him. Actually, I don't believe that. I mean, there's no logical reason for it.'

The taxi had reached Sloane Square. Tessa had meant to have a nice, long lunch but now, on the spur of the moment, she decided that a little shopping wouldn't go astray.

'Shopping for what?' Anna asked curiously, barely glancing around her. 'Do you need anything?'

'I think I need an entire overhaul, actually,' Tessa told her, smiling. 'I mean, look at me! I need a new wardrobe!' She hadn't actually even considered this until now, but, thinking about it, she wondered whether it wasn't true. No one would guess that she was only twenty-eight. Lucy was forever teasing her about her old-fashioned clothes and Tessa had always laughed off the good-natured criticism, but now she wondered if she was as much of an anachronism as Anna was.

'I like the way you dress. It's…comfortable.'

'Hmm. Sounds exciting.' They began strolling up the road. It was a gorgeous day. Bright skies, cold and dry and almost windless. A perfect day for shopping.

With each step, Anna's interest in the shop windows grew, and when she finally pointed out something she actually liked Tessa instantly pulled her inside, away from the drab, well-tailored grey skirt towards a rail of reds and burgundies, brief, beautiful short skirts with tiny, boxy jackets to match. She overrode the protests, hearing the insecurity in Anna's voice as she shied away from trying to turn herself into something she wasn't.

A beautiful mother, a father who was singularly drawn to women because of the way they looked... It wasn't too difficult to see how a timid child could turn into an adolescent who was convinced of her own plainness. In her head, Anna had come to the conclusion that she couldn't possibly compete with her mother or with any of the women she had seen her father with, and so she had gone in the opposite direction. She had taken refuge in sensible clothes and sensible shoes and no trace of make up, ever, that might signal a willingness to enter into the dressing game.

Tessa could identify with all that so she couldn't quite understand why she just didn't accept it.

It was very gratifying, though, to see Anna stare at herself in the small burgundy suit, eyes wide at the change in her appearance.

'Maybe I'll give it a go...' she conceded, pulling out the cash that was hers to use.

By the time they finally made it to the restaurant, there was a clutch of bags. A three-hour lunch hour! They bolted down their food and returned to the office, literally like guilty truants, to find Curtis there, waiting for them.

Anna ran and flung herself at him, and Tessa stifled a heartfelt urge to groan.

'We're late,' she said quickly. 'I'm really sorry. My fault. I decided that I'd take Anna out to lunch and—'

'My fault, Dad!' She stood back and gestured to all the carrier bags that had been summarily relegated to the ground the minute she had laid eyes on the unexpected sight of her father. 'I've been shopping!'

She ducked down to the bags strewn on the ground and,

in the intervening pause, Tessa made her way to her desk and asked him crisply how the trip had gone, whether it had been successful.

The lifeless computer screen sent another jab of guilt at the extended length of time she had been out of the office. It was unheard of. She had never, but never, sidelined her duties in favour of something frivolous. The work ethic was so deeply ingrained in her that she very rarely even made personal calls from work, so skipping off on a three-hour jaunt was almost beyond the bounds of belief. Worse was the fact that she had been caught out.

'Very good.' Curtis was watching his daughter with amused indulgence, perched on the desk, arms folded.

He was wearing faded jeans and a long-sleeved cream jumper, the sleeves of which he had pushed up to the elbows. Tessa took it all in as she industriously switched on the computer and sat down.

His mouth was curved into a smile of loving expectation as he looked at his excited daughter. Improbable as it seemed, given his relentlessly single image, he was a doting father. He didn't often make it to any school things, Anna had told her, but, she had quickly excused, that was because he was always so busy at work. When he *did* visit her at school, he invariably arrived with armfuls of gifts, and of course he was always the centre of attention. Her friends swooned over him. She had related this with great pride in her voice, never implying that she had ever longed for anything else. Reading between the lines, just having Curtis as her dad gave her some kind of indefinable street cred amongst her classmates.

One by one, Anna pulled her purchases out of their bags. She was so pleased with herself that she barely noticed the shift in his expression.

Tessa noticed, though. The smile remained in place, but

his eyes were narrowed as he took in the little burgundy outfit, then the soft dark green skirt that Anna had said might come in handy for a school thing she had been invited to, then the series of vest-tops, perfectly respectable but certainly nothing like what she had possessed before.

Tessa was tempted to offer some reassuring explanation for the choice of clothes. They looked a lot smaller off than on.

'Well! What do you think?' The clothes had all been neatly laid out now. They presented a startling and colourful divergence from what Anna was currently wearing, namely a sober grey trouser suit and some flat black shoes.

Curtis was still trying hard to maintain his relaxed smile and Anna must have sensed it because her face shadowed and she asked in a smaller voice, 'Don't you like them?'

'How can he *help but* like them?' Tessa stood up firmly, drawing attention to herself and giving Curtis the most professionally warning smile she could muster. She walked across to where they were laid out and gave Anna's arm a little squeeze. 'You ought to have seen your daughter in these.' She folded her arms and, with her back to Anna, managed to consolidate the warning in her eyes. 'She looked fabulous. She's been so excited buying that the time just ran away with us.'

'They're lovely, darling,' he ventured, skirting round Tessa. 'But perhaps you'd better gather them up. No, better than that, after a hard afternoon shopping, why don't you get a cab back to my place? I'll be an hour here, tops, and we'll go out somewhere special for something to eat.'

'I'll wear one of my new outfits, shall I? Which do you think, Dad? Where will we be eating? Somewhere smart? I can wear the cream skirt and top with my coat. Just so long as we won't have to do too much walking.' She looked lovingly at the new shoes. The shoes had been the very last purchase and had benefited from being bought at the very peak of Anna's excited embarkment into the world of glamour shopping. They were fur-lined, pointed-tipped fawn boots that fitted lovingly to mid-calf and had instantly transformed her into fashion-model height.

'That's a very nice outfit, darling, but perhaps a little too skimpy for this time of year? And those shoes, well, they might get scuffed. You wouldn't want to ruin such lovely things on your first foray, would you?'

'I suppose not.' The voice was uncertain now. She slowly began to gather up the various bits, folding them neatly before returning them to their expensive bags.

'Perhaps we'll go somewhere casual after all.' He yawned expansively. 'Long-haul travel is hideously tiring.' He pushed himself away from the desk and gave Tessa a veiled look, oddly lacking in its usual warmth. 'And there's a stack of things to get through before I call it a day. Tomorrow we'll do dressy, shall we?' He beckoned Anna across to him and swamped her in a big bear hug. When she emerged, her face was once again beaming, all uncertainty gone like a scattering of rain on a summer day. 'Why don't you help Anna down with her parcels—' he turned to Tessa '—make sure she gets a taxi and then meet me in my office?'

Anna was full of it. Her father had returned early! She had spent the past two nights in the company of her ex-babysitter, now a married woman with a toddler of her own, and had expected to be spending another night in her company. Her eyes were shining at the prospect of an evening out with her dad. Tessa wondered whether she should gently steer her away from wearing any of the clothes that had certainly met with his disapproval, however much he had tried to mask it, and decided against it.

But she was curious. In every way, he was utterly and

disconcertingly laid-back. He did things his way, sweeping everyone else up into his own unique personality, yet there he was, frowning like a Victorian stereotype the minute his own daughter displayed the slightest inclination to be a normal adolescent.

And curiosity was not something she wanted to feel. Certainly not when it applied to her charismatic boss. Hopefully by the time she got back to the office he would have moved on to some other thought. He was like that, possessed of a restless, brilliant energy that sometimes leapfrogged with dizzying speed. Every so often, even when he was dictating something to her, she would see that look in his eyes and realise that his mind was working ahead of itself, had jumped ahead to something new.

No such luck.

That clever, questing mind had focused on his daughter's brand new wardrobe and was staying there. The look on his face said it all as she walked into his office and shut the door behind her.

'So you and my daughter have been getting along.'

She could have faced up to him a little more confidently if he had chosen to sit at his desk like any normal human being. However, Curtis being Curtis, he was stretched out on the sofa, eyes closed, hands lightly linked behind his head. Tessa had to swivel the chair round to face him and then found herself reluctantly compelled to look at him, at that ridiculously good-looking face and those even more ridiculously long eyelashes.

'She's a lovely young woman. You must be very proud of her.'

'She's fourteen.' He opened his eyes and slanted her a glance. 'Not yet a *young woman.*'

'And what would you call it?'

'I would call it *a kid.*'

Tessa didn't answer.

'I asked you to provide Anna with some simple office duties to occupy her days. I didn't ask you to take her on an elaborate shopping spree.'

'You're right. You didn't. I'm sorry. She's been doing so well and I thought it might be nice for us to go out to lunch somewhere and before I knew it, we were shopping.'

'Before you knew it...'

He was looking at her now, his eyes narrowed slits. Ranting and raving, Tessa could manage. This soft, menacing voice, however, was a lot scarier.

'You're a secretary. Not a mother substitute for my daughter.'

Tessa drew in a long, deep breath and sat up straighter. 'I had no idea that part of my secretarial duties included babysitting the boss's daughter,' she said quietly, 'but that's fine. She's hard-working and enjoyable to have around. But having strayed from my original job description, I think it's a little unfair to start drawing boundaries. I don't know why you're so upset because Anna bought one or two things to wear. Teenagers *like* shopping, in case you hadn't noticed.'

'Of course I *know that!*'

'Then what's the problem? If it's the amount of time I took off, then I'm more than happy to make up for it by working late tonight and tomorrow night.'

'It's nothing to do with the amount of time you had off,' he said irritably, swinging himself up from the sofa and glowering at her on his way to his desk. He stood there, as if debating whether to sit down or not. 'And you're being deliberately obtuse. Since when have you ever seen me crack a whip because someone's running a bit late? More work takes place in these offices than in any other place I know, and that's *without* me having to pull the heavy-handed card.'

Tessa had now swung her chair around to face him. He still hadn't sat down. Maybe, she thought, he felt that if he sat down at his desk he would be more inclined to get down to the business of work. He propped himself up on the desk, palms flat on the gleaming surface, and continued to frown darkly.

'Then what is it?'

'I don't like the clothes you encouraged my daughter to buy.'

Tessa didn't know whether to shout at him or burst out laughing. Where had this puritanical streak come from? Here was the man who had thrown away the book of rules, who encouraged every aspect of creativity in the people who worked for him, who *had a sofa in his office,* for goodness' sake, *just in case he wanted to sleep*, just in case *he decided to spend a night in the office*. He must, she supposed, *somewhere,* keep a store of conventional suits, but she had yet to glimpse one.

Why on earth would he object to his daughter buying a few trendy clothes? There was nothing offensive in a single one of the outfits Anna had chosen. In fact, Tessa had dryly compared her choices to the ones Lucy had been making at the same age and marvelled at how she had managed to deal with her lovable headache of a sister all those years ago.

So where, she wondered, was the problem?

'I would never have expected it of you,' he said accusingly, and her head shot up at that.

'Meaning…?'

'Meaning that I thought I could trust you not to lead Anna astray!' He pushed himself away from the desk and began prowling around the room while Tessa sat completely still in her chair, counting to ten and refusing to swivel her chair in every direction just to keep up with his restless progress.

'Aren't you overreacting just a bit?'

The silence that greeted this was deafening. Tessa felt the hairs on the back of her neck stand on end and she realised, too late, that not having him within her line of vision was a major disadvantage.

She was oblivious to his stealthy approach until she felt the chair swivel round and found herself facing him, inches away from him, in fact, as he leant over her, caging her into her chair, leaning into her. She pressed herself into the back of the chair but, with nowhere to go, he remained close enough for her to feel his breath fanning her face.

Cool-headed composure shot through the window at a rate of knots, and in its place came a surge of panicky agitation. She wanted to push him back, but just the thought of her hand making contact with his hard chest made her quail.

'Maybe overreacting's a bit strong...' she retreated weakly. 'You're her father...'

'Damn right I am!' Curtis growled. 'I'm her father and there's no way I'm going to see my baby dressed like a tart!'

Tessa's eyes opened wide at this blatant display of double standards.

'A tart?' she spluttered. 'Did you actually *look* at the stuff Anna bought?'

'Sure I looked at it!'

'Those happened to be very expensive designer clothes!' Which was hardly an overstatement. At the time, Tessa had baulked at the price tags merrily dangling from the clothes, but she had swallowed back the temptation to hurry her charge along in the direction of more affordable places. This was a world she had never seen before. A world in which a fourteen-year-old girl had all the money she wanted at her disposal and was innocently ignorant of any need to go cheaper.

'I don't care if they were hand-finished by the Great Man up There himself!' he bellowed. 'I don't want my daughter wearing any of it! She was perfectly happy in clothes that *covered her up!*'

'How do you know that?' A delicate matter. Anna had confided in her that her father had always seen her as his little girl. He brought her back lavish gifts of coats and jackets that were beautifully tailored and cost the earth, but were not exactly the height of fashion, and she had never thought to rebel because she adored him.

'Because *she's never complained!*' He strode away from her and settled himself behind his desk.

Tessa released a long sigh of relief. Her legs were going stiff from sitting in the chair, rigid with tension, but a well-honed sense of survival told her that any mention of actually getting down to the business of work would be a big mistake. Curtis was still chewing on his thoughts and her options were basically reduced to staying put and trying to dodge the verbal missiles or else feigning a sudden, extreme illness.

'Well?' he prompted. 'What have you got to say to *that*? Hmm?'

'You're right.'

He looked at her suspiciously. 'Are you trying to calm me down?'

'No!' Tessa lied, protesting.

'Because if you are, I can tell you from now that that's one sure-fire way to get me enraged.'

At least he was no longer breathing fire and brimstone, though. Having the full force of his anger directed at her had been scary. Had that been yet another one of those elements of his interesting personality that his mother had casually mentioned? An ability to make other people aware of just how high their adrenaline levels could go? Working for a firm of accountants was beginning to seem like a stroll in the park!

'Look,' she ventured tentatively, 'Don't you think you're a little guilty of double standards?'

'I have no idea what you're talking about,' Curtis informed her with sweeping arrogance.

'You go out with beautiful women who wear provocative clothes. You employ beautiful women whom you *expect* to wear provocative clothes! Well, with the exception of me, obviously. You *like* attractive, glamorous women. I just don't see anything wrong with your daughter making the most of her youth. She's way too sensible to want to dress like a tart but she's *not a kid,* whatever you want to think! She can't go straight from frilly petticoats into slacks and jumpers a middle-aged woman would wear!'

'Said your piece?'

'I most certainly *have not*!' Lord, but how this man had the talent to get under her skin! 'How can you be so...*so authoritarian* when it comes to your daughter and *so relaxed* with everyone else?'

'Because she's my daughter. Believe me, I've seen firsthand how boys grow up looking at girls dressed in next to nothing...'

'Oh. Right.'

Black brows met in an irritable frown at her capitulation. But she didn't quite know what to say. They could keep going round in circles for hours because the plain truth was that Curtis wanted to protect his daughter and his version of protection was to insulate her behind a severely grown up image that would guarantee that no boys would be pounding at her door. While Anna was not unhappy with it, Tessa wondered whether she might be in time, whether her rebellion would take place later on and be all the more disastrous for that.

'Let me show you something.' He opened the bottom drawer of his desk, rummaged around, keeping his eyes firmly glued to her face, and eventually pulled out a photograph, which he slapped down on the desk in front of her. 'Have a look. Go on. It won't bite.'

Tessa tentatively went to look at the picture. A woman gazed back at her, her face propped thoughtfully in one hand, her mouth forming a little smile. She looked in her early twenties and was spectacularly beautiful. Silver-blonde hair framed a face that was perfectly chiselled, the sort of face that made men stare and then stare again and made women sigh with discontent at what they had been dealt. Laughter lurked just behind the pensive expression, as if she was holding back a boundless love of life.

'Chloe.' Curtis reached out for the photograph, glanced once more at it and stuck it back into the drawer.

All Tessa could think was that there was something poignant about him keeping that picture there, close at hand. Was that why he was so drawn to beauty? Because he had never really moved on from his wife?

'I was a kid when I met her and she was overwhelming, dazzling.' He grinned fondly at the memory and Tessa saw, for one second, a huge void open up in front of her, the void of being sensible and never dazzling anyone, then she was back to normal, listening, watching his expressive, gorgeous face as he spoke. 'We leapt into love as though tomorrow might never come, but of course it wasn't love. More like lust. We had a supremely lusty relationship. By the time she became pregnant, we were already drifting apart. Her looks, you see, that flamboyant way of hers…she couldn't resist the heads that were continually turned in her direction, she couldn't resist that pull she had over other people, something that made her want to just keep going. Anna grounded her for a while, but in the end it wasn't enough. I watch Anna pulling those clothes out of those bags and I see how easy it would be for her to start thinking that maybe education isn't that important, maybe having fun and all the attention that comes with being beautiful is a hell of a lot more appealing.'

'You're seeing things in black and white,' Tessa said uncomfortably. 'She'd hate to think she had disappointed you with her new wardrobe.' She stared down at her slender fingers, at the neatly trimmed fingernails shiny with clear polish. 'I won't take her shopping again and I wouldn't have if I had thought for a minute that you would have such violent objections to her splashing out on some pretty routine teenage gear. Not even really teenage, as a matter of fact. Just different from what she's accustomed to wearing.'

Why did he get the feeling that he was being verbally outmanoeuvred? Curtis looked at the smooth, bland face and frowned. He opened his mouth to say something, thought better of it and grunted instead.

'We'll have to agree to differ.'

'We will,' Tessa agreed, lowering her eyes, 'and, of course, there'll be no more corrupting shopping sprees.'

There was perfect acquiescence in that response except, he thought, for his perfect secretary to be acquiescent, she should also have been chastened, and chastened she certainly was not. In fact, in her own quiet way, he got the sneaking suspicion that she was reprimanding him. He moved swiftly away from the whole contentious subject and for the next hour they worked solidly and swiftly. As she was standing to leave he leaned back in his chair and asked her what she thought of his plans to consolidate a base in the Far East.

'Have you been reading up on this?' he asked, when she had finished her impressive monologue and Tessa relaxed enough to smile at him.

'Of course I haven't "been reading up on it". I've always preferred a good work of fiction to a computer magazine. No, I just happen to have a brain in my head and an ability to voice an opinion.'

'Which is why you're turning out to be such a good little secretary,' Curtis replied smugly. 'I'm going to have to admit to my mother that she may just have got it right when it came to hiring you. I never thought I'd hear myself say this, but a guy can get tired of beautiful girls sticking the wrong files in the cabinets and typing at a snail's pace.'

'I didn't think the misfiling and slow typing was a problem,' Tessa came back quickly, bristling under the composed surface. 'I thought Lizzie and Marge just picked up the slack.'

'There's way too much gossip in this office,' he said, grinning. 'I'll have to have a word.' He was an unrepentant sinner, though. Tessa, however, was in no mood to indulge him. From what she had seen, he was far too indulged already. He had been indulged at birth, by being blessed with staggering good looks, and from that it had probably only been a matter of time before self-assurance and charm had stepped into the equation. Add a brilliant mind and the world, she reckoned, had probably been his oyster from when he was a toddler.

'Will that be all?'

'You've gone prune-mouthed on me again.'

'Prune-mouthed?' Tessa flushed.

'You know what I mean. Tight-lipped. Like a schoolteacher inspecting a particularly offensive pupil.'

Tessa knew exactly what he meant and that in his own forthright way he had no compunctions whatsoever in airing his views, the way he always did. In all fairness, she knew that she could give him a piece of her mind and he wouldn't bat an eyelash, but naturally she wouldn't. She wouldn't fly off the handle and she certainly would never dream of telling him that being compared to a tight-lipped schoolmarm really hurt. It was just a little too near the mark for comfort.

She wasn't about to let him totally off the hook, however. She drew in a deep breath and said calmly, 'If you don't like my demeanour, then perhaps you'd like me to go?'

'Now you're offended.' He swept out of the chair and was standing by her before she had time to beat a tactical retreat. His voice was gushingly solicitous. 'And I like your demeanour!' He placed his hands on her shoulders and Tessa felt a peculiar surge of heat race through her, sending her heart into furious overdrive. 'It's very...bracing.'

*Bracing?* Was that a step up or a step down from tight-lipped? The worst of it was that he genuinely didn't recognise why she would be offended. Because she wasn't an airhead, she was virtually sexless. Infuriatingly, it bothered her.

'That's a huge improvement,' Tessa said, forcing a smile.

'Good. And I want you to know that you're a valuable member of the team.'

'Thank you.' She wished he would just remove his hands from her shoulders. Horrifyingly, he tilted her face to his and gave her a crooked smile, a smile that could turn lead to jelly.

'You're welcome. I like the way you speak your mind, I like your opinions and I don't want you to go away thinking that I ever make unfavourable comparisons between you and my previous secretaries. I use the term secretaries loosely.'

Something funny was happening to her inside, something confusing and frightening. 'Okay.' Quick agreement, quick exit.

He released her and she nearly fell backwards. 'Brilliant!' He remained where he was, watching as she left his office, only calling out behind her, 'Just don't see that as a licence to go shopping with my daughter, though!'

This time Tessa closed the door just a little too loudly behind her.

# CHAPTER FOUR

A QUIET weekend at home would be just what the doctor ordered.

Curtis's outspoken comments, not meant to be insulting but insulting anyway, had got to Tessa and she didn't quite understand why. In fact, she spent most of Saturday trying to work it out. It was proving annoying, as if the question were like a demon sprite, willing to be boxed in for intermittent periods, but only so that it could leap out at her just when she wasn't expecting it.

Lucy had gone away for the weekend and the house was blissfully calm.

At five-thirty, Tessa returned to the house after a hectic but essential visit to the supermarket. When she had been at her last job, she had always done her shopping on a Thursday night after work. Her hours had been fairly regular there and she had slipped into a routine that had suited her.

Now...

She had to do several trips from her small, second-hand car to the kitchen and it was half an hour before she had finally unpacked the last of the groceries, then she sat down wearily on a kitchen chair, tipping her head over the back and closing her eyes.

The demon sprite lunged out at her again.

She found herself thinking about him, thinking about the intense beauty of his face, the way his eyes crinkled when he laughed, the way they narrowed when he was thinking about something. She found that she had even committed to memory his various little habits, like the way he always yanked open the bottom drawer of his desk whenever he wanted to lean back in his chair and stretch out his long legs.

Tessa shook her head impatiently, snacked on a bar of chocolate, even though she knew that she would be eating in a couple of hours' time and was in the shower, in the process of washing her hair, when she heard the sharp buzz of the doorbell.

*Lucy,* was her first thought as she reluctantly turned off the shower, stepped out and wrapped herself in a bath sheet. Had she come home early from her weekend away? Lucy had a problem with keys. She continually went out and forgot to take them with her. Whenever she was faced with Tessa's wrath at having to drag herself out of bed at some ungodly hour to let her in, she invariably smiled sheepishly and swore never to repeat the same mistake again.

Her hair clung damply around her face, which was in a definite scowl as she pulled open the front door, lips parted to inform her sister that this was *absolutely the last time* she was going to go through this predictable charade.

No words came out. Something did but it was akin to a choking, strangled noise.

On the doorstep was Curtis, dressed in an impeccable charcoal-grey suit with a very conventional white shirt peeping out from between the lapels of his jacket. On one side was a highly disgruntled-looking daughter and on the other a leggy blonde with hair tumbling in disarray past her shoulders and a full complement of war paint. Her glossy red lips matched her glossy red fingernails, which in turn matched the glimpse of glossy tight dress that was only loosely covered by a startling terracotta-coloured silk trench coat. On anyone else the combination of colours would have brought on a sudden rush of nausea in the casual observer, but on her the clash of colour was dramatic and overwhelming.

Tessa shrank back and mortified colour crept slowly up her face. She still couldn't seem to string two words together to form a sentence.

She stared dumbly at Curtis and for once he didn't give her that lazy, amused grin.

'Do you normally answer the door with nothing but a towel wrapped round you?' he asked, levering his eyes upwards to her face.

'I thought it was my sister.' At last, she had managed to corner some vocal cords. 'What are you doing here?'

'You'd better let us in before you catch a death of a cold,' he said reasonably. Tessa was very tempted to slam the door on their faces, but he had already wedged one foot on the doorstep. She stood back, burning with embarrassment.

'Excuse me. I need to change.'

'Oh, don't put yourself out for us,' Curtis said, grinning now and raking his eyes over her semi-clad body in one wicked sweep. Just the sort of look she could imagine him giving the blonde at his side. That thought was enough to put frost into her voice.

'The sitting room's through there. I'll just be a minute.' She tried not to be affected by the thought of three pairs of eyes following her progress up the stairs towards the bedroom, but she was trembling when she shut the door behind her and hurriedly grabbed some clothes from the wardrobe. A pair of faded jeans and a long-sleeved black tee shirt that had faded through numerous washes.

Her hair was still a wet mess but, rather than waste time blow-drying it, she did what she sometimes did on a weekend to get it out of the way. She braided it into two plaits that just about reached her shoulders.

Now she looked about sixteen, but frankly she didn't care. How dared he waltz into her house without calling her beforehand to find out whether he was welcome?

*Because he was shrewd enough to guess the response,* a little voice said.

She slipped on some bedroom slippers, some garish black and gold pointy-tipped things that looked as though they would have been better suited to life in a Middle Eastern harem, which had been one of her birthday presents from her sister four months previously.

The three unwanted visitors were in the sitting room, although, when Tessa walked in, it was apparent that only one of them was at ease. Curtis had made himself at home in one of the comfy chairs while the other two were perched in rigid discomfort at opposite ends of the sofa.

'Sorry to barge in on you like this,' he said pleasantly.

'You didn't have to.' Tessa sat down, uneasy in her own house, which was ridiculous. 'You could have telephoned first.' She turned to Anna, caught her eye and smiled. 'How are you, Anna? Recovering from your first week at work?'

Anna made a valiant attempt to smile back but her eyes slid across to her father and the corners of her mouth turned down. It was a pout full of sulkiness. And, Tessa noted, she was back to wearing her neat, background clothes. A long-sleeved shift dress in brown, dark tights and flat brown shoes with a distinctive and recognisable thin gold designer band at the top.

'I would have if I had had the opportunity, but coming here only became an option on the drive over. Didn't it, Anna?'

'I just don't want to go to the theatre this evening,' Anna

said stiffly, 'and I don't know why you're making such a big deal of it.'

Tessa wondered what this minor domestic tiff had to do with her, but she refrained from saying anything. Out of the corner of her eye, the vision in red vibrated in silence on the sofa, her body language screaming discomfort.

Curtis must have read her mind because he finally introduced the woman, Susie, his date. His attention was obviously not on her, though, because he immediately reverted to his daughter, frowning as he looked at her. 'Anna insisted on the way over that we come here,' Curtis said patiently. She couldn't have imagined him ever getting cross with his daughter, with whom he was effusively affectionate, but he was cross now. 'She threw a tantrum, in fact.'

'I did not throw a tantrum, Dad! You just won't listen to me!' Tears thickened her voice and Tessa wanted to groan in dismay. 'You *said* that the two of us would be going out!'

So that was it. Poor Susie, the innocent participant in this small family drama. The girl looked close to tears herself and, having resolved to get rid of her guests as quickly as possible, Tessa now heard herself asking whether they wanted anything to drink. She could only offer wine in terms of alcohol.

'I'll come with you!' Anna sprang to her feet and disappeared out of the sitting room before her father could protest, and protest he most certainly was about to, judging from the expression on his face.

'I'm tired of it!' was the first thing Anna said as soon as Tessa was in the kitchen. She plonked herself down on a chair and glumly propped her chin in her hand. 'He promised we'd go out for a night, just the two of us, and then, lo and behold, the next thing I hear is the doorbell and there's Barbie-doll Susie on the doorstep!'

Tessa rested three wineglasses on the counter and turned round to face Anna. She, uncharitably, thought that the description was very accurate. In her head she had idly wondered what sort of women Curtis was attracted to. In the flesh, she realised that she hadn't been very far from the predictable truth. Glossy packaging without much of an intellect inside. She wondered whether his daily life was so full of creativity and challenge that beautiful bimbos were restful, a panacea at the end of a long working day.

She reminded herself sternly that, one way or another, speculation like that went nowhere because his private life was no concern of hers.

'He must have just forgotten about the theatre tickets, Anna,' she said gently, 'and I'm sure he didn't think you'd react the way you have. Surely you've been...well, out with him in the company of one of his girlfriends?'

'Of course I have.' She sighed laboriously. 'But when I was younger, I never minded, and anyway, he never made a habit of it. I know I'm behaving like a kid, but...'

'You *are* just a kid.'

'A teenager! And that's another thing.' She stuck her chin out belligerently, daring Tessa to side with her father. 'He said that the clothes we bought together don't suit me, that I look better in less gaudy stuff, but yet he has the *nerve* to go out with women who dress like...like teenagers!' The unfairness of it caused the threat of tears to become reality, and, try as she might, Tessa could find no easy comforting words to that adolescent protest because she basically agreed with his daughter.

She sighed inwardly and marvelled at how a man as clever and as worldly-wise as Curtis Diaz could be so hideously inept when it came to reading his own daughter and understanding what made her tick.

'You know what fathers are like,' Tessa said, playing down the situation. 'They can be a bit overprotective.'

'Was yours? I mean, when you were my age?'

'Different philosophy,' she hedged, thinking of her parents, who had quite rightly suspected that too many stringent guidelines ended up gestating bigger problems than allowing their girls a little leeway here and there, just enough never to make them feel as though they were being imprisoned against their will.

'I hate arguing with Dad.' Anna looked at her with such misery that Tessa's heart constricted. 'I don't see all that much of him. I mean, I'm at boarding-school and he does his best to see me whenever I'm on holiday or half-term, but, really, it's not an everyday thing. I just want us to go back to being how we were, but he can be such a tyrant!'

'Not always.' She poured wine into the glasses and offered Anna a glass of something light, which she refused, as she did the offer to come back into the sitting room, preferring to remain in the kitchen.

'We've ruined your evening, haven't we?' she asked in a small voice and Tessa laughed.

'I'd only planned on some pasta on a tray in front of the television. The most relaxing thing I can do when Lucy's not around.' She fished a circular tray out of a cupboard and carried the wine into the sitting room where active conversation was under way between Curtis and his Barbie doll, as Tessa now found herself thinking of the other woman.

'I'm dropping Susie back to her place,' Curtis announced, standing up and ignoring the wine. 'There's no point even thinking of going to any theatre now. The play will already have started anyway. Is there a chance you can hang on to Anna for about forty minutes?'

Tessa did not want to get caught up in this. She didn't want his private life to begin infiltrating into hers and she didn't want to find herself reluctant referee in a disagreement between him and his daughter. On the other hand, what choice did she have? She remembered Anna's forlorn face and felt sorry for her, so she just nodded.

Susie had her hand resting on his, and her face, raised to his, was disappointed. She looked, in fact, as though she had just been put through a wringer, as though, suddenly, from being the woman who was all dressed up, she had become the woman who was all dressed up with nowhere to go. And on top of that she couldn't even command her date's attention, which was very firmly focused on a sullen fourteen-year-old tucked away in the kitchen.

Curtis was back almost to the minute but the trip had done his tension no good. He was still unusually brooding when he stepped into the hall, glancing towards the small kitchen at the back.

'Thanks for that. Where is she? I'll take her home and let you enjoy the remainder of your evening in peace.'

'Bed.'

'Bed? You were going to enjoy your Saturday evening in bed?' Hard on the heels of that came a crazy thought, *And who's the lucky man?* He wasn't looking down at his efficient secretary who always had her hair pinned back and always, but always, wore neat little suits and blouses carefully buttoned all the way up. He was looking at someone with calm eyes but a stubborn chin, someone with glossy hair and a figure that managed to be boyish but very, very feminine.

He felt a dangerous stirring in his loins. Never had he felt this sudden, uncomfortable prickling under his skin when in the company of a woman. For a man who was highly complex underneath the easy charm and self-assurance, Curtis had never been drawn to his female counterpart. He liked his women to be easy on the eye and easy on the intellect.

He turned away abruptly and was aware of her following him into the sitting room. 'Anna? So where is she?' he demanded sharply, which drew an instant bristling response from Tessa.

'She's upstairs in my bed. Asleep.'

*'At this hour?'*

'She was upset, Curtis. I told her to head upstairs to wash her face and when she didn't come down I went to check her to find her fast asleep. Like a baby.' They stared at one another and Tessa felt her heart begin to race. He had disposed of his jacket, but he was still disturbingly tall and dark, especially in the confines of her house. She had a sudden feeling of being invaded and she had another spurt of resentment that he had brought his private life here, in her house, where she was defenceless.

'I'll go and wake her up.'

Good idea, Tessa thought to herself, and then you can both head off to wherever you had planned on going. Anywhere but here would suit her fine.

'Maybe you should let her sleep off her stress for a little while,' she said reluctantly. 'You can always come back if you want to take your girlfriend out. I'm home all evening and I don't mind keeping an eye on her.'

'You're home on a Saturday night?' For some reason that gave him quite a satisfied feeling and he relaxed enough to grin at her.

'Yes, that's right. Home on a Saturday night. How dull of me.'

'I never said that staying in was dull. In fact, I rather enjoy staying in sometimes myself...'

The implication behind that hovered tantalisingly in the air between them, the implication that stay in he might but he would be doing it in the company of a woman, a Susie clone. Champagne in bed. Certainly not pasta on a tray in front of the television.

'You never answered my question,' Tessa repeated coldly. 'I can babysit Anna if you'd like to pick up what you were doing with your girlfriend.' Neither of them had sat down. Curtis had strolled over to the window and was perched on the ledge, arms folded over his muscled chest. Tessa had stopped in mid-stride in the middle of the room and hadn't moved.

'Oh, I think Susie's better off where she is. No point making her endure my company tonight.'

'I doubt she would consider it hard work,' Tessa muttered sourly and he tilted his head politely to one side in a parody of someone doing their best to catch what was being said.

'I can't hear you when you mutter like that.'

Tessa panicked. What was she supposed to do with him if he stayed in her house till his daughter woke up? She had had enough experience of fraught teenagers to know that they could retreat for a quick nap only to fall into a deep four-hour sleep. Lucy had had a talent for just that when she had been younger. Tessa thought of Curtis Diaz prowling through her house for four hours while she tried to make conversation, and every ounce of self-composure went into immediate meltdown.

'I said that I thought she looked...well, very let down... that your plans for the evening had changed... I'm sure she'd appreciate you going over and, honestly, there's no point you being here if Anna's sleeping...' She wondered whether he had detected any desperation in her voice. He was still gazing at her with every semblance of attentiveness, though she had a feeling that she was getting precisely nowhere. 'And I...I hadn't planned on any company. There's nothing to eat in the house...'

'Nothing to eat in the house?'

'Well, nothing fancy...' He had managed to make her plausible-enough excuse sound ridiculous, as though a rooting-through of her cupboards and fridge would unearth nothing more than a few crusts of bread and some mouldy cheese.

'I'd prefer to stay here. I understand your evening's been spoiled, but I'm relieved you had nothing planned...'

Tessa felt her cheeks burn at what she thought was amusement in his voice. 'Lucy's away for the weekend...I enjoy the peace and quiet...'

'So you said. Now, what were you planning on eating?'

'Nothing! I mean, nothing much...'

'Nothing much. Sounds fine. Unless you'd rather I went and brought us back something? There's a supermarket I noticed on the high street. I'm pretty sure it'll still be open.'

'No, that won't be necessary,' Tessa said in a strangled voice. Visions of him returning in his fast car with shopping bags for an evening in cooking together was enough to bring her out in clammy perspiration.

It occurred to her that she had never entertained a man at home, not in the sense of make a meal together, sit and watch television. She had had a scattering of dates but no one important and she had always been happy to either go out somewhere or meet in a crowd. No wonder this man found her so amusing, accustomed as he was to the women he went out with.

'I was just going to make myself some pasta,' Tessa said

reluctantly. 'If you wait here, I can stretch it to two. I guess.'

He could hardly blame her for the lack of graciousness in her offer. He had descended on her with Anna in tow, ruined the peaceful evening she had planned, and she had now been further inconvenienced because his daughter had decided to fall asleep in her bed, leaving him here like a spare part.

That being said, Curtis didn't for a minute contemplate taking her up on her suggestion that he return to his date for the rest of the evening.

'I'll go and check on Anna,' he informed her, 'and pasta sounds great.'

'You can watch a little television if you like. Nothing much on and I'm afraid we don't have cable, but...quiz shows can be quite entertaining...provided you don't want to think too much...' She knew that she was gabbling on, but his eyes were mesmerising, that was the only word to describe it. She had to inhale deeply and turn away to break the connection, then she hurried top speed towards the kitchen, hearing him as he headed up the stairs towards the bedroom.

*Calm down,* she told herself! She took a few steadying breaths and switched on the portable CD player on the kitchen counter. Lucy found it hilarious that her big sister actually listened to *easy listening* music, but right now it was exactly what her jangled nerves needed.

A soft, soothing melody filled the little kitchen and she began to slow down, humming quietly to herself as she began chopping onions and mushrooms and tossing them into the plastic bowl next to her.

She imagined Curtis sitting in the room watching a tedious quiz show and couldn't stop herself from smirking.

In all her life, she could think of no one less suited to

being condemned to enforced immobility in front of a boring television programme. Curtis Diaz had way too much energy surging through him for that. Well, she couldn't help but think that there was a spot of justice to be found in the fact that he had wrecked her evening, intruded upon her private life despite her having made it absolutely clear from the word go that it was off limits, only to now find himself forced to sit down and kiss his own thrilling evening goodbye in front of the box. She began peeling the cloves of garlic, sniggering heartily at the thought.

The grin was still on her face when she swung around to grab a frying-pan from the cupboard, only to hear the subject of her musings say, in his smoky, sexy voice, 'Care to share the joke?'

Tessa looked up in sudden shock. She had been so absorbed in her pleasant thoughts, so lulled by the melodic strains of music, that she had had no inkling of his presence. She hadn't heard him approach! How long had he been there? Watching her? It made her feel as though he had been standing, spying on the workings of her mind.

'I thought you said that you were going to go and watch some television!' she accused hotly, snatching the frying-pan from the cupboard and proceeding to give him her most withering look.

'No, actually *you* said that I was going to watch television, so that I could be tucked safely out of the way…' He grinned with wicked amusement as his barb homed in with staggering accuracy.

Tessa recovered her aplomb quickly. 'And why aren't you?'

'I did make an effort…' He shrugged and walked into the kitchen where, infuriatingly, he began poking around in the bowl of chopped vegetables while Tessa watched in affronted silence. 'But...' he spun around and looked at her '...absolutely nothing on...'

'Not even a quiz show?' she asked sweetly.

'Oh, yes, a couple of those. I wasn't convinced. Can I help?'

'Yes. You can go and watch TV and leave me in peace to get this food ready.'

'I like your taste in music. What is this? Compilation?' Without asking, he gathered up the stack of CDs that she kept on the counter by Lucy's assortment of herbal tablets, and made himself at home on one of the kitchen chairs so that he could sift through them and give her his valued opinion on each and every CD.

'I think we should stick this one on,' he announced, waving one of the CDs at her in a satisfied manner. 'Lots of old numbers. In fact, I'm a little surprised you're not into more modern music!'

Tessa made an inarticulate noise and began her work with the frying-pan, some butter and garlic, and the vegetables.

With staggering arrogance, he put on the CD he wanted to hear, a compilation of old soul songs, from way back to Otis Redding, and the next thing she felt was his warm breath fanning her neck as he asked her for a dance.

Already hot from standing in front of the stove and having to contend with his presence in the kitchen, virtually right under her feet, Tessa now felt a surge of blazing warmth invade her body in a rush.

'Don't be ridiculous!' she snapped, jabbing the vegetables in the frying-pan with overdone savagery.

'What...not now? Not with me? Or not ever with anyone...?'

'Shut up!' She daredn't lift her eyes to his, even when she was aware of him drawing back. If he even glanced at her flushed face, she knew that he would read every shred of wild confusion inside her, every treacherous tug of excitement filling her veins like poison. 'Why?' he asked interestedly. 'Am I touching on a raw nerve? Don't tell me that you've never danced to a beautiful piece of music in the privacy of your own four walls? With a man?'

Actually, no.

Tessa added some herbs and cream to the mixture and stuck a saucepan of water on to boil for the pasta, hiding behind the pretence of busyness to avoid answering his prying questions.

'You're not *a man*,' she said, turning around to face him, arms folded protectively across her breasts. It was very important that she get that straight right now, she decided, before her wayward mind started taking too many unwelcome detours. Yes, he was attractive. Well, formidable, really. Yes, she had been aware of his sex appeal before now, but not like this, not in the claustrophobic confines of her own house. She had a deep-rooted fear that if she didn't lay down her boundaries, something from him, some oozing magnetism, might just seep into the walls around her, into the furniture and lie waiting in ambush for her whenever she returned home.

'You're not a *man*,' she repeated, 'You're *my boss*. You're the person I happen to work for, who just happens to have found himself in my house for reasons beyond my control, and it's no good you giving me a little speech about how you like to know your employees inside out, about how you like them being three-dimensional. I don't feel any need to be three-dimensional with you. So, no, I won't dance with you and whether I ever have at home with anyone is none of your business!'

That had wiped the grin off his face, she noticed. In fact, it seemed to have temporarily deprived him of the power of speech, which should have been good, should have been a clear pointer that she had won this particular battle, but for some reason the look on his face now was even more unsettling.

He had gone absolutely still and there was a dangerous quality to his stillness that had every pulse in her body racing.

'Wh-which isn't to say that I *resent* your probing...' she stammered, lying through her teeth. 'I mean, I know that it's part and parcel of your personality...'

'Being nosy?'

'Curious,' Tessa amended hurriedly. 'Interested in everyone and everything...which brings me to my cooking...you'll be interested to know that I'm not awfully good at it...' She fervently prayed that he would take the bait, accept the olive branch she was holding out, which was by way of apologising for her criticism while sticking to her guns. He did. He gave her one of those heart-stoppingly crooked smiles and suggested wine with the meal, reminding her that none of them had touched what she had brought in earlier, before he had driven Susie home.

Curtis could almost hear her shudder with relief. He was pretty relieved himself. Since he had arrived at the house, he had been too aware of her for his own good. Too aware of her clean smell, the enchanting freshness of her looks, the enticing depths of her personality which fought him off and beckoned him at the same time, and just for a minute there, when she had firmly put him in his place, reminded him that he was nothing more than her boss and a highly inconvenient one at that, he had felt as if someone had punched him in the stomach. Yes, he *was* her boss. A little technicality he didn't intend to forget. Despite his predilection for sexy secretaries, he had never been tempted to sleep with any of them. Why he felt compelled to hire them in the first place was something he had never questioned, although he was inclined to agree with his mother that it was all to do with delegation of duties. He could get away with giving them the minimum to do, ensuring that company confidentiality was never threatened. It had always suited him. Tessa was already winning his trust, slowly but surely, when it came to work. Jeopardising that on an insane whim would be madness. Added to which he was not, by nature, attracted to women like her, women of discreet charms, however alluring those charms might seem on the odd occasion. Like right now.

He struggled to recover his usual easy charm and not let his attention stray from her flustered face to the gentle swell of her breasts and the slimness of her legs encased in their tight jeans.

'Some wine, then. Food smells good, whatever you say…' He disappeared towards the sitting room, to rescue the untouched wine she had poured earlier on and returned with the tray. 'Gone a bit tepid, unfortunately…'

'No problem. There's some ice in the freezer.'

That unsettling moment had passed as ice was fetched and the table set and the food brought out, occupying most of the table top even though it was just one dish of pasta, one of salad and some dressing.

Or had it?

They sat opposite one another, but Tessa could feel her cheeks aching from having to force herself to smile. Just a few centimetres too far, and their knees would touch. A major disadvantage with a tiny kitchen table, she decided. To avert that possibility, she tilted her legs to one side, but every fibre in her being was aware of him, aware of the flex of his muscles as he dug into his food, aware of the way he twirled the spaghetti on his fork, aware of his dark eyes resting on her face during mouthfuls.

They talked about music, pleasant, unthreatening chit-chat that made her think about dancing with him. They talked a bit about work, about his ideas for the Far East, which made her wonder how he would look after a few weeks in the hot sun. Even darker and sexier than he did now. From that they moved easily into chatting about holidays abroad, and after she'd drunk two glasses of wine in record time she heard herself elaborating on her childhood, on how things had changed after her parents had died, on places she had seen and all the ones she wanted to but probably never would. At the back of her mind she knew that she would regret all the confidentiality in the morning, especially after her robust speech about keeping the lines between them clear.

But she didn't want any pregnant pauses to creep into the conversation between them.

'I hope it hasn't been too much of a strain,' Curtis said, when they had finished eating.

'What hasn't?'

'My being here with you tonight, taking advantage of your hospitality and good nature...'

He knew that she would blush. He also knew that he should be listening to his head, which was telling him to leave as soon as possible, even if that meant waking his daughter up.

'I...no, of course not...it's been fine...'

'Good.' He stood up and waved her down when she was about to follow suit. 'Don't even think about it! You cooked and I'll wash. Fair's fair!' He raked his long fingers through his hair and looked at her steadily. It required a superhuman feat of concentration. Her mouth looked so damned tempting, half parted like that...

'Why don't you go and check on my daughter?' he said

thickly, turning away. 'I'm a quick washer. By the time you get back I'll be done.'

Tessa stood up, thankful for something to do that required her to be out of the kitchen. 'Just make sure you do a good job,' she said lightly, addressing his broad back and wondering how she could possibly know that he was smiling. 'I don't accept shoddy work.'

She had expected a nightmare evening. It hadn't been. It had been good, and she wasn't sure whether that was worse...

# CHAPTER FIVE

TEN minutes later Tessa returned to the kitchen to find that the washing-up was certainly being done but in a cavalier fashion that entailed stacks of dishes balanced precariously on the draining-board. She watched, enjoying the sensation of being the observer rather than the observed, as Curtis's hand hovered, trying to locate a safe spot on which a wine-glass could be deposited without bringing the whole fragile balancing act crashing to the floor.

'Anna's up,' she announced. Without intervention, she doubted that the glass would survive in one piece. Before he could add it to the worrying pyramid of dishes, she grabbed a tea-cloth and removed it from his hand.

'Oh, good,' Curtis said, taking time out to watch her as she quickly dried the object and then moved on to remove crucially placed items back to the safety of the kitchen counter.

'Up and very apologetic about just falling asleep like that. Apparently she's been up very late most nights, doing emails to her friends, and what with exhaustion from work and all the stress of this evening, she just closed her eyes for one second and nodded off. I told her that she could have a bath and freshen up before she came down.'

'Well, let's hope she's in a slightly better frame of mind when she emerges,' Curtis replied, rinsing the last of the cutlery and dumping it into the upturned frying-pan, which was the closest thing to hand.

'I think she's hoping pretty much the same about you, actually.' Tessa carried on with the drying-up, not looking at him. 'There's a method to washing dishes, in case no one's ever told you,' she said, breaking the silence with nervous chatter. 'It usually involves using those convenient slots in the plastic for plates and the little attached rectangle at the front for cutlery.'

'I say that when it comes to washing dishes, speed is of the essence. I have no reason why Anna thinks I might be in a bad mood.'

'Because you were in one before she decided to lock off and go to sleep?' Tessa prompted, sticking the last of the dried-up dishes into cupboards and moving to stand behind one of the chairs.

'It's not every day a man gets attacked by his daughter because he happens to want to bring a woman along with him on a date.'

Tessa gave him a long, dry look and he returned it with one of innocent bewilderment.

'I really don't think she was objecting to you wanting to bring *a woman* along with you,' Tessa informed him succinctly. 'I think it was the *type* of woman you wanted to bring along.'

'Oh, I see.' He looked upwards, calculating how long Anna would be having a bath. Not long, from the sound of footsteps just above him. 'Look,' he said urgently, 'I really need to have a chat with you about this whole sorry situation. You seem to have built up some kind of rapport with my daughter and—'

'Forget it.' Yes, he was her boss, and, yes, there were limits. She could get a whiff of where he was heading with this one and she didn't like what she smelled. It had the fishy odour of trying to entice her into influencing a four-teen-year-old girl.

'Forget *what*? You haven't even let me finish!'

'I think I hear your daughter descending,' Tessa said

with heartfelt relief as the footsteps heralded a rush into the kitchen, where Anna immediately skidded to a halt.

'Sorry, Dad!' It was an apology without being apologetic and she eyed him warily, trying to gauge his mood from a safe distance. But her feathers were still ruffled. Not ruffled with the normal adolescent truculence and hostility. After a lifetime of absolute adherence to her father's wishes and adoration from afar, truculence and hostility would not be within her range of emotion. But Tessa could see all the signs of teenage rebellion, nevertheless.

'If you'd said you were tired, I would never have suggested we go out,' Curtis responded, shoving his hands in his pockets.

'It wasn't about whether I was tired or not.'

Tessa sighed.

In an hour's time they would both have forgotten their argument, but in an hour's time she would still be dealing with the fallout of having been dragged into involvement.

'Perhaps it's time both of you…sorted out your differences at home? By which I mean your own home?'

Two pairs of eyes swivelled towards her, neither displaying any wild enthusiasm for her suggestion for them to leave.

Tessa groaned inwardly.

'It's getting late,' she tried again, 'and Anna must be starving. She hasn't eaten, after all.' She turned to Curtis, appealing to his paternal side.

'I really don't want to go to a restaurant in this…' Anna said, flicking her head and staying her ground.

Tessa was puzzled. 'In what?'

'This.' One hand indicated her outfit in a smooth sweep.

'Oh, right.'

'You look beautiful, Anna. I told you that earlier!'

'Dad, you've been telling me that since I was a baby!'

'You've been beautiful since you were a baby!'

This was going nowhere fast. Having survived dinner, Tessa now recognised it seemed as though imminent departure was becoming tangled up in a quagmire of two people who, probably for the first time ever, had hit a rough patch. And they had hit it in her house.

'Would you like me to fix you something to eat, Anna?' she interrupted their exchange of words reluctantly.

'Have you got any pizza?' Anna asked hopefully and Tessa shook her head. 'Well, could you perhaps send out for some?'

'There's a pizza place just a few minutes' drive away,' Tessa said, brightening up. 'Why don't the two of you…? Well, it's not as though it's anything fancy…you needn't worry about your outfit there…'

'It's Saturday night. It's a pizzeria.'

'Right.' Tessa nodded in comprehension. She remembered the syndrome well. When *she* was fourteen and still enjoying her youth, she too would never have ventured into a casual, adolescent-ridden setting in anything but her most screamingly casual clothes. And when *Lucy* was fourteen and heading anywhere where she might possibly be seen by other teenagers, her outfits had involved whatever jeans had happened to be in fashion, the least practical of her tops and shoes that most normal people would have found it difficult to walk in.

'Explain, please,' Curtis interrupted from the sidelines of what looked like a female conspiracy, and Tessa turned to him.

'Pizzerias on a Saturday are usually home to teenagers wearing less…well, formal clothes. Anna thinks she might stand out a bit…'

'Stand out!' Curtis exploded incredulously. 'Stand out?

Yes, sure you'll stand out but only because you're a cut above the rest!'

Anna greeted this by turning on her heel and stomping out of the kitchen, leaving her father with a look of stunned amazement on his face. This quickly changed to glowering accusation as he looked at Tessa.

'This is all your fault,' he informed her. 'We never had these ridiculous problems until you decided to take her on a shopping trip. She was always fine with the clothes she had.'

'I think you need to go and talk to her,' Tessa returned with as much calm as she could muster given the unfairness of his accusation.

With a curt nod, he disappeared only to return minutes later. 'Where's your phone book?' he asked, pulling his mobile phone out of his pocket. 'It seems that eating out *anywhere* tonight isn't an option with my daughter. She's decided that she wants to sit in front of your television and eat some pizza so I've told her that I'll order some in.'

'Sit in front of *my* television? Why can't you both go home and she can sit in front of *your* television and eat the pizza?'

This was getting ridiculous. From a quiet night in, enjoying the peace of having the house to herself, she now found herself entertaining two people at loggerheads with one another, one of whom evoked all the wrong reactions in her. Worse, she could cope with him when he was at work, could cope with him when he was teasing her even though it made her insides squirm. Could even cope with him, just, when he was flirting with those dark eyes and that sexy smile. Flirting came naturally to him and meant nothing. In that context, it was possible to distance herself from some of the devastating effects of the odd wayward smile, the occasional crinkling of his eyes when he looked at her.

However, coping with him when he was like this, baffled and seemingly at a loss as to how to deal with a situation, was proving a nightmare. She wanted to plunge right in and stroke all his troubles away. Just the thought of that made her gulp with a hysterical swelling of pure alarm.

This was the essence of the charmer, she reminded herself. And the man was charm personified. It was a quality that couldn't be pulled out of a hat and then shoved back in; it was something that was there, always, enticing and beckoning. It was the quality that made women want to be near him, made them want to continue contact long after any relationship might have gone pear-shaped.

'Phone book?' he reminded her, bringing her thoughts to a skidding halt.

'I'm really very tired.' One last stab, she thought, one last attempt to propel him and Anna out of the door, leaving her in peace.

Curtis looked at his watch and then looked at her. 'It's not even nine-thirty as yet.'

'Yes, well, not everyone keeps late nights.' A deafening silence greeted this and it didn't take a rocket scientist to work out what was going through his head. Either he had reached the right conclusion, namely that she didn't want him around, in which case his active mind would already be jumping ahead to reasons and maybe, just maybe, coming up with the right one. Or else, she would be confirming his sweeping assumptions that she was as dreary as he thought she was, someone who retired to bed before ten with a cup of cocoa when all the world was out having a good time on a Saturday night.

Tessa fetched the phone book from the little bookshelf behind her and handed it to him.

'What did you say the name of that pizzeria was...?'

She gave it to him and watched in despairing silence as he rapidly phoned and placed his order before clicking off his mobile and sticking it back into his pocket.

'Forty minutes,' he informed her. 'I guess the place is so busy with hordes of appropriately dressed teenagers that the food orders are moving a little slowly.'

Tessa hesitated, torn between ignoring the light-hearted remark, made at her expense, and diving into a serious debate on his short-sightedness in not listening to what his daughter was trying to tell him. In the intervening silence, he solved the dilemma for her.

'Not funny? I suppose you think I'm making fun of a serious situation?'

'What I think doesn't matter and what you do doesn't concern me.'

'Very lofty sentiments,' Curtis mused, eyes narrowing on her. 'Must be easy getting through life when you can detach yourself from annoying situations with such ease.'

'I'm not detaching myself from anything,' she responded hotly. 'I'm just telling you that you have to sort out these temporary problems with Anna yourself. I can't be of any help.'

'You were a great deal of help when it came to rampaging the shops with her in hot pursuit of skimpy clothes.'

Tessa nearly laughed. Did he really see what those women he entertained wore? Had he really noticed Susie's outfit, which just about managed to cover her? If he thought Anna's new wardrobe was comprised of skimpy clothes, then how would he describe his girlfriends' choice of garments?

Silly assumption, she thought. What was good enough for his girlfriends was certainly not good enough for his daughter. Beneath the sharp, unconventional exterior, there beat the heart of a pure traditionalist.

'Would you like a cup of coffee?' Tessa asked, resigning herself to yet more emotional involvement in his life. 'Tea?'

'Coffee would be good.' He shoved himself away from the counter and sat at the kitchen table, watching in silence as she made them both a mug of coffee.

It was as clear as daylight that she wanted to get rid of them, or rather of him, he suspected. The decent thing would have been to leave her in peace, to enjoy the uneventful evening she had planned, but he decided that he really did want to talk to her about Anna, whose behaviour was as mysterious as it was unexpected. He also realised that he was rather enjoying himself here, watching her pad around preparing a meal, listening to her voice her opinions with absolutely no regard for whether she trod on his toes or not.

It was refreshing, he decided.

Refreshing to be in the company of a woman without the inevitability of sex.

He looked at her lazily from under his lashes, noting the slenderness of her body, the perfect jut of her rear, which was always so cunningly camouflaged at work underneath those asexual suits she insisted on wearing. There was nothing obvious about her, he thought. She didn't announce her sexuality, but look just a little deeper and there it was, as subtle but as fragrant as a summer breeze.

'Hello?' Tessa couldn't resist tossing his sarcastic mantra back at him. 'Is anybody there?'

'Hilarious,' Curtis responded, his mouth twitching at the corners. 'Sit down. You're making me nervous hovering over me like that.'

Tessa laughed, not one of those cultivated tinkling

laughs, but a proper laugh. 'I don't think it's possible for anyone to make you nervous.'

'Because, as I've mentioned before, I'm one hundred per cent man?'

'Because you're self-assured and arrogant.'

Curtis eyed her narrowly, trying to work out whether she was joking or being serious and realising that he didn't like it in the least that she thought he was arrogant. Coming from another woman, it wouldn't have bothered him in the slightest, but coming from her...

'Self-assured, yes. Arrogant, no.'

'Well, you seem to make a pretty good job of assuming you know exactly what's right for Anna without even considering that you might just be wrong.' Tessa sat down, rested her elbows on the table and sipped some of the coffee.

She hadn't been making an observation on *him*, he realised. She had been making an observation on one aspect of his behaviour. He shifted irritably in his chair, reluctant to engage in practical conversation, wanting to prod deeper into her and the workings of her mind. Insofar as they related to him.

'Why would I be wrong? I know my daughter.'

'You shouldn't have told her anything about the clothes she'd bought. I assume you did?'

'I mentioned that they seemed a little unsuitable.'

'Well, far be it from me to offer an opinion on how you bring your own child up...'

'But...?'

Tessa shrugged to lessen the impression that she might be voicing unwanted views. Also that his affairs might impact on her much harder than she wanted them to. 'But you should let her wear what she wants to wear, within reason, and please believe me when I tell you that Anna wouldn't push the boat out. She barely glanced at any of the ridiculously hipster trousers kids these days wear or any of the super-tight Lycra tops that leave nothing to the imagination.'

Curtis, head tilted to one side, half heard the gist of her remark. He just heard the telling way she referred to *kids*, as if she were a woman in her fifties instead of someone in their twenties.

'"Kids these days?"' he teased softly, holding her startled look and enjoying the sudden stillness hanging in the air between them. 'You're not exactly an old lady, Tessa.'

'No. I know that. I know I'm...' *A highly qualified and competent secretary, fully computer literate and with the references to show for it.*

'Yes...?' He cocked his head to one side.

'I'm pretty responsible for my age,' she conceded. The doorbell rang. In the nick of time, she felt, because she had uneasily been aware of ground shifting under her feet. She sprang to her feet, only to see that he had similarly stood up and was fishing into his trouser pocket for his wallet.

'You stay here,' he commanded. 'I'll pay for the pizza.'

Stay in the kitchen? Waiting for him to return so that he could resume their conversation, which was slowly sending her into a state of frantic panic? No way.

As soon as he had exited she went to the cupboard and quickly prepared a tray with plate, cutlery, a stack of paper napkins and a glass of orange squash. They coincided in the sitting room, where Anna was engrossed in an inane program featuring two muscle-bound women who seemed to be competing with one another in a series of frankly ridiculous tasks. She made a few appreciative noises when the pizza was put in front of her, barely aware of the pair of them looming to one side.

Curtis opened his mouth to ask what level of nonsense

she was watching, thought better of it and signalled to Tessa that they leave.

When she stood her ground, he tugged her gently but firmly out of the sitting room, keeping his hand on her arm until they were back in the kitchen.

'I get the feeling we might cramp her style if we stay in there with her,' he said, pushing the kitchen door behind him and killing the last vestige of noise wafting in from the television.

'Which is something you would never dream of doing.'

'Touché.' He was still holding onto her, enjoying it, and as though she had suddenly realised that she shrugged him off and sat back down.

'Okay. I get your point.' He reluctantly sat back down. 'Maybe I'm a bit overprotective and now's the time to start cutting the apron strings a bit.'

'That might be a good idea,' Tessa agreed, relieved that the conversation seemed to be back on an even keel. Discussing Anna was bad enough when it came to blurring the boundaries between Curtis and herself, but drifting into the unknown territory of discussing each other was off the scale altogether.

'I mean, lay down too many laws and you can sometimes find that a teenager will attempt to break them all.'

'Is that what you had to cope with when it came to your sister? You must have been pretty green round the gills when you found yourself having to deal with a teenager.'

'I coped,' Tessa informed him briefly.

'Ah, but I'm intrigued. How did you? Cope, I mean?' He smiled encouragingly. The urge to find out more about this woman was becoming irrational. His mind, which frequently drifted off in the direction of work whenever he was in the company of a woman, seemed to have developed extraordinary focusing ability.

His eyes wandered to her mouth, to the slender column of her neck. In his head he began to remove her top, bit by very slow bit.

'Lucy was a headache, but essentially a pretty good kid. No drugs, no alcohol, or at least not much, no staying out all night. I loosened some of her boundaries and she respected that. I think she knew that we'd both been thrown into a new situation and we had to help each other along the best we could if we were to survive. I gave her freedom within limits and she gave me her obedience within limits.'

The little speech fizzled out into the silence, which stretched unbroken until she became aware of the low hum of the fridge, just vague background noise suitable for magnifying the stillness.

'I suppose we've just…just got ourselves into a pattern…' she tripped on, losing the thread of what she was saying with each murmured word. 'She's the frivolous one and I…I indulge her…'

'And who indulges you?'

Tessa was aware of colour invading her face, a hot, burning flush that seemed to originate from within the deepest part of her. She had rested both her hands on the table and was now aware of exactly how small the table was. Certainly not big enough for the two of them when he was staring at her like that and she was responding in classic overwhelmed female tradition.

Then he did something so shockingly intimate that the breath literally caught in her throat, almost as if her brain had shut down and could no longer give the message to her lungs that she should inhale.

He reached out and gently, oh, so gently, began stroking the side of her thumb with his finger.

For such a small gesture, it was unbearably erotic. She felt the dampness of arousal spread through her and when she finally did manage to breathe, it was laboured and painful.

'Who does? Are you going to tell me?' he coaxed softly, and she had to blink several times before she remembered what he had been saying in the first place.

'I...I don't need indulging...' Her own whisper reached her ears with all the force of her forbidden excitement. For the life of her she couldn't remove her hand even though her head was telling her to scramble her wits together and run away.

'I don't believe that...' Curtis murmured. 'Not for a minute.' His finger moved from her thumb to the sensitive flesh of her wrist.

'No boyfriend?'

Fascinated by the movement of his finger, Tessa shook her head slowly.

'Ever?'

She shrugged. 'I've had boyfriends, but nothing serious...' Her lowered eyes flickered and he felt a sharp burst of exultation and an arousal that was so hard that it was almost painful.

Without removing his hand, he slid out of his chair until he was squatting right in front of her, looking up at her. And still he continued that lazy caress of her arm, just a feathering of sensation that was sending her body into a vortex of sensuous excitement.

'Poor baby,' he murmured huskily.

Tessa half opened her mouth to find a reply to this throaty observation, but before any words could emerge he straightened and she gasped as his mouth hit hers with a blinding, urgent passion that stifled every rational thought.

The force of his kiss pushed her head against the chair and she wrapped her arms around his neck, drawing him closer to her and returning the kiss with all the pent-up craving that had been stalking her for weeks.

He pushed her hair back so that he could nibble her ear and his warm breath had her squirming on the chair, panting softly with her eyes closed, arching her neck in open invitation for him to do what he was doing now, trailing his tongue against it, feathering it with kisses while his hand smoothed her taut skin above the waistband of her jeans.

Jeans that felt too tight, too clinging.

It was bliss when he parted her thighs with one hand so that he could position himself between them. Then he circled her waist with his hands, running them up along her ribcage and finding the restriction of her bra as impeding as she did.

Lord, Tessa thought on a soundless groan, this is madness. But as he pushed up her shirt and pushed up her stretchy bra, madness and her ability to deal with it were lost in a swirl of intense, aching desire.

She had never felt like this before. Had never even come close.

In a daze of wonder, she half opened her eyes as his mouth found one nipple and he began to suck it. Her body slid rapturously down a couple of inches in the chair and she surrendered to the ecstasy of his warm, wet mouth exploring the tight buds of her breasts, loving them with exquisite tenderness.

She was experiencing a sensation of total meltdown, and it was only the sudden noise of the television that alerted her numb senses to the awful reality of what they were doing and to the even more awful reality of Anna leaving the sitting room.

With a squeak of horror, Tessa pushed him away, yanked down her top and her bra in one swift movement, over breasts that were still throbbing, and scooted to the furthest corner of the kitchen.

God, she couldn't look at him. She just couldn't. It would be like looking her worst nightmare in the face and knowing that it wasn't about to go away.

*How could she?*

No point blaming him. She had responded enthusiastically, *desperately*, and the thought of that was like a flood of icy water rushing over her, straight through her body and right into her veins.

When she finally did raise her eyes Anna was pushing open the kitchen door and Curtis was back in his chair, outwardly as collected as she was torn apart inside.

'It's finished,' Anna said, yawning. She had brought through the remaining pizza in its box on the tray and she deposited it on the kitchen counter, resoundingly unaware of any atmosphere in the kitchen.

Tessa was deeply and profoundly grateful for the inherent selfishness of most adolescents, who rarely noticed anything that didn't pertain to them.

'Really?' Tessa's mouth ached as she forced herself to smile and appear relaxed. 'Who won?'

'The gigantic one with the straight black hair.' Another yawn. 'She had the muscles of a body-builder.'

'You're tired,' Tessa said lightly, arms folded, holding herself in and still not daring to look across at Curtis, who was sitting forward with his elbows resting on his thighs. 'So am I. In fact, I'm really going to have to be very rude and insist you both go home so that I can get some sleep.'

'Dad?'

'Uh. Yes.' He glanced at his daughter, then seemed to give himself a mental shake before he stood up and stretched, an unconsciously graceful movement that Tessa resentfully thought summed him up. The way he looked,

the way he spoke, the way he moved, it was all a work of
Art and she had succumbed with shameful alacrity.

'I'll be out in a minute, Anna. I just want to have a quick
word with Tessa about some work stuff she needs to do for
me on Monday.'

There was nothing Tessa could do to prevent Anna from
leaving the kitchen and, since she would have to face him,
this seemed as good a time as any. At least the experience
wouldn't last longer than a few minutes, not with his
daughter waiting outside and twiddling her thumbs.

'That should never have happened,' was the first thing
Curtis said when the kitchen door had closed behind Anna.
He stood up and crossed the small distance separating them
while Tessa steeled her features into a mask of frozen im-
passiveness. 'And I'm sorry.'

He raked his fingers in angry frustration through his hair.
He had wanted and he had just gone right ahead and taken,
he thought, sickened by himself. He hadn't stopped to think
that this woman was different, that this woman made him
feel as though that whole-relationship-thing, as he cynically
referred to it, might just be possible. If he could have turned
the clock back, he would have, but he couldn't.

And now she was freezing him out. He gently placed his
finger under her chin and, with a sharp flick of her head,
Tessa backed away and looked at him coldly.

Hadn't he called her *poor baby*? Before he had touched
her? Poor little Tessa, all alone on a Saturday night, with
nowhere to go. Had he thought that seducing her might
have been an act of kindness? He wouldn't even have had
to go down the complete road, just a kiss and a grope,
enough to inject a little colour into her drab life and a little
amusement into his. The pain of humiliation raced through
her, making her giddy.

She would hate him, she thought, but only after she had

hated herself. For closing her eyes and sipping from the poisoned chalice. It was no good telling herself that her body had let her down, that her emotions had been too awesomely powerful for her to withstand.

'I think we should both forget what just happened.' She was surprised at how composed she sounded. 'Things got a little out of control, that's all.'

*'That's all?'*

What more did he want her to say? she wondered savagely. Did he want her to confess how much he had blown her over? Did he want her to massage his already mightily healthy ego by agreeing that she had very nearly become yet another notch on his much-indented bedpost?

'That's right. I may not be as old as you or as experienced...' she shuddered at the dreadfully personal confidence she had shared with him in her heady moment of passion '...but nor am I a silly little fool.' She dismissed the unfortunate incident in a casual shrug. At least, she desperately hoped that she gave that impression. 'These things happen.' Except not to her. To him, yes. To those women with their short, short skirts and come-to-bed eyes, yes. But she knew herself well and the unfortunate incident went far beyond just being unfortunate. It was something that had opened her eyes to the very real fear that she was falling for her boss. Her wildly exciting, unorthodox and utterly unsuitable boss.

'These things sometimes happen, but—'

Tessa saw the yawning, hideous chasm open up in front of her and rushed in to cut him off in mid-correct assumption.

'Never again.' She drew herself up to her full height and mutinously stuck her chin forward. 'It was a mistake and I have to have your word that it will never happen again or else I shall have no option but to leave your company immediately.'

'Fighting talk,' Curtis murmured. 'What makes you think that I would be the perpetrator of any further mistakes?'

It took a few seconds for the meaning of what he had said to sink in, and then she uttered a little dismayed grunt. He was nothing if not direct. He was reminding her that she hadn't exactly been an innocent angel, passively having to endure his advances. She thought of her enthusiastic responses and a tidal wave of pure shame washed over her.

'Because I never make the same mistake twice,' she said forcefully. She had never even been in a situation like this before but even so she knew that she couldn't afford to let her emotions overtake her sanity as she had just done.

'I'll be taking next week off,' Curtis said, moving towards the kitchen door and opening it. 'Having some quality time with Anna as I haven't seen as much of her this week as I wanted to.'

Tessa breathed a sigh of profound relief. She managed to unglue her feet and follow him out of the kitchen, and even managed a smile when they were standing at the front door.

'It's been brilliant working for you,' Anna enthused, making it difficult for Tessa not to be moved by the sincerity. 'Guess I'll see you next time I'm home? Which would be Christmas?'

'I hope so,' Tessa said, directing her attention to Anna but reserving the significance of her words for Curtis.

'I'm sure Tessa will have no reason to leave the company before then,' Curtis murmured to his daughter, conversing with Tessa just below the surface, as she had done with him.

Because, Tessa thought, closing the door on them and then leaning heavily against it to stop herself from subsiding to the floor, he certainly would give her no reason to go. Those twenty ruinous minutes would be history for him because they had meant nothing, hence he could assure her, truthfully, that they would not be repeated.

For her, however...

She let her legs do what they wanted to do and sat down, back to the front door.

Thank goodness he wouldn't be around for a week. She could put everything in perspective and, really, she was not a silly, emotional girl. It was a calming thought. She simply wouldn't allow Curtis Diaz to get under her skin and the fact that he had played her for a fool was mortifying...but helpful.

After all, who, in the end, could be attracted to a man who had had no qualms in making a pass at a woman out of pity?

# CHAPTER SIX

'YOU'RE not still here!' Curtis stopped in the middle of the office and frowned. He, himself, wouldn't be here but for the fact that he had forgotten his mother's Christmas present in his desk drawer.

Tessa looked up guiltily and flushed.

Yes, here she was. Still. At four-thirty in the afternoon when the office was deserted because everyone had either gone home already or else had joined the group who had chosen to have a last lunch and drink at the pub down the road before the company closed for the Christmas break.

'I was just about to leave,' she said, switching off her computer and shoving things into her drawers, tidying up her desk. 'I wanted to finish all my work before the break.'

'How industrious,' Curtis said dryly, strolling over to where she was doing her best to ignore him by concentrating hard on flicking through the remnants of her filing tray. 'I think what's left can wait, don't you?' He reached out and circled her wrist with his fingers, stopping her in mid-tidy.

Tessa's heart did that familiar, lurching thing and she could feel every nerve in her body tense as she stilled and looked at him, at the lazy, perceptive eyes boring into her.

The past seven weeks had been a trial by ordeal. Her ordeal. After that incident in the kitchen, he had stuck rigidly to her request that they forget about what had happened. She had not seen him for the week after, when he had been out of the office, taking his daughter on various excursions, although they had spoken on the telephone regularly, at least twice a day, purely on work matters. When he had come back, things had returned to normal, the only difference between them that she could see was that he was slightly more aloof than he had been.

They settled back into a familiar routine, although he no longer pried into her private life. She was left to assume that the ease with which he had forgotten what had taken place told its own telling story about how much the misplaced episode had affected him. Not much.

'Why didn't you come to the pub with us?' he was asking her now. 'Don't tell me you preferred to stay here and make sure all your pencils were neatly arranged in your drawer before you left? I thought your excuse was that you had to go and do some last-minute Christmas shopping?'

He had released her hand and Tessa made good the opportunity to skirt round her desk and head towards the coat stand in the corner of the room. She could feel his eyes following her every movement.

'I do have a bit of shopping to do, actually,' she flung lightly over her shoulder as she put on her coat.

'Oh, yes. What?'

'This and that.' She shrugged and then, wondering whether he was going to stay on, hovered for a while. 'Are you going to be working now?'

'Yes,' Curtis informed her gravely. 'I thought I might just get in a couple of hours' work. You know, tidy my desk and get all my pens and pencils in some kind of order for when I return after the Christmas break.'

Tessa lowered her eyes, but her mouth was twitching. However much she knew that she should keep her distance from him, there were times, as now, when he made her want to grin. And it had been for ever since he had adopted that teasing tone with her, the one that made her toes curl and the hair on the nape of her neck stand on end.

'That's very important,' she returned with equal gravity. 'There's nothing worse than getting back to your desk after a little break to find that all your stationery's in a muddle.'

'Actually, I just came to get my mother's Christmas present from the drawer. Hang on a minute and I'll come down with you.' He disappeared into his office, fetched a box without bothering to turn the light on, and reappeared, still in his coat, which he hadn't removed.

Tessa picked the first neutral subject she could think of as they walked towards the lift, and asked him what he had bought for his mother.

'An antique brooch and some matching earrings,' he said. 'For some reason she's into things like that.' He was tossing the box lightly from one hand to the other. Tessa caught it in mid-air and handed it to him.

'I don't think you should be doing that,' she said sternly. 'What if it drops and breaks?'

'The shop has very carefully wrapped the contents in tissue paper,' Curtis said, pocketing the box, 'so I don't think there's much chance of that happening.' He looked at her sideways, amused and irritated to see the way she huddled against the side of the lift as though to stand any closer to him might bring her into contact with an infectious disease.

'What last-minute things have you got to buy?' he asked, stepping aside when the lift shuddered to a stop so that she could brush past him. In a minute she would be gone, eaten up by the black wintry evening outside. 'What are your plans for Christmas?'

'A stocking filler for my sister and not much, to answer your questions.' Tessa turned to him and forced herself to smile. What was *he* going to be doing for Christmas? He wouldn't be seeing Susie. She knew that for a fact. He and Susie were no longer an item. The company grapevine, with its usual irreverent efficiency, had long ago gleaned that Curtis and his Barbie doll had run their course. For the past four weeks, bets had been on as to what the replacement would look like and Curtis, fully aware of the furious speculation, had responded by informing them that he would be trying out celibacy for the foreseeable future. This in itself was sufficient to raise the tempo of the guessing games.

'Not much…hmm…sounds a little dull…'

Tessa had an instant replay in her head of him kissing her in the kitchen, caressing her, pushing up her shirt and bra so that he could attend to her breasts. All because he had felt sorry for her because she was dull. A spurt of anger made her turn to him.

'And what are *you* going to be doing?' she enquired with barbed sarcasm. 'Have you got a thrilling few days lined up? I mean, you never said…Susie the Barbie doll is no longer around, so who's the replacement? Have you decided to go for a different model this time or stick to what you know? Someone blonde and busty with a vocabulary that just boils down to the one word *yes*?'

She could have kicked herself when he smiled a long, slow smile at her.

She turned away abruptly and headed towards the exit, aware that he was following her, his footsteps as stealthy as a cat's.

'I didn't realise you'd been following the progress of my love life with as much gusto as everyone else,' Curtis murmured alongside her as they stepped out into the freezing embrace of a winter in full throttle. 'I don't recall ever seeing you adding any contributions to the board in the corridor.'

The board in the corridor had been the bright idea of one of the computer whizkids. It charted each and every speculation from anyone who cared to have input and entries ranged from petite brunette with Hollywood aspirations to older woman with a yen for toy boys. Curtis eyed it with amusement every time he walked past and occasionally wrote his own cryptic message on it himself.

'That's because I haven't,' Tessa said tartly. 'I'm about to head to the underground, so have a good Christmas.'

He fell into step with her. 'Now I'm hurt,' he said sorrowfully. 'I thought you cared...'

The mildly flirtatious teasing had been conspicuous by its absence and now it made her already heated skin begin to prickle with all the dangerous awareness she had successfully slapped down over the past few weeks.

'Well, you were wrong. Why are you following me?'

'Because I'm trying to persuade you to come and have a drink with me considering you never managed to make it to our little lunchtime party earlier.'

'I'm sorry. I can't.'

'Because you need to get that important stocking filler.'

'That's right.' The underground was now within sight, visible between the hordes of people who were also apparently on the search for last-minute Christmas gifts. The sight of that many people made her feel a little ill but now that she had told him she needed to shop, she had little choice but to honour the white lie, with him walking next to her like an unwanted shadow.

'In which case, I think I need to get a few things myself. We could go and have that drink afterwards.'

'No, we cannot!' Tessa refused vehemently, stopping to glare at him and irritating the flow of people who were forced to break their hurried stride around them.

'Scared, Tessa?' he taunted softly. 'You didn't manage to make it to the company do a couple of weeks ago either. A sudden cold, if I remember correctly?'

'I have to go, Curtis.' She spun around, blinded by rage

at what she could only assume was mockery in his voice. Never mind how clever and good looking and incisive and witty he was, she thought furiously, he was still the Man with the Oversized Ego.

She hurtled away from him, struggling against the sea of people, caught up in them as they began to cross the road as one on the go ahead of the little green man from the traffic lights.

Her thoughts were spinning off on a tangent, paying scant attention to the pavement, when her leg buckled under her. The crowd that had virtually carried her along in its surge from one pavement to the middle island had failed to be so accommodating as they'd hurried towards the far pavement.

Tessa gave a groan of pain, tried to maintain an upright position, but, with no one to hold on to, she slid inelegantly onto cold, hard tarmac and, had it not been for a couple of steel arms lifting her out of her embarrassed misery, she was convinced that people would simply have stepped over her in their haste to finish the rest of their Christmas shopping.

The owner of the steel arms spoke in an all-too-familiar voice and Tessa groaned again, this time with heartfelt dismay mixed in with the shooting pain in her ankle.

'You could have been trampled,' Curtis said and Tessa opened one eye to look at him. For once, there was no smile on his face as he fought his way across the road, belligerently ordering people to stand aside so that he could get through and cursing under his breath.

He briefly allowed her to stand on one foot for the ten seconds it took him to hail a taxi.

There was no point telling him that she was fine and would be able to make it back to her house without help. She wasn't fine. Her foot was killing her. She doubted she would have been able to call a taxi for herself, never mind anything else.

Once in the back of the cab, she managed to wriggle herself into a fairly upright and dignified position and turned to him stiffly.

'Thank you.'

'You're welcome. How does it feel?'

'Awful.' She experimentally tried to move it and winced. It was already beginning to swell and she didn't protest when he gingerly eased it onto his lap so that he could remove her shoe.

'We need to get you to a hospital. Get this properly seen to.'

'No!'

Curtis ignored her, leaning forward to tell the driver to get them to the Kensington and Chelsea Hospital as quickly as he could without killing anyone, then he sat back and reached his hand along her thighs.

'What are you doing?' Tessa yelped, trying to tug her leg away from him but greatly hampered by the pain in her foot every time she moved it. 'Get your hands *off me*!'

'Shh!'

'I will not *shut up*!' Her uncooperative leg refused to sprint off his lap.

'Look,' he said bluntly, 'There will be some gravel, probably, embedded in your ankle and knees where you took the brunt of the fall. With your leg swelling up at the rate it is, the gravel is going to become glued to your tights and it'll be a hell of a job removing them later on. If I could guarantee that we'd be at the hospital quickly, fine, but look at the traffic. It's Christmas and a half-hour drive could end up taking a lot longer.'

Tessa looked out of the window. The traffic was moving like treacle.

'Now I'm not too sure what you think I might get up to in the back of this taxi, but if you want to try and remove your tights yourself, then go ahead. I'll do the gentlemanly thing and look away, shall I?' There was a sharp, bitter edge in his voice that made her wonder whether he had now added the adjective *ridiculous* to the *dull* one he had already attached the minute he had first clapped eyes on her. Maybe he thought it frankly pathetic that she might overestimate her desirability to the extent that he would make a pass for her again. Again and especially in the back seat of a public transport vehicle.

Tessa still made a go of trying to do it herself, but manoeuvring her foot was next to impossible.

'Done trying?' Curtis asked, watching her with detached, cool interest.

By way of answer, Tessa sighed and leant back, closing her eyes so that she didn't have to witness the spectacle of him disrobing her.

Which didn't stop her feeling the slide of his cool fingers along her legs, up past her thighs to her waist, where he gently eased the tights down, pausing and taking extra care when he came to the swollen ankle.

'Mission accomplished,' he said, holding the tights up in one hand. 'You can open your eyes now.' His voice was still edged with suppressed impatience, as was his face when Tessa did open her eyes to look at him. She snatched the tights and stuffed them into her handbag.

'Thanks.' Her legs were still tingling from where he had touched them, even though there had been nothing personal in the touch. 'I'm sorry to be keeping you from...from whatever it was you had planned... There's no need for you to stay with me once we get to the hospital. I know Casualty can be busy at these places, and I'm more than capable of sitting quietly on my own till I get seen to.'

Curtis didn't answer. He had replaced her feet on his lap and he looked at them. Perfect, narrow feet with delicately painted pink toenails. Hardly the sort of feet to be cooped up in tight court shoes, which was what she had been wearing. But then, didn't this woman wear her clothes like a suit of armour? Stiff little suits that stifled every scrap of femininity? Except he knew, didn't he, that take the clothes away and she was highly feminine?

They spent the next twenty minutes in silence, while the cab driver did his best to beat the traffic.

By the time they reached the hospital, Tessa's nerves were fraying badly at the edges. She had never known Curtis to be quite as silent as he had been in the taxi. He wasn't garrulous in the manner of some people who talked even when they had nothing of interest to say. He talked *because* he was interested. It was all part and parcel of his charm, of that bigger-than-average personality that grabbed people and had them hooked and hanging onto every word he uttered.

She let him help her in, stifling the temptation to insist on paying for the taxi herself, considering she was the one who had needed it. As soon as they were through the door, though, she turned to him with a bright smile, trying to ignore the pounding in her ankle.

'Thanks again. I can take it from here.'

'I'm going to help you to that chair over there and then you're to sit down. I'll be ten minutes.'

'Look,' Tessa said, politeness giving way to irritation because she *just didn't want him around her*, 'there's no need.'

He ushered her to the one free spot, still protesting under her breath, and sat her down, then he leaned over her, supporting himself on the metal arms of the chair.

'Don't even think of staging a protest by doing anything. I'll only be a few minutes.'

'This is ridiculous. It's my fault I'm here and I don't feel very happy about...'

Any further protest was stifled as he placed his mouth very firmly over hers, administering one hard, swift kiss that succeeded in removing all power of speech.

'Well, at least there's *something* that can shut you up,' he murmured.

She was still struggling with a mixture of shock, outrage and stupid, uninvited pleasure when he returned, in less time than he had said.

'Right. Come on.'

'Come on *where*?'

'I'm getting you in for a quick look at that foot. Should take a few minutes unless they feel you need an X-ray.'

'But...but *we're queue jumping*!' She squeaked as he lifted her up in one smooth movement and began striding down the corridor, pushing open the double doors at the end with one foot.

'That's a very English response. Don't worry. This doctor is a personal friend of mine and doesn't work on Casualty. You're taking him away from nothing but his regulatory break.'

'Which he probably needs!'

She was relegated to sidelines when, minutes later, she found herself sitting in a room while Curtis and a young, bespectacled doctor discussed her foot, as though she were only rudimentarily attached to it.

The pronouncement was as Curtis had expected. Sprained but not broken. It was bandaged, a prescription for painkillers was given to be taken only as necessary, two on the spot to ease some of the immediate discomfort, and then the two men chatted briefly before she was established in a wheelchair, feeling an absolute fraud.

'I suppose some time today I might be able to stop thanking you.' Tessa forced gratitude into her voice. Of course, he would not allow her to return home on her own. Even though he must have gleaned by now that she didn't actually *want* him around her, he was still insisting on playing the knight in shining armour.

'Why do I get the feeling that it sticks in your throat?' No ready smile in return to her remark. If she was putting him out that much, she thought nastily, then he had been given more than ample opportunity to shed his duties.

'No one likes to think they've made a burden of themselves.'

'And no one likes to think that they're encouraging resentment simply by being humane.'

'No one asked you to be humane!'

'Would you have preferred me to have left you lying in the street? To get on with it?' Curtis snarled.

Tessa offered him a silent profile. She expected him to direct a few more verbal missiles at her, but when the silence lengthened she couldn't resist peeking, just a little. He was staring out of the window and even though she couldn't actually see his face, she could pretty much guess the expression on it. Sheer anger. He had been kind enough to try and break her *dull* routine by inviting her out for a drink, had been *humane* enough to rescue her when she needed help, had in fact pulled a few strings so that she had avoided a five-hour wait in Casualty on a bleak winter's night, and what, he must be thinking, did he get in return? Certainly not the flowery, dewy-eyed declarations of gratitude he had expected.

Tessa could almost feel sorry for him. Except the fact that he was so busy feeling sorry for *her* stuck in her throat and she had to bite back the temptation to hit him right over his egotistic, masculine head. With her perfectly good right arm.

They reached her house and she politely allowed him to help her to the door, even take her inside.

However, extending the gentlemanly routine to making her a cup of coffee and fetching her something to eat while she rested her leg was beyond the bounds. And she didn't want him in her house. Leaving his mark in yet more places for her to have to deal with at a later date.

'That's very kind,' she said from her disadvantaged position on the sofa where he had laid her, 'but I can manage from here. And besides, you don't want to let that taxi driver go. It'll be hell trying to get hold of another one at this time of year.'

He gave her a brief nod and disappeared, leaving her on the sofa to nurse a certain amount of disappointment. Well, he *would* have better things to do than sit around taking care of his secretary because she had been foolish enough to sprain her ankle. Susie's mystery replacement waiting in the wings wouldn't be too overjoyed to find herself sidelined by some woman to whom he felt obligated because she happened to work with him!

'He'll be back in a couple of hours.' Curtis reappeared, a dark, brooding presence by the sitting-room door. 'And there's no point wasting your breath telling me what I should and shouldn't have done.'

'How did you manage to get him to agree to come back for you?' Tessa asked in a small voice.

'Money. Now, I'm going to make you some egg on toast and some tea.' He handed her the remote for the television. 'Watch some TV. It'll take your mind off your foot.'

But not off *him*. Unfortunately. Despite raising the volume on the television, she was still acutely aware of him in the kitchen, rustling something up, handling her cooking utensils. He would have dumped his coat and jacket in the hall, and would have shoved up the sleeves of his faded denim shirt, exposing his strong, muscular forearms. He always had to loosen his clothing when he worked, undo a couple of buttons on his shirt, push up the sleeves, as though being buttoned up stifled his creative genius.

He returned with the promised egg on toast and a pot of tea, all on a tray that he placed on her lap, having first made sure she was comfortable by puffing up the cushions behind her and dragging over a pouffe on which she could rest her legs.

Tessa thanked him and ate, feigning deep concentration on the Christmas programme on the TV, and he let her get away with it, allowing her to think that she might, just might, be able to ignore his presence for the next hour and a half.

She realised how much she had misread his obliging silence when, as soon as she had finished eating, he removed the tray to ask her what time her sister was expected back.

'Tomorrow morning,' Tessa said dryly. 'She's out with a crowd of her college friends and I told her to stay with one of her friends who lives in central London rather than risk trying to find a taxi late at night to bring her back here. I've booked her one for the morning.'

'In which case—' he held out one hand, which Tessa looked at dubiously '—you need to have a bath and I intend to help you.'

'You must be mad!'

'I think I must be...' Curtis muttered under his breath. He leant down and, before she could launch into her routine of shoving him away, he picked her up, ignoring her shrieks and flailing limbs.

The bathroom was very easy to locate, sandwiched next

to the airing cupboard and between the main bedroom and the guest room which, judging from the art on the walls, would belong to Lucy.

'Now,' he said in a steely voice, 'are you going to carry on kicking and screaming, in which case I'll just continue holding you till you tire yourself out, or are you going to be a nice little girl and do what you're told?'

'Put me down!' she snapped.

'Sure. In a minute.' Still carrying her, he clicked the key to the bathroom door, locking them both in, and pocketed it. Tessa let out a howl of outrage.

*'How dare you?'*

Curtis placed her on the wooden linen basket and stood up, arms folded. 'Don't get into a state, Tessa. I said I would help you have a bath, not get in it with you!'

'I don't need a bath and *I don't need your help*!'

'I'm going to run the bath. You can get out of your clothes. You should be able to do that just fine but you'll need me to help you in, especially as this Victorian bath is so high-sided.'

He began running the bath, tipping bath foam in and testing the temperature with his hand. 'Okay. I take it from the lack of tell-tale rustling that you haven't removed a stick of clothing. If, when the bath is run, you're still glaring at me and trying to pretend that you're comfortable with being grubby, then you'll leave me no choice but to abandon my gentlemanly approach and undress you. On the other hand, you have my word that I'll look away if you undress yourself and leave the bathroom as soon as you're in the water. Deal?'

*'Deal? Deal?* You've got a nerve, Curtis Diaz! You know that, don't you?' Under the simmering anger, she could feel her heart hammering inside her and her heightened state of awareness was making her limbs go weak,

and it had nothing to do with her sprain. In fact, the tablets had reduced the sharp pain to a bearable discomfort.

'I reckon you've got roughly two minutes,' he answered, with his back still to her.

He meant it! The arrogance of the man left her speechless, but that didn't take away the fact that he meant every word. If she didn't clamber out of her clothes, he would do it for himself. Tessa hurriedly removed her blouse, leaving her bra in place, then, standing on one leg, she shuffled her skirt down, leaving her underwear similarly in place.

He switched off the bath.

'The bra and pants stay on,' Tessa said, folding her arms. 'If they get wet, they get wet. I'll get them off myself once I'm in the water.'

'Fair enough.' He lifted her up, breathing in, catching the mutinous set of her mouth out of the corner of his eye. Also catching the way the bra gaped as he held her, the way he could see the curve of her breast, the hint of her nipple just partially hidden by the lacy fabric. His breathing thickened and he had to tear his eyes forward as he placed her gently in the water and her body was hidden from view by the layer of bubbles.

'Right,' he said roughly, turning away and not looking over his shoulder as he slotted the key back into the door and opened it, 'I'll be back in fifteen minutes. Okay?'

He cleared out of the bathroom as quickly as he could. One more minute in there and he would be in need of a bath himself, an ice-cold one.

What was happening here? he wondered. The woman was not the type he was drawn to. When the work was over and the office door was shut, he liked his women to be fun. He enjoyed the chase, knowing where it would lead, enjoyed the beautiful packaging even though he always knew that he would inevitably get bored with the toy inside. He suspected that if this particular woman was ever chased by him, she wouldn't hesitate to whack him over the head with a hard object, just as he suspected that what was inside the packaging was way too complex for him. Was that why he couldn't take his eyes off her? Because she took challenge to new heights and what red blooded male could ever resist a good challenge?

That, he thought, washing the dishes and keeping an eye on his watch, must be it.

He was whistling as he headed back up to the bathroom, knocking before entering.

The steam from the bath had softened her cheeks and made them pink and the ends of her hair that had dipped into the water were damp strands. She looked all of eighteen.

'You get the bath sheet,' were her first words, issued as a firm command. 'Hold it up and look away. I'll stand up, I can manage that, and I'll wrap the towel around myself and then you can lift me out.'

'Yes, ma'am.' He had enacted many a bath scene in his life and none of them, he thought wryly, had taken on this format. But he obediently did as he was told, fighting off the urge to look, to savour, to rein in his frantic imagination by actually giving it something real to feed on. It physically hurt, it was so difficult.

'Okay,' Tessa said crisply, when the towel was safely around her. 'You can carry me to my bedroom now.' There was just no point pursuing the protesting damsel business. He would just ride roughshod over her if he figured he had to, and she was too vulnerable to allow him to do that, to really invade her privacy by seeing her naked, touching her bare skin. Bad enough having him lift her now with nothing but a towel between them.

The only way she knew how to counterbalance her

screaming nerves was to pretend to be someone else, someone in control, briskly matter-of-fact about what he was doing. And it had been blissful to get clean, to wash off the scraping of dirt on her legs that had penetrated through her sheer tights when she had fallen.

'Feel better?' Curtis asked, sitting her on the edge of the bed and taking a few healthy steps backwards. 'Refreshed? I've brought you up a couple more tablets in case the pain's beginning to kick back in.' He nodded to the table by the head of her bed. Now seemed a very good time to retreat downstairs. He had helped her home, done the whole rescuing-of-the-damsel-in-distress lot. He could watch a little telly while he waited for his taxi to return, leave her up here to get changed, maybe lie down and rest her foot.

He remained where he was, hands thrust into his pockets. The towel had ridden up her thighs and there was no denying that she had very nice thighs. Great legs, in fact, pale and smooth like satin, and very slender.

He cleared his throat. 'I'll be heading downstairs now,' he said. 'Catch up on some award-winning Christmas reruns while I wait for the taxi.'

'Thanks for everything, Curtis,' Tessa said. 'I'd see you to the door but…' She shrugged and gave him a little smile, which he returned.

'Take the tablets.' Nothing left to be said now. He turned, left the room and was about to head downstairs when one more thing occurred to him. In fact, he had meant to ask her while they were in the office, before a series of unexpected events had landed them up here in her house.

He spun round, pushed open the bedroom door and stopped dead in his tracks.

Tessa, on the bed, on all fours, was reaching out for the glass of water and the tablets. The towel, which she had protectively wrapped around her, had slithered to the ground. The moment between them was electric and it seemed to stretch on and on and on.

There was a savage intensity in his blue eyes that made her feel weak because she could read messages there that were firing into her brain and connecting with it in ways she wouldn't have dreamed possible.

When he took a step towards her, she almost moaned. She knew, in every fibre of her being, that she should cover herself up immediately, that she should *want* to.

So why wasn't she yelling at him to leave the room?

Curtis quietly closed the door behind him and that click was like a decision made.

Tessa fell back against the bed, watching, her eyes dark with hunger as he moved towards her.

All these weeks of looking at him from under her lashes, absorbing every little thing about him, and fighting it off because she recognised the dangers, were like nothing now.

She just wanted him to touch her...

# CHAPTER SEVEN

TESSA lay down on the bed, drinking Curtis in with her eyes as he walked slowly towards her, finally to sit on the edge of the bed. 'I know,' she said, sitting up so that their faces were only inches apart. 'This is a bad idea. It's madness.'

By way of response, he smoothed his hand along her thigh, curving his fingers over the dewy silk of her buttocks.

'Your foot...' He had wondered whether he would actually be able to speak, whether his vocal cords might not have dried up altogether, but his voice was low and only shook a little.

'Is still sprained.' Tessa tried twisting it and winced. 'It only hurts when I try to move it.' It seemed a little silly to be discussing her foot when she was naked next to him.

Even though the room was dark, with only the side light switched on, she could still make out the fine lines around his eyes, laughter lines, giving his face character.

The realisation that she loved this man, had fallen head over heels with his impossible, unpredictable, utterly mesmerising personality was just something that she accepted. It didn't leap out at her like a bolt from the blue, more revealed itself finally and inexorably. And yes, she should protect herself from him, from getting hurt by him, but hadn't the damage already been done? He had wormed himself deep into the very core of her and pretending that he hadn't wasn't going to make her feel any better. It was a ploy that certainly hadn't worked over the past few weeks.

'You have a beautiful body,' Curtis said thickly, looking down at her and reaching out to cup a breast in his hand. He felt her shudder as he rubbed the pad of his finger over her nipple. It stiffened and the reaction made him draw his breath in sharply.

This was no game. It was nothing like the romps he had had with the women he had dated over the years. He felt suddenly disoriented and when he raised his hand to caress the nape of her neck, it was shaking.

'Your foot...' he murmured roughly. 'I don't think the doctor would advise...'

Tessa lay back, spreading her arms wide, revealing herself to him in a gesture of pure, abandoned trust.

No, she thought, she didn't trust that he wouldn't hurt her. In fact, it was a dead cert that he would. Curtis Diaz wasn't into all those things that came with relationships, proper relationships. But she could only say how she would feel if she carried on denying the truth to herself.

A slow, thick wave was washing over Curtis, making his thinking sluggish. Lying there, she was bewitching. It went way beyond the contours of her body. It was something glimpsed in her eyes, in the soft, suggestive smile curving her lips. She was the perfect combination of woman and child, tempting and cautious at the same time.

His hands were shaking as he began to undo the buttons of his shirt, watching her watching him. He tugged the shirt out of the waistband of his trousers and pulled it off, feeling like a man performing a striptease.

'All I need is some music,' he joked huskily. He hoped to God he wasn't blushing. That was something he had never done in his life before, but right now, the way those eyes were making him feel, he might just be breaking the habit of a lifetime.

The gossip columnists might have overrated his sexual prowess, but Curtis Diaz was no shrinking violet when it came to the fairer sex. He enjoyed the company of women and he enjoyed making love with them. He certainly never felt nervous in their presence but right now, he was as nervous as hell.

She was leaning up on one elbow, half smiling as his hand rested on the top button of his trousers. Instead of wresting them off, however, Curtis squatted down next to the bed so that his eyes were level with hers.

'Do this often, do you?' The clichéd line sounded a little strangled and he was disturbed to find how much he was hanging on for her answer, even though he knew what it would be.

She was an innocent. He had sensed that from the very first. But what if he was wrong? What if she had a secret side? It was known to happen, wasn't it? Secretary by day, stripper by night…?

When he thought about that possibility, his blood seemed to freeze over in his veins.

'You know I don't,' Tessa confessed truthfully. She sighed and stroked the side of his face. 'And I make a particular habit of staying away from my bosses.'

Curtis captured her hand and turned it palm upwards, so that he could press his lips against the soft flesh. With his trousers still on, he joined her in her bed so that he was lying next to her.

'Funnily enough, I make it a policy of separating work from pleasure myself,' he murmured. The temptation was too much. No matter how hard he concentrated on her face, willing himself to rise above this strange, sinking feeling that was enveloping him, he couldn't resist the lure of her breasts. And touching them wasn't enough, not nearly enough. Not when he could lower his head so that he could take one demanding nipple into his mouth and tease it with the wet caress of his tongue. And that breathless groan was enough to draw his hand along her leg, along that smooth thigh, until it made contact with the soft dampness that she offered to him by parting her legs. His finger found the crease that brought forth a gasp of pure pleasure and he rubbed it gently and rhythmically, struggling to control his own pounding arousal.

*Take it easy,* he told himself, but, when her sweet moistness was enveloping his exploring fingers, that was nigh on impossible.

He reluctantly drew his hand up to her stomach, kissing her when she protested.

'What about conversation?' he murmured, sprinkling little kisses on her mouth and stroking the swell of her breasts.

'Were we talking? I can't remember...' She hooked her hands behind his neck. If she had thought that she could get away with being more agile, she would have, but the dull ache in her foot was just waiting for an opportunity to become a jabbing pain. Right now, being as still as she could manage was pretty much the best idea, but, Lord, what she wouldn't have done to have been able to curl up into him.

'I was telling you that I don't mix business with pleasure either.'

'Despite the exotic flora you've had decorating your office before I came along?'

'What makes you think that you're not as exotic as the rest of them?' Curtis asked, while through his head the disturbing thought took root that she went beyond exotic. She was positively dangerous.

'The mirror?' Tessa touched his lips with the tip of her tongue and he moaned and closed his eyes for the briefest of seconds.

'Then you need to buy yourself a new one,' he muttered inaudibly. Something, somewhere, was telling him that this was getting way out of control, and that that was definitely not good for a man who had always had everything very much under control. He laughed off the uneasy sensation and tilted her head so that he could kiss her neck.

'Are you going to get undressed?' Tessa asked huskily. Their eyes met for a second.

'Making love can be vigorous,' Curtis said, and simply hearing himself say that threw so many graphic pictures into his head that his now painful erection ached even more. 'Vigorous isn't what the doctor ordered for you.'

'Stop worrying about my foot,' Tessa pleaded. 'The tablets have taken care of most of the pain...'

'Which means that you probably wouldn't feel it too much if I hurt you, at least right now, but as soon as those painkillers wear off, you'll be in agony.'

He flipped onto his back, breathing thickly and not knowing quite what was going on with him. He had to remind himself that reining himself in was not a choice, it was a necessity.

Tessa carefully rolled towards him, slowly drawing one leg to cover his, and he looked at her with dark, frustrated hunger.

He had to go. Something deep inside him, some place that had never existed before, was telling him that he had to leave before...before *what?* Before he could no longer put the brakes on his rampaging desires.

He blindly kissed her upturned face, his tongue probing her mouth while one hand sought what it needed to find, the soft, wet bud pulsing for his touch. He felt her shiver.

It sent the last of his coherent thoughts scattering to the four winds. With a stifled groan, he urgently began to explore her body, pinning her arms back and straddling her so that he could devote equal attention to her breasts. He flicked each one with his tongue and, when she twisted beneath him, took first one then the other into his mouth, sucking hard and watching her arched, flushed face with a deep, thrusting satisfaction.

He began to move lower, trailing his tongue along her flat belly, enjoying her rapid breathing. When he looked up, their eyes tangled, hers dark with hunger, his slumberous with the need to satisfy that hunger.

Before he could lower his head to continue his ministrations of her body, she coiled her fingers into his dark hair, tugging him so that he was looking at her once more.

'Curtis…you can't…'

'Can't what, my darling?'

'I've never…'

'Never…what?' Comprehension dawned and with it came another of those destabilising thrusts of pure satisfaction. 'Never been touched down there before…? In the way I mean to touch you…?'

Tessa nodded. He saw the apprehension in her eyes and his heart did something funny inside him, then he broke eye contact so that he could kiss his way down past her belly button, pausing only for a fraction of a second to breathe in the sweet femininity of her. He blew gently on the soft pubic hair, but the need to taste her was just too overpowering. The musky scent had filled his nostrils and he wanted more, much more.

And tasting her was every bit as good as he had imagined it would be. He could feel her bucking against him, writhing, and he stilled her growing need by flattening his hands on either side of her thighs.

Her groans had increased by several octaves, sweet music to his ears, and as his tongue slid remorselessly over that tightened bud, the essence of her naked hunger, he felt her reach her inexorable climax, arching back, shuddering and finally coming down in restless waves from the peak.

Her eyes were slumberous when he edged himself up so that he was lying next to her.

'That wasn't quite what I had in mind,' she whispered, drawing him to her with drowsy contentment, 'but it felt... well...' Modesty deprived her of voicing a suitable description and Curtis smiled.

With reality weaving its tentacles around him, that uneasy, dangerous feeling was back, although he couldn't put his finger on where it came from.

'I should go...' he murmured.

'But...'

'But you need to get some rest, and, Lord knows, the taxi's probably come and gone.'

*Shouldn't he want to stay with her?* Tessa suddenly felt very vulnerable. She consoled herself with the thought that she was a modern woman and there was absolutely nothing wrong in fulfilling her needs, especially with the man she loved. Even though he didn't love her back. Still...she pulled the duvet cover from one side to partially cover her exposed body.

When he heaved himself off the bed, the vulnerability feeling grew stronger. This time she swamped herself under the duvet and pushed herself into a sitting position, leaning back against the headboard so that she could watch him as he slipped back on his shirt and slowly began doing up the buttons.

'I never got to mention why I came back into your room,' Curtis said roughly. 'I meant to ask whether you and your sister would like to come over on Boxing Day.

Anna wants to see you and it makes even more sense now that you probably won't be able to do very much with your foot.' He grinned crookedly at her. She looked so damned edible lying there, all bundled up under that duvet. His hands itched to rip it away but he knew that if he did, he would be lost, would end up never wanting to leave. No, he corrected uncomfortably, not wanting to leave in a hurry...

He took one step back, as though he had been standing too close to an open fire, and then turned at the sound of the doorbell.

'Your taxi awaits you,' Tessa said.

'Hang on. I'll just tell him that I'll be down in a minute.'

'It's Christmas. He may not be prepared to wait that long.'

It was suddenly chilly in the room the minute he vacated it. In fact, it had become pretty chilly in the bed the second he had got out, but there was no point moaning about what had happened or about the fact that she felt a great deal more vulnerable now than she had before.

She had wanted him. She had wanted to feel his big body next to hers. Just thinking about it now made her shiver.

And she was a realist, wasn't she? Had she really expected declarations of love in the heat of passion? The cold clutch of uncertainty gripped her and she fought it off, listening for the sound of his footsteps approaching.

When she finally did hear him, she felt her body tense.

'No taxi,' Curtis said, standing by the door for a few moments before coming into the room and gently pushing the door shut behind him. 'I phoned for another, but there's a waiting list, apparently, as long as the Great Wall of China.'

'Then who was it at the door?' Tessa asked, forgetting what he had said about the non-appearing taxi.

'Your sister.'

'Oh!' She froze while a thousand possible scenarios raced through her head like a swarm of bees. 'Oh. I thought...I wasn't expecting her to come home until tomorrow,' Tessa said breathlessly.

'Seems she decided that an all-night drinking binge wasn't such a good idea.'

'Oh, right.' She looked anxiously at Curtis, wondering how to phrase the unavoidable question, but in all events he read her mind and answered it without having to be asked.

'I told her that you had sprained your ankle and I had done the good employer thing and brought you back. I told her that you were up in bed, nicely settled, and that I was on my way out.'

*What did you think of her?* Tessa wanted to ask him, but she bit back the temptation. Instead, she said, 'I must get up and go down to see her.'

'Don't be ridiculous. Your foot needs rest. The last thing you want to do is leap down the stairs to make sure your sister is all right. Trust me, she's fine.'

'I wasn't planning on leaping anywhere!' Tessa retorted. 'Would you mind passing me some clothes if I tell you where to find them?' Before he could answer, she was pointing to her chest of drawers, directing him towards her underwear, a long-sleeved tee shirt and her most comfortable pair of jogging bottoms. All items of clothing that the fashion police would have her hung, drawn and quartered for wearing, but she needed to get changed quickly, something that she did with his help. Lord, but it was difficult, when her body kept having a mind of its own and, as much as she kept hurrying him up, so he took his time. She protested but could hardly prevent the groundswell of excitement every time his fingers brushed against her skin.

Once she was fully dressed, she informed him that he could take her down.

'Would that be a command?' he asked, amused at the change between the woman with clothes on and the woman with them off.

'I could always try and go it on my own.'

'I take that back. It wasn't a command. It was a cunning piece of emotional blackmail.'

He lifted her up and carried her down the stairs while she protested futilely on what her sister would say.

Lucy, as it turned out, said nothing for a few seconds. She just looked as Curtis brought Tessa in and deposited her on the sofa.

'I see you've been swept off your feet, sis!' Lucy's face broke into a smile of pure charm and she flashed Curtis an approving look.

It was the sort of look that inspired jealousy in other females. Tessa had never, ever, been jealous of her sister. She had been proud of the lovely child who had matured into a gorgeous adult. Lucy had all the hallmarks of the glamorous bimbo. Long, streaming blonde hair, perfectly chiselled features, wide blue eyes and a figure that screamed out for very tight clothing. However, she was saved from being the archetypal blonde by nature of her personality. Her eyes danced and her mouth looked as though it was permanently ready to laugh. There was something sweetly wicked about her and it had got men hooked time and time again.

No, Tessa had become used to sitting back and enjoying her sister's impact.

Not quite so now. She couldn't bring herself to look at Curtis just in case he, too, was falling under her sister's spell.

She caught herself. This was the man who had just made

love to her! Touched her in ways that had set her body alight!

But then…a little voice of malice said, he hadn't exactly been shouting out his love, had he? Or even his attraction. And it hadn't really been *making love*, had it? Not really. Not technically. He had pleasured her…

Lucy had flopped into one of the chairs, with one leg dangling over the arm and her head thrown back.

She was managing to turn brown into a colour everyone might conceivably want to wear, in the hope that they might pull it off too. Brown, flared jeans, brown tight cardigan cropped at the waist, exposing a terracotta-coloured silk vest. Nothing else. No jewellery, nothing brash, just utter simplicity.

Tessa roused herself sufficiently to answer Lucy's questions about how she fell and where and how and why and wasn't she so lucky to have had her boss there, on the spot, ready to charge into action and rescue her from being trampled to death by crowds of people intent on Christmas shopping.

Lucy made a feeble attempt at a joke about Christmas, turkeys and shoppers, forgetting the punchline three times, but still managed to evoke a hearty chuckle from Curtis when she did finally remember. Tessa's laugh was a little more forced.

'You seem pretty sober for a night on the tiles, Luce,' she said, changing the subject from herself, and Lucy snorted, sitting up straighter and tucking her legs under her.

'Started too early,' she explained. 'Lunch time, in fact. Just a quick one at the pub and you know how it goes. I barely drank a thing, actually. I'd planned on doing a bit of, yes, shopping, and I spent half my time checking my watch and wondering whether I could leave and catch them all up a bit later. Which is what I did, except by the time

I caught them up I was as sober as a judge and they were rolling in the aisles.'

'Not a good situation,' Curtis said sympathetically. Tessa's acidity levels rose accordingly. The warm glow she had felt in the immediate aftermath of their love-making was fading fast. Too many doubts had set in, and now, when she sneaked a look at Curtis, it was to find his attention focused on her sister.

'Hence,' Lucy was saying airily, 'my early night. Well, early compared to what I had planned on. I would have come home a lot sooner if I had known about your leg, sis.' Her voice became serious. 'You should have called me.'

'I didn't think you'd hear your phone amid the noise,' Tessa hedged. Actually, calling her sister hadn't occurred to her at any point in time. Why would it? she thought sourly. How many damsels in distress would choose being rescued by a disgruntled sibling dragged away from a hell raising pre-Christmas pub-crawl over a knight in shining armour? Especially when said damsel in distress was in love with the knight in question?

'True,' Lucy admitted readily enough. 'Although it does vibrate. I would have felt it in my bag. Maybe. Well, much more fun being rescued by a tall, gorgeous hunk, anyway.' She giggled and Curtis shot Tessa a look that very much resembled a cat in possession of the proverbial cream.

'Oh, good grief,' Tessa said, 'that sort of remark is just the thing to go to his head. Which,' she added, 'is already heavily inflated anyway.'

'Though not by your sister, I hasten to assure you,' Curtis addressed Lucy, who gave them both an odd little look from under her lashes. 'So...' he leaned back and relaxed '...I've heard enough about you. Tell me what you do, Lucy.'

Tessa butted in before this particular conversation could kick off. 'Shouldn't you be thinking of leaving, Curtis? I mean, taxis…Christmas…long wait…'

'Oh, I'll drop him back! If you'll let me borrow your car, Tess. I can guarantee that the alcohol levels in my blood are non-existent, despite original plans.' She giggled and Tessa frowned, not liking this suggestion but not really knowing how she could deflect the inevitable acceptance of the offer from Curtis.

Jealousy ate away like a poison and she knew why. Lucy was just the sort of girl Curtis went for.

When she tried to tell herself that he had slept with *her,* had made love to *her,* the little nasty voice she was becoming accustomed to reminded her that she had been the one to put temptation in his way, that he was a commitment-free zone who hadn't once mentioned anything normal like, When shall we meet again? On a date? She, the little voice continued remorselessly, had wanted him because she felt more than mere physical attraction. He, on the other hand, was the same person who had felt sorry for her and still did.

In the middle of her protracted internal debates, she was aware of Curtis quizzing Lucy about her course, asking her a million questions about the kind of things she designed, on what she intended to do once she was through with college. As usual, intently curious, leaning forward with his elbows resting on his thighs, his amazing eyes focused on Lucy's face as she spoke, his head inclined in the attitude of the avid listener. Pure animal magnetism flowed off him in waves. The sort of waves that women could easily drown in.

Lucy, enjoying the single-minded attention, was happily talking about Lucy and Tessa noticed that she seemed to be a heck of a lot more forthcoming about her possible future with him than she was with her. None of her usual vague 'oh, I'll just wait and see what happens when the course is finished' nonsense. Oh, no. Apparently she had ideas of going into advertising! Starting at the bottom and working her way up the ladder!

Tessa sourly thought that a few magic words of interest from Curtis Diaz and suddenly her sister was a miracle of revelation.

'I think I'll be heading up now.' She yawned and they both looked at her. 'Sorry if I'm spoiling the party,' she muttered and Curtis threw her an amused smile.

'I'll carry you up, m'lady.' He stood up and bowed lavishly to Lucy's merriment and Tessa's annoyance.

'It's okay. You've already done enough, thanks. I'll try and make my own way upstairs. I think I should get as much practice using this foot anyway. It's not as though it's broken or anything.'

'Don't be ridiculous. Treat that foot properly and you'll be ready for dancing in a couple of days' time. Walk on it and you'll end up laid up for the next two weeks.'

'Which would be fine considering I won't have to go to work,' Tessa retorted, standing up and delicately placing a bit of pressure on the foot in question.

Before she was aware of it, he was next to her and sweeping her up in one easy movement. Out of the corner of her eye, Tessa could see her sister grinning like a Cheshire cat and she scowled, unfortunately into Curtis's chest.

She couldn't work out where things had all gone so horribly wrong. The feel-good factor that had been there in the bedroom, the sensation that everything she was doing, mad though it all was, was somehow *right* had disappeared like a puff of smoke.

*What had she done?* Bit late in the game to start asking

questions like that, she thought, but they still kept coming at her thick and fast and Curtis, with his usual impeccable perception, had obviously clocked into that because as soon as he deposited her on the bed he stood back, arms folded, every inch the forbidding male.

'What's the matter with you?' he asked her without preamble.

'Matter?'

'Don't play dumb, Tessa.'

Tessa decided to drop the act. She had never been very good at playing dumb anyway. She shrugged and went for the outright lie instead. 'I didn't want to say anything but my foot was beginning to act up a little.' She looked at it mournfully. The painkillers were doing a brilliant job. 'You were right. It needs to be rested if it's to mend.' Curtis being a man, she thought that that little piece of ego flattery would deflect him from his perceptive appraisal of her mood, which was something she didn't want to dwell on.

'Sweet of you to agree with me on that one.'

Tessa's eyes flickered to his face. His expression was serious but there was just enough of an edge of sarcasm to his voice to make her think that the syrupy appeal to his male ego hadn't been as accurate as she had hoped.

'So, what do you think of Lucy?' she asked, idly brushing some non-existent fluff from her jogging bottoms. Her body tensed. To have not asked the question would have spared her any unwanted truths but she knew that she had to find out. For her own peace of mind. She wasn't looking at him but she could almost hear him thinking.

'Not what I expected.'

'What did you expect?'

'Someone a lot more frivolous.'

But you found her attractive, didn't you? Tessa wanted

to press on. In other words, you were attracted to her, weren't you? In ways you could never be attracted to me?

'She's got some interesting things to say. Would you like to look at me when I'm talking?'

'Sorry. Just a little sleepy, that's all.' I have a stunningly attractive, deep and interesting sister. More silly, foolish, unfamiliar, unacceptable jealousy seared through her. She wanted to point out that, gorgeous and interesting though she might be, she hadn't invented a cure for cancer, for goodness' sake! 'What?' she asked irritably, because he looked as though he was about to say something.

'It's nothing,' he said eventually. 'You're tired. You need to get to sleep.' He stepped towards her, undeterred by the wall of frost she had erected, and sat on the bed next to her. When he lowered his head to gently kiss her on the lips, she wanted to pull back. Pride should have made her pull back. But the pressure of his mouth was so sweet, so unbearably sweet, that she closed her eyes and kissed him gently back. And hated herself for it the minute her eyes were open again and he was back by the door, lounging against it and eyeing her with brooding speculation. The kind of brooding speculation that made her wonder what exactly he was thinking and what he had been on the verge of saying to her before he changed his mind.

For someone who could be flamboyantly open, he possessed a talent for self-concealment, she thought uneasily.

Catching herself thinking and staring, Tessa made a show of yawning widely before snapping off the bedroom light and rolling onto her side.

He left quietly, without shutting the bedroom door. The corridor light will keep me up, she thought, but the effort of doing something about it was too much. Besides, now that she was lying down, she discovered that she really was tired. Exhausted from the battle that had been raging inside her.

She expected to hear the sound of the front door any minute, but in fact she nodded off before the anticipated click came and only awoke, groggily, some time later. She didn't know how much later because she had left her watch on the dressing table.

She was only aware of two things. The sound of voices from below and an urgent need to go to the bathroom.

Her foot had stiffened up and was aching, but it struck Tessa that it was amazing how Nature's setbacks could be circumnavigated provided the incentive was right.

In this case, the incentive was her burning curiosity to find out what was being said at the bottom of the stairs.

Shouldn't Lucy have dropped him off and be back home by now? Because, even though she couldn't discern the words, she could instantly recognise the timbre of Curtis's voice.

She hobbled to the door, pulled it slightly wider and then dropped to all fours. Ludicrous but necessary. If she walked, or rather staggered, to the top of the stairs, they would both notice her, unless they coincidentally had their backs both turned. They would see her the minute she emerged from behind the wall, from which the staircase down went directly to the small hallway.

On the other hand, it would be highly unlikely that they would notice if she just peered round the wall at ground level.

She slithered into position, peeped and saw Lucy and Curtis both by the front door, which was open. Through it Tessa could see the back end of a taxi. He had somehow managed to find one. That momentary distraction didn't last long.

They were making no attempt to keep their voices low,

obviously expecting her to be well away in the land of Nod, so she didn't have to strain to hear what was being said.

All the usual pleasantries. And they didn't appear to be standing too close to one another. Tessa wondered whether she had mistakenly jumped to wrong conclusions. Her mind was halfway wandering off, dreaming up impossible scenarios, when he said it, appropriately dropping his voice to a lower decibel.

'So are you sure it's okay if I get in touch with you…?'

Lucy laughed and pinkened. 'Absolutely.' She tiptoed and kissed him demurely on his cheek. Tessa's heart, which was in full plummet, fell even further. 'I never thought when I came home tonight that I would end up meeting someone who could turn out to be so good for me!'

From where he was standing, with his hand on the door, he smiled, and Tessa squeezed her eyes shut very tightly, fighting back the tears of self pity.

'But not a word to your sister. Not yet. I thought of saying something when I said goodnight to her, but let's just see where we're going with this before…before, well, we say anything…'

'I agree.'

'And I'll see the both of you on Boxing Day!'

Tessa didn't wait to hear the remainder of the damning conversation. She crawled back to her bedroom, hobbled to the bathroom and practically sprinted to her bed before Lucy could make it up the stairs and discover that her sister was still up.

Although, Tessa thought bitterly, no girlish sharing of confidences would be forthcoming. Not when there was so much to hide…

One thing she knew for sure…she would not be going to spend Boxing Day with him. No way was she going to witness Lucy and Curtis flirting surreptitiously with one another while she skulked in the corner with various assorted relatives, pretending that everything was fine and dandy!

# CHAPTER EIGHT

CHRISTMAS DAY was a miserable, protracted affair that involved a great deal of jaw-aching jollity as Tessa pretended that everything was all right. In the absence of any other family members, they had always made a big thing of Christmas lunch, making sure that all the trimmings were there, from the traditional turkey to the mince pies. With her foot still too sore to handle the cooking, Tessa watched as Lucy took over, displaying nerve-jangling cheeriness as she flitted across the kitchen, keeping up a steady stream of conversation. It would have been too much if there had been just the two of them over the Christmas lunch, but thankfully three of Lucy's friends, all Australians who were over for the duration of the course, joined them for lunch and, from the relative safety of onlooker, Tessa felt free to observe her sister undercover.

Was it her imagination or did Lucy seem to be over-bright? She was like a wind-up toy into which new batteries had been inserted. Tessa thought that her sister could have continued for days, chattering and laughing and brimming over with gaiety. It was infectious. At least for the guests. Never flat at the best of times, the Australians were positively bursting with good cheer.

At seven, Tessa could stand it no longer and made her excuses. A headache, she apologised, avoiding Lucy's probing, concerned eyes. As excuses went, it was pretty feeble, but it could prove useful in the morning when she pulled it back out of her hat and produced it as a reason why she couldn't possibly go to any Boxing Day thing at the Diaz residence.

Purely to avoid a confrontation on Christmas Day, Tessa had allowed her sister to assume that their little outing on Boxing Day was a foregone certainty. A so-called headache accompanied by a weak smile would at least give her some warning that ill health was destined to make an appearance first thing in the morning.

'I'll walk you up.' Lucy shot to her feet, all worried concern.

'No need. You...you stay here with...your friends. I'm more than capable of making it up some stairs without hurtling down backwards!' She gently tried to prise her arm out of her sister's grasp. Just the feel of those treacherous fingers on her made her want to recoil in misery.

But none of this was her sister's fault. She had told herself this over and over again. Lucy had had no idea that she and Curtis were involved. As far as she was concerned, she wasn't treading on any toes. Curtis was up for grabs and he had clearly not seen fit to enlighten her. The blame lay fully at his door.

Still...Tessa couldn't bring herself to look at her sister so she remained staring glassily at the assembled trio still sitting down, who stared back at her with varying degrees of intoxication.

'What on earth is *the matter with you*?' Lucy hissed, tugging her towards the door, one hand around her waist. 'You've been acting very strange today.'

'Have I?' Tessa muttered. She wondered how Lucy would react if she started pouring out what was in her head. Of course, she wasn't going to do that. Not now, not ever. Opening up those particular dam gates would be a very bad idea. For a start, she would end up having to confess why it hurt so much, having to admit that she had fallen head over heels in love with a man whose feelings towards her were casual at best. Her sister would be horrified. God, she would probably join the Pity Crew, of whom Curtis Diaz was a platinum-card member!

'You know you have! You've barely said a word all day! And after I slaved over a hot stove cooking up Christmas lunch for us!'

'Poor Lucy,' Tessa said unsympathetically. 'Awful having to take care of yourself for a change, isn't it? Not to mention, take care of me as well!'

'I was just joking, Tess.'

'Well, I'm not. I'm tired and my head hurts and I want to go to bed.' She debated whether she should just go for it and inform her sister that the headache would still be ongoing in the morning so she could squash any idea of her trudging over to the Diaz place for Boxing Day frivolities.

'Okay,' Lucy said hurriedly, 'but I'll get you some painkillers and I have something here…' She fumbled in one of her pockets and extracted a small silver object, which she handed to her sister. 'It's a whistle,' she explained sheepishly. 'No single girl is complete without one.'

Tessa took it and turned it over in her hand. 'I know what it is, Lucy. I'm just wondering what I'm supposed to do with it.'

'You're supposed to blow it every time you need me.' They had reached the bedroom and Lucy turned so that the sisters were facing one another. 'Just in case I've not got round to saying this, Tess…I'm really grateful for everything you've done for me since Mum and Dad died… and…well, all the stuff you're still doing now. I know I've been hard work in the past…'

Some of the frozen ice in Tessa's heart melted. Or maybe

just got redistributed to the ice block weighted against Curtis.

'I'm so used to seeing you up and about in control of everything that…it's been salutary to know that you can be as helpless as anybody else…'

'What do you mean *helpless*?' Tessa feverishly scanned back to how she had behaved throughout the course of the day. Quiet, yes, but had she come across as *helpless*? Had she been that transparent? She felt her face blanch, which increased Lucy's level of sibling concern, and she found herself gently propelled into the bedroom and onto the bed.

'Well, *ill*, you know…' Lucy said awkwardly, looking across from where she was rummaging in her sister's drawer for a nightdress. 'Not physically able to do the caring thing that you normally do so well.' She handed the nightdress to Tessa, unable to resist commenting on the baggy nature of it.

'I like baggy,' Tessa said, allowing some help with the process of getting undressed and then lying back on the pillows once she was in the baggy, thigh-length nightie with its Tigger motto.

Already sensitive to the unfolding nightmare between Lucy and Curtis, she mentally added a postscript to this statement. She liked baggy but men didn't. Men liked women like Lucy, sexy women who wore sexy lingerie. Not that her sister favoured the kind of lacy jobs that were touted as sexy. More little strappy cotton vests and very brief briefs, which were perfect at tantalisingly showing up every inch of skin.

'So what did you think of Curtis?' Tessa asked, not meaning to but unable to help herself. She noticed the brightness in her sister's eyes when the name was mentioned, as though someone had lit a lightbulb inside her.

Just the way *she* had felt whenever he was around, Tessa thought painfully.

'Very dishy.' Lucy pretended to sigh but her eyes were still bright and excited when she glanced at her sister. 'Don't you think?'

Tessa shrugged. 'He's all right, I suppose, if you go for that kind of thing.'

Her heart clenched painfully even though her voice was perfectly modulated, even dismissive. If Lucy ever found out about the two of them, she would be appalled, but Tessa was quite sure that Curtis wouldn't breathe a word. Even a fool would know that to spill those particular beans would be the death knoll of any burgeoning relationship and Curtis was no fool. Not by a long shot.

'It's not just the way he looks.' Lucy looked seriously at her sister. 'I mean, he's good looking enough, but...he's...well, I just get the feeling that he's one of the good guys...'

Which shows how savvy you are when it comes to members of the opposite sex, Tessa thought. She closed her eyes, feigning exhaustion, and was pleased when her sister immediately took the hint.

The headache she had pretended now really did feel as though it was coming on. Her temples throbbed and her eyes were hurting from unshed tears. She finally drifted off to sleep with snatches of overheard conversation providing a rich foundation for a series of disturbing, disjointed dreams in which she pursued a faceless couple who disappeared out of reach whenever they came within touching distance.

She woke up at a little before nine, feeling as though she hadn't slept at all. The same snatches of conversation that she had gone to bed contemplating resumed their relentless torture and not even the laborious process of having a bath and thinking about what to wear could push them to one side.

She emerged from the bathroom to find Lucy waiting for her, along with an immaculately prepared breakfast tray, complete with a flower in a vase.

'You should have blown the whistle,' Lucy said, frowning. 'That's why I gave it to you. You blow and I come. Still. Never mind. Look, I've made you breakfast. Am I or am I not the perfect sister? Toast, scrambled eggs, juice, coffee...' She hovered like a sergeant major, watching as Tessa made her way over to the chair by the window, then she deposited the nicely arranged tray on her lap.

'Course, you'll have to gulp it down.' She folded her arms and waited in expectation that her sister would obey orders. 'I told Curtis that we'd be over by eleven, in time for some pre-lunch drinks, which leaves...' she looked at her watch and did some mental arithmetic '...a little over an hour and you know how long it takes me to get going.'

'My headache...' Tessa made a wincing gesture and tucked into the breakfast, head downturned just in case Lucy spotted the little white lie. 'I don't think I'm going to be able to make it. My head...and my foot...I'd be better off resting up... But you go!' The false brightness in her voice threatened to overspill into tears. She would have to watch that.

'I can't go on my own!' Lucy's voice was horrified. 'You *have* to come, Tess!'

'Have to? I don't think so.' When she glanced up at her sister, she saw that Lucy was stricken. *Stricken!* One hour in the man's company and she was already distraught at the thought of not seeing him! 'You'll be fine without me,' she said coolly. 'Face it, Luce, you've never needed me around to hold your hand when it came to dealing with the opposite sex.'

'You don't understand. Anyway, staying here will be horrible and grim and depressing. What will you do? Hang around watching television in your Tigger nightie?'

Sounded fine to Tess.

'He might think that you're annoyed with him for some reason,' Lucy continued with a shrewdness that Tessa would never have expected.

It did make her think, though.

Lucy had a point. If she chickened out, Curtis would immediately come to the conclusion that he had offended her, and, since she was determined to emerge from her ill-conceived race into bed with him with dignity, showing any sign of offence was number one on the forbidden list.

Also, Curtis was unpredictable. He didn't obey conventions. She wouldn't put it past him to come to the house and confront her. If there was one thing Tessa knew she couldn't handle, it was that. She shuddered over the remainder of her toast and egg and hurriedly gulped down a mouthful of coffee.

'He probably wouldn't even notice my absence,' she said lamely, and Lucy made a stern tut-tutting noise under her breath.

'False modesty and you know it!' She removed the tray from her sister's lap. 'You just have to come. Now, what are you going to wear?'

'Why is it so important for us to go, Luce?' The question was innocent enough but Tessa's eyes narrowed speculatively on her sister's face, which reddened. The most conclusive sign of guilt Tessa could imagine. Her heart hardened. It was a good job Curtis Diaz wasn't around, she thought bitterly. Her famed composure might have undergone some serious fracturing. Along with his head.

'I thought I might take along some of my work,' Lucy

said, her colour deepening. 'Curtis seemed very interested in the sort of stuff I'm doing at the moment.'

'Oh, did Curtis?'

The inveterate charmer, she thought, her heart clenching. Always showed interest in other people and not just mild curiosity, but real interest. Or so it seemed. Poor Lucy. If she could have warned her, she would have, but she could hardly admit to speaking from experience and, besides, when it came to men, Lucy was a law unto herself.

But there were other ways of warning...

She stood up. Her foot, after that initial day of pain, was already strong enough to take some of her weight, though not comfortably. She still allowed herself to be helped to the bathroom and while she was doing her usual morning routine, even allowed Lucy to rifle through her wardrobe and choose some clothes for her to wear.

The choice was a pair of sand-coloured cord trousers, a similarly coloured roll-necked jumper and Lucy had completed the ensemble with a Burberry scarf of her own and a tan jacket, also hers, which fashionably came to mid-thigh. In terms of combating winter cold, it wasn't very practical but it did look very fetching. Besides, Tessa didn't have the energy to complain. Her energy was all being used up by the tide of emotions running amok inside her. There was just none left to distribute anywhere else.

They arrived at the Diaz house promptly at eleven, a minor miracle considering Lucy never arrived anywhere on time.

An intimate family gathering was Tessa's greatest fear, and her fear was misplaced because they arrived to find a throng of guests. Family members, of which there were many, mixed alongside old family friends and various members of *their* family. And, of course, Anna was there, ready to usher them in.

In one corner of the enormous room stood the most impressive Christmas tree Tessa had ever seen. It stretched from floor to ceiling and glittered with tiny white lights and what looked like an entire Harrods department's worth of stunning baubles, all in various shades of cream and ivory.

And lounging by the tree in a group was Curtis, dressed in his usual unique way. Faded jeans and a jumper with an off-puttingly elaborate pattern of reindeer. He saw her as soon as she walked through the door and Tessa felt that electric feeling of primitive awareness, as though her body had suddenly become alive. She smiled stiffly and then turned her attention back to Anna, asking her a thousand questions about her work at school and how she was getting on, whether her brief stint at filing was proving useful.

'Very!' Anna said, grinning. 'Now I just file away anything I don't like the look of, straight into the bin by my dressing table.'

'Well, something useful *did* come out of your working stint,' Tessa said teasingly, 'aside from that valuable filing art. Look at you! Very trendy. I recognise the top. Isn't that the one we got in that little boutique by the shoe shop?'

'Yes. The one Dad thought was a little too tight and a little too colourful and a little too...unwearable for his precious daughter!' Anna laughed. 'Mr Pot decides to call Miss Kettle black. I mean, look at him...' Her voice was soft with affection. 'He's the only one who would dare come to a do like this dressed in a pair of his oldest jeans and that jumper! A present from one of his ex-girlfriends, apparently.'

Tessa thought that she would rather not look at him, but she did anyway. The magnetic pull of his personality from across the room was just too much to bear. And besides, she and Anna were now being descended upon by various other people, Curtis's brother, Mark, his wife, and a delicate, elderly lady who seemed to be a godmother to one of the boys. Tessa smiled and went onto autopilot when they asked her about her foot, which was in an endearing bedroom slipper, but her eyes strayed over to Curtis. Now, the little group that had surrounded him had disbanded. In their place was an animated Lucy, cheeks flushed, glass of champagne jiggling precariously as she talked and gesticulated. Like someone who had known him for years instead of the perfect stranger that she was. The portfolio that she had lugged over was nowhere in evidence and Tessa assumed that it had been dumped somewhere, that it had been no more than a plausible excuse for Lucy's real reason for wanting to make it over here.

Jovial conversation continued to swim around her as she looked furtively at the chatting couple by the Christmas tree. Now Lucy must have said something about the tree, because she leant forward and gently touched one of the baubles, twirling it in her fingers.

She was dressed perfectly for the occasion. A deep burgundy skirt reaching to mid-calf and a small, long-sleeved top in a matching colour with a neckline designed to discreetly attract attention to what God had so generously given her up top. She had pinned up her long fair hair in an untidy pony-tail and a few artful strands danced around her cheeks as she leant forward to admire the bauble on the tree.

'Great tree,' Tessa said, looking away. 'Must have taken for ever to decorate.' She took time out to look at Curtis's brother, who was clearly older and far more traditional than his younger sibling. He was also fairer, without the dramatic looks that Curtis possessed. An affable, charming man married to an elegant woman with two very good-looking children, both under the age of five. Tessa drank her first glass of champagne, decided that it was doing won-ders for her spirits and accepted another from the tray that was being passed around by a young girl in uniform.

She had almost convinced herself that she had forgotten about Curtis's presence in the room, when she felt a soft tap on her shoulder and looked around to find him smiling down at her, telling her that her foot would be the size of a beach ball if she continued standing on it for much longer.

'Don't worry.' He grinned at his brother. 'I'll make sure she doesn't want for drinks, nibbles or amusing company.'

They were friends, Tessa thought, not merely two men who happened to share the same gene pool. The look that passed between them was full of mutual affection. A bit like she and Lucy. She automatically glanced around and saw that Lucy was being Lucy with two elderly gentlemen.

'There's no need to treat me like an invalid,' Tessa said in a prickly voice. 'My foot's actually a lot better. It must have been a very minor twist.' She was acutely aware of his long fingers curled around her forearm as he led her towards one of the deep chairs in the corner of the room. 'How was your day yesterday? It must have been marvellous sitting under that tree opening presents!' Her voice was high and light and stunningly polite.

'Oh, marvellous.' He pulled up a footstool and perched on it, one arm resting lightly on the arm of her chair. 'I was up at three in the morning, of course, all excited at what Santa might have brought for me.' He grinned, inviting her to share his amusement, and Tessa looked back at him blankly.

When she thought of his little tête à tête with her sister, when she imagined the sizzling lust that must have sprung into life the minute he'd clapped eyes on Lucy, just the thought of sharing any kind of joke with him made her feel physically sick. But she still held onto her smile.

'And what *did* you get?' she asked politely. He had positioned his body in such a way that he effectively blocked out the rest of the circulating party. Most of the older people had found chairs for themselves and were catching up on a year's worth of anecdotes. Mark and Emily's two children were whizzing round the room, with Anna in attendance, and Lucy had moved on to another group with the effortless ease of the born mixer.

'This magnificent jumper from an ex-girlfriend of long ago who's now happily married with a child and apparently thinks I need taking care of in the way of clothing. I like it.' He plucked at it and made a show of trying to make sense of the gaudy pattern.

'It's very cheerful.'

'Which is more than can be said about you,' Curtis said, with his usual lack of preamble. His blue eyes took on a wicked glint and Tessa quickly looked away.

'Yes, well…I didn't sleep all that well with my foot…'

'Which you said was definitely on the mend…'

'On the mend but not quite there yet,' Tessa informed him irritably, knowing that the foot was the last thing that had disturbed her sleep patterns.

'Lucy said you went to bed early with a headache,' Curtis remarked, and Tessa flinched at the intimacy implied in discussing her behind her back.

'Your brother's very nice.' She changed the conversation abruptly and cast her eyes around him, scanning the room and hopefully giving off signals of restlessness. 'He was telling me all about his house in Scotland and what it's like living there…'

'Riveting stuff.' Curtis's eyes were narrowed speculatively on her face. 'Ground-breaking social repartee, I would say.'

'I'd like to go and meet your mother.' Tessa dodged the verbal missile that she knew was designed to stimulate a response in her. As was his body language, leaning into her, elbows resting on his thighs. When did he plan to tell her about Lucy? she wondered. Once she had been eased gently off the scene? 'She's caught my eye a couple of times. I must seem very rude coming here and then ignoring the hostess.'

'I shouldn't worry about it.' Curtis could feel his irritation growing as she glanced across the room, cleverly avoiding the blue eyes that were trying to pin her down. 'Right now, Mum's as busy as the proverbial bee. It's the same every Boxing Day. Mark and I tell her just to do something light and trouble free, beg her to get the caterers in...'

'And...?' Tessa reluctantly looked at him, charmed by the evident love in his voice when he discussed the members of his family.

'And she agrees wholeheartedly. All through the month of November. At which point she begins letting slip the odd remark that people always preferred home-cooked food instead of all that plastic perfection that caterers were so good at, that *light food* was fine but that it had to be *interesting light food*. Then Boxing Day arrives and she's rushed off her feet, even though Anna does her best to try and help out. Despite the distractions...' They both looked at his daughter, who was now involved in amateurishly face-painting one of his brother's children.

'You let her wear the clothes she bought in London,' Tessa couldn't help remarking. 'She looks beautiful.'

'You can take the credit for that,' Curtis said lazily. 'Actually, you did me a favour. I was a little overprotective, thought I could keep her in strait-laced frocks suitable for the over forties when actually she would have asserted herself sooner or later. Better she asserted herself when she happened to be with you than later on, in the company of someone her own age with a taste for provocative clothing.'

'Or Lucy, even,' Tessa murmured, and when he frowned and leaned forward to catch what she had said, she smiled brightly and nodded in the direction of her sister. 'I said, here's Lucy!'

Curtis felt another spark of intense irritation and the uncomfortable feeling that she was somehow getting away, though there was no reason to think that. He would corner her later on, somehow, but in the meantime he smiled as Lucy approached and pulled a low, fabric-covered stool next to them.

'I always wondered how Boxing Day things were conducted in the houses of the Great and Good,' she exclaimed, grinning and flopping down on the stool, which was so low that she had to stretch her legs out in front of her at an angle.

'The Great and Good. Hmm. Not sure too many of my family members would allow me into that particular club, but does it live up to expectations anyway?'

'An awful lot of hard work, from what I see. Don't you agree, Tess? I mean, on Boxing Day we normally run to a couple of people, left-over turkey sandwiches and drunken games of charades once we've polished off all the chocolates in the house.'

'Which just goes to show how far apart our worlds are, Luce!' It was an opportunity too good to pass up. The opportunity to project just the smallest of warnings to her sister that this man was definitely not all he cracked himself up to be. 'This is Curtis's reality, even though he does such a brilliant job at being one of the ordinary people!'

Lucy seemed stunned by this observation, but then giggled a little nervously. Curtis looked enraged. Quietly, darkly and silently enraged. Tessa smiled blandly at him, as though there were absolutely nothing wrong in stating the obvious.

She wondered whether she should push the boat out with another ingenuous observation, but those narrowed, furious eyes, so far from the teasing charm that came naturally to him, made her think again. She stood up and excused herself.

'I'm going to see if I can find your mum,' she said, scanning the room. 'If not, I think I'll corner Anna again. I'll leave you two to it. Oh, you can have a look at Lucy's portfolio! She said you were interested in some of the stuff that she was doing!' If the portfolio had been some kind of ruse, then too bad. Lucy would have to sit through an inspection and suffer any consequent embarrassment.

She saw them exchange a quick look and then Lucy hurried into speech, apologising in advance for the quality of her work but unable to suppress the excitement in her voice.

Tessa slowly walked off, head held high, feeling Curtis's eyes boring into her from behind.

If she could spend the remainder of the time avoiding him, then she would.

It largely worked out that way. His relatives were all highly sociable people and she found that her foot was an immediate ice-breaker with them. The fact that she worked for Curtis was a further source of conversation, most of it highly entertaining. And Isobel, busy and flustered, was a delight, since Tessa had only ever thought of her as the embodiment of elegance and calm. It was nice to see this big family group, with their long-time friends, enjoying the fact of being together.

From wherever she was in the room, she was aware of Curtis with Lucy, aware of his eyes following her, trying to puzzle out her mood, was even aware when they disappeared for a short while, Lucy with her portfolio under her arm.

She saw them slip away, towards the middle of the afternoon, just when the curtains were being drawn and coffee was being served with liqueurs. Her heart seemed to stop beating for a few seconds and she was aware of the catch in her throat as she continued to chat to Anna and Isobel, while her mind swelled with images of what they might be getting up to.

A quick, cursory flick through some pictures and then what...? A kiss? One of those hungry, urgent kisses that she herself had been a victim of? A kiss aimed at catapulting down any barriers? Not that there would be any barriers between them. Lucy wasn't a barrier kind of girl. Tessa didn't think there would be any angst-filled questions, any doubts. She had to force herself back into the conversation, but her body was taut when they eventually emerged, both talking urgently together, his dark head inclined to meet her fair one.

Curtis spotted her immediately. She was sitting down on one of the plump chairs, foot resting on a small, velvet-covered footstool, chatting to old Colonel Watson, one of his parents' friends. For a few seconds he just stared at her, drinking in that calm, serious expression as she listened to whatever George Watson was rambling on about. She had tucked her hair neatly behind her ears, but every time she moved her head some escaped and swished against her cheek and then she would automatically tuck it back into position.

Lucy had wandered off to play with the kids, and for a moment his eyes lingered between the two of them, musing on how physically different they were. Blonde and vivacious stacked against brunette and wary.

From across the room, Tessa caught that look as his eyes

followed Lucy thoughtfully. He was comparing them. She
read that as clearly as if he had it written in large script
across his forehead. Comparing and contrasting. Or perhaps
just contrasting. She couldn't remember a time when she
had been jealous of Lucy. Lucy was Lucy and her stream
of boyfriends and adoring admirers had been a source of
amusement for Tessa but nothing else. But now jealousy
filled her like a poison and she closed her eyes for a few
fleeting seconds. When she opened them it was to find that
Curtis had bridged the space between them and was standing by her, gazing down from his great height.

'Oh!' Tessa said, flustered that she had been speculating
about him and now here he was, as if he had read her
thoughts and decided to wander over to find out more.
'You're back.'

'Back?'

'From having a look at Lucy's portfolio. What did you
think of her work?' She turned to the colonel and began
explaining what her sister did, taking much longer with the
explanation than was necessary, just to garner some self-
control, while Curtis stood and stared down at her.

The colonel made one or two jocular remarks about his
lack of artistic talent, his admiration for anyone who knew
what to do with some charcoal or a paintbrush, and then
excused himself to check up on Isobel, make sure she
hadn't collapsed from overexertion. Which left her all alone
with Curtis.

He sat down in the colonel's chair. When he spoke, his
voice was normal enough but his blue eyes were watchful
and assessing. Assessing what? Assessing how she would
react to his budding involvement with her sister? The sickening, faint feeling that had plagued her since she had first
overheard that conversation was replaced by a dead, still,
cold calm.

He was asking her something about whether she was having fun. Tessa nearly laughed aloud at that one.

'Absolutely,' she said neutrally. 'Your relatives are all so nice and it's great seeing Anna again. She looks wonderful.'

'In her twenty-first-century clothing.' Curtis grinned, trying unsuccessfully to drag her from her zoned-out state. 'I think she's done a ritual burning of the old-fashioned frocks and Alice bands.'

'She hasn't, has she?' Tessa gasped, momentarily distracted, and he laughed and touched her cheek with one brown finger.

'I hope not. Those clothes cost quite a bit. I've told her that the least she could do is give them to charity. I'm keeping my fingers crossed that she doesn't interpret that as free rein to go and buy whatever she wants in the expectation that I now have no right to object.'

Where he had touched her had left a hot, stinging trail. It was all she could do not to wipe it away with the back of her fist.

'I'm sure she's far too sensible to do that,' Tessa said obligingly, and he gave her another quick, frustrated look from under his lashes.

'Tessa, what's goi—'

'Lord, is that the time?' she interrupted quickly, before he could start on any difficult conversations. 'Work tomorrow. We really must go. I wonder if your mother needs any help with the clearing up?'

'No, she definitely doesn't need any help with any clearing up,' he grated, catching her by her wrist as she began to stand. 'She might insist on doing all the cooking but she does relent when it comes to the aftermath. She has people come in to do that for her. We've barely exchanged two words all day, do you realise that?'

'It's difficult at something like this,' Tessa said on a note of desperation. Caught in mid-motion, she didn't know whether to sit back down or wrestle her hand out of his vice-like grip. 'So many people around,' she elaborated vaguely.

'You should try my mother's New Year's Eve parties.' Curtis relaxed enough to grin. 'Always starts small, just a few close friends, and by the time December the thirty-first has come round, the few close friends has always managed to swell into eighty-odd and counting. We have to talk. There's something I need to tell you...' The grin got a little wider and Tessa felt panic hit her like a fist right in her stomach. She just knew, with sudden foreboding, that somewhere in his next sentence her sister's name would be mentioned.

'It's about Lucy...'

# CHAPTER NINE

REFLECTING back, Tessa was amazed that those three little words, unintentionally aimed straight at her heart, hadn't resulted in an immediate breakdown. Right there, half standing, half sitting, with Curtis's firm hand closed over her wrist. In fact, her utter composure had been a great reminder to her that she would be able to get through this and put it behind her. An ability to keep up appearances was everything. After all, didn't you eventually believe the myths you started creating about yourself? Show the world that you were strong, that you hadn't been hurt, and sooner or later you would find yourself no longer having to pretend.

She had smiled brightly and exclaimed that there was no need to launch into this particular conversation about her sister, that she already knew. And then, when he had still been in his stunned phase, she had managed to release herself from his fingers and return to the noisy bustle of the party, where several people had conveniently been paying their respects to the hostess before taking their leave.

She and Lucy had managed to slip out before she could be cornered again by him and forced to hear the quiet letdown, the rueful sheepishness that her sister's attractions were just so much greater and more inviting. She had even managed to avoid the worst-case scenario, which was being asked, urgently and passionately, whether she would mind not saying anything about what they had got up to just in case it jeopardised his chances with her sister.

However, she had known what she had to do.

Nevertheless, she could feel a wave of nauseous nervousness sweep through her as she walked through the familiar doors of the office building.

The feeling intensified on the ride up, where she maintained a glassy-eyed, fixed stare in front of her, ignoring every other person in the lift.

She had decided to arrive as early as possible, in the hope that she would get to the office before him. Time for a strong cup of coffee and a few stern lectures to herself before she had to face the reality of his overwhelming presence.

As luck would have it, he was there. Tessa spotted him the minute she walked into her office, through the open door that led to his. He was sprawled back in his chair, legs propped up on the desk, surveying something on his computer. His jeans were faded to almost white in patches and he was wearing a long-sleeved black tee shirt. Conservative dressing by his standards and he looked shockingly sexy.

'God, you're early!' His eyes crinkled in an appreciative smile. 'Half the staff are off for a couple more days and the other half will be taking their time getting here.' He beckoned her with one finger and, though he was still smiling, his eyes were serious.

Just in case he was thinking of continuing the conversation he had been obliged to abort the evening before, Tessa rooted through her bag and carefully placed the envelope on the desk in front of him.

He looked at it for a few seconds, then said brusquely, 'What's this?'

'Open it and you'll find out. Can I get you some coffee?'

'No, you can stay right there until I see what you've given me.' He dropped his feet to the ground, leaned forward and took the envelope, opening it in one swift movement as he slid back into his reclining position.

Tessa didn't look at him as he read, and re-read and re-read again. She focused on her fingers instead, spread clammily on her skirt.

'It's a letter of resignation,' Curtis said eventually, his voice devoid of any intonation, and this time she did look at him. His lips were narrowed in a thin line and he was frowning, but not in a puzzled way. More in a savagely grim way.

'I know what it is. I wrote it.'

'Mind telling me why? Or do I have to guess?'

'Well, as I mentioned in the letter, the job is brilliant, but it's just not for me.'

'Why not?'

'We did say from the start that there would be a three-month probationary period,' Tessa hedged. 'You would be free to give me my walking papers if you didn't like what you got and I would be free to do the same.'

'And you've decided to go down that route even though you've spent, let's see now, eight lines extolling the fabulous nature of the work.' He leaned back, folded his hands behind his head and proceeded to give her the full benefit of his attention. It was like being hosed down in freezing water. His eyes were chips of ice.

In her head, Tessa had imagined that her resignation, after the first few platitudes of regret and maybe a token attempt to tempt her to stay, would be happily accepted. After all, wasn't she freeing him up to commence a full-blown affair with Lucy, without having her around like a guilty conscience draped round his neck?

She hadn't thought that she would have to account for her decision.

'Do you mind if I sit down?'

For a few seconds, he looked as though he might just insist that she remain standing, but eventually he nodded briefly at the chair in front of his desk and she sank into it with a feeling of relief.

'So...you were about to explain why you feel the need to leave this job even though...' he picked up the letter lying on his desk and quoted from it '''...It is enjoyable and invigorating and has provided an invaluable window of experience which will prove very influential when seeking a new position elsewhere...'''

'I just think...' What *did* she think? Quoting her own resignation letter back to her had been a dirty trick. Now she was supposed to come up with some plausible reason why she was quitting a supposed dream job. And she could hardly start waffling on about the money because the money was just another dreamy aspect of it.

'Cut the crap, Tessa. We both know why you've suddenly decided that you have to quit.'

Silence. Tessa cringed into her chair and stared firmly down at the tips of her shoes. So, she had managed to dodge the inevitable let-down chat the evening before and now she was going to have it drummed into her head.

She didn't notice him vacating his chair and wasn't aware of what he was doing until he was leaning right over her, hands gripping the sides of her chair, his face thrust aggressively close to hers.

'I just want to hear you say it,' he grated softly.

That did it. This time she looked him straight in the eye, her rising anger matching his own.

As if it wasn't enough that she knew what he was up to! Oh, no, he was determined to have it out in the open so that they could discuss it! Presumably like two adults. Maybe he needed to talk about it so that he could put any tiny speck of conscience he had to bed.

'Okay. I'm leaving because I know what's going on between you and my sister and I don't think it's appropriate for me to continue working for you under those circumstances.'

'You *know what's going on between me and your sister*?' Bafflement was quickly replaced by cold, dawning comprehension. Tessa wondered, for a few fleeting seconds, whether she might have made a mistake, but then decided that she had heard what she had heard, and, as if that weren't enough, she knew what she knew. That Lucy was his type. In Tessa's view, too many problems were caused by people trying to hide from the truth. She had seen enough of her friends and Lucy's to know that ignoring certain glaring facts always proved very costly emotionally. Woe betide the poor woman whose boyfriend started avoiding phone calls, when her response was to make excuses on his behalf instead of interpreting the situation the way it really was.

Their fling, if it even deserved to be in that category, had been, Tessa thought, fragile from the word go. He had never been going to hang about for very long and if she had made the fatal mistake of falling in love with him, then that was her fault and her fault alone.

'Care to elaborate?' There was a dangerous softness to his voice that she chose to ignore.

'I don't see the point of that. Would you mind moving? I can't breathe properly with you so close.'

He pushed himself away from her to go by the window where he proceeded to lean against the broad ledge, arms folded, like a judge contemplating a seriously irritating miscreant.

'You think…what *exactly*?'

'You know what I think! And there's no point trying to deny it. I heard the two of you whispering by the front door, discussing that perhaps it would be best to keep the situation from me. I heard! And, for heaven's sake, don't even try to patronise me by pretending that you don't have a clue what I'm talking about!'

'I wouldn't dream of patronising you and I remember the conversation distinctly.'

'Right. Good. In that case...' In that case, she thought, I'll just get my act together and leave.

'So in you jumped with your conclusions because, naturally, I'm the sort of bastard who sleeps with a woman and then has no compunctions about sharing himself with her sister. You wouldn't say that you know me better than that?'

'I never accused you of sleeping with Lucy,' Tessa mumbled uncomfortably.

'A minor technicality.' Curtis overrode her interruption coldly. 'Conspiring to meet up behind your back is as good as. And what a quick worker I am! Twenty minutes and I've already managed to make an assignation with a girl I didn't know from Adam! What a lot of faith you have in me! Not forgetting your sister, of course.'

'Lucy wouldn't have known about...about us...'

'Oh, that's all right, then. For her to arrange to meet me after a couple of minutes and some polite conversation. Does she normally do that sort of thing? Get involved with a perfect stranger without bothering with the niceties of getting to know him?'

'If you arranged to meet, then that would be step one in getting to know one another, wouldn't it?' Tessa shrugged. 'Hence my resignation. Working with you under those circumstances would be too uncomfortable. For both of us.'

'So, really, having written me off as a serial womaniser, you're doing the big-hearted thing and giving me the space to move on to another model without having to work with model number one.'

'That's about it.'

A deathly silence lengthened between them. Tessa could feel the vein in her neck pulsing and her heart hammering inside her like a steam engine.

'Fine.'

'I beg your pardon?'

'I said fine. You can go now. You're released from your employment with immediate effect. Any money the company owes you will be forwarded to your address and, naturally, I will provide a good reference for you when you find yourself another job.'

Tessa stared at him. She had got what she wanted. She was being released from the agony of working alongside him while he cavorted with her sister. In the long run, it had been the only option. Lucy might come and go in the blink of an eye, but there would be others, a long line of them. Fun-loving blondes, the sort he enjoyed having around brightening his office, the sort he enjoyed going out with. If she had stayed put, she would have had to endure each and every one and how thick could one person's skin be?

Logic and good, solid reason were no match for the awful loneliness spreading through her, though.

She made her legs move, made herself stand up and even propelled herself in the direction of him, stretching out her hand in the final, utterly polite, gesture of farewell.

Curtis looked at the outstretched hand with contempt.

'I don't think so,' he said icily.

Her hand dropped to her side and she felt tears well up and prick the backs of her eyes. That expression in his eyes was the very worst thing. It sliced right through her like a blade.

'I—' she began.

'Don't say a word,' he snarled. 'I think you've already said quite enough.' With that he spun round on his heel and stared out of the window, affording her the sight of his ramrod-straight back.

Let her go, Curtis thought savagely. He was aware of her hovering behind him, but there was no way he was going to rescue her from her self-inflicted discomfort. He continued to stare broodingly out of the window, not that there was much worth looking at. With spectacular pre-dictability, it had failed to snow yet again and the skies were typically leaden. Everything looked monochrome and depressed.

He was aware of her departure with the sound of the door clicking shut, and only then did he slowly turn around and return to his chair, making no attempt to immerse him-self in his work. He had no idea how long he sat there, staring at the wretched screen saver, while thoughts jostled in his head. He only knew that the next time he glanced out of the window, it had begun to snow. He guessed that all over London kids would be staring out of their windows in wonder, praying that the flurries would turn into some-thing more substantial, something they could build a snow-man out of. He had promised Anna that he would be home early, in time to take her and his mother out for an early supper somewhere. It had been his intention to invite Tessa along as well.

Clearly now out of the question.

He swivelled so that his chair was squarely facing the window and told himself that he had had a very lucky es-cape.

He had deviated from his usual course, had been blinded by a combination of seriousness, intelligence and humour, not realising that seriousness, intelligence and humour added up to a woman who would not be content to simply have a spot of fun.

Curtis frowned darkly at the window. He worked damned hard all year long. Relationships were about releasing him from the tensions of his job. Relationships were all about putting guilt-free fun into his life. They weren't about making him feel like this, feel like throwing things at the window and walking for hours in the snow because he needed to clear his head.

He swore softly and ineffectively under his breath, cursing the fact that there was no one in the office with whom he could indulge in some casual banter, just until his head got sorted. Flexitime had distinct drawbacks occasionally.

He slung his jumper on over the long-sleeved tee shirt, stuck on his coat and headed down, only remembering that his computer was still running when he was almost out of the office.

He wasn't too sure where he was heading. Only when he was outside, with the flakes gathering momentum around him and all trace of sun stifled under the thick grey skies, did he realise that he needed to see her.

She certainly didn't need to see him. In fact, Tessa thought as she turned the key to her front door, he was the last person in the world she ever wanted to clap eyes on again.

A tiny voice in her head pointed out that her wish had certainly been granted. He had made no move to stop her from leaving the company. A careless shrug had been all she had been worth at the end of the day. He hadn't even mentioned what they had had together. It had been so meaningless to him that he couldn't even be bothered to bring the subject up.

She dashed a couple of wayward tears from her eyes and pushed open the door.

Of course, just when she wanted to be on her own, Lucy was in. She could hear her sister clattering around in the kitchen, and, knowing that she could hardly avoid her, Tessa removed her coat, hung it on the coat stand by the door and reluctantly made her way to the origin of the noise.

'Would you believe it's snowing?' Lucy greeted her triumphantly, as though the fall of snow were something she had personally been involved in. As an afterthought, she added, frowning, 'Why are you home, anyway? I thought you'd gone off to work?'

Tessa sighed and sat down. 'Long story.'

'Will it be one of those long stories that I'll want to hear?' Lucy flopped into the chair facing hers and looked at Tessa with concern. 'You didn't have a relapse of your twisted-foot syndrome, did you?'

'Oh, no. Foot's fine.' It's the heart that's not doing too good, she added silently to herself. 'But, as of this moment, I'm officially on the dole.'

Lucy gaped. For a few seconds, Tessa forgot her worries and actually laughed because it took a lot to reduce her sister to speechlessness.

'You're joking!' Lucy searched her face for some semblance of humour, found none and sank back into her chair. 'Oh, my God, *why*?'

'Oh, you know. Not the job for me.'

'But...I thought you enjoyed working there. You told me that it was a lot more fun than your last place, that fuddy-duddy accountancy firm...I don't understand...'

Now came the careful tiptoeing-round-the-minefield part. To put off the dire moment, Tessa asked whether she could possibly have a cup of tea, and then thought about her next approach, while Lucy gabbled away in the background, expressing curiosity and surprise at the same time. Finally,

mug in hand, she plonked it in front of her sister and said
sternly, 'You've made a huge mistake. You had an invigorating, well-paid job and Curtis Diaz was most probably
the best boss you could ever hope to find.'

'Curtis Diaz is a workaholic and a womaniser.'

'That doesn't make sense. Workaholics don't have time
to womanise and, anyway, what do his private habits have
to do with how much you enjoy your work?'

'Stop quizzing me about this, Luce,' Tessa said irritably.
'I'm tired and I have another headache. I don't need you
to start playing older sis with me.'

'Because you think you've monopolised that position!'
Lucy retorted quick as a flash. 'Well, I just want to tell you
that quitting your job has really jeopardised things for me.
I mean, did Curtis mention anything about me? No, I don't
suppose he would have. If he knew that you'd made your
mind up, he wouldn't have wanted to put you under any
pressure to stay. Mind you...' she stared off into the distance, oblivious to Tessa '...there's no real reason why everything should come to a halt just because you've suddenly decided that you hate working for him...'

'Lucy, *what are you on about*?'

'I mean...he really *did* like what he saw yesterday. I
know he did. He *said* he did, but I just get the feeling that
he's not one of those guys who says something just for the
sake of it...do you?'

'Liked *what*?' This conversation was getting surreal.
What had Curtis seen that he had liked? Had they been
playing some kind of adult doctor-and-nurse game for the
half an hour that they'd been closeted away in his mother's
house? Surely they couldn't have been that overcome with
lust? A sick feeling clawed away at her stomach, threatening to make her bring up the few mouthfuls of tea she
had just swallowed.

'Well…we were going to tell you this together but…' She couldn't help it. She smiled. A broad, thrilled smile that lit up her face. 'God, Tess, it's the most exciting thing ever!'

Tessa could think of nothing to say. Her throat had closed up and really she doubted whether she would have been able to speak even if she had wanted to. The truth was going to come at her from every angle, she now realised. It didn't matter how much she tried to deflect the blows, they would still come because they would never be able to keep a relationship between them silent.

'You know when Curtis came round the other evening…Lord, but it feels like a thousand years ago!' Her eyes sparkled as she leant forward, propping her chin in her hand. She had wonderful, tumbling hair that she occasionally straightened, when she wanted to look glamorous. Now, it was a riotous jumble of curls cascading past her shoulders.

'Yes, I remember.' Tessa sighed quietly.

'Well, he asked me all about what I was doing at college and then he told me that I might be just the person to work on some logos for him. You know he's thinking about extending parts of his operation to the Far East…'

What she was hearing seemed to be coming at her from a long way off. In fact, it took a few seconds for it to sink in, then she said, on a whisper, 'What are you talking about, Luce?'

'My work! What else? We decided not to say anything to you because I know you. I knew you'd be disappointed if you thought that I'd been rejected, but yesterday, after he had a look at my portfolio, he said that he was prepared to give me a stab at it. He was so sweet about it! Not patronising at all. He said he liked my work, that it was quirky and inventive, which would be just the sort of thing he would be looking for...'

'Your work...' Tessa said hollowly.

'Why aren't you excited?' Lucy demanded, pausing in her breathless excitement to realise that the expected reaction had not arrived.

'I am. Excited and thrilled.' Tessa forced herself to smile but the smile was strained. Why hadn't he said anything? Why hang on to his silence, letting her fling herself into accusations that were wildly off target?

She remember the puzzled look on his face when she had informed him that she knew about his feelings for her sister.

'What about your course?' she asked faintly, dragging the subject back to the prosaic and leaving her restless mind free to wander unimpeded. 'You can't possibly give that up. Not when you've come so far...'

But Lucy had everything sorted and Tessa half listened, only stirring herself when mention was made of food and, buoyed up by the prospect of her first successful dip into the brave world of advertising, Lucy actually volunteered to go out and buy some. With her own money.

Once she was gone, Tessa went into the sitting room and just let the sound of silence drift over her. Peaceful though it was, it wasn't nearly peaceful enough to end the nasty tangle of thoughts writhing around in her head like hungry serpents. She moaned softly and closed her eyes.

She still had them optimistically closed when the doorbell went.

The prospect of lunch, even though it might be procured and prepared by her sister in a very rare excursion into domesticity, did not appeal. Tessa didn't feel hungry. In fact, she felt as though she had crashed headlong into a brick wall.

Which was *good*, she told herself, trundling to the front door. Because, face it, even if things hadn't gone utterly pear-shaped now, they would have further down the line. She and the brick wall would *still* have become close acquaintances somewhere in the future.

She pulled open the front door and her eyes travelled up, and up, and up until they finally rested on Curtis's dark, glowering face. At which point something like electricity shot through her veins, making her take a step backwards from the impact.

In that brief instant of stunned hesitation, Curtis pushed his way inside and slammed the door shut behind him, then he leaned heavily against it and stared down at her.

'What are you doing here?' Tessa asked in a small voice. She took a few more steps backwards, putting distance between them. Her hands fluttered nervously and she clasped them together in front of her.

'Just passing by. Thought I'd drop in. About now, you should start hurling more accusations about me and your sister, wouldn't you say? Something along the lines of what a bastard I am?'

'You should have told me.'

'Told you what.'

'That I was wrong about you and Lucy. That you were interested in her work. That that was what all the hushed voices were all about, as well as her desperation to get to your mother's Boxing Day do. Because she wanted to show you her portfolio. I shouldn't have had to hear it all from my sister.'

'And what...stop you in mid-rant?' He had spent the last hour cooling his heels at his usual coffee shop close to the office, giving his composure time to return to working condition. In fact, he had never had so many about-turns in his life before. One minute he had wanted to storm over to her place and give her a piece of his mind, because why the hell should he allow her to drag his reputation into the mud without murmuring a single word of protest? The next minute, he was telling himself that she wasn't worth the effort of an argument, that she could think precisely what she wanted and the fact that he knew the truth was enough.

In fact, he had worked his way through two espressos and a bacon roll before coming to the decision that he was a man of honour and, as such, had a right to put her straight on one or two of her assumptions.

In a very cool, very detached, laudably rational way, of course. After all, all he would be doing would be to put her straight and move on with a clean slate. Get right back to the sort of woman he understood. Some uncomplicated, fun creature. The world was full of them, as he had always found.

Looking at this particular woman now, though, was doing nothing for all his good intentions. He didn't feel very cool or detached or even rational, come to think of it.

'No,' he drawled, moving towards her until they were doing a weird dance, with Tessa retreating in the face of Curtis's slow, relentless advance. 'How cruel would I have been not to have allowed you the pleasure of ripping my personality to shreds?'

'I didn't rip your personality to shreds,' Tessa mumbled, wincing. She had now backed herself into the sitting room and she scuttled into the closest chair, curling into it.

'No?' Curtis intoned silkily. He was no longer advancing on her, but, almost as bad, prowling through the room like a great jungle cat exploring the limits of its cage. And he was every bit as threatening as any great jungle cat. 'If I remember accurately, you accused me of seducing your sister in this very house, when I was still fresh from sleeping with *you*, of arranging to meet her with your smell still lingering in my nostrils. Now, I'm not sure what school of morality you attended, but the one I went to clearly stated that those types of accusations come into the category of *personality shredding!*' Each sibilant, vicious word was like a drop of poison.

He had ceased his restless prowling and was now standing in front of her, hands shoved into his trouser pockets, his face a mask of freezing contempt.

'You should have said something,' Tessa flung at him. She lifted her chin and eyed him mutinously. 'You let me jump to all the wrong conclusions and now you think you can just walk in and throw it in my face!'

Had he thought for one minute, seriously, that she would open the door, meekly and tearfully accept what he had to say, fall at his feet with hands clasped in apology, simply because she had made a mistake? Her cheeks were two burning patches of colour and the stubborn tilt of her chin spoke volumes for her determination to fight him right back.

Let her.

Yes. Yes, he had done the right thing in coming here. Every muscle in his body was pulsing and it was a damn sight healthier than that impotent, frustrated, dead feeling he had had earlier.

And he still wanted her. With all her complications, her intolerance of his basic ground rule of *just have fun*, her wild accusations. A sex thing. But he felt his rage ratchet up a notch and this time it was directed solely at himself.

He angrily stalked off and sat down, glowering. 'I was going to let you walk away. Of course I knew you'd find out the truth sooner or later, but guess what? Why should I drop it? Why should I allow you to get away with defamation of my character? I notice you haven't even had the common decency to *apologise!*'

'Okay. I'm sorry. I'm *sorry*. I jumped to the wrong conclusions. Satisfied?'

'Not really, no.'

'Because…?'

'Because it's more than just jumping to the wrong conclusions, isn't it? It's about trust. What kind of man do you think I am? That's the basic question, isn't it?'

'What was I supposed to think?'

'You were supposed to think that a few overheard snatches of conversation just might not add up to the worst possible conclusion. You were *supposed to think* that you knew me well enough to presume me innocent before condemning me to the guillotine.' He knew how he sounded. Cold, indifferent, composed. He knew that only he would be able to discern the awful truth behind what he was saying, which was that he had been hurt. Curtis Diaz, the man who had always burnt the candle at both ends, the man who worked hard and played hard, had been hurt.

Tessa's face was closed as she looked at him. Now *this* argument, she thought, was one she could really get her teeth into. He obviously hadn't followed through with his logic. Unusual for him, since he had the most logical brain of any man she had ever met, but everyone had a blind spot and this was his. He was a charming, dangerously sexy man who nurtured a reputation for never staying with one woman for too long, whose tastes had always run to a very specialised type of female, and yet he naively thought that he should be seen as Mr Trustworthy. The ego of the man!

Tessa focused very hard on that side of him. The side that wasn't witty and thoughtful and sharp and ironic. She concentrated on his house-sized ego. Safer.

'Why do you think I should have done that?' she asked, with a coldness that almost matched his but didn't quite. 'Why do you think I should have heard what sounded like a very compromising conversation and immediately come to the conclusion that it was innocent?' She would have done, she knew it, if she'd thought that he loved her, because mutual love was all about trust. But she was just a passing fancy and passing fancies didn't necessarily qualify for exclusivity. That was life.

'Look at you!' Tessa continued, gathering momentum as her heart protected itself by projecting a one-dimensional cardboard cut-out image of him. 'You're not exactly noted for your celibate nature...'

'Meaning that I see nothing wrong in overlapping relationships?'

'I never said that you would have gone out with Lucy while I was still trailing in the background like some inconvenient unfinished business. But you're not exactly the solid type who places a whole lot of emphasis on cultivating long-standing relationships, are you?'

'Why did you sleep with me if I didn't fit into that niche?'

'Because...' Tessa glared back at him, carelessly lounging there in the chair as if he had a perfect right to be there.

'You're upset because you thought that I had lived down to my reputation. Upset enough to quit a job you loved doing. But when we went to bed together, I was still that man, so why did you decide to come to bed with me? Were you hoping that somehow I'd change? That you'd be able to turn me into a domestic dream who wanted nothing more than to slip into commitment and live happily ever after with a few kiddies running around and a dog in front of the Aga?'

# CHAPTER TEN

'I THINK it's time you left.' Tessa got to her feet with as much dignity as she could muster. Curtis's question had shaken her to the core. How could she have thought for a minute that his lessons in logic might have been incomplete? With a few short observations, he had stripped her reaction down to the bone. What she didn't want to do was give him any opportunity to go further.

'I'm not ready to leave.' And he wasn't. He really wasn't. Because he was back in the driving seat, utterly and totally in control. When he left, he would have put her straight on her vast misconception of his character. He wasn't a commitment guy. That was for his brother, who loved the routine and order of his life. He, himself, had never cared for routine. His job predicated against any sort of routine, anyway. That had been the beauty of his wife, when she was alive. She too had been full of the joy of living and pregnancy had not really interfered with that.

His only grounding now came from being a father. For Anna he would take time off work, for Anna he would postpone meetings and attend school concerts whenever he could. But that was it. Absolutely. The thought of having some wife in the background nagging about his hours and reminding him of deadly dinner parties she had arranged for the weekend was just not on his agenda.

'Since you happen to be in *my* house, whether or not you're ready to go isn't the point. The point is I want you out. You've got your apology and now we have nothing left to say.' Her breath caught in her throat at that. The house-sized ego she had been focusing so intently on vanished like a puff of smoke. All she thought was, You were such fun, you could make me laugh and make me abandon every ounce of common sense just to feel you close to me. You could make me love you.

The dangerous thoughts crept into her head like thieves, stealing her will-power.

'You haven't answered my question,' Curtis said, not budging. 'And you might as well sit back down. I'm not ready to leave, not yet, and I don't see how you can force me out. I'm all for equality of the sexes, but when it comes to physical strength, we're still poles apart.'

'Oh, right! When in doubt, just fall back on the caveman principle, why don't you?'

'Answer my question and I'll go.'

Tessa sat back down, furious and helpless at the same time. 'I never saw you as relationship potential,' she spat out. 'Never.'

'Then I expect you'll be wanting your job back, in that case? Now that we've established that there's nothing going on between me and your sister?'

'And slide back into being your casual fling till you get bored of me? No, thanks!' The words were out before she could take them back, and they flew through the sudden, thick silence with the efficiency of the contents from Pandora's box. Tessa could feel the blood rush to her face and she had to stop herself from groaning out loud. Everything she had been trying so hard to deny was wrapped up in those few careless words and he knew it. She could see it on his face.

'Because that wouldn't be enough for you, would it?' Curtis said softly. 'You're just not the type of woman who can have flings.'

Tessa hoped he wasn't expecting an answer to that because he wasn't going to get one. She would just have to let him spin his yarn and then he would leave. His life would carry on its own merry way and she would pick up the pieces and start again.

'I'm sorry,' he said. Horribly, he sounded as if he meant it. Tessa cringed inwardly and wished she could somehow magic herself out of the room, out of the house, maybe even out of the country. Anywhere she could escape to where those piercing blue eyes couldn't bore into her soul and read what was written there.

'I don't want commitment. Not yet. Maybe not ever.' He stood up slowly. 'I don't get turned on by the prospect of shopping for rings or by the thought of coming back home to the smell of home-cooked food.'

He had an image of her, waiting for him at the end of the day, smiling when he walked through the door, asking him how his day had been.

'I don't need anyone asking me how my day went,' he ground out more forcefully than he had intended. 'Aren't you going to say anything?' he snapped, angry with her because somehow she had made him think thoughts he had no business thinking.

'What's there to say?' Tessa asked wearily. 'You're right. I'm not a casual kind of girl and I never could be. I was stupid to ever have gone to bed with you, but we all make mistakes.'

Curtis didn't much care for being called a mistake. Why, he didn't know.

'I thought I could just have fun, but I was wrong. I knew that when Lucy appeared on the scene and I thought you were interested in her.'

'You were jealous, in other words.' That was much better. He really rather liked the idea of Tessa being jealous. More than liked it. It made his heart sing crazily. What man's heart wouldn't? he thought to himself. Perfectly normal human reaction.

'I was realistic,' Tessa corrected coldly. 'You've chosen the road you want to go down, and good luck to you. It's not the road I want and I don't intend wasting time indulging in something that's going nowhere.'

'I couldn't agree more.' Curtis moved towards the door, waiting for her to stand up to see him out, which he soon realised she had no intention of doing, although she wanted him out. That was pretty clear from the shuttered, cool expression on her face. 'I don't personally see it as wasting time, but there you go. Different strokes for different folks.'

'That's right.'

He hesitated, wanting to ask her about her foot but knowing that that was stupid when they had just waged World War III, bar the shooting. 'Tell Lucy to get in touch with me so that we can formally discuss details of this job. And tell her to make sure that her passport's up to date. She might need to fly out to one or two proposed sites at short notice.'

'Sure.' Tessa looked at him, taking him in for the last time.

'You can come in with her and collect your pay-cheque,' Curtis heard himself say. His face darkened at the sudden crack in his armour but if she noticed anything, she didn't show it.

'I'd rather you posted it to me.'

'Look, we're adults. There's no need for you to avoid me like the plague. Chances are that we'll even bump into one another in the course of things, if Lucy takes on the commission and things go according to plan...'

The thought of *bumping into him* was enough to make her feel sick. Since when did convalescents expose themselves witlessly to the cause of their illness?

'I don't see any reason why we should meet again. And I'd really rather Personnel posted the cheque to me. I'm going to be out and about looking for a job. I can't guarantee that I'll be able to pop in at the drop of a hat.'

'Sure. Well, whatever.'

'Just slam the door behind you. It self-locks.' With that, she turned away, dismissing him.

Suited him just fine, Curtis decided, striding out of the room and slamming the front door behind him.

It had all gone according to plan. Really. He had come to state his case and state it he had. What she had said had only confirmed his suspicions that she had been a dangerous near miss. She had wanted more and she had told him so in no uncertain terms. He was a free man. He would spend the rest of the school holidays juggling his work so he could take Anna out, maybe even buy her some new clothes in the sales, before she went back to school. He thought back to that day when his daughter and Tessa had gone shopping, the glow of achievement on her face. Well, he didn't think he would be able to match that as far as shopping partners went, but so be it.

It would be his first step in getting his life back to normal, back where he wanted it to be, where he was in control. Leave the unpredictability for his job.

He drove to his mother's house, having originally planned to return to the office where he would be able to submerge himself in work. In his head he played out the conversation he had just had with Tessa. He didn't want to. What he wanted was to now wash his hands of her altogether. But his mind was refusing to co-operate.

He had done what he had set out to do. That was good. Leaving her with the impression that he had somehow, ludicrously, managed to get involved with her sister was a misconception he hadn't been able to ignore in the end and he had sorted that out.

Frowning as his logical brain backtracked and fitted pieces together, he very nearly went into the back of someone at some traffic lights that had turned red. A minor interruption to his concentration. There was some link he should be making, he thought restlessly, some vital connection, and then as his car purred away at the traffic lights it happened and it was like being catapulted into the air at full speed.

Tessa was a commitment girl. She had said so herself. What she had failed to mention was what he was now figuring out for himself.

Commitment girls would never get involved with a man purely because it promised to be a spot of fun, no matter how powerful the attraction might be. He knew that in the depth of his bones and from the very summit of his experience. Women who seriously sought commitment wouldn't even be *attracted* to a man like him. They might look, but they would never venture near.

Which meant that Tessa had become involved because... because...

The conclusion that he had been inexorably working towards now presented itself to him. She had fallen in love with him. Maybe she didn't realise it herself, maybe she was just pretending to herself that, really, it had all been fun and she had got out before it was too late, but he thought otherwise. He thought that she had fallen in love with him even before she had slept with him and, subconsciously, her physical capitulation had just been the logical consequence of her emotional involvement.

He found that he was driving on automatic, not even realising where he was going, and was startled when his car suddenly appeared to be at his mother's place. His head felt fuzzy, almost as though important brain connections had been subtly altered so that his responses weren't what they should be. Everything was just a bit off kilter. And there was a pounding rush deep inside him, which he couldn't understand or deal with. He just knew one thing. His narrow escape must have been a hell of a lot narrower than he had imagined. He felt as though he had been too close to a fire and had been singed.

Singed but not burnt. Lucky him. And tomorrow he would probably be fully healed and ready to move forward. He would have her out of his head. In a week's time, he might even be seeing someone else, someone uncomplicated, straightforward and up for some fun, no strings attached…

A mere three days later, when Tessa spotted him in the gossip column of the newspaper, cavorting with a blonde, she made her mind up. She needed a break. The thought of seeing the new year in with Lucy around, puzzled and curious and waiting for the right time to launch into a detailed interrogation, just wouldn't do. Nor would the inevitable sleepless night, heady fuzzy with thoughts of him kissing the blonde as the clock struck twelve.

She had to get away, right away. Be on her own in different surroundings. The familiarity of the house stirred up too many painful memories. The four walls were no longer her haven but her torture chamber, impregnated with his dynamic, restless personality, and she needed time out from it.

She didn't even bother to tell her sister face to face. She couldn't face the concern and the questions.

So she left a note on the kitchen table. She would be in Dublin. She gave the name of the hotel and the phone number in case of an emergency, but failed to mention when she would be back.

And it felt glorious to walk out of the house, with a holdall, two good books and no one asking her what she was doing.

The feeling persisted on the flight over, and even the reality of checking into the hotel wasn't sufficient for Tessa to doubt for a single minute that she had done the right thing.

The place she had managed to find so close to New Year was small and cosy. She took a deep breath and filled her nostrils with the fragrant scent of polished wood and lavender. There were intimate touches everywhere, from the pretty furnishings to the pictures on the walls. She would shop during the day and then just read in the communal, oak-panelled sitting room with the roaring fire and clumps of deep, worn chairs. Read and forget. She could feel herself forgetting already!

It was a mantra she kept up for the remainder of the day, which was spent browsing in the shops, having lunch in a café where she watched the world hurry by under brilliant blue but freezing skies, and reading book number one in front of the fire. The couple who ran the tiny hotel were charming and showed no curiosity at her request to eat early so that she could retire to her room before midnight. By dinnertime, as she was ushered to a small table at the back of the discreetly lit dining room, now festive in preparation for celebrations later, Tessa was convinced that she was finally beginning to unwind. Maybe, she considered lazily, she would move to Dublin permanently. Start afresh. Forget everything and most of all forget Curtis Diaz.

Which was why, taking her time with her soup and letting her mind toy with the fantasy of a time ahead when she could barely remember his name, let alone what he looked like, Tessa almost managed not to see the tall, dark figure that was suddenly looming at the far end of the room. He was talking to Bill Winters, the owner of the hotel while his eyes drifted slowly across the expanse of the dining area. And those blue eyes connected with hers just as realisation hit home with a resounding crash. Even so, the sight of Curtis *here* was sufficiently unbelievable for her to take it in. So she watched as he crossed the room, blinking in disbelief. The vision didn't clear. It continued to come closer until her shocked brain forced her to acknowledge that this was no dream. Curtis Diaz was here. At which point she gently returned her soup spoon to its bowl, before it clattered to the floor, and eyed him with gaping horror.

'Your sister told me where you were,' he said heavily. 'Carry on eating. I don't want to disrupt your meal.'

*Disrupt her meal? What about disrupting her life?* He had no right to be here, Tessa thought with uncurling anger. He had no right to just show up when she was trying so hard to forget all about him!

'I seem to have lost my appetite.' He was staring at her and she couldn't fathom what was in those dangerous, deep blue eyes. 'Why have you come here?' she demanded in a low, shaking voice. 'It's New Year's Eve…shouldn't you be out somewhere?' *With a leggy blonde?*

'Do you think I want to be here?' Curtis rasped, raking his fingers through his hair. 'I came because I had to.'

Which smelled to Tessa of work. Curtis Diaz only felt obligated to do things that impacted on his professional life. Mr No Commitment had no such qualms when it came to emotions, she thought bitterly.

'If it's to do with work, forget it. My replacement can deal with whatever I left behind. There's no way I'm going back to hold anyone's hand and walk them through my filing system.'

'It's not to do with work, for God's sake!' He banged one fist on the table and Tessa started back in alarm, heart beating like a sledgehammer.

'Then what? We've talked already. Too much. There's nothing left to say.'

'You never told me that you loved me.'

His words dropped like lead pellets into the thick pool of silence and every ripple that spread outwards was more horrifying than the last. Tessa felt her face whiten. She opened her mouth to speak and nothing came out.

'I...I...well,' she finally managed to say in a voice she didn't recognise as her own, 'I didn't because it's a ridiculous idea.' As if to lend edge to what she had said, she laughed hysterically, a little too hysterically.

Someone came to remove her soup bowl and she was aware of Curtis telling him to wait a while before he brought the next course. The instruction was accepted with a deferential nod. Tessa watched all this through a haze of sickening panic.

'It's not a ridiculous idea,' Curtis said quietly, leaning forward so that his elbows were on the table and the space between them was diminished to suffocating proportions. 'You're not the kind of girl to sleep with a man for no better reason than she wants to test the water or have a bit of fun. You're the kind of girl who sleeps with a man because she's involved with him, because her heart tells her it's the right thing to do.'

'I thought we'd established that,' Tessa muttered uncomfortably. 'Which is why I wasn't interested in a fling with you...'

'We established *that*,' Curtis agreed. 'Which made me wonder why you slept with me in the first place...'

Tessa's struggle to deny the truth collapsed. And she didn't even feel angry with him any more. She still wondered what he had had to gain by coming here, by cornering her, but even that curiosity was a pale shadow compared to her own sense of utter defeat.

'You're right,' she said. 'Did you think that this would be unfinished business unless you happened to drag the whole truth out of me?' She gave a short, mirthless laugh, but her eyes stung from the pressure of unshed tears and her fingers were compulsively twisting the serviette on her lap. 'Well, we wouldn't want that, would we? After all, Curtis Diaz is a man who *always* finishes business, isn't he? Even though this could have waited! So I'll help you out here. Yes. I didn't mean to and I knew that it was stupid, but once your heart starts galloping down a certain path, then it's impossible to catch up with it. I fell in love with you. Against all my better judgement, I fell in love with you and you're absolutely right. That's why I slept with you, because it just felt right. My only saving grace was that I knew from the word go that you weren't looking for a relationship. But I stupidly thought that maybe I *could* just enjoy something temporary. Thinking that you and Lucy were going to become an item made me realise that I couldn't. So, there you go, Curtis. Happy?'

'Amazingly, wondrously, fabulously happy.' He sent her a slow smile that made her toes curl and her mouth tighten.

'Good. I'm so glad for you. And now you've got that confession out of me, why don't you do me a huge favour and leave? Let me ring in the new year without you around to spoil it for me!'

'You seem to make a habit of asking me to leave when I don't want to.' He reached out and stroked her cheek before she had time to pull back. Now, it wasn't just her toes that were curling, but everything inside her as well.

'Do you really think that I just came here because I wanted the satisfaction of hearing you tell me?'

Tessa gave an eloquent shrug. Where he had touched her cheek burnt as though he had branded her.

'I came here because...' A dark flush spread across his cheekbones and he suddenly looked vulnerable and uncertain, two traits not normally associated with him.

'Because...?' Tessa prompted out of hateful, treacherous curiosity, when he lapsed into silence.

He met her eyes quickly and gave a slight shrug. 'Because I was that man. The one you described. The one who never wanted to put roots down. I felt that I had all the roots I needed with Anna and, besides, work never left time to cultivate anything, not that I couldn't have made the time if I'd wanted, but I didn't. I liked the life I had, or at least I thought I did.'

Tessa felt her breath catch in her throat. She didn't want hope to interfere with reality but the way he was looking at her...

'As you said, different strokes for different folks,' she said neutrally.

His hand reached out to cover hers, though, and she didn't remove it. The pressure of his palm against hers was warm and still and strong and as seductive as she remembered. Everything about him was.

'And I thought I meant it at the time, I really did.'

Tessa opened her mouth to speak and he briefly placed one finger over her lips.

'In fact, I told myself a lot of things a couple of days back, including that I was relieved to have escaped the possibility of getting caught up in a relationship I couldn't handle...no, wait, let me finish. I figured that I could walk away, breathe a sigh of relief, and get back to my life. I've been trying as hard as I could...'

'I know. I saw the picture in the newspaper of you trying with a blonde.'

Curtis snorted. 'I think *trying* would certainly be the word she would use to describe me. God, I can't even remember her name. She was just part of my Master Plan to get my life back and, in all fairness, she didn't mind being photographed with me. Upped her credibility in the world of glamour.'

*He couldn't remember her name!* Tessa's heart flipped a few times and reality gave up trying to put the dampener on hope.

'All I've succeeded in doing is drinking more than I should, storming around the office like a bear with a sore head, bellowing at anyone who crosses my path, not that I've had much of an audience, thank God, and staring at computer screens without managing to achieve very much.'

'Oh, I see,' Tessa said weakly.

'Do you? Can you? See, I mean? How much I missed you? I don't think you can. If someone had told me six months ago that I'd be running towards commitment as if my life depended on it, I'd have laughed them out of court.'

'You're saying…'

'I'm saying that…' He looked around uncomfortably and cleared his throat. 'I'm saying that I love you. Not just lust after you, although I do that as well, excel at it in fact, but need you and want you and can't bear the thought of you not being by my side. In fact…'

Their eyes tangled and Tessa smiled slowly back at him, reading his mind. 'I don't think anyone would miss us if we had a bit of a breather before the main course…'

They slunk out of the dining room like two teenagers, with Curtis just about managing to mutter something to their host on the way out about needing to fetch something before they carried on with the meal, that they would be back very shortly.

'Very shortly?' Tessa quizzed, half running up the stairs with him to her bedroom.

'Oh, yes. Remember what I said about lusting after you...? Well, it feels as though it's been years and I don't think my body is capable of behaving itself properly right now...' To demonstrate exactly what he meant, as soon as the key turned in the door he pushed it open and pulled her to him with a low groan, pressing her against the door to shut it, muttering thickly against her pliant mouth.

And his urgency matched hers. Hands collided as they tugged to free each other of unwanted clothes. Actually making it to the bed was not an option. 'We can spend all the time we want in bed later,' he promised roughly, 'but I want you right here and right now...'

With perfect understanding and feeling shockingly debauched, Tessa coiled her hands around his neck and groaned as their bodies found the perfect position. Her legs wrapped round him and, with a gasp of absolute fulfilment, she felt him move strongly inside her, thrusting and manoeuvring her with expertise so that her breasts bounced against his chest.

They came as one, shuddering on that final thrust, and Tessa curved lovingly against him as he carried her to the bed.

'Next time, my darling, we'll take all the time in the world, but I just couldn't wait...'

'Nor could I...' she murmured. She ran the palm of her hand against his chest and, with a smile, he did the same to her, pausing to cup her swollen breast in his hand and eliciting a tiny moan when he began rubbing her stiffened nipple between his fingers.

'You're the most beautiful creature on the face of the earth,' he said solemnly. 'Next to you, every woman seems to fade into the background.' As if unable to help himself, he lowered his head so that he could take one nipple into his mouth and suckle on it and Tessa was more than content to let him stay there, feasting, with her hand resting lightly on his head. She smiled when he finally looked up at her.

'My life only has meaning with you in it,' he told her, and she tugged him up so that their faces were once more on a level and she could gently kiss his mouth, pressing her body against his and moving sinuously against his already stiffening member.

'You don't know how I've longed to hear you say that,' she confessed, smiling and arching back as his hand curved along her thigh, seeking and finding the wetness that spoke of her desire. She drew her breath in sharply as his fingers rubbed insistently, sending shooting stars through her. 'What about the meal waiting downstairs?' She giggled, moving against his hand and then, reaching down, guiding his hardness against her sensitised softness.

'Mmm. Good question.' He grinned and rotated the tiny bud of femininity, loving the way she squirmed in response. 'I just had to touch you, Tessa…had to tell you how much I love you…how much I'm committed to a lifetime with you. I want you to have my kids, brothers or sisters for Anna, and I want you to grow old with me. And, yes, I really want you to ask me how my day went when I get back from work and arrange dinner parties with people when I'd rather just stay in and have a meal with you.'

'You mean with me and Anna and all those babies you want us to have…' How was it possible that she wanted to laugh and cry at the same time?

'That's right, my darling. The old year is on its way out, just like my old life is. The significance of the timing wasn't lost on me as I pulled out all the stops to get here, to see you. The end of something and the beginning of something else, something wonderful. For ever is in front of us…and it's perfect…'

'Yes,' Tessa breathed. 'Isn't it?'

'So what do we do? Go back down or just stay up here…?'

'Go back down, I think…' She smiled at him lovingly. 'But now I don't think I'll be coming up to my room to avoid the midnight hour…'

Was it her imagination or did Bill and his wife exchange a look of satisfaction when she told them that dinner would now be for two and that they would both be enjoying the celebrations together?

It didn't matter. All that mattered was that the man she loved was by her side and when the clock struck twelve, the lips that touched her own promised a future she had never dared dream of…

# CONTRACTED: CORPORATE WIFE

**JESSICA HART**

For Diana, with love

**Jessica Hart** was born in West Africa, and has
suffered from itchy feet ever since, travelling and
working around the world in a wide variety of
interesting but very lowly jobs, all of which have
provided inspiration on which to draw when it
comes to the settings and plots of her stories. Now
she lives a rather more settled existence in York,
where she has been able to pursue her interest in
history, although she still yearns sometimes for
wider horizons. If you'd like to know more about
Jessica, visit her website www.jessicahart.co.uk

# CHAPTER ONE

THE lift doors slid open, and out stepped Louisa Dennison, bang on time. As always.

Watching her from across the lobby, Patrick was conscious of a familiar spurt of something close to irritation. Dammit, couldn't the woman be five seconds late for once?

Here she came, in her prim little grey suit, whose skirt stopped precisely at the knee, not a hair of her dark head out of place. She looked sensible, discreet, well groomed, the epitome of a perfect PA.

Patrick knew that he was being irrational. He had been lucky to inherit such an efficient assistant when he'd taken over Schola Systems. Lou—her name was the only relaxed thing about her, as far as he was concerned—was a model secretary. She was poised, punctual, professional. He never caught her gossiping or making personal phone calls in the office. She showed no interest whatsoever in his personal life, so Patrick never felt obliged to ask about hers. No, he couldn't ask for a better PA.

It was just that sometimes he found himself wishing that she would make a mistake, just a little one. A typing error, say, that he could pick her up on, or a file that she couldn't lay her hand on immediately. Maybe she could ladder her tights, or spill her coffee. Do something to prove that she was human.

But she never did.

The truth was that Patrick found Lou secretly intimidating at times, and it annoyed him. If there was any intimidating to be done, he was the one who liked to do it. Grown men had been known to tremble when he walked into the room, and his reputation as a ruthless executive was usually enough to make people tread warily around him.

Not Lou Dennison, though. She just looked at him with those dark eyes of hers. Her expression was usually one of complete indifference, but sometimes he suspected it also held a quiet irony that riled Patrick more than he cared to admit. It wasn't even as if there was anything particularly special about her, he thought with a tinge of resentment. She was attractive enough, but she had to be at least forty-five, and it showed in the lines around her eyes.

That cool, composed look had never done anything for him, anyway. He liked his women more feminine, more appealing, less in control. And younger.

'I'm not late, am I?' Lou asked as she came up to him, and Patrick repressed the urge to glance ostentatiously at his watch and announce that she was a good fifteen seconds overdue.

'Of course not.'

He forced a smile and reminded himself that it wasn't actually Lou's fault that high winds had forced the closure of the east coast line that evening, that it was too far to an airport, or that he would rather be having dinner with almost anyone else. There had been no way he could have got out of asking her to share a meal with him since they were both stranded, but he was hoping they could get it over with quickly and then go their separate ways for the rest of the evening.

He nodded in the direction of the restaurant. 'Shall we go straight in? Or would you like a drink first?'

The drink option was such a patent afterthought that Lou was left in little doubt that Patrick was looking forward to their meal with as little pleasure as she was. Clearly she was supposed to meekly agree to eating straight away, but Lou didn't feel like it.

She'd had a long day. It had begun with a five o'clock alarm call, progressed to getting two squabbling adolescents out of the house earlier than usual, continued with delays on the tube, followed by a stressful train journey with Patrick Farr. This was the first time they had had to travel to secure a contract, and she hadn't thought her presence was necessary, but Patrick had insisted.

In the end, the meeting had been successful, but it had been long and intense, and Lou had been looking forward to getting home and enjoying a rare evening on her own to wind down with a stiff gin and a long bath without her children banging on the door and demanding to know what there was to eat or where she had put their special pair of torn jeans, which they needed right *now*.

And now she was stuck in this hotel with her boss instead. It wouldn't have been too bad if Patrick hadn't felt obliged to invite her to have dinner with him, or if she'd been able to think of a way of refusing without sounding ungracious. As it was, it looked as if they were both condemned to an evening of stilted conversation, and for that she definitely needed a drink!

'A drink would be lovely, thank you,' she said defiantly, ignoring the way Patrick's thick brows drew together. He was evidently a man who was used to getting what he wanted—especially as far as women were concerned, if rumours were anything to go by. No doubt Lou was expected to fall in with his wishes like everyone else.

Tough, she thought unsympathetically. If he didn't like it, he shouldn't have asked her!

'Let's try the bar, then,' he said, with just the suggestion of gritted teeth.

Lou didn't care. In the three months since Patrick Farr

had taken over Schola Systems he had made it obvious that he had no interest whatsoever in his new PA. Not young and pretty enough, clearly, Lou thought dispassionately. She didn't mind that, but she didn't see why she should pander to his ego in her free time. She wasn't actually working this evening, and it wouldn't do Patrick Farr any harm not to get his own way for once.

The bar was even worse than Patrick had feared. By the time they had realised that there would be no more trains to London that night, and that all road and air traffic was equally disrupted by the weather, all the best hotels had been booked out.

It was a long time since he had stayed anywhere this provincial, he thought, looking around the bar with distaste. It was overflowing with vegetation, and so dark that they practically had to grope their way to a table, which did nothing to improve his temper.

'What would you like?' he asked Lou as he snapped his fingers to summon the barman, although whether the man would be able to find them in the gloom was another matter.

'A glass of champagne would be nice,' said Lou composedly as she settled herself and smoothed down her skirt.

Patrick was surprised. She hadn't struck him as a champagne drinker. He would have thought champagne too fizzy and frivolous for someone so efficient. He could imagine her drinking something much more sensible, like a glass of water, or possibly something sharp. A dry martini perhaps. Yes, he could see her with one of those.

Lou lifted her elegant brows at his expression. 'Is that too extravagant?' she asked, thinking that a glass of champagne was the least that he owed her after the day she had had. And it wasn't as if he couldn't afford it. The Patrick

Farrs of this world could buy champagne by the truckload and think of it as small change.

'We did win that contract,' she reminded him, a subtle edge to her voice. 'I thought we should celebrate.'

'Of course.' Patrick set his teeth, perfectly aware that he should have suggested a celebration given the size of the contract they had just won. 'I'll have the same.'

The barman had fought his way through the artificial jungle and was hovering. Opening his mouth to ask for two glasses of champagne, Patrick changed his mind and ordered a bottle instead. He wasn't going to have Lou Dennison thinking that he was mean.

'Certainly, sir.'

Sitting relaxed in her chair, she was looking around the gloomy bar, apparently unperturbed by the silence while they waited for the barman to come back. She was quite unlike the women he was usually with in bars, Patrick reflected. He liked girls who were prepared to enjoy themselves a bit.

Take Ariel, for instance. Ariel was always *thrilled* to be out with him. That was what she told him, anyway. If she were here, she'd be chatting away, entertaining him, exerting herself to captivate him.

Unlike Lou, who was just sitting there with that faintly ironic gleam in her eyes, unimpressed by his company. What would it take to impress a woman like her? Patrick wondered. Someone must have done it once. She was Mrs Dennison, although he noticed that she didn't wear a wedding ring. Divorced, no doubt. Her husband probably couldn't live up to her exacting standards.

Uncomfortable with the situation, Patrick leant forward and picked up a drinks mat, tapping it moodily on the low table between them. It took a huge effort not to glance at his watch, but chances were he wouldn't be able to read it anyway in this light. It looked like being a long evening.

Lou was thinking the same thing. Patrick's moody tapping was driving her mad. It was just the kind of thing Tom did when he was being at his most annoying. Her fingers twitched with the longing to snatch the mat out of his hand and tell him to stop fiddling at *once*, the way she would if Tom were sitting there irritating her like this.

But Tom was her son and eleven, while Patrick Farr had to be in his late forties and, more to the point, was her boss. And she couldn't afford to lose her job. She had better hold back on the ticking-off front, Lou decided reluctantly.

She was gasping for a drink. Where was that champagne? The barman must be treading the grapes out there. It couldn't take that long to shove a bottle in an ice bucket and find a couple of glasses, could it? If it didn't arrive soon, she was going to have to take that mat anyway and shove it—

Ah, at last!

Lou smiled up at the barman as he materialised out of the gloom, and Patrick's hand froze in mid-tap as he felt a jolt of surprise. He hadn't realised that she could smile like that.

She never smiled at *him* like that.

She smiled, of course, but it was only ever a cool, polite smile, the kind of smile that went with her immaculate suit, her perfectly groomed hair and her infallible professional manner. Not the warm, friendly smile she was giving the barman now, lighting her face and making her seem all at once attractive and approachable. The kind of woman you might actually want to share a bottle of champagne with, in fact.

Patrick sat up straighter and studied her with new interest

as the barman opened the bottle with an unnecessary flourish and made a big deal of pouring the champagne.

The boy was clearly trying to impress Lou, Patrick thought disapprovingly, watching his attempts at banter. She had only smiled at him, for heaven's sake. Anyone would think that she was hot, instead of nearly old enough to be his mother. Just what they needed, a barman with a Mrs Robinson fixation.

And now he was tossing his cloth over his shoulder in a ridiculously affected way as he placed the bottle back in the ice bucket, and telling Lou to enjoy her drink. Patrick noticed that *he* didn't get so much as a nod, which was a bit much given that he was paying for it all.

'Thank you,' Lou was saying, with another quite unnecessary smile.

Patrick glowered at the barman's departing back. 'Thank God he's gone. I was afraid that he was planning on spending the whole evening with us. I'm surprised he didn't bring himself a glass and pull up a chair.'

'I thought he was charming,' said Lou, picking up her glass.

She would.

'Don't tell me you've got a taste for toy boys!'

'No—not that it would be any business of yours if I did.'

Patrick was taken aback by her directness. She was normally so discreet.

'You don't think it would be a bit inappropriate?' he countered.

Lou stared at him for a moment, then sipped at her champagne. 'That sounds to me like a prime case of pots and kettles,' she said coolly, putting her glass back down on the table.

'What do you mean?' demanded Patrick.

'I understand that your own girlfriends tend to be on the young side.'

Patrick was momentarily taken aback. 'How do you know that?'

She shrugged. 'Your picture is in the gossip pages occasionally. You've usually got a blonde on your arm, and I've got to say that most of them look a good twenty years younger than you.'

That was true enough. Patrick didn't see why he should apologise for it. 'I like beautiful women, and I especially like beautiful women who aren't old enough to get obsessed with commitment,' he said.

Ah, commitment-phobic. That figured, thought Lou with a touch of cynicism. She knew the type. And how. Lawrie had never been hot on commitment either, but at least he had warmth and charm. Patrick didn't even have that to recommend him.

She studied him over the rim of her glass. He was an attractive enough man, she admitted fairly to herself. Mid to late forties, she'd say. Tall, broad-shouldered, well set up. He had good, strong features too, with darkish brown hair and piercing light eyes—grey or green, Lou hadn't quite worked that one out yet—but there was a coolness and an arrogance to him that left her quite cold. He seemed to go down well with young nubile blondes, but he certainly didn't ring any of *her* bells.

Not that that was likely to bother Patrick Farr much. She was a middle-aged woman and it was well known that you became invisible after forty, particularly to men like him. She doubted that he had registered anything about her other than her efficiency.

'I'd no idea you took such an interest in my personal life,' Patrick was saying, annoyed for some reason by her dispassionate tone.

'I don't. It's absolutely nothing to do with me.'

'You seem to know enough about it!'

'Hardly,' said Lou. 'The girls in Finance have taken to passing round any articles about you so that we can get some idea of who's running the company now. You took us over three months ago, and all we know about you is your reputation.'

'And what is my reputation, exactly?' asked Patrick.

Lou smiled faintly. 'Don't you know?'

'I'd be interested to hear it from your point of view.'

'Well...' Lou took a sip of her champagne—it was slipping down very nicely, thank you—and considered. 'I suppose we'd heard that you were pretty ruthless. Very successful. A workaholic, but a bit of a playboy on the side.' Her mouth turned down as she tried to remember anything else. 'That's it, really.' She glanced at him. 'Is it fair?'

'I like the successful bit,' said Patrick. 'As for the rest of it...well, I certainly work hard. I know what I want, and I always get what I want. I like winning. I'm not interested in compromising or accepting second best. If people think that's ruthless, that's their problem,' he said. Ruthlessly, in fact.

'And the playboy side?'

He made a dismissive gesture with his glass. 'People only say that if you're rich and don't tie yourself down with a wife and children. I like the company of beautiful women, sure, and I meet lots of them at the parties and events I'm invited to, but I'd much rather work than swan around on yachts or waste money in casinos or whatever it is playboys do.'

'I see. I'll tell the girls in Finance that you're really quite boring after all, then.'

Patrick looked up sharply from his glass and met Lou's

eyes. They held a distinct gleam of amusement and he realised to his amazement that she was teasing him.

There was a new sassiness to her tonight, he thought, and he wasn't at all sure how to take her. Lou Dennison had always been the epitome of an efficient PA, quiet, discreet, always demurely dressed in a neat suit, but he had had no sense of her as a woman beyond that.

Now, suddenly, it was as if he were seeing her for the first time. The dark eyes held a challenging spark, and there was a vibrancy and a directness to her that he had never noticed before. Patrick's interest was piqued. Perhaps there was more to Lou than was obvious at first glance.

He knew nothing about her, he realised. If he'd thought about it at all, he might have imagined her going home to an immaculately organised flat somewhere, but the truth was that he had never really considered the fact that she had any existence at all outside the office. What did she do? Where did she go? What was she really like?

He ought to know, Patrick thought with a twinge of shame. She had been his PA for three months. Of course, they had been incredibly busy trying to turn the failing firm around, and she wasn't exactly easy to get to know. She never encouraged any form of social contact...or was it just that he had been too intimidated by her composure to make the first move?

Patrick wriggled his shoulders uncomfortably. He should have made more of an effort. She was the closest member of staff to him, after all. The truth was that he was more used to women flirting and fluttering around him. No way would Lou Dennison indulge him like that. She wasn't the flirting kind.

On the other hand, what did he know? Maybe it was time to find out more about her.

'So what about you?' he asked her. 'Do you live up to *your* reputation?'

Lou looked surprised. Well, that was better than indifference or irony, anyway.

'I don't have a reputation,' she said.

'Yes, you do,' Patrick corrected her. 'I heard all about you before I got to Schola Systems. I heard that it was you that ran that company, not Bill Sheeran.'

Lou frowned. 'That's rubbish!'

'Don't worry, I don't believe it for a minute. If you'd been running the company, you would never have let it go under. You're too competent to let that happen.'

She grimaced slightly. 'Competent?' It didn't sound very exciting. Not like being a playboy. 'Is that what people think of me?'

Her glass was empty. Patrick lifted the bottle and held it over the ice bucket to let it drip for a moment. 'Competent…efficient…practical…yes, all those things.'

'You don't have much choice about being practical when you've got kids to bring up on your own,' said Lou with a sigh.

'It's easy to be laid-back when you've just got yourself to worry about,' she said, oblivious to the fact that his head had jerked up in surprise. 'It's different when the rent is due and there are bills to be paid and every morning you've got a major logistical operation just to get the kids up and dressed and fed, and to check that they've got everything they need and that all their homework is done and that they're not going to be late for school.'

Patrick hadn't got over the first revelation. 'You've got *kids*?' he said, ignoring the last part of her speech. He stared at her. Children meant mess and chaos and constant requests for time off, none of which he associated with Lou Dennison.

She had raised her brows at the incredulity in his expression. 'Just two. Grace is fourteen, and Tom's eleven.'

'You never mentioned that you had children,' said Patrick accusingly.

'You never asked,' said Lou, 'and, to be honest, I didn't think you'd be the slightest bit interested in my private life.'

He hadn't been—he *wasn't*, Patrick reminded himself—but, still, she might have said something. He felt vaguely aggrieved. Two children, adolescent children at that, were a big thing not to mention.

'Why have you kept them a secret?'

'I haven't,' said Lou, taken aback. 'There's a framed photo of both of them on my desk. If you're that interested, I'll show you tomorrow!'

'There's no need for that, I believe you,' said Patrick, recoiling. He had no intention of admiring pictures of grubby brats. 'I was just surprised. I've had secretaries with children before, and they were always having time off for various crises,' he complained. 'After the last time, I vowed I'd never have a PA who was a mother again.'

'Very family-minded of you,' said Lou.

Patrick's brows drew together at the unconcealed sarcasm in her voice. 'I haven't got anything against families,' he said. 'It's up to individuals whether they have a family or not, but I don't see why I should have to rearrange my life around other people's children. I had a PA once whose children ended up running the office. We'd just be at a critical point of negotiations, and Carol would be putting on her coat and saying that she had to get to the school.'

'Sometimes you just have to go,' said Lou, who had somehow managed to get to the bottom of another glass of champagne. 'Especially when your children are smaller. At least my two are old enough to take themselves to and from school, but if anything happened, or they were ill, then I'm afraid that I would be putting on my coat too.'

Patrick looked at her as if a dog he had been cajoling had just turned and snapped at him, but he refilled her glass anyway. 'Am I supposed to find that reassuring?'

'I'm just telling you, that's all,' said Lou. She looked at him directly. 'Is it going to be a problem for you that I have children?'

'Not as long as they don't interfere with your work,' said Patrick.

'You know that they don't, or you would have known about their existence long before now,' she said in a crisp voice. 'That doesn't mean there won't be times when I *will* need to be flexible, and, yes, sometimes at short notice.'

'Oh, great.' Patrick hunched a shoulder and Lou leant forward.

'You're obviously not aware of the fact that Schola Systems has always had a very good reputation for family-friendly policies,' she admonished him. 'I was lucky to get a job there when I had to go back to work and the children were small, and especially to have such an understanding boss. Bill Sheeran was always flexible when people needed time at home for one reason or another.

'It won him a lot of loyalty from the staff,' she added warningly, 'so if you were thinking of holding parenthood against your employees, you might find yourself without any staff at all!'

'There's no question of holding anything against anyone,' said Patrick irritably.

He didn't want to hear any more about how marvellous Bill Sheeran had been. Not marvellous enough to save his own company, though, Patrick thought cynically. It was all very well being friendly and flexible, but if Patrick hadn't taken over all those admiring employees would have been spending a lot more time at home than they wanted. There was no point in being family friendly if your firm went bust and your staff found themselves out of a job.

'I just wish you'd told me, that's all,' he grumbled to Lou.

Lou didn't feel like making it easy for him. Honestly, the man never even asked her if she'd had a nice weekend on a Monday morning. 'If you'd shown any interest in your new PA at all, you would have known.'

'I'm showing an interest now,' he said grumpily. 'Is there anything else I need to know?'

'Is there anything else you want to know?' she countered.

'You don't wear a wedding ring,' said Patrick after a moment.

'I'm divorced. Why?' The champagne was definitely having an effect. 'Don't tell me you've got a problem with divorce as well as children?'

'Of course not. I'm divorced myself.'

'Really?'

'Why the surprise? It's not exactly uncommon as you'll know better than anyone.'

Quite, thought Lou. 'You're right. I don't know why I was surprised, really. I suppose it's because you don't seem like the marrying kind,' she said, thinking of his lifestyle. Playboy or not, he clearly didn't spend much time at home.

'I'm not,' said Patrick with a grim smile. 'That's why I'm divorced. We were only married a couple of years. We were both very young.' He shrugged. 'It was a mistake for both of us. That'll be a bit of news for the girls in Finance,' he added, not without a trace of sarcasm.

'I'll pass it on,' said Lou, smiling blandly in return.

Patrick held up the bottle and squinted at the dregs in surprise. 'We seem to have finished the bottle,' he said, sharing out the last drops and upending it in the ice bucket. 'Do you want another? Your toy boy is probably longing for an excuse to come over and see you again!'

Lou rolled her eyes. 'I think I'd better eat,' she said, ignoring the toy-boy crack.

The champagne had slipped down very nicely. A little too nicely, in fact. She was beginning to feel pleasantly fuzzy. She might even be a bit tipsy, Lou realised, hoping that she would be able to make it to the restaurant without falling over or doing anything embarrassing. They hadn't had time for a proper lunch and it was all starting to catch up with her.

She felt better in the restaurant. The waiters fussed around, bringing bread and a jug of water without being asked. Obviously they could see that she needed it.

Lou took a piece of bread, and spread butter on it. This was no time to worry about her diet. She needed to line her stomach as quickly as possible.

She tried to focus on the menu, but kept getting distracted by Patrick opposite. He had been easier to talk to than she had expected. Of course, the champagne had probably helped. He certainly wasn't as brusque and impersonal as usual. She had even found herself warming to him in a funny kind of way. It was as if they had both let down their guards for the evening. It must be something to do with being stranded away from home and tired…and, oh, yes, the champagne.

She really mustn't have any more to drink, Lou decided, but somehow a glass of wine appeared in front of her and it seemed rude to ignore it. She would just take the occasional sip.

'So,' said Patrick when they had ordered. 'What's happened to your children tonight? Are they with their father?'

'No, Lawrie lives in Manchester.' There was a certain

restraint in her voice when she mentioned her ex-husband, he noticed. 'I knew I'd be late back to London even if the trains had been running, so I arranged for them to stay with a friend. They love going to Marisa's. She lets them watch television all night and doesn't make them eat vegetables.'

Which was probably more than Patrick needed or wanted to know. He was only making polite conversation after all. She was getting garrulous, a sure sign that she had had too much to drink. Better have another piece of bread.

'Have you got any children?' she asked, thinking it might be better to switch the conversation back to Patrick before she started telling him how good at sport Grace was or how adorable Tom had been as a baby.

'No,' said Patrick, barely restraining a shudder at the very idea. 'I've never wanted them. My ex-wife, Catriona, did. That's one of the reasons we split up in the end.' His mouth pulled down at the corners as he contemplated his glass. 'Apparently I was incredibly selfish for wanting to live my own life.'

Lou frowned a little owlishly. 'But isn't the reason you get married precisely because you want to live your life with another person, that you want to do it together and not on your own?'

She'd spoken without thinking and for a moment she thought she might have gone a bit far.

'I told Catriona before we got married that I didn't want children,' said Patrick, apparently not taking exception at the intrusiveness of her question. 'And she said that she understood. She said she didn't want a family either, that she didn't want to share me with anyone else, not even a baby.'

He rolled his eyes a little as if inviting her to mock his younger self who had believed his wife, but Lou thought she could still hear the hurt in his voice. He must have loved Catriona a lot.

'We *agreed*,' Patrick insisted, even as part of him marvelled that he was telling Lou all this. 'It wasn't just me. I thought we both wanted the same thing and that everything would be fine, but we'd hardly been married a year before she started to lobby for a baby.'

He sounded exasperated, and Lou couldn't help feeling a pang of sympathy for poor Catriona. You'd have to be pretty brave to lobby Patrick Farr about anything.

'It's quite common for women to change their minds about having a baby,' she said mildly. 'It's a hormone thing. You can be quite sure you're not interested, and then one day you wake up and your body clock has kicked in, and suddenly a baby is all you can think about. I was like that before I had Grace.'

'Yes, well, I've learnt the hard way that women change their minds the whole time,' said Patrick grouchily. 'If I'd known then what I know now, I wouldn't have believed Catriona in the first place. But I was young then, and it was a blow.'

'It must have been a blow for her too,' Lou pointed out. 'It doesn't sound as if you were prepared to compromise at all.'

'How can you compromise about a baby?' demanded Patrick. 'Either you have one or you don't. There are no halfway measures, no part-time options, on parenthood.'

That would be news to Lawrie, Lou couldn't help thinking. He seemed to think that he could drop in and out of his children's lives whenever it suited him.

'Plenty of fathers don't have much choice but to see their children on a part-time basis,' she said, struggling to sound fair. 'It can work.'

'I didn't want to be a father like that,' said Patrick flatly. 'I don't believe in half measures. Either you do something properly, or you don't do it at all.'

Not the king of compromise, then.

# CHAPTER TWO

'YOU could say that about marriage too,' said Lou, courage bolstered by all the champagne she had drunk.

Patrick twisted a fork between his fingers, his expression bitter. 'I would have stuck with our marriage no matter what, but Catriona wanted a divorce. So that's what happened. We didn't do it at all.'

'What happened to Catriona?'

'Oh, she met someone else. She got her children...three of them...but now she's divorced again. Her husband ran off with his secretary for a more exciting and child-free life, I gather, so she's on her own again.'

'You know,' he confided slowly, 'Catriona always used to say that if only she could have a baby, she would never be unhappy again, but I still see her occasionally, and she doesn't look very happy to me. She's got the children she wanted, but she looks exhausted and worn down.'

'I'm not surprised if her husband's left her and she's dealing with three children by herself,' said Lou.

'She's got help,' said Patrick unsympathetically. 'She got the house and she'll have someone to clean it and an au pair to take care of the kids. She doesn't even have to work. And when it comes down to it, it was her choice.'

'It's tiring bringing up children,' said Lou, although she was feeling less sympathetic since hearing about the cleaner and the au pair and the lack of a mortgage.

A cleaner, imagine it! Imagine having a house with no rent or mortgage to pay. Even better. She'd hold on the au pair though. Grace would make mincemeat of the poor girl.

23

'Kids can be very consuming,' she said.

'I know,' said Patrick. 'That's precisely why I've chosen not to have them. You can keep all your dirty nappies and your grazed knees and your adolescent tantrums. I don't want to be bothered with any of that.'

'But are you any happier than Catriona?'

'Of course I am!'

Lou looked unconvinced. 'You say she's not happy, but I bet she is. I bet she doesn't regret having those children for an *instant*. Of course it's hard work. There are days when I'm so exhausted just getting through the day, and it all seems a never-ending battle, and then I'll look at the back of Tom's neck, or hear Grace laughing, and they're so…*miraculous*…I feel like my heart's going to stop with the sheer joy of them. Do you ever feel like that?'

'I do when I look at my Porsche,' said Patrick flippantly.

'Enough to make up for a failed marriage and losing your wife?'

'Look, I was bitter when Catriona left. Of course I was,' he said, a slightly defensive edge to his voice. 'I'm not going to pretend I've been ecstatically happy all the time, ever since, but I've moved on. I've been successful in a way I would never have dreamed of when I was married to Catriona. I've built up some great companies, and I've made lots of money while I was at it. I've worked hard and I've had a good life. And I've got the kind of car most men can only fantasise about.'

'Oh, well, as long as you've got a nice *car*…'

'You may mock, but it means a lot.'

'I think you may need to be a man to understand that one,' said Lou. Tom and Lawrie certainly would.

'Let's put it this way,' said Patrick, pointing a fork at her for emphasis. 'I can do what I want. I can go where I want, when I want, with whoever I want. You don't think that makes me happy?'

'Right.' Lou nodded understandingly as she buttered another piece of bread. She hoped the food was coming soon. She was starving. 'So when was the last time you went away? You certainly haven't been anywhere in the last three months.'

'I've been busy, in case you hadn't noticed,' said Patrick, thrown off balance by this new, combative Lou. 'I had a company to save!'

'Hey, we managed for years before you came along! We wouldn't have fallen apart if you'd taken a long weekend. You didn't even go away at Easter. Don't you ever wish that you were working for something more than to make more money? That you had someone to go home to at the end of the day?'

'Aren't you trying to ask me if I ever get lonely?' said Patrick sardonically.

'Well, don't you?'

'I don't need to be on my own if I don't choose to. I've had plenty of relationships, and I'm not short of female company.'

So Lou had gathered from the gossip columns.

Perhaps it was just as well that the food arrived before she had time to frame a tart retort. Patrick had to watch while Lou went through her smiling routine again, and the waiter, this one old enough to have known better, fell over himself to serve her. He picked up her napkin, refilled both of her glasses, offered to fetch her more bread and ground pepper from an extremely suggestive-looking mill.

Extraordinary, thought Patrick. He studied her across the table. She had taken off her jacket and was wearing a simple, silky sort of top with a scoop neck, its plainness set off by a striking silver necklace. OK, she was elegant in a classic way and she had a charming smile—it seemed to work on waiters and barmen, anyway—but there wasn't anything particularly special about the rest of her.

Well, she had nice eyes, he supposed, amending his opinion slightly, and all the assurance of an older woman, but there was no way you could describe her as beautiful. Not like Ariel, who had all the bloom and radiance of youth. Still, now that he was looking at her properly, he could see that she *did* have a certain allure with that dark hair and those dark eyes.

Funny, this was the first time he had really been aware of her as a woman. He must have seen the line of her throat and the curve of her mouth almost every day for the last three months, and yet tonight was the first time he had noticed them at all.

Patrick frowned slightly. He wasn't sure he really wanted to start noticing things like that about Lou. There was something vaguely unsettling about thinking of her as a woman, warm and real, as opposed to the impersonal PA who ran his office so efficiently. About realising how oddly the generous curve of her lips sat with that air of cool competence or the ironic undertone in her voice sometimes.

And there was something *very* unsettling about noticing the way that top shifted as she leant forward to pick up her glass. The material seemed to slither over her skin, and it was impossible not to wonder how it would feel beneath his hands, how warm and smooth her body would be underneath…

Patrick looked abruptly away. Enough of that.

'What about you?' he said, struggling to remember what they had been talking about. She had been making him cross, and that was good. Anything was better than watching that top slip and slide as she breathed. 'Are you Mrs Happy?'

'I think I'm pretty happy,' she said, swirling the wine in her glass as she considered the matter. 'Content, anyway. I'm not joyously happy the way I was when I was first married, and when Grace and Tom were babies, but I've got a lot to be happy about. My children are healthy, I've got a dear aunt who's like a mother to me, I've got good friends... It's just a shame about my awful job. I've got this boss who makes my life an absolute misery.'

'What?' Patrick did a double take. He had been so busy not noticing what was going on with that damn top—why couldn't the woman sit still, for God's sake?—that it took him a moment to realise what she had said.

'That was a joke,' said Lou patiently.

'Oh. Right.' Patrick was surprised by how relieved he felt. 'Ha, ha,' he said morosely, and then was startled when Lou laughed. She had a proper laugh, not a giggle or a simper, and it made her look younger, vibrant, interesting, really quite...*sexy*. Was that what the waiter had seen too?

'Sorry,' she said. 'Just checking to see if you were listening!'

Patrick had the alarming feeling that things were slipping out of control and he got a grip of himself with an effort. There must have been something very odd in that champagne. He wasn't feeling like himself at all.

'You're on your own, though.' That was better; think of her as a sad divorcee. 'Don't *you* get lonely?'

'When you live in a tiny flat with two growing children, I can tell you that you long for the chance to be lonely sometimes!' said Lou.

'That's not what I mean, and you know it,' he said.

'No, OK,' she acknowledged. 'I miss being married sometimes,' she said slowly, pushing her plate aside so that she could lean her arms on the table and prop her face in one palm, oblivious to what that did to her cleavage, or what the effect on Patrick might be.

'It's hard bringing up children on your own,' she told him, while he fought to concentrate. 'There's no one to talk to in the evening, no one to share your worries with, no one who cares the way you do about their little triumphs.'

She was gazing at the candle flame, miles away with her children, and Patrick wondered if she had forgotten that he was there. If she had, he didn't like it, he realised.

'It would just be nice sometimes to have someone to support you when everything seems to be going wrong,' she said.

'Someone to hold you?' he suggested, his voice harder than he had intended, and Lou's dark eyes flashed up from the candle to meet his for a taut moment while both of them tried not to think about being held.

Her gaze dropped first. 'Yes, someone to hold me,' she said quietly. 'Sometimes.'

Patrick had a sudden memory of Lou walking across the lobby earlier that evening. She had seemed so prim and proper then, so cool and composed. Not appealing at all. He was almost appalled to realise how warm and soft and inviting she looked now, her eyes dark, gleaming pools in the candlelight, and her hair just a little tousled. He wondered what it would be like to touch it, to run his fingers through it and let the dark, silky strands fall back against her cheek.

What had happened? Then the neat suit and the demure top had struck him as merely dull. Now they seemed tantalising, as if they were specifically designed to make him wonder what she might be wearing underneath. If she were warm and willing in his lap, would he be able to slide his hand over her knee and under that businesslike skirt and discover that she was wearing stockings?

Patrick swallowed. God, he had to stop this right now. Talk about inappropriate. He didn't want Lou to think that he was just another lecherous businessman fantasising about secretaries in tight skirts and stockings and high heels.

Although if the cap fitted…

Picking up his glass, he took a gulp of wine and made a sterling effort to pull himself together.

'Yes, being held…I do miss that,' Lou was saying thoughtfully, unaware of Patrick's confusion. 'I think what I miss most, though, is the feeling that you don't have to deal with *everything* on your own, that someone is interested in you for yourself, and not just because you're a mother and there to be taken for granted. I don't mind when the kids do that, I know that's part of their job, but still…'

She glanced at him, evidently hesitating, and Patrick cleared his throat and nodded encouragingly.

'Go on, tell me. This is confession time, remember? Nothing to be remembered or held against you tomorrow!'

Lou laughed in spite of herself. 'OK, then, but you get to tell me an embarrassing fantasy too.'

'It's a fantasy? Better and better!'

A slight blush crept up her cheeks, but she hoped the candlelight would disguise it. 'Mine's not a very exciting fantasy, I'm afraid. I imagine that I can skip the awkwardness of meeting a man, dating him, getting to know him, all of that. I don't want the falling-in-love bit again. It's too consuming, and it hurts too much when you lose it.'

'So where does the fantasy come in?'

'I just want to wake up and find myself comfortably married to someone,' she confessed. 'Someone nice and…*kind*. Someone I could lean on when I needed to, and support when he needed it, and the rest of the time we'd be…I don't know…friends, I suppose.'

'What's embarrassing about that?' asked Patrick, his mind straying distractingly back to Lou's stockings. If they *were* stockings. He really, really wanted to know now.

Could he ask her? Patrick wondered, and then caught himself. What was he *thinking* of? Of course he couldn't ask his PA if she was wearing stockings. That would be sexual harassment.

'It's so politically incorrect,' said Lou guiltily. 'I'm a strong, independent woman. I shouldn't need anyone to look after me. I can look after myself. And I do, most of the time,' she said, recovering herself. 'I only think about having someone else when I'm tired, or feeling down, or one of the kids is being difficult.'

Which was a depressing number of times in the week, when she thought about it.

'It doesn't sound to me like an impossible fantasy,' said Patrick carefully. 'You'll just have to keep an eye out for someone suitable.'

'Oh, yes, and there are so many kind, supportive, single men out there!'

'There must be someone,' said Patrick. 'You're an attractive woman.' Rather too attractive for his own comfort, it appeared.

'I'm also forty-five and have two bolshy adolescents who consume every moment I'm not at work,' she pointed out. 'Would you want to take that on?'

'Not when you put it like that.'

'There isn't any other way to put it,' said Lou. 'I've been divorced over six years now, and I've learnt to cope on my own. I'm not looking for a man.'

'I've heard that before,' said Patrick cynically, thinking of the women who had assured him that they were just out for a good time and then started dawdling past jewellers'

windows and dropping heavy hints about moving in
with him.

This was good. He wasn't thinking about stockings any
more.

Much.

'It's true.' Lou fixed him with one of her disconcertingly
direct looks. 'Frankly, I haven't got the energy to put into
finding a man, let alone maintaining a relationship. When
you work all day, and go home to two children who need
all your attention, it's hard to imagine being with anyone
new.'

'And even if I did by some remote chance meet someone
who didn't mind only meeting every few weeks when I
could persuade a friend to babysit, and wasn't put off by
Grace's moods, or the fact that I don't have a bedroom of
my own, and was happy with only ever getting the fraction
of my attention that was left over from my children, I'd
still hesitate,' she said. 'It's taken me a long time to build
up my life again after Lawrie left. I'm not going to let it
all come crashing down in smithereens like before.'

'You mean if you were hurt again?' said Patrick.

'Yes. I won't expose myself to it.' Draining her glass,
Lou set it down firmly in front of her, absolutely definite.

'So you won't even take a risk?'

'If it was just me, maybe I would,' she said, and then
thought about the pain and the heartache she'd been
through. 'Maybe. But I've got two children who were
caught in the fallout of a failed relationship. I won't do that
to them again. Anyway,' she said, going on the counter-
attack, 'I notice you haven't rushed to remarry either!'

'No, once was enough for me,' Patrick agreed. 'I wasn't
good at being married. I hated the endless negotiations and
guessing games.'

'It doesn't have to be like that,' Lou pointed out. There

had never been any question of negotiating with Lawrie. He had gone his own charming way without ever considering that she might be affected by what he was doing.

'No, but it often is. Every relationship I've had since my divorce has been the same. The thing about women is that they're never satisfied. You give them what they ask for, and then they want more.'

'I don't think that's very fair,' said Lou, trying to remember the last time she'd been given what she asked for by a man.

'Isn't it?' Patrick demanded. He was feeling more himself now. Good. The stockings thing had obviously just been a momentary aberration.

He leant forward, counting off the points on his fingers. 'You're getting on well and having a good time together, but then they want to leave their hair-dryer or something at your house. Just something small to stake a claim on your space. They want you to say you love them, and when you say you love them, they want commitment. And when you've committed yourself, they want you to move in with them, or marry them, and then they want babies…

'And those are just the big things,' he said. 'At the same time they're working on you to change your life completely, they want you to understand them and talk to them and surprise them with little presents and weekends away. They want you to send them flowers and emails and to ring them from work so they know that you're thinking about them the whole time. I tell you, it's never-ending demands with women.'

He drained his glass morosely. 'Basically they want to take over your whole life.'

Lou was unimpressed by his suffering. 'So what you're saying is that you want to have sex but you don't want a relationship?'

'What's the big deal about relationships anyway?' Patrick grumbled. 'Women are obsessed with them! I thought I might get on better if I dated younger women. I figured they'd be happy to have a good time and not care about settling down, but, oh, no! We've only been out a couple of times and they're talking about *our relationship*.'

He sighed. 'Before you know where you are, you're in the middle of all that emotional hassle again.'

'It must be awful for you,' said Lou, not bothering to hide her sarcasm.

Patrick shot her a look. 'Why do women *do* that?' he complained.

'Well, you see, we tend to have these awkward things called feelings,' Lou explained with mock patience. 'It's annoying of us, I know, but there's nothing we can do about it. We *will* go and fall in love without thinking about how tedious it is for you to have someone who adores you and will do anything for you.'

She shook her head in pretended disbelief. 'I mean, how selfish is *that*?'

'I'm serious,' said Patrick. 'I just wish I could find a woman who was happy to take things as they are without always fretting about the future or what it all means or what will happen between us. As it is, we only go out for a few weeks before she starts to get clingy and I start to get claustrophobic.'

He grimaced. 'The thought of tying myself down for life is too horrible to contemplate. I'd be bored within a month.'

'You didn't get bored with Catriona,' Lou pointed out.

Patrick thought about living with Catriona. They had both been so young and excited to be living together. They had argued a lot, but it hadn't been boring. He had missed her when she had gone.

'That was different.'

'How?'

Patrick wished that Lou would stop asking difficult questions. 'It just was,' he said.

'Nothing to do with the fact that you and Catriona were the same age, and now you're twice as old as any girl you might contemplate marrying?'

And she could stop putting her finger on the nub of the matter while she was at it.

'No.' He scowled at her. 'It's just that the older I get, the more I value my freedom. I like my life as it is. I work hard, I play hard and if I find a woman attractive, I can do something about it.'

Although clearly that wasn't always the case, he added mentally, remembering Lou's stockings.

Damn. Patrick cursed inwardly. He was supposed to have forgotten about them.

'That's not to say it wouldn't be very handy to have a wife sometimes,' he said, pushing the stockings to the back of his mind once more. 'It would be good to have someone who could deal with the domestic and social side of things. I can't be bothered with all of that, but there are times when I have to entertain and it would all be a lot easier if I were married.'

'You can always have a housekeeper to take care of the house, and there must be any number of caterers falling over themselves to cook for people like you.'

'Quite. That's exactly what I do at the moment. But it's not quite the same as having a hostess who can welcome people and introduce them to each other and do all the chit-chat.'

'Have you ever tried any of your girlfriends?'

'No.' Patrick looked horrified. 'It's bad enough taking them along to receptions and parties. They're not interested in business. They get bored and end up more of a liability than an asset. I can just imagine what would happen if I asked them to help me entertain business associates to dinner. That would be *commitment*.' He sneered the word. 'They'd be off buying wedding magazines the next day.'

'I can't believe that all these girls are really that desperate to marry you,' said Lou, exasperated by his attitude. 'It's not like you're *that* big a deal.'

Of course, incredibly wealthy, single, intelligent men in their forties weren't that easy to come by, she had to admit. And it wasn't as if Patrick were grotesquely ugly, either. He probably had a pretty fair notion of how attractive he was.

Not her type of course. The cockiness of Tom Cruise and the cool of Clint Eastwood was how she had described him to Marisa. 'Tell me he's got the looks of George Clooney and I'll come and work for him myself!' Marisa had said.

But Patrick was no George Clooney. He was too cold, his features too austere. He had none of Lawrie's rakish good looks, or his easy charm, but still… Lou considered him anew. There was something *definite* about him, she decided, something solid and steady, and when he listened he concentrated completely on what you were saying. He looked at you properly, instead of letting his eyes wander around looking for something or someone more interesting the way Lawrie's had done.

Funny that she had never noticed that before, thought Lou. Or his mouth, so cool and firm and intriguing. The kind of mouth you couldn't help wondering about, how it would feel, how it would kiss. Not that she would want to, Lou reminded herself. It was just funny that she hadn't noticed it until now, that was all.

Funny to realise what a difference a gleam of humour

made, too, lightening his expression and warming the cold eyes.

Funny how his smile made her heart jump, just a little.

Must be all that champagne she had drunk.

'Why don't you try going out with women who've got bigger ambitions?' she said, forcing her mind back to the subject at issue. 'Someone who's got a career of her own and who doesn't want to settle down any more than you do?'

'Believe me, I would if I could find a girl like that,' said Patrick. 'I might even be prepared to marry her.'

'What, and give up your precious freedom?'

'At least it would shut my mother up. She's constantly going on at me to get married again. She thinks it would be good for me to have someone else to think about. She says it would stop me being so selfish.'

He sounded aggrieved and Lou smothered a smile. She rather liked the idea of him having a mother who was no more impressed with him than his PA.

'Does she want grandchildren? Is that why she's keen for you to get married?'

'I think she's accepted that she's not going to get them from me,' he said, and pointed a finger at Lou's expression. 'Don't you go feeling sorry for her! She can't complain. She's already got eleven grandchildren. I'd have thought that was more than enough.'

'Eleven?' said Lou, trying to adjust to the idea of Patrick as part of a large family.

'I've got three sisters, all of whom seem to be very fertile, and all of whom also think I should get married. Every time I see them, they ask me what's the point of having all that money and not enjoying it. Just because they've got big families of their own, they think I should have that too,' he grumbled.

'I tell them I'm perfectly happy living on my own, and I am, but sometimes when I go home the house *does* seem a bit empty,' he admitted, and gave a rather shamefaced smile. 'There, that's my embarrassing confession!'

'That's a confession, not a fantasy,' said Lou light-heartedly.

She was feeling extraordinarily mellow. It was oddly comfortable to be sitting here with him, talking to Patrick about things she would never normally *dream* of discussing with anyone at work, let alone her boss, talking to him as if he were a friend.

It was strange now to think that she had been perfectly happy to have a cool working relationship with him. For a fleeting moment, Lou wondered whether she would regret her confidences in the morning, but she pushed the thought aside. She would just blame it on the champagne.

Not to mention the wine. They seemed to have made major inroads into that bottle in spite of her plans to stick to the occasional sip.

She wasn't going to worry about it now, anyway. She was here, away from home, away from the children. It was like being in a bubble, time out from the day-to-day reality of commuting and cooking and preparing lunchboxes. Everything felt different.

Patrick even *looked* different. Warmer somehow, more human, more approachable. Much more attractive than he should for a man who wasn't her type, anyway.

'Go on,' she told him. 'You said it was confession time, and that we'd forget it all tomorrow. I told you my fantasy, so I think you should tell me yours.'

Patrick thought about leaning over the table and whispering that she should forget pudding, that he wanted to take her upstairs and press her against the bedroom door, that he wanted to explore the back of her knee while he kissed her, to let his hand smooth insistently up her thigh, pushing up that prim little skirt until his fingers found the top of her stocking, and then—

'One of them anyway,' said Lou, unnerved by the way his eyes had darkened. She didn't know what he was thinking about just then, but she was pretty sure it would leave her blushing.

And more than a little jealous. There had been something in his expression that had made her pulse kick in a way it hadn't for a very long time. Now was not the time for it to start doing that, and her boss was not the man to set it off either. Whatever he had been fantasising about doing with one of those blonde stick insects he liked so much, she didn't want to hear it.

'A fantasy that will embarrass you, not me,' she specified firmly.

It was just as well she had said that, thought Patrick, a mixture of amusement and horror at the narrowness of his escape tugging at the corner of his mouth. For a minute there he had got a bit carried away. Fortunately, her intervention had given him time to unscramble his brains. Reality had slotted back into place and all the disadvantages of explaining to your PA that you were fantasising about her and her choice of lingerie had presented themselves starkly.

Not a good idea, in fact.

'OK...' he said, drawing out the syllables. He drank some wine while he tried to focus. Surely he could think of something to tell her? A fantasy...a fantasy...and keep right away from stockings...

'Right,' he said after a moment. 'Well, how about this one? It's not that different from yours, actually. What I'd really like is all the advantages of marriage without any of the drawbacks. So in my fantasy, I would have a wife who was there when I needed her. She would be the perfect hostess, remember all my sisters' birthdays, and mysteriously vanish whenever I met a new and beautiful girl so that I could continue to have guilt-free affairs.'

Lou rolled her eyes, unimpressed. 'Oh, the old fantastic-sex-without-a-relationship chestnut! I don't think that's like my fantasy *at all*,' she objected. 'But I can see why it appeals to you.'

Patrick wasn't quite sure how to take that. 'Well, since it's likely to remain a fantasy, I'll reconcile myself to an empty house, to hiring caterers and disappointing my mother.'

Thinking about it, Lou absently held out her glass for another refill.

'What you really need,' she said, 'is someone who's prepared to marry you for your money, and treat marriage like a job.'

'That's not very romantic!'

'You don't need romance,' she told him sternly. 'You need someone to run your house, to be your social secretary, to be pleasant and interested when you go out as a couple but turn a blind eye to your affairs and generally expect absolutely nothing from you other than access to your bank account.'

Patrick was impressed by her assessment and said so as he topped up her glass. 'That's exactly what I need.'

'In fact,' said Lou, 'you need to marry me.'

# CHAPTER THREE

PATRICK'S hand jerked and he missed her glass, spilling wine on the tablecloth. 'Sorry,' he said as he mopped it up with his napkin. 'I thought you said that I should marry you there!'

'I did.' Lou accepted her glass back with a smile of thanks, quite unfazed. 'Someone like me, anyway. But actually, now I come to think of it, I'd be the perfect wife for you.'

'You would?' Patrick wasn't sure whether to be amused or appalled.

'Of course.' Lou gestured grandly with her glass. 'I know your business, and I could do all that social stuff easily. I know who you need to charm and who to impress, and I'm under absolutely no illusions as to what you're like!'

'Right,' said Patrick, fascinated.

'You'd be much better off with someone sensible like me who wouldn't make a fuss about your girlfriends, or expect you to pay me any attention,' she pointed out. 'You wouldn't need to email me every day or buy me flowers or surprise me with mini-breaks to Paris.'

'O…K,' he said slowly, buying time until he worked out whether she was joking or not. 'But why would you want to marry me?'

'Oh, I'd be marrying you for your money, of course,' said Lou cheerfully.

'I thought you didn't want a man?'

'I don't, but I do want financial security. Do you have

any idea how tough it is to be a single parent living on a limited income in a city like London?'

Patrick raised his brows. 'Is this a very roundabout way of complaining about your salary?'

'No.' She shook her head. 'My salary is fair. More than fair, in fact. If it wasn't, I would have got another job. It just doesn't go very far when you have to pay an extortionate rent and feed and support two growing children into the bargain.'

'Yes, I've heard that children are expensive nowadays,' said Patrick, thinking of his sisters' complaints.

'They are, and the older they are, the more expensive they seem to become.' Lou sighed and sipped her wine reflectively. 'I'd like to be able to say that I had raised a couple of thoughtful, unmaterialistic, community-minded children who understood that the love and security you strive to give them mattered more than the latest brand of trainers or the newest computer game, but sadly they're not like that at all!'

'Oh?' said Patrick, rather taken with the idea that Lou's children weren't the paragons he would have expected them to be. He found her attitude refreshing. He'd had to listen to too many mothers telling him how clever and talented and generally marvellous their children were.

'They're not bad kids,' said Lou, 'but they're like all their friends. They want to be in with the in-crowd, to be like everyone else and to have what everyone else has. At least I haven't been able to spoil them,' she added with a wry smile. 'The silver lining of living on a strict budget. Although naturally Grace and Tom don't see it that way!'

'Doesn't their father give you any financial support?' asked Patrick, ever the businessman. As a man who specialised in taking failing businesses and turning them round, he was clearly offended by the idea of losing control of your finances.

Lou sighed a little, thinking of Lawrie. 'He's always willing in principle, but when it comes to transferring money there's always some great scheme that he needs to buy into temporarily which will solve all our problems.'

'And does it?'

'No. The last time he had any real money to invest, he lost us our house,' said Lou, trying to make light of it. 'There's no way I'm getting back on the property ladder in London now.'

'Unfortunate,' commented Patrick, looking disapproving. He was far too canny a businessman ever to take the kind of risks Lawrie ran all the time.

Lou thought of the day Lawrie had come home and confessed that he had borrowed against the house, and lost it all on some idiotic venture that a child of six could have told him would fail.

Oh, and that by the way he was leaving her for a younger, prettier woman who wasn't so boring about being sensible about money.

Of course, the other woman didn't have two children to worry about, so it was easy for her.

Lou had lost her home and her husband on a single day. A double whammy as her world fell apart. Not one of the best days of her life.

'It was a bit,' she agreed, smiling bitterly at the understatement.

There was a pause. Patrick was having to adjust his ideas about Lou. She had always seemed so cool and in control, it was hard to imagine her dragged down by a feckless husband, having to scrape and make do.

'So marrying for money might solve some of your problems?' he said, trying to lighten the atmosphere, and Lou was glad to follow his lead.

'Well, I've got to admit that I haven't given it a lot of thought as an option before,' she said, 'but I really think it might. In fact, I wonder if marrying you might not be just the thing!'

'I'm glad you think I might be of some use to you!'

'When you're in my position, you can't afford to be proud,' said Lou frankly. 'I'm sick of scraping by and worrying about money the whole time. And I hate not being able to give Grace and Tom the kind of life I want for them.'

'You said you didn't want to give them things,' Patrick reminded her, and she nodded.

'I don't. They don't need things, but they do need more space, for instance. If you saw where we live now...'

She trailed off with a grimace at the thought of the flat. 'I know we're better off than some, but it's a tiny apartment for the three of us. Grace and I have to share a bedroom, and Tom's is barely more than a cupboard. If you want to have any privacy, you have to go into the bathroom, and even then there's always one of them banging on the door.'

Lou sighed. 'It's so small we all get on top of each other, and that makes everyone scratchy. I'm sure we wouldn't argue nearly so much if we had more space.' She cocked her head at him. 'You've got a big house, haven't you?'

'I've got three.'

'There you go, then. Plenty of room to spread ourselves. And I bet you don't have neighbours going through a marital crisis on one side of you, while those on the other put the television on full blast at seven in the morning and don't turn it off until well after midnight?'

'I don't know what state my neighbours' marriage is in,

or what their viewing habits are, but I certainly can't hear them,' agreed Patrick.

'I didn't think so. And you probably don't have people upstairs either?'

'No, I've got the whole house to myself.'

Lou sighed enviously. 'Our neighbours upstairs are perfectly nice, but every footstep reverberates through the ceiling, and we can hear almost everything they say above a whisper.'

'It sounds as if marrying me would certainly improve your accommodation prospects,' said Patrick dryly.

'Oh, don't worry, I'd want your money too.' Lou waved a piece of bread at him gaily. 'Not millions, just enough to be able to do the kind of things I could have done for them if Lawrie had stayed and we hadn't lost the house. I'd love to be in a position where I could encourage their interests, give them a chance to develop their talents, open their eyes to how other people live...'

She trailed off wistfully. 'I'd really like to be able to take them abroad for a holiday one year. Grace has friends whose father took them to the States last summer. They had a week in Florida, and a week in New York, where they stayed in some swish apartment and got taken round the Statue of Liberty in a private speedboat. Grace was so jealous, she could hardly speak to Alice and Harriet when they got back. I know she'd love a holiday like that, but all I can afford is to take them to see my aunt in the Yorkshire Dales. It's not that exciting for a fourteen-year-old.'

It didn't sound that exciting to a forty-eight-year-old either, thought Patrick, and then sucked in an exasperated breath as he saw the waiters bearing down on them once more with their main courses. They had to go through the whole rigmarole as before, both waiters hovering sycophantically around Lou and vying to top up her glass or express the hope that she would enjoy her meal.

And Lou just sat there, encouraging them with that smile of hers.

Patrick watched them grovel off at last with a disgruntled expression. 'If things are that tight, wouldn't it be cheaper for you to move out of London?'

'Yes, I often think that,' said Lou as she picked up her knife and fork. 'It's the rent that's so expensive anywhere within commuting distance of London. I'd love to live in the country, and I'm sure I could get some kind of job, although it's not easy starting in a new place when you're over forty.'

'So why don't you do it?'

'Because the kids would hate it. They're both settled at a good school in the centre of London. London's all they've ever known, so they're real metropolitans now. It's bad enough taking them to the Dales for a week. They just droop around and say that they're bored. Tom's not too bad when you get him up and out, but Grace pines for her friends.'

'You can't arrange your whole life around your children,' said Patrick, looking down his nose disapprovingly.

Lou put down her knife and fork and looked at him in wonder at his lack of understanding. 'But that's *exactly* what you have to do,' she corrected him. 'That's the thing about having children. They always come first.

'And the fact is that Grace and Tom would be miserable living in the country now,' she went on, picking up her cutlery once more so that she could tuck into her meal. 'All their friends are in London. That's their home. They're used to taking the tube and jumping on and off buses.

'No,' she said with mock resolution. 'It's a choice between marrying you or winning the lottery.'

Patrick was enjoying Lou's novel approach. Not that he had any real intention of getting married, but at least her frankness about his money made a change from tears and protestations of love and tedious conversations about why he wasn't prepared to commit.

'Let's just say for the sake of argument that I did marry you,' he said. 'How would it work?'

'It would be a meeting of our two fantasies,' said Lou, warming to the idea. 'We wouldn't have to pretend to be in love or any of that nonsense. I'd do the dutiful-wife act. I'd run your house, turn up for business dos and remind you to ring your mother, but other than that you'd hardly know I was there. You could chase girls all you liked and I wouldn't be the slightest bit jealous. I'd just wave you off, tell you to have a nice time and remind you to leave me your credit card!'

She laughed at the absurdity of the idea. Honestly, she must have had far too much to drink, but she was at the merry stage where she couldn't bring herself to care.

Patrick was having a bit of trouble disentangling the fantasies they had discussed from the one they definitely hadn't. Clearly, Lou wasn't talking about the one with the stockings, anyway. He'd certainly know she was there in that one.

With an effort he remembered what she had told him about her fantasy. Something about having someone to talk to, wasn't it? Nothing about stockings, that was for sure.

'So what would I have to do?'

Lou was enjoying herself. 'Oh, you'd just have to be there occasionally for me to have a moan about things, but it shouldn't cut into your seduction time too much. All I'd really want would be the run of the house and the security of knowing I wasn't going to find myself homeless again.'

'Does that mean if it was all a disaster and we ended up getting divorced I'd have to give you my house?'

'Well, if you've got three, you could probably spare one,' said Lou frankly. 'It doesn't seem very fair though, I agree.'

She pondered the matter, her brows drawn together in concentration as she continued to sip her wine absently. 'I'm sure we could draw up some kind of pre-nuptial contract. You know, like they do in Hollywood. We'd just put in some clause that said you had to give me some money if you got fed up of me,' she decided.

'But, hey, why would you want to divorce me?' Lou went on breezily. 'A marriage of convenience would solve all your problems. In fact, we'd both get exactly what we wanted.'

'Right,' said Patrick, a grin twitching at the corner of his mouth. 'Remind me again where our fantasies collide.'

'I want financial security. You want sex without commitment. Honestly, it's ideal,' said Lou. 'We would both know exactly where we were. There'd be no question of falling in love, or any of those messy emotions you're so afraid of. I don't want to get involved any more than you do.'

Patrick studied her with amusement. She had obviously had even more champagne than he had. He had the feeling that they would both regret this conversation in the morning, but for now he was finding it very entertaining.

'So you think you're the ideal wife for me?'

'I do,' she said with owlish dignity. 'I'm offering you a great deal here!'

'What about the two stroppy adolescents that come with you?'

'Yes, I'm afraid that Grace and Tom would come as part of the package, and I can see that they could be a bit of a drawback from your point of view,' Lou conceded, determined to be fair. 'But you did say that your house feels empty sometimes, and they would fill it up nicely. I presume you've got bedrooms for us all?'

Patrick did a quick calculation. 'Six.'

'*Six?*' She paused for a moment to consider how much a six-bedroom house in Chelsea must be worth. The answer made her mind boggle, and she shook her head.

'What on earth were you doing buying a house with six bedrooms when you live on your own?'

'It had good off-road parking.'

He sounded quite serious, too.

'Well, it's high time you filled up some of those rooms, if you ask me,' she said, recovering her nerve. 'It sounds excellent for us. There would be plenty of room for the kids to spread themselves, and we can all have a room each, *and* have two spare for visitors.'

'Oh, so you and I wouldn't be sharing a room, then?' said Patrick, having worked out the bedroom allocation.

Dark eyes met his squarely across the table. 'Not as long as you're sleeping around,' she said.

Ah. Not quite *that* intoxicated, then, thought Patrick.

'Some wife you'd be,' he pretended to grumble.

'You don't want to sleep with me,' Lou pointed out, 'and I certainly don't want to sleep with you!'

So much for his stockings fantasy. 'Well, that seems clear enough.' Patrick knew that she was right, but couldn't quite prevent the slight edge to his voice.

Lou heard it, and realised belatedly that she hadn't been very flattering. 'That's not to say that you're unattractive,' she tried to reassure him, even as part of her wondered why she was bothering to prop an ego that was already quite big enough. 'In fact, you're much more attractive than I thought you were.'

Oh, God, she'd had far too much to drink! She hadn't meant to say that at all. 'When I said I didn't want to sleep with you, I didn't mean...at least, I *did* mean... Well, I was just trying to say that it's not that—'

She stopped abruptly. There was no way that sentence was going anywhere she wanted it to, so she might as well give up on it now.

'I know what you meant,' said Patrick, keeping his face straight with difficulty. 'I think! I can see it would still be a pretty good deal for me,' he added, taking pity on Lou's confusion.

'It would be.' She beamed at him, grateful for rescuing her from the great big hole she had dug for herself there. She picked up her glass. 'You should think about it.'

Patrick looked at her, pink-cheeked and distinctly dishevelled by now. He could hardly recognise his prim and proper PA.

'Maybe I should.'

Lou stared fixedly at the lift button and tried not to sway. Really, she must have drunk more than she thought.

'I don't usually drink this much,' she confided to Patrick, with the nasty feeling that she was slurring her words. Getting to her feet had been more difficult than it usually was, too, and the walk across the hotel lobby to the lifts had involved a lot more concentration than it should have done.

'Honestly, no one would ever guess,' he said, and grinned. 'Perhaps I'd better see you to your room!'

Lou thought about walking along the dimly lit hotel corridor to her bedroom with him by her side, thought about saying goodnight. With anyone else, she wouldn't hesitate about kissing them on the cheek to thank them for dinner, but Patrick wasn't anyone else. She couldn't imagine kissing him.

Or was that quite true? Perversely, her mind proceeded to imagine it perfectly well. With unnerving clarity, in fact. Lou saw herself leaning in to brush his cheek with her lips and breathe in the smell of male skin and clean shirt, saw the corner of Patrick's mouth curve into that smile she had been noticing all evening as he turned his head slightly and his lips met hers.

Uh-oh. Lou was dismayed to discover that her subconscious had been working on this for some time. Evidently it had already thought about *exactly* what his kiss would feel like, had spent some time calculating the way her bones would melt and her lips would part at the surge of pleasure at his touch, so it was all there for her to imagine, ready prepared.

She would be able to press into him, to wrap her arms around his lean, hard body and kiss him back while he tugged her top free and slid his hands under the silk and—

Good grief, what was she *doing*? Lou sucked in a deep breath as if surfacing after a dive and tried to still her hammering heart. Suddenly her body was humming, her mouth dry, and there didn't seem to be enough oxygen in the air. She was terrified to look at Patrick in case her thoughts were plastered all over her face.

Lou's cheeks burned. This was *it*. She was never touching alcohol again.

Where was the lift? Please, please, hurry up, Lou prayed.

As if catching her impatience, Patrick leant forward and jabbed impatiently at the button again. 'What are they doing—cranking the thing up and down by hand?' he asked irritably.

Lou didn't feel that an answer was expected, which was

just as well, given the extraordinary shortage of breath in her lungs right now.

In spite of herself, her eyes slid sideways to where Patrick was standing, looking conventional and utterly devastating in a suit, blue shirt and dark blue tie. The mere sight of him was enough to make her senses snarl with longing, to make her hands itch with the need to reach out and touch him, to make her throb with wanting to crawl all over him.

And she didn't even like the man!

Or she hadn't at the beginning of the evening, anyway.

Lou swallowed desperately and willed the lift to appear. This was *awful*. She didn't feel like herself *at all*. She just hoped the feeling would go away as soon as the alcohol had worn off. The sooner she got to bed—alone!—and had a good night's sleep, the better.

*Ping.* At last! The lift doors slid open and Patrick stood aside to let Lou in first. She walked primly past him, being very careful not to touch him and stood pressed against the back wall so that there was no chance of accidentally brushing against him. The way she felt, she wouldn't put it past herself to burst into flames, and then there really *would* be a nasty mess.

'Which floor?' asked Patrick as the doors began to close.

Oh, God, she wasn't up to answering questions that involved thinking! 'Um…four, I think.'

He turned from the control panel to look at her in surprise. 'You don't sound very sure. Do you know your room number?'

'Of course,' said Lou, flustered. 'It's…it's…' She dug around in her bag for the key card, but typically it wasn't marked with anything useful like a number. 'Four O seven,' she remembered with a gasp, and Patrick shot her a curious glance as he pressed the button marked four, and five for his own room, which was on the floor above.

Of course the lift *would* have to be empty, thought Lou bitterly. Had it been this small on the way down? There wasn't really *room* for two people, she decided, sucking in her stomach in a vain attempt to make more space between them. Patrick seemed to be very *close* somehow. How was she supposed to stop her hands grabbing for him when he was only inches away?

She clutched her bag to her chest to keep them under control.

Silence. It seemed to thrum in the enclosed space and Lou gazed desperately at the numbers above the door as they slid slowly upwards. After talking non-stop all evening, she now couldn't think of a single thing to say, and it was a huge relief when the doors pinged once more.

'Um…well…thanks for a lovely evening,' she gasped as the doors opened. 'See you tomorrow.'

Edging round Patrick, she stumbled out. Thank God, for that. Now all she had to do was get herself to her room, close the door and hope against hope that this evening had never happened.

'Lou?'

She turned to see Patrick holding open the lift doors.

'This is only the second floor,' he explained kindly.

Lou looked around her. That would explain why nothing looked familiar then.

'Oh. Yes. How silly of me.'

Mortified, she got back into the lift. Her face burned with embarrassment. Excellent. Here she was, aged forty-five, responsible mother of two and top-flight PA, making a complete and utter fool of herself.

'Here's four,' said Patrick as the doors sighed open once

more. 'Are you sure you don't need me to see you to your room after all?'

Lou couldn't look at him, but she could hear that he was smiling. 'I don't think there's any need for that,' she said with as much dignity as she could muster, which wasn't much. 'I'm perfectly all right,' she said and promptly tripped on the edge of the lift, only just recovering herself before she fell flat on her face.

Great.

'Lou, are you OK?'

'I'm fine, fine.' Lou summoned a bright smile and straightened her jacket. 'Absolutely fine.'

A smile hovered around Patrick's mouth, but she had to give him credit for not laughing out loud. 'Well, goodnight, then.' He released the doors and they closed slowly.

'Goodnight,' said Lou just in time as Patrick disappeared from view.

It took her ages to get the stupid card to release the lock on the door, but finally she made it into her room, kicked off her shoes and flopped onto the bed.

Could it really only be eleven o'clock? Lou peered at her watch. It had taken her just over three hours to ruin her image and probably destroy her career in the process. She was going to write a stiff letter of complaint to the chairman of the east coast line, just as soon as her head stopped spinning.

If they hadn't cancelled all the trains because of one piddly little storm, she would have been safely home alone by now. She would still be thinking of Patrick Farr as an arrogant businessman with whom she needed to have a coolly polite working relationship, but in whom she otherwise had no interest at all.

Instead of which, she had talked to him and got drunk with him and confided her fantasies to him, and now she was stuck with *liking* him, dammit. She wasn't going to be stuck with finding him attractive, though, Lou reassured herself. That was definitely off the agenda come tomorrow.

She just wished she hadn't made such a fool of herself in front of him.

Pulling her mobile phone out of her bag abruptly, Lou rolled over onto her front. She needed advice and Marisa never went to bed before midnight.

'I think I've just asked my boss to marry me,' she said when Marisa answered the phone.

'This would be the boss who never asks you about your weekend and is rude and arrogant, and doesn't look a bit like George Clooney, is that right?' said Marisa, who never minded phone calls that began in mid-conversation.

'Yes, except I don't think that he's that bad.' Lou rolled back so that she could look up at the ceiling and remember Patrick's face and the look in his eyes when she had asked about his fantasy. A squirmy feeling shivered down her spine at the memory. 'He's OK when you get to know him.'

'OK is not good enough for you to marry,' said Marisa firmly. 'You deserve someone who is fantastic at the very least.'

'I don't want to marry him,' said Lou, suddenly realising the implications of what she'd been saying to Patrick in the restaurant.

'Then why did you ask him to marry you?' asked Marisa, not unreasonably.

'I didn't really ask him,' Lou tried to explain. 'He was just talking about the kind of wife he wanted, and I said he needed someone like me.'

'And he responded to that how?'

'He said he'd think about it.'

'He sounds a cold fish to me,' said Marisa.

'I don't think he is really. He seems cold, but actually I think he could be quite…well, *hot*…'

There was a pause. 'Have you been drinking?'

'A bit.'

'Louisa Dennison, I'm going to tell your children on you!'

'Oh, please don't,' she begged. 'They'll never let me forget it! How are they, anyway?' she asked belatedly, feeling like a bad mother for not asking about them first.

'Fine. Sound asleep, and don't change the subject,' said Marisa. 'I want to know what's going on with you and Patrick What's-his-name.'

'Nothing's going on. We just had dinner.'

'And a vat of wine and talked about getting married!'

Lou cringed at the memory. 'The thing is, do you think when I see him tomorrow morning that I should apologise?'

'What for?'

'For all that marriage thing. I might have got a bit carried away,' Lou remembered uncomfortably. 'I told him I would be the perfect wife for him.'

'More to the point, would he be a perfect husband for you?'

'Definitely not,' said Lou. 'Patrick likes his women a good twenty years younger, with perfect bodies and an allergy to commitment of any kind.'

'Ah, he's a man, then!'

'This is serious,' said Lou crossly. 'My job's at stake.'

'He's not going to sack you for getting a bit drunk in your own time,' Marisa pointed out. 'It's not as if you were offensive…were you?'

'Of course not!'

'Well, then, I wouldn't worry about it. It sounds as if he had a fair amount to drink as well, and if he's anything like the men I know, he'll have a built-in ability to wipe any conversation concerning marriage from his memory. He'll either ignore it completely, or say that was a jolly good idea of yours and why don't you get married after all?'

Lou was appalled at the thought. 'I wasn't being serious! I've got no intention of marrying again. Once was enough for me!'

'Shame,' said Marisa lightly. 'I saw this wonderful hat the other day. It would be perfect for your wedding.'

'Buy it and keep it for Grace's wedding,' said Lou. 'She'll be getting married long before me!'

Marisa just laughed. 'We'll see.'

# CHAPTER FOUR

'I WAS wondering if you'd like me to find you a temporary assistant,' said Lou as she gathered up her notebook and stood up to go.

Patrick looked up over the rim of his glasses from the letter he was reading. 'What on earth for?'

'I've got a week's holiday booked at the end of May. I did tell you about it,' she added as she saw him about to object.

'I don't remember,' he said unhelpfully. 'Does it have to be the end of May? We'll be busy preparing for the Packenham contract then.'

'Yes, it does have to be then,' said Lou crisply. 'It's half-term, and I need to spend that time with my children. And don't start about what a liability children are,' she warned him as he opened his mouth. 'This is the first time I've needed time off, and I booked it at the beginning of the year. I don't think that's unreasonable.'

It wasn't, but Patrick didn't feel inclined to admit it. The truth was that he didn't like the thought of Lou not being there. He *needed* her to run the office. He wouldn't be able to find anything without her, he'd get over-committed and nothing would work properly.

And he was used to her now.

In a funny kind of way.

Patrick had wondered if things might have been awkward after that evening they had spent together in Newcastle, but, in spite of the fact that neither of them had alluded to their conversation that night, in many ways the atmosphere between them was much easier. It was hard to stay frosty, after all, when you'd talked and laughed and confided your fantasies to each other—although not all of them, in Patrick's case.

Of course, Lou had reverted to her crisp and efficient self the next morning, but Patrick was no longer intimidated by her. He had seen her tipsy. He had seen her fall out of the lift. She couldn't fool him now. He knew she wasn't the ice-cold superwoman she had once seemed. Now that he let himself notice the glint of dry humour in her face, the warmth in her smile, the ironic undertone in her voice.

Too often for his own peace of mind, in fact, Patrick found himself thinking about the contrast between his cool, practical PA and the warm, vibrant woman he had glimpsed as she'd leant across the restaurant table, her dark eyes bright and her face vivid.

*I'd be the perfect wife for you,* she had said.

It was nonsense, of course. If he ever contemplated marriage again, it would be to someone beautiful and passionate and sexy. He certainly wouldn't be tying himself down to a middle-aged mother of two, no matter how good her legs were.

And they *were* good. Patrick knew because every time she walked into his office he would find himself looking at them and remembering his fantasy about whether she was wearing stockings or not. Her legs were great, in fact. He couldn't believe that he hadn't noticed them before.

He knew it was pathetic. He knew it was politically incorrect and deeply inappropriate, and probably perverted, but once the thought had slipped into his head it was impossible to get rid of it. It wasn't that Patrick hadn't tried. Life would be a lot easier if he had been able to carry on thinking of her suits as dull and demure instead of sexy as hell, which was how they now seemed to him. He began to think that it would be easier if Lou turned up for work in a miniskirt and plunging top. The kind of thing Ariel wore, in fact.

It was getting too distracting, that was the trouble. Patrick decided to stop noticing anything. It wasn't as if he were sex-starved, after all. Ariel was much prettier than Lou. She had a much better body, even better legs. What was more, Ariel was concerned when he was in a bad mood. She didn't just lift an ironic eyebrow, the way Lou did. Ariel never made him feel a fool. She never said cutting things.

But, then, she never made him laugh either, or left the office feeling empty when she had gone in the evenings.

Now Lou was talking about being away all week!

'It'll be very inconvenient,' he grumbled.

'That's why I'm asking if you want me to arrange for someone to cover the office,' said Lou patiently.

Patrick scowled. 'It won't be the same,' he said. 'I can't be bothered to explain everything.'

'Well, you can always answer your own phone,' said Lou, unperturbed. 'Or take the week off yourself.'

'What?'

'Take the week off, have a holiday, relax,' she said, stopping just short of rolling her eyes, although she might as well not have bothered, Patrick thought. It was perfectly obvious that she was doing it mentally. 'Or would that be too much like having a good time?' she asked, quite unnecessarily, in his opinion.

'I'm perfectly capable of having a good time,' he said, stung.

Lou didn't say anything. She just raised her brows and smiled faintly, in that deeply annoying way she had.

'All right.' Provoked, Patrick took off his reading glasses

and threw them onto his desk. 'I'll take the week off as well. You can book it tomorrow.'

Lou was already at her desk when Patrick came in the next morning. Her heart had developed an exasperating habit of jolting at the sight of him, but at least it didn't show—at least, she hoped that it didn't. She worked hard to keep her expression as indifferent as ever.

It had been a huge relief when she had met Patrick in the lobby the morning after that night she had made such a fool of herself in Newcastle. As Marisa had predicted, he appeared to have wiped the whole incident from his memory.

'How's the head?' was all he had said.

Lou had grimaced. 'Not good,' she'd admitted.

'I don't feel so hot either, to tell you the truth,' Patrick had said.

And that was it.

Nothing more had been said, and gradually Lou had let herself relax. It had just been a silly evening. Patrick was obviously prepared to pretend that it had never happened at all, and that suited her fine. She had other things to worry about, like Grace's determination to have her nose pierced, and Tom's run-in with his English teacher. She would forget it.

Only it wasn't that easy to forget. Lou was uncomfortably aware of Patrick now in a way that she had never been before. It had been awful on the train. Sitting opposite him in the first-class carriage on their way back to London, she had kept noticing his hands, his mouth, the line of his jaw, the crease of concentration between his brows.

Once Patrick had glanced up and caught her watching him, and her heart had jerked at the keenness of his eyes. Flushing, she had looked away and cleared her throat as

she'd held out some papers. 'You wanted those budget figures for last year...'

Since then it hadn't been too bad, though. Patrick had
no shortage of faults to concentrate on, so Lou made herself
notice his abruptness rather than his mouth, his impatience
rather than the way his eyes glinted when he smiled.

It was fine. Lou decided that she had made quite enough
of a fool of herself in Newcastle. She certainly wasn't going
to make things worse by getting obsessed with a ruthless,
workaholic boss who was fixated on younger women. Even
if her heart did jump a bit when she saw him.

Patrick paused by her desk on his way to his office.

'You can book me a holiday when you've finished that,'
he told her.

Lou looked up, thought about asking him if he had ever
thought of learning the word *please* and decided against it
when she saw his face. Most people managed to look happy
or excited at the idea of a holiday, but obviously not Patrick
Farr.

'You're going?' she said, a little surprised.

'It was your idea,' he reminded her grouchily.

'Well, I do tend to have good ones,' she said, composed.

There was a short silence while the memory of her idea
that they get married shimmered in the air between them.
Patrick didn't need to say anything. Lou knew perfectly
well that he was thinking about it. A flush crept up her
cheeks and her poise slipped a little.

'Sometimes,' she said.

Patrick's eyes gleamed. 'Get me flights to the Maldives
and a hotel for that week you're away.'

Lou raised her brows at his choice of destination, but
made a note. 'Where do you want to stay?'

'Wherever's best,' he said indifferently. He had picked

up a report from her desk and was leafing through it. 'Book a suite, or a cabin, or whatever it is everyone has out there.'

'Best for what? Best location, best food, most luxurious?'

'I don't know.' Patrick gestured irritably. 'The most expensive.'

'Right.' Lou set her jaw. 'I take it you're not travelling alone?'

'No.' He closed the report with a slap and dropped it back onto the pile. 'One of the tickets should be in the name of Ariel Harper.'

Ariel. How charming, thought Lou, teeth mentally gritted. No doubt Hazel in Finance would be able to supply a photo, but Lou would take a bet on Ariel being blonde and ethereal. Oh, and twenty-five, tops.

'Put it through on my personal account,' said Patrick, and was about to turn away when he caught the look on Lou's face. 'What?' he demanded.

'Nothing, I'm just surprised at your choice of destination,' said Lou. 'I can't imagine you lying on a beach for a week.'

Patrick couldn't imagine it either. He was always bored of the beach after an hour. But, stung by Lou's implication that he didn't know how to relax and have a good time, he had asked Ariel the night before if she wanted to go away for a week. She had leapt at the idea, as he had known that she would. The Maldives had been her choice, and, as Patrick couldn't think of anywhere else he wanted to go, the Maldives it was.

'I have hidden shallows,' he told Lou, who was surprised into a laugh.

Patrick wished she wouldn't do that. It always startled him to see how vivid she looked when she laughed, how very different from the prim and proper PA he half wished she had remained.

'It's a long way to go for a week,' she warned. 'Why don't you make it a fortnight?'

Patrick thought about a week on a beach with Ariel's chatter. She was an extraordinarily pretty girl, but she did *talk*. 'A week will be quite long enough,' he said. 'You're only taking a week anyway.'

'Yes, but that's because Grace and Tom have to go back to school the following week,' she pointed out. 'And we're only going to the Yorkshire Dales, which is a bit different from a long-haul flight to the Maldives.'

He didn't want to remind her that he was only going on holiday because she was. It would sound a bit pathetic. 'Why Yorkshire?' he asked instead.

'My aunt lives there. My parents died when I was quite young, and since then Fenny has been the closest I've got to a mother. She lives in a lovely village, right in the Dales, and she's got the most beautiful garden. It's not quite the Indian Ocean,' she said, 'but it's always like going home for me. I'll be happy grubbing around in the garden and bullying the kids into long walks in the hills.'

And she had the nerve to imply that he wouldn't enjoy lying on a beach! 'Whatever turns you on,' he said, and then wished he'd chosen another phrase. Practically snatching the letters Lou was holding out to him, he headed towards his office before he could get distracted by wondering what else might turn her on.

It took Lou the best part of the morning to investigate hotels in the Maldives. She chose one whose prices made her eyes boggle, and then booked two first-class return flights, trying not to think about the train tickets she had bought with her family railcard the day before.

She had barely put down the phone to get on with some

of her own work when a quite distractingly beautiful girl drifted into her office. She had the kind of long, streaky blonde hair that looked as if she spent her life in the sun, and she constantly drew attention to it by shaking it away from her face.

As if that weren't bad enough, Lou noted sourly, she had glowing skin and enormous blue eyes and a perfect body, much of it visible given that she was only wearing a tiny skirt looped with a belt almost as big as it was, and a flimsy top that looked as if it consisted of a few scraps of material pinned together in a fit of absent-mindedness, but that probably cost a fortune.

Just being in the same room as her made Lou feel faded and grey and matronly.

'Can I help you?'

More shaking of the sun-streaked hair. 'Is Pat in?'

Pat? It took Lou a moment to work out whom she was talking about. *Pat?* Pat sounded far too warm and cuddly for Patrick. He wasn't a man who did warm and cuddly.

'I'm afraid he's in a meeting,' Lou said as pleasantly as she could.

'Oh.' The girl pouted, her beautiful mouth drooping. 'I need to talk to him about our holiday.'

'You must be Ariel,' said Lou. She had been dead right in her earlier speculations. Ariel could only be in her early twenties. Really, Patrick ought to be ashamed of himself. 'I've been booking the holiday for you this morning,' she told her.

Ariel's eyes flickered over her without interest. 'Oh, ya, Pat said he would ask his secretary to arrange it all.'

Oh, did he? Clearly she didn't even merit a name when he was talking to Ariel. Lou couldn't help feeling a little hurt.

'Well, don't worry, it's all arranged,' she said brightly.

Back went the hair again. 'I hope you've booked the Kandarai Beach Hotel?'

'No,' said Lou, keeping her voice determinedly even. 'I wasn't asked to book that. I've booked a really beautiful hotel on the grounds that it was the most luxurious one I could find.'

'Oh, but I wanted to go to the Kandarai Beach!' Ariel's beautiful face crumpled and for a moment she looked extraordinarily like Grace on the verge of a tantrum. 'That's what I wanted to talk to Pat about. I've been talking to my friend. She says it's *fabulous*. I didn't think you'd book it so quickly, but you can change it, can't you?'

'I can certainly mention it to Patrick,' said Lou. Frankly she had had enough of booking other people's luxury holidays in the Maldives for one morning.

'Mention what?' said Patrick's voice from the doorway. His eyes fell on Ariel, and he frowned, although Ariel didn't seem to notice his marked lack of delight at her unexpected appearance in his office.

'Oh, Pat, there you are!' she cried, wafting over to wind her arms around his neck and kiss him.

Patrick had little choice but to kiss her back, but as he lifted his head his eyes met Lou's, dark and ironic, over Ariel's blonde hair. He glared at her expression, but Lou just looked up at the ceiling, all innocence.

Annoyed, he put Ariel away from him. 'Ariel, what are you doing here? You know I don't like mixing work and pleasure.'

'Oh, *you*!' Ariel gave a girlish moue that made Lou cringe. 'I was just so excited about our holiday, I wanted to make sure that it was all perfect, and it's just as well I did,' she said. 'Pat, she's booked the wrong hotel!'

'You mean Lou,' said Patrick, frowning.

'Whatever.' Ariel waved Lou aside as unimportant. 'Oh,

Pat, please, please, *please* tell her to book the Kandarai Beach! I'll be so happy.' She was clinging girlishly to his arm, gazing up at him with her big blue eyes. 'I'll love you for ever!'

Oops, *big* mistake, Ariel, thought Lou, a reluctant witness to this simpering display. Even Ariel couldn't have missed the flash of irritation in Patrick's face.

He glanced at Lou in naked appeal. Clearly his only concern right then was to shut Ariel up and get her out of the office.

'I'll see what I can do,' she told him coolly and his features relaxed a bit.

Apparently Ariel had missed his look of irritation. Either that or she was monumentally thick-skinned. 'Ooh, thank you, thank you, thank you,' she said to Patrick, although he wasn't the one who was going to spend the afternoon on the phone. Ariel was wriggling with ecstasy. 'Let's go and have lunch and celebrate!'

'I haven't got time for lunch today,' said Patrick abruptly. 'I've got a meeting.'

Ariel shook more hair around so that it shone like spun gold in the light. 'I'll see you tonight, then,' she said, with a little pout.

Patrick evaded that neatly. 'I'll call you,' he said. 'Now, I'm sorry, Ariel, but I'm very busy.'

Lou didn't know whether she was glad to see Ariel go, or outraged at the passive way the girl accepted Patrick's brush-off. Ariel seemed perfectly happy, though, as well she might given that she was getting a free week in a luxury hotel in the Maldives.

At the door, she turned back with a final shake of her tresses and blew Patrick a kiss. 'Enjoy!' she said, and drifted off.

Patrick met Lou's eyes. 'Don't say a word,' he warned.

Lou preserved an innocent expression. 'I wouldn't dream of it,' she said, and picked up a file. 'Here are those figures you wanted.'

'Thank you.'

She couldn't resist it. 'You know, that would sound so much more sincere if you said it three times and promised to love me for ever,' she said sweetly, just as he reached his office door.

Patrick turned to glare at her, but Lou just laughed, and blew him a kiss in perfect imitation of Ariel. 'Enjoy!' she simpered and had the huge satisfaction of making Patrick stomp into his office and slam the door behind him.

She was less amused when Ariel took to calling every day, having evidently decided that Lou was her own private travel agent. After many phone calls and a lot of string-pulling, Lou had finally managed to book a suite at the Kandarai Beach Hotel, but this wasn't enough for Ariel. It turned out that she didn't want a suite, she wanted one of the luxuriously furnished huts that were built out over the water, so Lou had to rearrange it all again.

Then Ariel wanted to leave a day later so that she could go to some party, and as soon Lou had done that she wanted her ticket changed again so that she could come back via Mombasa. A day later, she needed Lou to find out whether the hotel would be able to provide soya milk as she was allergic to dairy products.

By the time half-term came round, Lou's jaw was aching from keeping her teeth in a permanently gritted position. Ariel hadn't bothered to remember her name, but was constantly on the phone throwing her insubstantial weight around.

Hazel in Finance said that Ariel was a model. Lou wasn't surprised. Ariel certainly had the looks for it. She had the personality, too. Lou knew she was being unfair, and that there were probably loads of perfectly nice, pleasant models out there, but Ariel fulfilled every stereotype of a spoilt and manipulative prima donna, constantly demanding attention. Lou couldn't imagine what Patrick ever found to talk to her about.

But then, they probably didn't do a whole lot of talking, Lou realised, feeling depressed. It had been so long since she had slept with anyone, she could hardly remember what it was like. She was sure that she had forgotten how to do it. Most of the time she just accepted the absence of physical comfort as the price of refusing to get emotionally involved, and since she couldn't imagine sleeping with a man unless she loved him, and she wasn't going to risk the pain and heartbreak that accompanied love, it looked as if she might as well carry on accepting it.

She was better off sticking to gardening, Lou told herself. She might not be spending a week of passion and romance in the Indian Ocean, but she would have a week weeding instead, and very happy she would be with it.

It was a relief to leave Ariel and her ceaseless demands behind when they left for Yorkshire, but Lou couldn't help comparing her crowded train journey with Patrick's first-class flight. She cheered herself up by remembering that, although he might be surrounded by all the trappings of luxury, he would still have Ariel yakking non-stop beside him.

Then she looked across at Grace, slumped in the seat opposite, her mouth turned down sulkily, and Tom, riveted to his Game Boy, and she sighed to herself. Patrick probably wouldn't envy her her travelling companions either.

Fenny met them at the station in Skipton and drove them home. That tended to be a nerve-racking experience, as both the car and Fenny were getting on, and her aunt had only ever been an erratic driver at best, but as soon as Lou got out of the car and took a deep breath, savouring the clean, sharp air of the hills, she felt better. Even the children perked up. They might grumble and groan about being taken to the country, but they loved Fenny.

Yes, it had been a good idea to come here, Lou decided. She wasn't going to think about the bills waiting to be paid. She wasn't going to think about work. She wasn't going to think about anything.

Especially she wasn't going to think about Patrick.

But at odd times during the week Lou found her mind drifting to the Indian Ocean in spite of herself. She'd be pulling out weeds in Fenny's front garden, and suddenly she'd be wondering what Patrick was doing right then. Was he walking along a palm-fringed beach, hand in hand with Ariel? Were they frolicking in the minty green waters of a lagoon? Probably not, Lou decided on that one. She couldn't picture Patrick frolicking.

Or were they simply spending the entire week in bed?

'You seem very distracted at the moment, Lou,' said Fenny. She had brought out two cups of tea, and they sat companionably together on the doorstep as they drank them.

'I'm sorry, I didn't mean to be,' said Lou guiltily. 'I suppose I've just got things on my mind at the moment.'

'What kind of things?'

Patrick in bed, his body bare and brown against white sheets...

'Oh, you know...the usual things. Bills to pay, new shoes to buy for the kids.' She smiled, but it didn't quite work. 'It would help if they would stop growing!'

'I thought it might be a man,' said Fenny casually.

Since when had her aunt been telepathic? Lou attempted a laugh. 'Oh, Fenny, I'm too old for all that now!'

'Nonsense!' Fenny sounded quite cross. 'You're never

too old for *all that*!' She sighed. 'I keep hoping that you'll tell me you're getting married again,' she admitted. 'It would be such a shame if that Lawrence put you off men altogether. They're not all low-down, irresponsible cheats, you know.'

Fenny had never liked Lawrie and the feeling had been mutual. 'It would just be so much *easier* for you if you had a husband. Someone to help you. It's very hard for you to deal with everything on your own.'

Lou couldn't help thinking about the fantasy she had confessed to Patrick. 'It sounds good, Fenny,' she said lightly, 'but it's not that easy to find men who want to do that.'

'I know.' Fenny shot her a speculative sideways glance. 'I just wondered if you had met someone likely already. There's something different about you,' she said thoughtfully.

For some reason, Lou's mind flashed to Patrick, and a tiny blush crept up her cheeks. 'No, there's no one.'

No one the slightest bit likely, anyway.

She had herself well back under control by the time she got into work the following Monday, though. She was standing in front of her desk, glancing through the pile of messages, when Patrick strode in, and although her heart did its usual little lurch Lou was proud of the cool way she could smile at him.

'Hello,' she said, quite as if she hadn't spent most of the previous week imagining him stretched out in bed, his body lean and brown, a lazy grin on his face.

Patrick stopped at the sight of her, neat and dark and as immaculately turned out as ever. She was wearing a straight grey skirt and pale pink shirt, with just a glimpse of pearls at her neck. Not an exciting outfit, but after a week of women in bikinis, or shorts and skimpy dresses, Lou looked cool and classy.

'Oh,' he said. 'It's you.'

Lou lifted her brows. 'It *is* my office,' she pointed out. 'It shouldn't be that big a surprise to find me here.'

'I didn't think you'd be in yet,' Patrick said, hating the way she could make him feel like a fool sometimes.

'I wasn't expecting you either.' No one knew his flight times better than Lou, who had had to change them so often. He wouldn't have got back until late the night before. 'Did you have a good holiday?'

'No,' said Patrick, and went into his office, shutting the door with a snap.

'I had a lovely week too, thanks,' said Lou to the closed door. 'Nice of you to ask!'

At his desk, Patrick switched on his computer with a scowl. It had been a long week and he was glad to be back in the office and away from Ariel, who had taken the invitation to spend a holiday together as a sign of irreversible commitment on his part. Alternately possessive and coyly flirtatious, she had simply ignored his increasingly blunt attempts to explain that, as far as he was concerned, there was no question of a long-term relationship, let alone marriage.

Patrick cursed himself for ever asking her. He had only done it to prove something to Lou, and it didn't help that he couldn't now remember what that something was. All he knew was that it was somehow Lou's fault.

In the evenings he had sat and watched the sun set over the Indian Ocean in a spectacular blaze of colour, and inexplicably his mind had drifted to the Yorkshire Dales. As the hot wind had soughed through the palm trees, Patrick had found himself thinking about clean, fresh air and green hills. He had imagined Lou, sitting and talking in a fragrant garden as the light faded in the long, unspectacular English summer twilight, and he had been alarmed at how appealing it had all seemed.

There was something wrong with him, Patrick had decided irritably. There he was, on a beautiful tropical island, in unimaginable luxury, unobtrusive staff on hand to gratify his every whim. With him was a girl who made every other man on the island look at him enviously. Ariel was gorgeous, there were no two ways about it. Beautiful, sexy, with glowing skin, a fantastic body and legs up to her armpits, she was every man's fantasy come true.

So why was he sitting there thinking about a middle-aged woman with lines starring her eyes? Lou had good legs, but she was hardly the stuff of fantasy, was she? It was just that Patrick had found himself longing for a dose of her cool irony in place of Ariel's inane chatter, for her crisp retorts, for the gleam of humour in her dark gaze, and the direct way she looked into his eyes instead of coyly sweeping down her lashes and peeping from beneath them the way Ariel did.

And then he had found himself remembering how warm and vivid Lou had seemed that night in Newcastle, how she had let down that barrier of poise and let him glimpse the sensuous woman beneath, and he had found himself wishing, too, that he could see her that way again.

He had thought about what she had suggested that night, too. He had thought about it a lot.

Patrick threw himself down in his chair and swung it round in exasperation. He hated feeling like this, edgy and uncertain about everything. He wasn't himself.

Look at the way he had behaved just now. He'd been thinking about Lou, and when he'd walked into the office and found her there his heart had leapt ridiculously. She had smiled, but it had only been her polite smile, and then she had lifted her brows and he had felt an idiot. Clearly she wasn't overjoyed to see him, the way he was to see her, and Patrick had been so disappointed that he had just grunted and slammed into his office.

He would have to apologise. If only she didn't make him feel so unsettled. Patrick drummed his fingers on the desk, wondering how to word what he wanted to say.

'I'm sorry I was a bit abrupt earlier,' he said when she had come into his office and they had been through the urgent business.

'That's all right,' said Lou. 'I'm sorry you didn't have a good time. Was there a problem with the hotel?'

'No.'

'Did you have good weather?'

'Perfect, and, before you ask, the flights were on time and all your arrangements worked precisely.' He hesitated. 'How was your holiday?'

'Well, the trains were late and the weather was awful, but it was beautiful and Fenny's a great cook, so it was a very relaxing break. Just what I needed.'

'Good,' said Patrick, but he knew that he sounded grouchy. Obviously she hadn't missed *him* at all. She'd been quite happy having a good time with her children and aunt.

That seemed to be the end of the holiday interrogation. It didn't look as if there would be a friendly exchange of holiday snaps when the photos were developed. Lou gathered up her notebook and pen and rose from her seat.

'Don't go,' said Patrick brusquely. 'I want to talk to you.'

Subsiding back into her chair, Lou opened her notebook once more and held her pen at the ready.

'You won't need to take notes,' he said, disconcerted by her businesslike demeanour.

He was doing this all wrong, he realised. He should have waited until the evening and taken her out for a drink, but it was too late for that now. He shrugged mentally. He might as well deal with it now that he'd got this far.

'This is personal,' he explained.

'Oh?'

Lou laid down her pen and regarded him with a certain wariness.

Having got this far, Patrick wasn't sure how to proceed. He got to his feet and prowled around the office, his hands thrust into his pockets and his brows drawn together.

'I've been thinking about what you said,' he said at last, coming to a halt by the window.

'What *I* said? When?'

'That night in Newcastle.' He turned to look at her.

Tell-tale colour crept into Lou's cheeks. Trust Patrick to bring that up now, just when she had allowed herself to relax and think that the whole sorry incident was forgotten.

'I shouldn't pay any attention to anything I said that night.' She tried to make a joke of it. 'I'd had far too much champagne.'

'You said I should think about marrying you,' said Patrick. 'And that's what I've been doing. I think you were right. I think we should get married.'

# CHAPTER FIVE

Lou stared at him. 'I wasn't being serious!'

'I know, but the more I think about it, the more sensible it seems.'

Sensible…? 'Hang on,' said Lou. 'Is this a joke?'

'If you'd had the week I've just had, you'd know I'm not in a joking mood,' said Patrick. 'It was a mistake taking Ariel on holiday, I can see that now. She took it to mean that I was ready for commitment. And you didn't tell me that the Maldives were full of honeymooners,' he added accusingly.

'I'm not responsible for you knowing what anyone who's ever picked up a holiday brochure knows,' said Lou at her most crisp.

Patrick glowered. 'It was a disaster. Ariel spent her entire time angling for an engagement ring. I told her that it wasn't going to happen, but that didn't stop her giggling about weddings with new brides and picking up tips about dresses and table decorations and what the best man ought to wear,' he said with distaste.

'I came home vowing that I was never going to get in that situation again. I've decided that the only way to convince girls that a relationship with me doesn't involve any measure of commitment is to show them I'm already married.'

Lou could hardly believe what she was hearing. 'You don't think that's taking your fantasy about sex without a relationship a bit far?' she asked acidly.

'Why? It would make the point, wouldn't it?'

She shook her head in disbelief. 'Why would you want to get involved with a woman who was prepared to sleep with a married man?'

'But that's the whole point,' said Patrick impatiently. 'I don't want to be involved. I'm not interested in anything beyond a purely physical relationship. I always make that clear anyway, but maybe they would believe me if they knew I had a wife in the background.'

'There is such a thing as divorce, you know,' said Lou, exasperated. 'What's to stop these poor deluded girls hoping that you'll fall in love with them and leave your wife?'

Patrick thought for a moment. 'I'll tell them that I've signed a pre-nuptial contract so my wife gets seventy per cent of my assets if there's a divorce.'

Lou goggled at him. 'It might even be worth marrying you for that!' she said, still half convinced that he was joking.

'I'm serious,' said Patrick. He came back to sit opposite her and folded his hands on the desk. 'I'm offering you the chance of a life where you never have to worry about money again. All I ask in return is that you be a visible wife, that you'll help with corporate entertaining and play the convincing part of a wife in front of my business associates—and my mother and sisters,' he added as an afterthought.

'It's true that you're not absolutely ideal,' he went on, apparently unaware of Lou's expression of growing outrage. 'You're certainly not the kind of wife I ever envisaged for myself,' he admitted, 'and it's a pity that you've got children. I don't see myself as a stepfather, but I expect that we could work something out.'

There was always boarding-school, he thought to himself.

'I don't see why we'd need to have that much to do with

each other,' said Patrick, dismissing that objection. 'So while you're not exactly what I want, you have got other advantages to offset that, especially your knowledge of the business, as you pointed out yourself. And being older means that you're mature enough to understand that marriage would be a purely practical arrangement on both sides. And, of course, you've got more of an incentive than most,' he finished. 'You need the money.'

'Not that much,' said Lou distinctly. Now she knew how Elizabeth Bennett had felt when Mr Darcy had insulted her family and her connections and then tossed a proposal of marriage her way.

She got to her feet.

'Where are you going?' asked Patrick, taken aback.

'Back to work.'

'But what about my proposal?'

'Oh, that was a *proposal*, was it?' said Lou in her most sarcastic voice. 'I didn't realise an answer was required.'

'Of course I want an answer,' said Patrick crossly. What did she think, he was just having a chat?

'Oh, OK.' Lou put her head on one side and pretended to think about it for an insultingly short time. 'No.'

'*No?*' He was outraged.

'No,' she repeated firmly. 'As proposals go, that one sucked! There's absolutely no question of me marrying you, Patrick. You'd better find someone else to solve your commitment problem, because it's certainly not going to be me!'

Patrick got to his feet too. 'Just a minute, this was *your* idea,' he said angrily.

'I can't believe you took me seriously,' said Lou, just as angry. Angrier, in fact, and getting more and more angry the more she thought about it. 'I'd been guzzling champagne all evening, for heaven's sake! Of *course* I wasn't serious!'

'You were pretty persuasive!'

'I certainly wouldn't have been if I'd known you were going to take a joke and use it to insult me!'

'I've just asked you to marry me,' said Patrick, livid by now. 'How is that insulting you?'

'What kind of woman do you think I am?' she demanded furiously. 'Do you really think I'd marry a man I don't love, a man I don't even *like* very much, just for his money? A man who tells me outright that he can't be bothered with my children, a man who doesn't really want me at all or find me that attractive, but thinks I'll do and that I'm desperate enough to agree?

'I've got to tell you, Patrick, that I find that pretty insulting,' she told him. 'I mean, I've heard of some insensitive proposals in my time, but yours has to take the biscuit!'

'What was I supposed to do, go down on one knee and wrap it up in a lot of romantic claptrap? Don't tell me you expected me to tell you I loved you?'

Lou drew in a sharp breath. 'I *expected* you to treat me with some respect,' she said in an arctic accent.

'I was being honest!' he protested.

'Oh, yes, you were honest, all right. You made your position crystal-clear. You think you can buy me the way you can buy all the other women in your life. Well, I may not have a lot of money, but I'm not for sale!'

Patrick struggled to control his temper, not very successfully. 'Listen, it was you who were so full of what a perfect wife you'd be and what a good thing it would be for you if you married me. It would be your fantasy, you said.'

'I can assure you that a proposal like that has *never* figured in a fantasy of mine,' said Lou, her voice still glacial. 'I've already been told by one husband that I'm not really the kind of wife he wanted,' she added bitterly. 'I can do without another husband thinking the same thing. And if you think I'm going to expose my children to the kind of attitude that treats young women as objects, and women over forty as past their sell-by date, you've got another think coming!

'Your mother's right,' she swept on, too consumed by hurt and anger to care about her job any more. 'You *are* selfish. You think that because you're rich, you can have whatever you want, and never have to give anything in return. Well, I'm sorry, but that's not a lesson I want Grace and Tom to learn. They've got few enough role models as it is, and I'm certainly not going to provide them with one of such monumental selfishness!'

'I never suggested not giving you anything in return,' Patrick ground out. 'I was proposing to give you quite a lot of money, if you remember.'

'I'm not talking about money,' said Lou contemptuously. 'I'm talking about feelings.'

'Oh, *feelings*!' he sneered.

'Yes, those things you don't have and the rest of us do. You go on and on about how your girlfriends hassle you about commitment, but have you ever thought what it's like for them to be with you and get their emotions thrown back in their faces all the time?'

'Listen, nobody's forcing them. If they don't want to go out with me, they can say no.'

'Yes, well, I'm saying no too,' said Lou. 'I want my children to believe that it's possible for adults to live together in a loving relationship. They're not stupid. They're not likely to find that very convincing if they saw you carrying on with your…*floozies*…and treating me as a house-keeper, only coming home whenever it suits you.'

Patrick raked his hands through his hair in frustration. 'You might want to think some time about exposing your children to the realities of life,' he bit out. 'All those romantic ideals aren't going to be much use to them when they get out into the big, bad world and realise that nothing is free. If you want anything, you have to work for it, one way or another. Why should marriage be any different?'

'Because unless it *is* different, there's no point in getting married!' Lou exploded. 'It shouldn't be about who gets what, it should be about sharing.'

Tears of sheer anger, and more than a little hurt, were perilously close. She turned for the door. 'I'm sorry if I gave you the wrong impression in Newcastle. I had hoped that you would be able to forget that conversation. I'll certainly try to forget this one,' she said in a freezing voice.

'If that's what you want,' said Patrick, equally icy.

'I'll let you have these letters to sign as soon as I've done them,' said Lou coolly and went out, closing the door carefully behind her.

As soon as she had gone, Patrick vented his feelings on his chair, something that hurt him a lot more than the chair. He couldn't believe that she had said no and walked out like that. Not once had he considered that she would turn him down. He was Patrick Farr and he always got what he wanted.

Until now.

He raged silently as he hopped around, nursing his sore foot. How dared Lou talk to him like that? He had offered her a solution to all her problems, and he would have been generous. Did she have any idea what she was giving up?

Well, if she didn't want to marry him, that was fine, he told himself. It was probably a good thing. He could have done without the last few humiliating minutes, but he'd be perfectly happy to carry on his life as before. *He* wasn't the one who had lost the chance to change his life. Oh, no, he wasn't going to be the one with the regrets.

'Mum, I need a new pair of trainers,' Tom greeted Lou when she picked him up that night.

Lou's heart sank. Tom was growing so fast. He seemed to need a new pair of trainers every few months, and they were always so expensive. They had to be the right brand and the right style and the right colour. In her day they had just had plimsolls. Whatever had happened to them?

'We'll get you some this weekend,' she promised.

'Cool. Can we go into town to where Charlie got his?'

Charlie was Tom's best friend and rival in everything. He was a nice boy, but Lou sometimes wished his parents didn't indulge him quite so much. But then she would feel guilty about being unfair. If she could afford it, she would probably want to do the same for Tom as Charlie's parents did for him.

'Charlie's going to a brilliant sports course in the summer,' Tom told her, hoisting his backpack onto his thin shoulders. 'You go off to this place for two weeks and they give you special coaching and you get to try a lot of new sports as well. Can I go?'

Lou looked down at his eager face and her heart twisted. The only thing Tom loved more than sport was cars, and fortunately he was still too young to indulge that particular taste. He would get so much out of a sports course like that, but it was bound to be expensive.

'We'll see, Tom,' she said and his face fell.

'It's not fair,' he said, scuffing his shoes along the pavement. 'Whenever you say, "We'll see", it means no. I'm just as good at football as Charlie, but he'll get extra coach-

ing and I'll be left behind. I probably won't even get in the
team next year,' he said bitterly.

There was worse to come when Grace danced in. She
had always been a volatile child, changing moods with be-
wildering speed. When she was happy, she was wonderful
company, but she could just as easily make life a misery
for everyone in the vicinity. The latter had been her preferred option since turning teenager with a vengeance, although there were still moments when Lou recognised the
enchanting child she had been when she was small.

'Mum, look!' she said breathlessly, waving a piece of
paper around. 'There's going to be a skiing trip to the
Rockies next year. *Please* say I can go!'

'Skiing?' Tom's face lit up. 'Can I go? I want to try
snowboarding.'

'It's not for your year, squirt,' said Grace, whipping the
paper out of his reach. 'What do you think, Mum?' she
added anxiously. 'Can I go?'

Lou's head was aching with tension after that row with
Patrick, and she had come home to find three bills and an
ominously worded letter from her bank suggesting that she
make an appointment to see her personal manager.

'Can I see what it says?'

Grace relinquished the piece of paper reluctantly. She
was too excited to sit still and kept jumping up and down
from the kitchen table. 'Emily went last year, and she was,
like, it was so excellent. They stayed in this log-cabin-type
place and went out every night and the snow was this high.'
She gestured up to her shoulder for Tom's benefit.

Lou listened to her chattering on, and tried to concentrate
on the details the school had sent out. She fastened at last
on the cost of the trip. As suspected, she couldn't even
afford the deposit as things stood at the moment.

She bit her lip. Grace was so excited, she couldn't bear

to disappoint her. And Tom deserved a chance at that course. She would have to see if Lawrie could help. He might be going through a flush period. You could never tell with Lawrie.

'Let me talk to your father,' she said.

'Oh, Mum, he won't do anything,' wailed Grace. 'He said he was going to take us to Greece this summer, but then he went and bought that stupid sports car, and now he says he can't afford to go anywhere.'

'It's a cool car,' said Tom loyally. 'It's an Audi Quattro coupé. He's got a personalised number plate too.'

Lou wanted to scream. A sports car! Why could Lawrie never think of his children first? Oh, there would be some plausible excuse. He would explain very patiently that he needed the car to project the right image for his new company, a company that would no doubt go the way of all the others Lawrie had lost interest in.

'Mum, Dad won't help,' said Grace bitterly. 'He never does. He'll say that he will, and then he won't.'

That just about summed Lawrie up.

Lou hated the look on her daughter's face. There wasn't anything she could do now about Lawrie's relationship with his children, but she wished he understood how much he hurt them whenever he let them down. Grace and Tom loved their father, but they had learnt not to rely on him.

Lou knew what that felt like.

She sighed. 'I'll see what I can do,' was all she could promise Grace, who slumped down at the kitchen table, her excitement evaporated.

Lawrie wasn't a bad man. He wasn't malicious or deliberately hurtful. He was intelligent and funny, and charm itself when it suited him, but he was also thoughtless and utterly self-centred. Lou didn't mind for herself any more, but she did mind for the children. It wasn't the life she had wanted to give them. She had tried so hard for so long to shield them from the consequences of their father's feckless attitude to life, but the reality was that Lawrie had chosen to leave them. He had chosen a new family, and there was nothing she could do to make that better for them.

They had lost their father and their home, and it hadn't been easy for either of them. Lou was doing her best. She loved them unconditionally, she comforted them when they were upset, she fed them and cared for them and encouraged them, and gave them the security and stability they didn't know they needed. She had been careful never to talk bitterly about Lawrie in front of them, great as the temptation was at times. It was Lou who rang him to remind him when their birthdays were, who suggested ways he could meet up with Grace and Tom, and who made sure they rang him regularly.

And she tried to give them as much fun as she could, although she was bitterly aware that a lot of the time she was too worn down by work and worry to give them as much of that as they needed. Lawrie was always good at fun, but Lawrie wasn't always there.

Lou ached for them sometimes. At times like now, knowing that she was going to end up disappointing them both, she would do anything to make things different for them.

About to lay aside the note Grace had given her, Lou stopped with her hand outstretched.

*Anything?*

Including marrying Patrick Farr?

She looked down at the note once more. Where else could she possibly find the extra money she'd need to send Grace on this holiday? And if Grace went skiing, Tom could go on his sports course…

At the kitchen table, Grace was slumped in a familiar posture, leaning on one arm, her dark curly hair hanging over her face. Lou could just see the tip of her nose as she traced despondent patterns on the tabletop with one finger. Opposite her, Tom had dropped his backpack on the floor and was crouched over it, tossing pens, bits of paper and chocolate wrappers carelessly aside as he rummaged through it. Probably *not* looking for his homework, judging by his enthusiasm.

As she watched them Lou felt the familiar clutch of love so intense it was almost painful. It was easy to say, 'I'd do anything for my kids', but was she prepared to do it?

Thoughtfully, she opened the fridge and took out some tomatoes. Pasta again tonight. It was cheap, cheerful and nutritious, but sometimes she got so sick of cooking it. She picked her way through Tom's discarded mess and removed the ironing basket so that she could get into the cupboard and find some oil. That was another thing about this flat. There was no room to put anything.

If she married Patrick, there would be plenty of room for them all to spread themselves. She thought about his six bedrooms. Perhaps if they weren't living on top of each other the way they were now, they wouldn't be so irritable with each other.

Outside, it was a beautiful summer evening, but it was hard to tell from in here, overshadowed as they were by the backs of the house behind them. The backyards in this area were dark and gloomy at the best of times, but at least if you had one you could step outside and look up at the sky.

Patrick probably had a garden, mused Lou. She could grow fresh herbs, and when she was making pasta like this she could go out and pick some basil, some oregano, maybe, or some parsley. She could stand with the herbs in her hand and smell the grass and feel the sun on her face.

All she had to do was marry Patrick.

*    *    *

Lou moistened her lips nervously. 'Could I have a word with you?'

Patrick had been in meetings most of the day, which was a relief in one way. The atmosphere that morning had been inevitably arctic, but Lou was desperate not to lose her nerve. Having made her decision, she hadn't got a chance to even raise the matter until Patrick had come back at five o'clock, which meant that she had spent the entire day dithering about what to say.

Daunted by his air of chilly reserve, Lou gave him his messages and made her request. It was now or never. She couldn't spend another night like the last one, tossing and turning in an agony of indecision.

Patrick looked at her properly for the first time that day, his eyes a glacial green. 'A word?'

'Well, a few words.' Lou took a deep breath. 'I...I wanted to apologise for the way I reacted yesterday,' she said. 'You made a fair offer. I just...wasn't expecting it, and I overreacted. I'm sorry.'

Something shifted in Patrick's expression. 'I'm the one who should be apologising to you,' he said gruffly. 'I didn't express myself well. When I thought about it afterwards, I wasn't surprised you were angry. So I'm sorry too.'

'The thing is...' Lou stopped, not sure how to ask if the offer was still open. She couldn't really blame Patrick if he had changed his mind after the fuss she had made.

'Look, why don't we start again?' said Patrick, coming to her rescue. 'But let's go somewhere we can talk properly, away from the office.' He looked at his watch. 'Do you have to go and pick up the children, or can you come and have a drink?'

Grace was going to do her homework with a friend, and Tom had football. 'A drink would be nice,' said Lou gratefully. She had a feeling she was going to need it.

Patrick glanced quickly through his messages. 'All of this can wait till tomorrow. Let's go now.'

Lou was very aware of him as they caught the lift down to the ground floor. He seemed guarded, which was fair enough after the way she'd spoken to him yesterday, but not as angry as she had expected. She wasn't sure what she was going to say. It seemed a colossal cheek to ask him to marry her after all—and without the benefit of a bucketload of champagne either.

Patrick took her to a quiet pub not far from the river. To Lou's delight it had a garden hidden away behind, with a couple of trees and some shrubs, and a few jolly geraniums in pots. They had beaten the rush-hour exodus and there was still a table.

'You sit there and make sure no one else gets it,' said Patrick, overbearing Lou's attempts to buy the drinks.

Closing her eyes and tipping her face to the sun, Lou felt some of the tension begin to seep out of her. It felt good to be outside, even in a crowded pub garden with the traffic roaring away at the front of the building. Of course, it would feel even better if she didn't have to ask her boss to marry her when he came back from the bar.

'Here you go.' Her eyes snapped open as Patrick set the drinks down on the table and sat opposite her on the bench. He had left his jacket in the office and was in shirtsleeves, rolled up to his wrists.

The sight of him was giving Lou curious flutters inside, and it was difficult to know whether they were caused by nerves or a much more primitive attraction. Either way, they had left her in the grip of a paralysing shyness, and she sipped her gin and tonic nervously, trying desperately to think of a way to start.

She couldn't do it. There was no way she could calmly

ask Patrick if she could change her mind about marrying him, after everything she had had to say yesterday about not being the kind of woman who would marry for money. No way. She must have been mad to have even considered it.

She would pretend she wanted to talk about her overtime, Lou decided.

But then she remembered Grace's face, lit up with excitement at the thought of a skiing holiday, of going somewhere different and doing something different and meeting different people. And she remembered the way Tom's shoulders had slumped when she had said, 'We'll see.'

She thought about the cramped flat where sometimes it felt hard to breathe, and where the neighbours conducted their arguments at the tops of their voices so that Grace and Tom knew more than they ought to about the most intimate details of married life.

And then she thought about being married to Patrick and her insides squirmed and fluttered and generally made it impossible to get to grips with anything else.

The silence stretched uncomfortably. Lou's eyes wandered desperately around the garden, but she was very conscious of Patrick sitting opposite her. With his shirtsleeves rolled up, she could see his forearms, browner than usual after a week in the Maldives, and her gaze kept snagging on the fine hairs at his wrist and the strong, square hands playing with his glass.

Patrick was nervous too, she realised slowly. It gave her the confidence to launch into speech.

'I've been thinking—'

She began just as Patrick said, 'I probably shouldn't say this, but—'

They both stopped, feeling foolish.

'You first,' he said awkwardly.

Lou squared her shoulders and took a breath. Just do it. 'Look, you were honest with me yesterday, so I might as well be the same today. I was furious when you made that proposal, but I thought about it a lot last night and I was wondering…well, if it was too late to change my mind.'

There, it was done.

Patrick had spent the previous night trying to convince himself that he had had a lucky escape. The whole idea had been ridiculous, and if he hadn't had such an awful holiday he would probably never have considered it. What if Lou had accepted him? He would have been saddled with two adolescent stepchildren and a middle-aged wife. Madness.

So the rush of relief he felt at her words didn't make much sense. He was still raw with hurt and humiliation at her flat rejection—*a man I don't even like*, she had told him—mingled with guilt at the botched way he had handled things. He had hurt Lou, too, and it wasn't a nice feeling.

He drank his beer carefully. 'What made you change your mind?'

'Money,' said Lou bleakly. She told him about the skiing trip and Tom's sports course. 'I'm tired of struggling and disappointing the kids. Yesterday you offered me a chance to change that.'

She hesitated. 'I know I had a lot to say about not being the kind of person who married for money, but maybe I am that person. Maybe I have to be. I've tried marrying for love, and that didn't work out, so this time perhaps I should think about marrying for a different reason, for my children. That may be the right thing to do.'

'You don't sound that convinced,' commented Patrick, his eyes still guarded.

'I'm not entirely convinced,' Lou admitted. 'That's really

what I wanted to talk to you about. I wanted to ask you if I could think about it a bit. I can't decide anything until Grace and Tom have met you, and you've met them.' She managed a feeble smile. 'You might change *your* mind then!'

Patrick's expression was unreadable, but at least he wasn't shouting at her or carrying on the way she had carried on when he had made *his* proposal. Lou ploughed on.

'I was wondering if we could keep our options open,' she said. 'Perhaps we could have lunch or something together, and then see if we think it could still work?' She swallowed. 'We might decide to forget the whole idea, or we might decide it could work after all, in which case we could talk about what we would both expect out of a marriage like that.'

'That makes sense,' said Patrick. A lot more sense than springing the idea on her, tossing down a proposal and demanding an immediate answer. It was what he should have suggested in the first place. 'All right, let's do it that way.'

For the first time a smile touched the corners of his mouth. 'What are you doing this weekend? Why don't you bring them to lunch on Sunday? It would give you all a chance to see where you could be living if nothing else.' He hesitated. 'I've got to say that I've got no experience of entertaining children of that age, but there's a pool if they like swimming. They just need to bring their things.'

By Sunday, Lou had talked herself in and out of the idea so many times that she didn't know *what* she thought any more. But it was too late to back out of lunch, so they would all go. She had this idea that if she could just see Patrick with the children, she would know what to do.

It was hard to imagine them getting on, though. Patrick

had no interest in children, and Grace and Tom would make it very clear if they didn't like him. Lou foresaw a disastrous lunch.

Well, if it was a disaster, her decision would be made, she decided resolutely. She would just tell Patrick that marriage wouldn't work, and she would find some other way to send Grace skiing. And Tom would get his sports course as well.

She would do it. Somehow.

But she would try Patrick's option first.

# CHAPTER SIX

PATRICK lived in a quiet street in Chelsea that positively smelled of money. Lou felt as if, somewhere between there and the tube, they had wandered into a parallel universe that had no relation whatsoever to the busy road in Tooting where they lived. She had known Patrick was wealthy, of course, but this was the first time she had come face to face with the reality of how different his life was from hers.

It felt very uncomfortable. This was a street peopled by different beings and the three of them didn't belong here. It had been a mistake to come.

Lou had done her best to make the children presentable, but she wasn't sure that Patrick would appreciate the chains looped around Grace's waist or her enormous clumpy boots. Her curly hair, inherited from her father, was a mess. Lou's fingers itched for a comb, but Grace had absolutely refused to brush it. She was going through a Goth phase, and she considered that she had made enough concessions by not wearing black lipstick.

Tom was less trendy, but no more neat. Lou was resigned to that by now. He was one of those boys that you could send out of the door looking well scrubbed and immaculate, and by the time he was at the end of the street his hair would be sticking up in tufts, his top would have parted company with his trousers and his shoelaces would be undone.

Today he was wearing scruffy trainers, saggy jeans and a T-shirt that had been clean when they'd left the house, but which had mysteriously acquired a dirty mark somewhere along the line, probably when he'd been messing around on the underground escalators.

Only the promise of a swim in a private pool had re-signed the children to a boring lunch, but they were clearly impressed by the wealth that practically oozed out of the front doors of these houses. There were no terraced houses here. No flats, no shops, no take-aways or minicab firms. Each house stood in its own grounds, partially hidden by high hedges, so that you just caught the odd glimpse of the luxury within through the gates.

Tom's steps slowed down as they passed each entrance, straining to get a look at the cars parked on the crisp gravel. 'Wow, look at that!' he said, offering a running commentary of the vehicles on display as he craned his neck to see through the gates. 'BMW…Mercedes…Mercedes…Rolls Royce…Porsche…Jaguar…'

'Your boss must be rolling in it if he lives here,' said Grace.

Lou didn't answer. She felt slightly sick, and her nerve was rapidly deserting her. It was all very well wanting financial security, but this kind of wealth was just obscene. She couldn't possibly marry Patrick. It would never work. She was much too old to play Cinderella.

'Is this it?' Grace had stopped and was staring at a house set back from the road, her voiced awed.

Lou dug out the address and checked the number. 'Thirty-three…yes, it looks like this is it.' She swallowed as she looked at the house. 'Gosh.'

Joining her daughter at the iron gates, she peered through at a large, handsome house with large windows, its cream stucco front softened by a wonderful climbing hydrangea. A sweep of gravel led up to the imposing front door, and the front garden had been cleverly planted to keep the house as private as possible without overshadowing it.

Tom trailed up and the three of them stood there looking at it, their hands on the railings of the gate, like prisoners staring longingly at the outside world.

'Mum…' Tom drew a deep breath of wonderment. 'Mum, is that his car?'

Lou hadn't even noticed the car sitting in front of the house. 'Er…maybe. I don't know,' she said nervously.

'How do we get in?' said Grace more practically.

There was an intercom on the massive gate post. Lou pressed the button, half expecting some venerable butler to answer. Or more likely a beefy security guard complete with snarling Rottweiler. But it was Patrick's voice that emerged from the speaker, crisp and unmistakable.

'It's me,' she said weakly. 'Lou. We're here.'

'Good,' he said. 'Come on in.'

The great gates swung open, and they slipped through, unnerved by how quickly the gates began to close behind them. 'It's like being in a prison,' whispered Grace as they headed towards the front door, their shoes crunching on the gravel, the sound unnaturally loud in the silence.

Ahead of them, the front door opened and suddenly Patrick was there, wearing chinos and a blue shirt open at the collar, but looking as formidable as ever in spite of his casual clothes.

For some reason, Lou was finding it hard to breathe properly. 'Hi,' she said in a stupid high voice, and felt Grace flick a surprised glance in her direction.

'Hello. Glad you could make it.' To her annoyance Patrick sounded exactly the same as usual. Shouldn't he be nervous too at the prospect of meeting her children? He might have seemed a little bit more effusive, or looked as if he was trying too hard. But no. He was just the way he always was, faintly brusque and to the point.

Clearing her throat, Lou put an arm round Grace. 'This is my daughter, Grace.'

Patrick and Grace sized each other up. At first all Patrick saw was a young girl with messy hair, dressed alarmingly in Goth gear, but when he looked closer he could see that she had an enchantingly pretty face, a very stubborn chin, and her mother's dark, direct eyes.

For her part, Grace saw a tall man in boring, conventional clothes, but she couldn't dismiss him the way she really wanted to. There was something uncompromising about him, a coolness to his eyes and a set to his mouth that indicated that he wasn't someone to mess with. Also, he wasn't trying to impress her, which she liked.

'Hello, Grace,' he said.

'Hi,' she said warily.

Lou let out a breath she hadn't realised she'd been holding. It might not sound like much of an exchange, but Grace was liable to take violent dislike to people on sight, often on the flimsiest of grounds—I didn't like his shoes, I didn't like the way she smiled at me, that sniff really annoyed me.

'And this—'

She stopped, realising for the first time that Tom wasn't by her side. Turning, she saw to her horror that her son had gravitated towards the car and had his nose squashed up against the driver's window, grubby hands pressed into the immaculate paintwork, oblivious to the greetings taking place at the door.

'Tom!' she said, aghast. 'What do you think you're doing? Come here at once.'

Tom didn't even turn round. 'Mum, do you know what this is?' he said reverently. 'It's a *Porsche 911*! Twin turbo!'

'I dare say,' said Lou, a distinct edge to her voice now. 'But leave it now and come and meet Patrick. *Now*, Tom.'

Tom glanced over his shoulder at that. 'But, Mum, you don't understand! This is *the best car in the world*!'

Lou looked helplessly at Patrick. 'I'm terribly sorry. He loves cars.'

'I can see.' Patrick went over to join Tom at the Porsche, surprised but pleased to discover a kindred spirit at last, even in the unlikely form of Lou's eleven-year-old son. He loved that car, but he never seemed to meet anyone else who understood how beautiful it was.

Women just didn't get it. They might like the idea of a sports car, but in Patrick's experience they didn't have a clue what made it really special. He had given up talking to them about cars. He was pretty sure, for instance, that if he asked Lou what kind of car she liked she would reply something annoying like 'one that goes' or 'a red one' as his sisters did.

'You're right,' he said to Tom. 'It *is* the best car in the world. Do you want to get in the driver's seat?'

Tom's eyes shone. 'Could I?' he breathed.

Patrick fished his key out of his pocket and pressed a button that sent the soft top sliding smoothly back as Tom opened the driver's door with the kind of awe usually reserved for cathedrals. Delighted at the chance to show off his car to someone who would really appreciate it, Patrick got in beside him, and soon the two heads were bent together over the dashboard.

Lou and Grace stood on the front steps, and listened as snatches of animated conversation about spoilers and revs per minute and six-speed manual gearboxes floated across the gravel.

Lou looked at Grace and Grace looked at Lou.

'We'll never get lunch now,' sighed Grace. 'You know what Tom's like.'

Lou went over to the car. 'We'll go in and make ourselves at home, shall we?' she suggested pleasantly.

The startled pause that followed made it pretty clear that Patrick had forgotten all about the two of them left stranded on the steps.

'Oh, yes, yes…do you mind?' he said, wrenching his attention from the dashboard with an effort. 'I'll just show Tom the engine. We'll just be a minute…'

It was clearly going to be a very long minute. Lou and Grace left them to it. Inside, there was a vast hall with a grand staircase leading up to a landing, and doors opening off it. Lou was dying to explore, but she didn't want to seem too nosy, so they followed the light through to the back of the house where an enormous, elegant conservatory housed a gleaming turquoise pool.

'Wow,' said Grace.

Quite.

A glass door led onto a sunny terrace straight out of *Homes and Gardens You'll Never in a Million Years Be Able to Afford*. Grace sat at the table under a classy cream parasol and tried desperately not to look too impressed, while Lou wandered round the garden, too jittery to sit still. It had been cleverly designed on a green and white theme. Elegant, Lou decided, but lacking in heart somehow. Personally she liked a bit more colour and chaos in a garden.

She was absently dead-heading some busy lizzies—white, of course—when Patrick and Tom eventually appeared, having clearly bonded without bothering with any introductions.

'I'm sorry about that.' At least Patrick had the grace to

sound a bit embarrassed at how long they had been. 'We got a bit carried away.'

Tom's face was glowing, not embarrassed at all. 'You should go and have a look, Mum,' he said eagerly. 'It's, like, a dream car! Patrick let me have a go with the gears. It's got *six*, and four-wheel drive, and guess what its top speed is?'

'Pretty fast, I should think.'

'A hundred and eight-nine miles per hour!'

'That's handy,' said Lou, wondering what was the point of a car that went at a hundred and eighty-nine miles an hour when the speed limit was seventy.

Grace was equally unimpressed, having heard her brother go on for hours about cars before. She let her elbow slip off the table and mimed falling asleep with boredom, but Tom wasn't to be deflated.

'It can go from nought to sixty-two miles an hour in four point two seconds,' he told his mother in a reverent tone, ignoring his sister. 'And when you're going really fast, these spoilers fold out and that gives you extra stability.'

'Spoilers? Really?' Lou didn't have a clue what her son was talking about, but she loved watching his face when he was lit up with enthusiasm like this. 'Jolly good.'

Patrick grinned at her expression. 'What's the betting your mother doesn't know what a spoiler is, Tom?'

'It's a kind of wing, Mum,' Tom explained kindly. 'It's sort of upside down. It folds out and keeps the car steady at speed. Patrick showed me. It's like the opposite of planes, isn't it, Patrick?' He was struggling a bit, obviously dying to show off his new knowledge but not that confident. 'You tell Mum,' he said to Patrick.

'Tom's right. Planes have wings designed to give them up force,' said Patrick obediently. 'On a high-performance car the wing is the other way, to keep them grounded. They generate so much force that you could drive a Formula One car upside down on a ceiling at two hundred miles an hour.'

Tom nodded eagerly. 'Can you imagine it?'

Frankly, Lou couldn't. Why would anyone want to drive upside down in the first place? Still, she appreciated that wasn't really the point.

'Wow,' she said dutifully, and then caught Patrick's eye. He was smiling, and looking so much more relaxed than she had ever seen him that she felt oddly hollow inside.

'I didn't realise that you were a petrol head too,' she said lightly to cover the sudden stumble of her heart.

'My mother always complained that cars were my only passion,' said Patrick cheerfully.

'I suppose they're less demanding than women,' said Lou in a dry voice, and he flashed a look at her.

'Exactly. I don't often meet anyone else who feels like I do about them, though. Tom knows a lot about cars,' he said, sounding genuinely impressed, and Lou felt herself flush with pleasure.

'He gets that from his father. Lawrie's mad about cars too.'

'Wait till I tell him I've been in a Porsche 911!' said Tom. 'He'll be really jealous.'

Much more jealous than he would be to hear that she was thinking of getting remarried, Lou couldn't help thinking.

'What about a drink?' said Patrick. 'Then we can have lunch. It's cold, so we just need to put it on the table.'

'Have you been slaving away in the kitchen all weekend?'

'My housekeeper has,' he admitted. 'She left it all for me yesterday.'

They ate in the kitchen, a bright, sunny room opening

out onto the terrace. Patrick said the dining room was too gloomy. 'I only use it for formal dinners.'

His housekeeper lived out, he told them, but had come in specially on Saturday to prepare the lunch, and she had done them proud, with a very simple but delicious spread.

'It must get a bit lonely rattling around in this great big house on your own, doesn't it?' said Lou, looking around her and calculating that they could probably fit their current flat into Patrick's kitchen alone.

'Only occasionally,' said Patrick. 'I'm out a lot.'

Ah, yes, with all those leggy blondes. Not a subject Lou wanted to raise in front of the children.

Fortunately Grace changed the conversation by asking Patrick if he had ever been skiing. 'I saw those photos of mountains in your loo,' she explained, and was soon telling him all about the trip she was so eager to go on, her sullen Goth pose quite forgotten.

'I wish I could go too,' said Tom enviously. 'Charlie's been snowboarding. He says it's really cool.'

'It sounds a great way to start,' Patrick said to Grace. 'When are you going?'

Grace's face closed as she remembered. 'I might not go at all,' she muttered. 'It's quite expensive. Mum's going to see what she can do, though.'

Patrick glanced across the table at Lou, who met his eyes for a moment before looking away. 'Could I have some more of that delicious salmon?' she said.

So that was why she had changed her mind, he thought, passing her the dish. Marrying him must have seemed the only way she could ever afford to send Grace on the trip she wanted so much.

It wasn't as if he hadn't known she would only consider marrying him for his money, Patrick reminded himself, puzzled by the slight pang he felt. Nobody could say she hadn't been honest with him. And that was what he wanted too. He didn't want a wife who would marry him because she loved him. That would just end in tears, the way all his other relationships did. He wanted it to be different with Lou.

There was something unfamiliar about her today. Patrick couldn't work out what it was until belatedly he realised that it was the first time he had seen her without one of her prim little suits she wore to work. Instead she had on cool linen trousers and a silky sleeveless top, with silver bangles on her wrist and silver drops hanging from her ears. She looked casual, but cool and elegant, and Patrick enjoyed the contrasting picture she made to her children, Grace with her outrageous outfit and wary charm, and Tom, hair standing up on end, still elated by encountering the car of his dreams.

The children lobbied for a swim after lunch. Lou's eyes followed Patrick as he led Grace and Tom off and showed them where they could change. It was very strange seeing the three of them together. Strange, too, to remember how nervous she had been about how they would get on. They all seemed fine, Lou thought. Bang went that excuse for not marrying him.

And now she had seen him with the children, she wasn't sure she wanted an excuse any more.

When Patrick came back, she was clearing away the lunch dishes.

'Leave all that,' he said. 'You go and sit in the garden. I'll bring you coffee.'

There was no doubt that it was nice to be looked after. Lou protested but Patrick was insistent, and in the end she wandered back out to the terrace as instructed. She paused for a moment to watch Tom and Grace splashing excitedly in the pool, then sat at the table with a little sigh. It was a perfect temperature under the parasol, with a soft breeze just ruffling the leaves, which fractured the sunlight. The whole garden seemed to sway with splashes of light and shade.

Lou watched a butterfly hovering by a white buddleia and breathed in the scent of the roses growing up the wall behind her. It was so quiet and peaceful here, the silence broken only by the shrieks from the pool. Incredible to think that they were right in the centre of London.

It would be easy to get used to this. Dangerously easy.

'What do you think of the garden?' Patrick asked, setting the coffee tray down on the table.

'It's lovely,' said Lou, looking around her.

A subtle change seemed to come over her when she was surrounded by plants, almost like a slackening of tension. Patrick had noticed it before, when he had come out of the bar and seen her sitting in the pub garden, her eyes closed and her face tipped back as she'd breathed in the scent of growing things, her mouth curved with pleasure.

He liked that about her, the way every now and then he got a glimpse of the secret, sensuous Lou who hid behind the practical façade and the prim suits and the cool, ironic gaze.

'I'm glad you said that,' he said, pouring out the coffee. 'I spent a fortune having it redesigned a couple of years ago.'

'It shows,' said Lou.

'Ouch,' said Patrick wryly. 'That wasn't the idea.'

'No, honestly, it's beautiful,' she said, trying to explain. 'It's just a bit too perfect for me, that's all.'

'Too perfect? That's a new one on me.'

'Well, you can tell that it's a garden that's been designed. It hasn't grown up gradually. It's not full of cuttings your neighbour has given you, or plants that have just put themselves in and are so determined to flower that you haven't got the heart to dig them up, even if they do clash with everything else.'

Lou gestured at the immaculate garden. 'There's no campanula running riot because you put it in without thinking a few years ago and it's now out of control.' A terrible thug in the garden, Fenny always said about campanula. 'I suppose it just doesn't seem like a garden that's loved,' she finished lamely.

Patrick looked at her curiously. She was always surprising him nowadays. 'I thought you would have liked everything neat and orderly, the way you keep things in the office.'

'No.' There was a pot of exquisite white lavender beside her, and Lou pulled a stem through her fingers. 'I like order in my life, but not in my gardens.' Lifting her hand to her nose, she sniffed the wonderful lavender fragrance. 'My perfect garden would be all jumbly and colourful, with plants tumbling everywhere, and thick with scent on a summer night...' She sighed wistfully, just thinking about it. One day...

'You're a romantic,' Patrick discovered, amused. 'I never had you down as one of those!'

Lou's face closed as she thought of Lawrie. 'I used to be. I'm not a romantic any more, though. You tend to lose your faith in romance when you've been through a divorce.'

'What happened?' asked Patrick, and then paused, wondering if he'd been tactless. 'Sorry, it's not my business.'

'No, it's OK.' He had told her why his marriage to Catriona had broken down, after all. 'If we're going to get married, it probably is your business anyway.'

Lou sipped her coffee, her eyes on the sunlight wavering

through the trees. 'It wasn't all a disaster. For a long time, we were really happy. I was happy, anyway.' She sighed a little. 'I was a real romantic then. I used to think that if you loved each other enough, nothing could go wrong, and I couldn't have loved Lawrie more. I loved him from the first moment I laid eyes on him.'

'Love at first sight?' Patrick looked sceptical. Lou wasn't surprised. Patrick was never going to be a love-at-first-sight kind of guy.

'I didn't believe in it either,' she said. 'Until it happened to me. One look, and I was lost. I'd never met anyone like Lawrie before. He was so good-looking and funny and he had charm oozing from every pore. I couldn't believe he'd look at a nice, sensible girl like me. He made me feel... wonderful...alive...*exciting*. He made me feel like I wasn't such a nice, sensible girl after all.'

Her eyes were alight with memories, her face soft and warm, and she smiled in spite of herself at the memory of those heady days.

Watching her, Patrick felt something stir inside him. Had he ever been able to make a woman glow like that, just thinking about him? It was a disquieting thought and he frowned down at his coffee.

'Of course, if I'd really been a sensible girl, I would never have married him,' Lou was saying. 'Being with Lawrie was like being on a roller coaster. One minute you were having the best fun you'd ever had, and the next you were in despair. He wouldn't call, he wouldn't turn up when he said he would, he'd be adoring you one minute and chatting up some other girl the next...'

She made a face remembering those bad times. 'Fenny said that I was mad to marry him, but I was besotted. It wasn't that I couldn't see Lawrie's faults, but none of them mattered against the fact that just being near him gave me the biggest thrill I'd ever known.'

'So what changed?' asked Patrick, vaguely disgruntled by all this. He was beginning to wish that he hadn't asked.

'I did.' A little of the warmth faded from Lou's face. 'It was great until Grace was born, but you have to think differently when you've got a baby to look after. You can't both be irresponsible and free spirits. Babies don't need excitement and romance, they need security and a routine, and Lawrie wasn't good at either of those. He didn't like feeling tied down by responsibility, and I didn't like not being able to count on him when it mattered.

'I could deal with it when it was just me,' she said. 'His unreliability was part of his charm, I suppose, but what made him fun and unpredictable as a lover was less endearing as a father. There were so many times when the children waited for him and he didn't turn up when he said he would, or looked forward to some treat he'd promised, which he changed his mind about at the last minute.'

'Disappointing for them,' said Patrick, thinking that Lawrie sounded a jerk. Why had Lou stuck with him for so long? She must have loved him a lot.

'Yes, nearly as disappointing as discovering that your husband has borrowed against the house to finance some wild scheme that's gone bust, so you've lost your home,' said Lou, her voice dusty dry. 'Or even being told that you're so boring and wrapped up in domesticity that he's decided to trade you in for a younger and more exciting model.'

'Why did you stay with him for so long?' demanded Patrick, angry for some reason.

'Because of the children. And because I loved him.'

'Are you still in love with him?'

Lou glanced at him, surprised at the harshness in his

voice. Patrick was surprised by it too. He hadn't meant to ask her that, but the question was out before he could stop it.

'I guess that isn't my business either,' he said.

*Did* she still love Lawrie? Lou twisted her coffee-cup in its saucer.

'I think part of me will always love him,' she said slowly. 'I can't imagine ever loving anyone else that deeply, and I don't want to. Lawrie hurt me so much in the end. I couldn't go through that again. I just couldn't,' she said. 'I'll never fall in love again. Not like that.'

She risked another glance at Patrick. He was looking a bit grim. Probably dreading an outburst of emotion.

'That's the only reason I could think about marrying you,' she told him. 'Knowing that you wouldn't expect me to love you, or even want me to.'

'No.' Patrick could hear the edge of doubt in his own voice, and he frowned. Where had that come from? 'No, I wouldn't,' he said more firmly. A bit too firmly, in fact. Almost as if he were protesting too much.

Fortunately Lou didn't seem to notice. 'And I wouldn't expect you to be faithful,' she said. 'I know you'd have other relationships, and I would accept that, of course.' She hesitated a little. 'The only thing is that I wouldn't want the children exposed to that fact. All I'd ask is that you were as discreet as you could be, and that you didn't bring any girlfriends back to the house if we were there.'

When she put it like that, the idea of carrying on a relationship when he was married to her sounded degrading somehow. Patrick shifted uncomfortably. Maybe it was a bit degrading. He hadn't really thought about how it would work in practice. He had just been determined to avoid emotional entanglements and keep all his options open. Wasn't that the whole point of marrying Lou?

But he certainly didn't want to hurt or humiliate her. How could she think that he would be that crass?

'I don't have a problem with that,' he said gruffly. 'I won't bring anyone back, I promise.'

'It looks like you might be able to have that fantasy of yours after all, then,' said Lou.

'Does this mean you're thinking about marrying me after all?'

She bit her lip. 'If you still want to.'

'Hey, you've just offered me my fantasy. How could I not want to?'

'Well, when you put it like that...' Lou tried to smile, but it didn't quite come off.

'The point is, do *you* want to?' said Patrick.

'I'm just worried about Grace and Tom. You were pretty clear that you weren't interested in being a stepfather, and I wouldn't be able to go through with it if I thought that you would resent them.'

'I wouldn't resent them,' said Patrick. 'I'd never thought about having kids around, that's all. But now that I've met them, I feel different. I didn't think I'd like them, to be honest, but I do.'

'You're not just saying that because Tom admired your car?'

He half smiled. 'No, it's not that.' He thought about it for a bit. 'I suppose they were just complications before, but now they're individuals. I can see now how important they are to you. I think I understand more why you'd be prepared to do this.'

They listened for a moment to the sound of Grace and Tom in the pool. There seemed to be a lot of shouting and splashing going on, thought Lou. They were obviously having a great time. When they had to entertain themselves and forgot to fight, the two of them got on very well.

'I don't suppose I would be a very touchy-feely stepfather,' Patrick said, 'but I would do my best. You want Grace to go skiing, don't you?'

'Yes,' said Lou in a low voice.

'She can go if you marry me. I can take Tom snowboarding if he wants to have a go at that. You can give them all the opportunities you want.' He paused. 'You could have your fantasy too, Lou. You wouldn't have to worry about things on your own any more. You'd have someone to talk to at the end of the day. You'd even have someone to hold you, if that was what you needed.'

Lou had been listening quietly, but her eyes jerked to his at that.

'As a friend,' Patrick clarified quickly. 'You've been frank about how you're not going to love me. Well, I won't love you either. We won't complicate things with sex.'

And it *would* be a complication, he thought. A quite unnecessary one too. Much better to put the whole idea out of his mind completely.

'We'd be partners,' he assured her. 'Friends rather than man and wife in the usual sense. We've got a chance here to make both our fantasies come true, Lou,' he said gently.

There was a pause. Lou watched a bee zooming over the thyme and thought about what Patrick had said. It all seemed to make such perfect sense when he talked like that. Why was she hesitating? Surely it couldn't be the way he had assured her that he wouldn't love her?

'Lou, I made a real mess of this before,' said Patrick after a while. 'Can I ask you again now?'

She nodded, her mind made up. 'Yes, ask me again.'

'Will you marry me, Lou?'

Lou took a breath and looked straight into his grey-green eyes. 'Yes,' she said. 'I will.'

# CHAPTER SEVEN

THERE was an awkward pause as they looked at each other uncertainly. If they were a real couple, they would fall into each other's arms at this point, but clearly a passionate kiss wasn't appropriate in their case.

'We could shake hands on the deal,' Patrick suggested, making a joke of it. 'But it does seem a bit businesslike. I think we should kiss, don't you?'

Lou's heart did an alarming somersault at the very thought. 'Kiss?' she echoed, horrified at how squeaky her voice sounded.

'We may not be going to be lovers, but I hope we can be friends,' he said.

Right. A kiss between friends. That was all he meant. *Right.* Calm down, Lou told her still-stuttering heart and firmly squashed a sneaky and quite irrational sense of disappointment. Friends, that was fine. She could do friends. She had been very clear that that was all she wanted, and she was glad that Patrick had got the message.

Very glad. Of course.

She cleared her throat to get rid of that ridiculous squeakiness. 'Sounds good to me,' she said, super casual.

'Good,' said Patrick, and leant across the table to kiss her on the cheek.

Lou had a dizzying sense of his nearness, and a sudden terrifying desire to turn her head and kiss him back, but it was over in a moment, and he was sitting back with a smile.

'Good,' he said again, looking across the table at Lou, and his smile widened. She looked somehow right, sitting

109

there in his garden. He liked the idea that there would be other days when he would come home and find her here. The girls might come and go, but Lou would always be there. It was a good thought, and Patrick beamed with satisfaction. Everything was working out perfectly.

'Let's get married soon,' he said.

Lou swallowed nervously and decided to take the plunge. 'I want to talk to you both,' she said as she ladled baked beans onto toast. They had had such a good lunch that she thought she could get away with a Sunday-night snack.

'Baked beans? Great!' Tom sat up in his chair. 'My favourite,' he said excitedly, and Lou smiled in spite of her nerves. There had to be something to be said for a child whose tastes ranged from a car that even second-hand cost as much as a house to beans on toast.

'I hate beans,' said Grace, but she picked up her knife and fork anyway.

'There's something I want to say,' Lou began again as they started eating.

She couldn't face anything herself. She was too churned up at the decision she had made, and anxious about how the children would react.

Not to mention appalled at how shaky a mere kiss on the cheek had made her feel.

Patrick had suggested that they tell the children when they finally dragged them out of the pool, but Lou had wanted to do it on her own. So he had driven them home instead, putting the seal on Tom's day by letting him sit in the front passenger seat and play with all the buttons.

'Dad's got a sports car too,' he told Patrick. 'But it's not as good as this.'

The two of them talked cars while Lou and Grace were squeezed into the back seat. Sitting behind Tom, Lou found her eyes resting on Patrick's profile, on the strong neck and the line of his jaw and the sudden gleam of his smile that made her heart clench uncomfortably.

She had said that she would marry him.

She was going to *marry* him.

What had she let herself in for?

Panic, elation, terror and a weird kind of excitement churned around inside her at the thought, and she hardly noticed the drive across London until Patrick drew up outside the flat. Tom must have directed him.

It seemed unlikely that the neighbourhood had ever seen a car like this. 'I'd ask you up, but I don't think you should leave the car here,' Lou said nervously.

Patrick merely laughed. 'I'll see you tomorrow,' he said, and then he drove back to his fabulous house and his garden and his pool and Lou was left to make beans on toast.

'Earth to Planet Lou!' Grace waved a hand in front of her face. 'Wake up, Mum! You're weirding us out here.'

Weirding them out? Where did they get these expressions?

'Sorry.' Lou pulled herself together. 'Yes. So.' She cleared her throat. 'Um…did you enjoy today?'

'It was cool,' said Tom. 'I can't believe he's got a Porsche 911! I liked the pool too.'

'Yeah, the pool was great,' said Grace.

'And did you see that television?' Tom put in, and launched into a description of all its technical features before Lou cut him off.

'Forget about his things,' she said sharply. 'What about Patrick? Did you like him?'

Tom offered the ultimate accolade. 'He was really cool.'

Typically, Grace was less enthusiastic. 'He was OK,' she offered grudgingly. 'At least he didn't talk to us like we were children.'

Instead of the grown-ups they were at fourteen and eleven. Lucky Patrick had avoided that elementary error.

Still, he hadn't done badly to merit an OK. That was high praise from Grace.

'Well, I'm glad you liked him,' said Lou, squaring up to the challenge at last. 'That's what I want to talk to you about, actually. The thing is, Patrick and I are thinking of getting married.'

Lou often read about children wisely picking up on adult signals, but if she had hoped for a cosy admission from either of them that they had secretly suspected that Patrick was madly in love with her, she was due for a disappointment. Grace and Tom were dumbfounded.

They stared at her, their beans forgotten. 'You're kidding!'

'Er…no, I'm not, actually.'

'You mean *Patrick's* in love with *you*?' There was no mistaking the incredulity in Grace's voice. Lou couldn't blame her.

'No,' she said. She wanted to be honest with them. They deserved that at least. 'No, he isn't. And I'm not in love with him.'

At least she hoped she wasn't. She had certainly reacted very strangely to a little peck on the cheek. It might be a smidgeon of lust, perhaps, but love? No. She wasn't falling in love again. She had told Patrick that.

Lou paused, wondering how best to explain. 'Patrick and I aren't in love with each other, but we are friends, and we respect each other, and those things mean a good deal in a marriage. Ideally, we would love each other as well, but sometimes two out of three is good enough. I think we can have a strong, honest relationship.'

She was just confusing them, Lou could see. 'Look, if you don't like the idea, I won't marry him,' she tried to reassure them. 'Patrick knows that. The important thing is

that the three of us are a family. We'd still be a family if
I married Patrick, though. He'd just be there as well.'

'Would we still see Dad?' asked Tom anxiously.

'Of course you would. Patrick wouldn't try and be your
father. He knows you've got your own dad. And it's not
as if everything would change. You'd still go to the same
school. We just wouldn't live here any more.'

'You mean we'd live in that house with a pool *all the
time*?' Tom's eyes were huge.

'Well, yes, probably.'

Grace sat up straighter. 'Could I have my own room?'

'Yes, you could.'

'And go on that skiing trip?'

'Yes,' said Lou. 'You can go skiing.'

Grace looked at her mother for a long moment, and then
she smiled. 'Thanks, Mum,' she said, and for some reason
Lou felt tears prick her eyes.

'I know it will mean a big change for both of you,' she
said, blinking them back fiercely. 'But nothing's going to
change about *us*, I promise you. I know I've rather sprung
this on you, and it may take you a bit of time to get used
to the idea, but—'

'It's cool, Mum,' Tom interrupted her kindly. 'I don't
want to be mean, but Patrick's house is a lot nicer than
this. Living there will be better than living here, won't it?'

Lou looked around the poky kitchen, where the three of
them were squeezed around the table. Upstairs, feet
clomped across the ceiling, and the television blared from
next door. Whenever she wondered if she'd made the right
decision, she needed to remember this.

'Yes,' she said. 'It will.'

Lou stood on top of the hill and lifted her face to the wind.
It was the end of July, mid-summer, but here high in the

Yorkshire Dales there was little sign of it. Grey clouds scudded across the sky, bringing the occasional splatter of rain, and the wind had a distinct chill to it.

Patrick poured coffee into the lid of a flask and handed it to her. Taking it, Lou sat next to him on a rocky outcrop and cradled the mug between her hands as she gazed down at the village below. She could see the river, the huddle of grey stone cottages around the sturdy church. Across the valley, half hidden in trees, was the hotel where they would be married the next day.

It had been a busy couple of months. Lou had thought it would be too difficult to carry on working for Patrick once they were married, so she had recruited a new PA for him and handed the office over in perfect order, not without a pang or two. She had plans to do a garden design course eventually, but it was sad leaving behind the people at Schola Systems who had been friends and colleagues for so long.

She had fewer regrets about leaving the flat. It was empty now, their things packed up and waiting for them in Chelsea. They were to move in with Patrick after the wedding, and life for all of them would change completely.

Patrick was obviously thinking about the future too. 'I can't believe we're actually going through with it,' he said, following her gaze to the hotel.

'It's not too late to change your mind,' she pointed out.

'What, and disappoint Fenny? I couldn't do it,' he said. 'She told me that she'd been hoping for years that you would find someone like me to marry!'

Lou had been relieved and more than a little surprised at her aunt's ready acceptance of Patrick. She wouldn't have thought that they would get on at all.

'I hope you appreciate what an honour that is,' she told

him, putting down her coffee to unwrap the packet of sand-wiches Fenny had made for them that morning before or-dering them out of the house. 'Fenny's like Grace. She doesn't give her approval easily.

'She never had any time for Lawrie,' Lou remembered, offering the sandwiches to Patrick. 'She told me that he had a weak chin and couldn't be trusted, and Lawrie thought that she was a rude and eccentric old woman. I used to have to come up to see her by myself. He flatly refused to come, and Fenny probably wouldn't have had him in the house anyway.'

Not wanting to have any secrets from her aunt, she had told Fenny the truth about her marriage to Patrick. She had expected her to be shocked and disapproving, but Fenny had merely listened carefully and nodded.

'Very sensible, dear,' was all she had said. 'You can get married from here as soon as the children break up for their summer holidays.'

Patrick brushed breadcrumbs from his trousers. 'Do *you* want to change your mind?' he asked carefully. 'I wouldn't blame you after being cornered by my mother last night.'

The two families had met for a pre-wedding party at the hotel, which had been virtually taken over by Patrick's sis-ters and their offspring. Grace and Tom had slotted effort-lessly into the big group of nieces and nephews, one of whom had discovered the pool table. Lou had hardly seen them all evening.

She had liked Patrick's mother and sisters a lot. They were all down-to-earth and had teased Patrick mercilessly, unimpressed by his wealth.

'What on earth were the two of you talking about for so long?' he asked, taking another sandwich.

'You, of course,' said Lou. The wind was whipping her

dark hair around her face and she tried to hold it back with one hand while she ate her sandwich.

'I'd given up hope that Patrick would ever marry again,' Kate Farr told Lou when they found themselves on their own. 'The silly boy has been running around with quite unsuitable girls for far too long. I can't tell you how pleased I am that he's come to his senses at last and found himself a real woman!'

Lou couldn't help being amused at hearing Patrick roundly described by his mother as a 'silly boy', but she felt a little uncomfortable about the warm welcome she had received from his family. He obviously hadn't told his family the whole truth about their marriage.

'It's a shame that his father died when he did,' Kate was saying. 'Patrick was only fifteen, and I often think that he grew up too fast after that. And then there was Catriona. She was a nice enough girl,' she said fairly, 'but all wrong for Patrick. That marriage was never going to last. The divorce was supposedly amicable, but I know Patrick was much more hurt about it all than he wanted to admit.

'He threw himself into his work after that, and I think he made too much money too soon. That playboy lifestyle wasn't what he needed.' Kate shook her smartly coiffed grey head. 'He built up this image of Mr I-Don't-Care, but of course what he was afraid of was caring too much.'

'I know what that feels like,' Lou confessed and his mother studied her with eyes that were uncannily like her son's, and quite as shrewd.

'I thought you might,' she said. 'That's why you're right for him. I just hope that you know that much of what Patrick shows the world is just a façade. Underneath he's generous and dependable, and he's got a kind heart. Nothing's too much trouble for the few people he really cares about. You know that, don't you?'

Lou looked across at Patrick, and felt something shift inside her. He was surrounded by his sisters, laughing and throwing up his hands in defeat as if resigned to being the butt of their jokes. It was hard to recognise the cold, hard man she hadn't wanted to have dinner with in Newcastle.

'Yes,' she said to his mother, 'I know.'

She was pretty sure that if she asked him, he would do anything for her or the children, just as Kate said. But he would do it because they had signed a pre-nuptial contract to say that he would.

Lou wanted him to do it because he cared for them too.

And that wasn't in the contract.


The grey clouds cleared miraculously for Lou's wedding day. She woke to sunshine pouring through the bedroom window and a knot of nerves in her stomach. A perfect summer day. A perfect day to get married.

If only you were marrying a man who loved you.

Lou's fingers shook as she laid out her outfit. There had been no question of a white dress—the wedding was going to be enough of a fraud as it was—and she had chosen a pale pink suit to wear with the string of pearls Fenny had given her.

'I'd like you to wear these at your wedding,' she had said, unwrapping the velvet cloth in which the pearls had lain unworn for years.

'Oh, Fenny, they're beautiful!' Lou held them against her skin, admiring their warm lustre.

'My neck's too scraggy to wear them now,' said Fenny. 'And they're not really suitable for gardening, which is all I do nowadays.' She put her head on one side to study Lou who was fastening the pearls around her neck. 'Donald gave them to me when we were married, so goodness knows how long ago that is now... It certainly makes them something old for you to wear with your wedding outfit, anyway! I'd like you to have them.'

Marisa had approved. 'I've brought some pearl earrings to lend you that'll go perfectly with Fenny's necklace,' she announced, breezing into the room as Lou was getting changed. She had insisted on coming to help Lou dress, in spite of everything Lou had to say about it not being a proper wedding.

'So now you've got something old and something borrowed,' she said, picking up a lipstick from the dressing table. 'I trust you've bought yourself some new underwear at least for today, so all you need is something blue.' She pulled the top off the lipstick and frowned. 'I hope you're not planning to wear this with that suit, are you?'

'I bought it specially,' Lou protested.

Marisa was shocked. 'It's far too pale! You need something much brighter than that. I'll see what I can find.' She dug in her bag for the vast cosmetic case she never travelled without. 'Are you OK, Lou? It's not like you to make a mistake when it comes to style!'

'I'm nervous.' Lou fiddled edgily with the pearls. 'What if I'm doing the wrong thing?'

Marisa put the cosmetic case on one side and concentrated on Lou. 'OK, what could go wrong?' she asked patiently.

'Everything! The children might not get on with Patrick; he might not get on with them.'

'They seem to get on fine at the moment.'

'They do now, but what if Patrick gets bored with us? He might meet some...some *supermodel* with no bottom and legs up to her armpits and decide he wants to have babies with her!' said Lou wildly.

'I agree Patrick's more likely to meet a supermodel than most men,' Marisa conceded, 'but if he'd wanted to marry someone like that, he could have done. It's you he's marrying.'

'Yes, but not for the right reasons,' said Lou wretchedly. 'If it all goes wrong, I'll have given my children an absolutely terrible example of how to form adult relationships, won't I?'

Marisa sighed. 'I hate to be tactless, but that low life Lawrie isn't exactly a shining role model when it comes to relationships, and you married *him*.'

'All the more reason not to make the same mistake again. Shouldn't I be teaching the children about adults loving each other, not making deals?'

'It's always a deal, Lou,' said Marisa stringently. 'Yes, you've made a deal, but it's an open and honest one. It's a good start—and who's to say that you and Patrick won't come to love each other?'

Lou shook her head. 'No, we're not going to do that,' she said. 'I told you, we've agreed that's not what either of us want.'

'Well, it seems a sinful waste to me.' Her friend sighed. 'I can't believe you haven't noticed how attractive he is. I wouldn't be letting any ditzy blondes get their paws on him if he was mine!'

Lou turned away to pick up the pearls. 'I don't want to get hurt again,' she said. 'I'd rather he hurt the blondes.'

'If I were you, I'd just relax and see what happens,' Marisa advised. 'I don't think Patrick would hurt you, anyway.'

'You can't know that.'

'Well, I told him that if he *did* hurt you, I would personally come after him with a pair of shears—and it wouldn't just be the sleeves of his suits I'd be chopping off!'

Lou couldn't help laughing and immediately felt better. 'Poor Patrick! What did he say?'

'Very sensibly, he said that he wouldn't.' Marisa grinned and made a scissoring gesture with her fingers. 'But he has been warned!'

Once the knotty question of the lipstick had been sorted out, Marisa insisted on bringing Lou a glass of champagne. Lou was doubtful at first.

'It was champagne that got me into this mess in the first place!'

'Hey, you're marrying a millionaire,' said Marisa. 'You're also getting married for the second time, when some of us are still looking for a guy to waltz us up the aisle once, let alone twice. Don't knock it!'

Grace sidled into the room when she was gone in search of a bottle. Lou swung round on the dressing-table stool, her heart squeezing at the sight of her daughter who had eschewed her normally gloomy wardrobe for a pretty mint-green dress covered in pink dots. On her feet she wore pink ballerina shoes in place of her usual clumpety black boots.

Lou had told her that she could wear whatever she wanted, and she had been very touched when Grace had opted for a dress that she had known would please her mother. She had even brushed her hair.

'You look lovely,' said Lou sincerely.

'Thanks. You look nice too, Mum,' Grace muttered. She brought a hand out from behind her back. 'Marisa says you need something blue.'

It was a perfectly hideous bracelet, made up of blue plastic cubes on an elasticated band, but Lou knew how treasured it was. A boy at school, about whom Grace was unusually coy, had given it to her the previous Christmas.

'You can wear this if you want.'

It was a real sacrifice, Lou knew, and her throat was tight

as she got up and hugged her daughter. 'Thank you, Grace. I'd love to wear it.'

Grace was not normally a tactile child, but she clung to her mother for a moment. 'I just wanted to say thank you,' she said in a rush. 'I know you're doing this for me, and for Tom.'

Lou held her close, her heart full. 'I'm doing it for all of us, Grace,' she told her quietly. 'Everything's going to be fine.'

Stepping back with a smile, she slipped the bracelet onto her wrist. It threw out all Marisa's style rules, and her friend would have a fit when she saw it, but it meant more to Lou than anything else that day.

'I'll take great care of it,' she promised Grace.

Afterwards, Lou remembered little of the wedding itself. The simple ceremony was held in the garden of the hotel, and, although they had decided just to invite family.. and Marisa, who was an honorary member of the family, as Fenny pointed out...there seemed to be a lot of people grouped around them and smiling.

As they waited for the celebrant to gather her thoughts together and begin, Lou saw Patrick's mother, who had pulled out all the stops with an imposing hat, before her eyes skipped on to Fenny, eccentrically dressed in a striped dress that had to be at least thirty years old. Then there was Grace, and Tom, his shirt tail already hanging loose, and Marisa, who gave her a discreet thumbs-up sign.

Lou managed a smile for them all, and then she turned to Patrick and everything else faded into a vague background. It was as if the rest of the party were no more than a blur of faces and figures, cut off from the two of them by an invisible barrier.

Only Patrick was real and solid. He looked very smart in a grey suit, an immaculate white shirt, and a pale grey tie. Lou found herself staring at his face as if she had never seen him properly before. That jaw, that cool, firm mouth, the hard line of his cheek…had he always looked like that?

Her gaze travelled over him as if fascinated until her eyes reached his. Light, more green than grey today, and somehow disturbing, they held a quizzical smile at her scrutiny, and Lou blushed as she looked quickly away.

The celebrant cleared her throat. 'Shall we start?' she asked in an undertone, and Patrick turned to face her. After a moment's hesitation, Lou did the same.

Getting married was a strange experience this time. She heard the words, and made the right responses, marvelling at the steadiness of her own voice, but part of her didn't seem to be there at all. It was like watching herself in a film.

Then Patrick was taking her hand, sliding the ring onto her finger and suddenly it all felt horribly real. His fingers were warm and sure, and Lou felt herself go hollow inside at his touch. Her own hands shook slightly as she picked up the ring to push it onto Patrick's finger, but at last it was done.

They were married.

Patrick smiled and turned to Lou quite naturally, putting his hand under her chin and lifting her face so that he could kiss her. At the touch of his mouth the ground seemed to drop away beneath Lou's feet. His lips weren't cool, the way she had imagined them to be. They were warm and firm and dangerously exciting, and her heart jolted in response. Unable to resist it, Lou leant slightly into him, and Patrick's mouth lingered on hers for a moment longer than necessary before he forced himself to lift his head.

She looked almost as startled as he felt. Patrick felt ridiculously shaken by the unexpected sweetness of that one kiss. He couldn't believe such a brief gesture could have thrown him so off balance, or what an effort it was to muster a flippant smile.

'Well, we did it,' he said.

'Yes,' said Lou, and smiled a little uncertainly back at him.

Patrick was conscious of a sudden urge to pull her back into his arms, but she was already turning, her smile widening as Grace and Tom reached her. He watched as she hugged them both to her, aware of a feeling that it took him a little while to identify as jealousy. Just because Lou loved her children and they loved her and got to be gathered close into her softness and her warmth whenever they wanted her or needed her.

How pathetic was it to feel jealous about *that*?

Patrick suddenly realised that Grace was smiling tentatively at him, and he pulled himself together. He opened his arms, and to his surprise she stepped into them for a quick, hard hug. 'Thank you, Grace,' he said, meaning it. He had known her long enough to know that Grace only hugged the people who meant most to her, and he felt a sudden rush of pride and pleasure to be included.

Ruffling Tom's hair, he glanced over at Lou and found her watching him with her children. The expression in her dark eyes was impossible to read, but she smiled at him, and Patrick felt something unlock inside him. He longed suddenly to be alone with her, the way they had been on top of that hill yesterday, but there was no chance of that with all these people here, all wanting to congratulate him and kiss Lou.

And things didn't get any better. At one point in the afternoon, it seemed to Patrick that he was the only one not getting to kiss the bride. It was hard to get near her. He kept getting glimpses of her dark head and her warm smile and then somebody else would come up and want him to be pleasant to them.

Patrick grew more and more frustrated. 'Don't worry, you'll get her to yourself soon enough,' his elder sister said, coming up behind him. She laughed at his disconcerted expression. 'We're all enjoying the sight of you besotted at last. You haven't been able to take your eyes off Lou all day.'

Besotted? He wasn't besotted, Patrick thought crossly. What a ridiculous idea. He had never been besotted with anyone in his life. Everyone knew that he was the one who ran a mile at the faintest hint of emotion. It was just a groom's job to keep an eye on his bride, that was all.

Unthinkingly, he sought Lou in the crowd. She was standing with his mother and Fenny, and they were all laughing. Lou's face was alive, her dark eyes sparkling, and his chest felt suddenly tight.

She looked wonderful in that suit, so different from the demure grey ones she wore to the office. The soft pink colour made her skin glow, and the silk jacket was fastened low to offer a glimpse of something that looked as if it were made of satin and lace beneath. The mere thought of it was enough to make Patrick catch his breath.

With those high-heeled shoes, she looked incredibly sexy, yet elegant at the same time. Patrick wasn't sure where the blue plastic bracelet fitted into the colour scheme, but it looked OK to him. Today Lou could carry off anything.

He *wasn't* besotted. He just wished that he were with her. Just wished that they were alone and that he were the one making her laugh. Wished that he could undo that jacket and find out just what she was wearing underneath...

Patrick swallowed.

'Besotted,' his sister confirmed with satisfaction. 'It was

about time you fell in love with a real woman, instead of all those bimbos you've been running around with for all this time, trying to prove that you weren't going to be middle-aged like the rest of us. Talk about an extended mid-life crisis. Oh, there's Michael!' She waved at a man through the crowd. 'I must go and have a word.'

Patrick was left outraged by his sister's candid remarks. He had not been trying to prove anything, he had never had any suggestion of a mid-life crisis and he most certainly wasn't in love with Lou.

In spite of himself, he glanced her way again. She was bending down to talk to one of his small nieces. He could see the way her breasts moved beneath that jacket, the way the silky dark hair swung against her cheek, the way she smiled with those lips that had tasted so piercingly, unexpectedly sweet. Patrick's head reeled and he closed his eyes briefly.

He was *not* in love with his wife.

A bit in lust, maybe, but that was all it was.

He was just frustrated. He hadn't had so much as a date since he and Lou had agreed to marry. Lou had made it clear that she would have no objections, but somehow Patrick hadn't felt like going out.

That would have to change. Lou had been definite that a physical relationship was out, and in any case Patrick had no intention of closing off his options with other women. That was the whole reason he had married her in the first place!

No, forget Lou's camisole, he told himself sternly. Stick with friendship, just as they had agreed before she'd started putting on pink suits and kissing him.

Patrick was glad now that he had got his new PA to arrange suites at all the hotels they were going to stay at on their way back to London. It hadn't seemed appropriate to book a honeymoon, but he had suggested that they make their way home slowly, visiting some gardens on the way if that appealed to Lou.

'But you're not interested in gardens,' she had protested.

'No, but I am interested in my car. I'll be happy to drive all the way.'

Lou laughed. 'Ah, now I understand!'

'All the hotels have got suites,' he added casually, 'so you should be quite comfortable. You'll be able to have a room of your own every night.'

She didn't even hesitate. 'Great,' she said. 'Thanks for organising that.'

So that was fine. Separate beds all the way. Patrick sneaked another glance at Lou.

It was fine by him too. Absolutely fine.

# CHAPTER EIGHT

IT WAS nearly seven before Patrick and Lou managed to say all their goodbyes. The roof was down as they drove off into a golden summer evening, and the car seemed to float along the winding dales roads. It should have been an idyllic start to a honeymoon, thought Lou, leaning her head back against the plush leather seat.

Only it wasn't a proper honeymoon, of course. They were just going to stay the night at a couple of hotels on their way back to London. There would be no intimate celebrations, no elation, no laughter, no kisses.

No making love.

Patrick had made it very clear that they wouldn't be sharing a room, let alone a bed. That was fine by her, Lou reminded herself firmly, but it did make the whole notion of a honeymoon a bit of a mockery. They might just as well have driven back with Grace and Tom, but Lawrie had, for once, turned up as arranged to collect them from the reception. The children were going to spend a week with him. It was good for them to see their father, Lou thought, but it did mean that she was now going to have to spend a week alone with Patrick.

Of course, they had spent plenty of time alone in the office, but it was different now. Lou stole a sideways glance at Patrick. Her *husband*. She still couldn't quite comprehend it.

His expression was preoccupied, but his hands were very sure on the steering-wheel. As she watched he shifted gear to round a tight bend, completely in control of the powerful car, and something tightened and twisted inside Lou. Something deep and disturbing. Something that brought back the memory of the kiss they had shared after the ceremony in a vivid whoosh, so that she could feel again the warmth of his lips, the touch of his hand against her face.

Awareness of him shivered through her, vibrating out to her fingertips and toes, and Lou had to force herself to look away. Feeling like this whenever you looked at your husband was fine, but not when you and your husband had agreed very clearly that there was no question of a physical relationship. It was just as well that Patrick had arranged separate rooms while they were away.

It took them less than an hour to reach the hotel he had booked for that night, and the manageress came out to give them her personal attention. 'You must allow me to congratulate you both, Mr and Mrs Farr,' she said unctuously as they checked in. 'I understand you were just married today.'

Patrick looked up sharply from signing the form. 'How do you know that?'

She checked her notes. 'A…let me see, yes…Marisa Brandon…rang up earlier. She wanted to arrange for us to put a bottle of champagne in the suite for you to enjoy when you got here, and she mentioned that you would be coming straight from your wedding, so of course we're absolutely delighted to move you to our special honeymoon suite. It's just been renovated and completely refurbished to create a really special intimate and romantic atmosphere.'

Patrick glanced at Lou, but she shook her head very slightly to indicate that he shouldn't insist on the original arrangement. She certainly didn't want to stand there while he explained that actually they would rather have separate rooms. Some honeymoon they would seem to be on then!

The manageress insisted on escorting them up to the honeymoon suite, talking proudly about it all the way.

'I do hope you'll like it,' she said, opening the door for them. 'It's the perfect place for a honeymoon, I think.'

'It's lovely,' said Lou dutifully, and tried not to look at the bed. There was just the one, naturally. How many honeymoon suites catered for couples who didn't want to sleep together on their wedding night?

She would kill Marisa when she saw her.

'Well,' she said when the manageress had finished her tour of the suite, evidently designed to ensure that they appreciated every last intimate and romantic detail, and had at last left them alone.

'I'm sorry about this,' said Patrick. 'This isn't quite what I planned.'

'It doesn't matter,' said Lou, who had been thinking about the situation while listening to the manageress with half an ear. 'It won't kill us to share a bed for one night,' she went on briskly. 'There's no need to be silly about it. Look, it's huge,' she said, pointing at the bed.

Yes, and what a great bed it would be to make love in, thought Patrick, and was immediately cross with himself for being able to imagine doing just that.

'There's plenty of room for both of us,' Lou was saying, determined to show that the situation didn't bother her in the slightest. 'I don't see why it should be uncomfortable. We've both agreed that our relationship is going to be about friendship and nothing else, and if we *are* going to be friends, we should be able to share a bed without making a fuss.'

Her matter-of-fact attitude was beginning to annoy Patrick. So she wasn't bothered by the idea of sharing a bed with him. That didn't help *him*, did it? Lou obviously hadn't spent most of the day speculating about what he was wearing underneath *his* jacket. If she had, she might find the prospect of climbing into bed with him a lot more problematic.

Well, he would just have to show that he could be equally cool.

'Right, well, if you're happy with that, it's fine by me,' he said, a little too heartily. 'But I'm quite happy to go and have a quiet word down at Reception to see if they can give us back the original suite.'

'There's no need for that.' Lou sat down on the edge of the bed and eased off her shoes, just to prove how totally and utterly relaxed she was about the whole idea of sleeping with Patrick. 'Now that we're married, we're likely to find ourselves in this situation again, so we'd better get used to it.'

Patrick opened the fridge bar. 'In that case, we might as well have some of this champagne Marisa has provided for us.' He could certainly do with a drink.

Massaging her sore feet, Lou watched him surreptitiously as he deftly opened the bottle. Patrick seemed convinced by her show of unconcern, even if her insides weren't. Her entrails were clearly still very dubious about the whole business, and were churning and fluttering frantically at the mere prospect of climbing calmly into bed with him.

Patrick poured out the champagne and put the two glasses down by the bed while he pulled off his tie. Loosening his shirt at the neck, he rolled up his sleeves, took off his shoes and swung his legs up onto the bed so that he could make himself comfortable against the pillows.

'That's better,' he said, adjusting a pillow behind him. 'At least we can relax now.'

Well, *he* might be able to relax, thought Lou, still perched prissily on the edge of the bed. He was used to sharing beds with the likes of Ariel Harper.

And that meant that he was hardly likely to be overcome by lust at the idea of *her* on the other side of the bed, was he? Lou reminded herself, and her churning entrails quietened a little. Really, she was just being silly. She was forty-five, for heaven's sake. Far too old to be getting in a state about something so ridiculous.

So when Patrick patted the other side of the bed and urged her to put her feet up, Lou calmly scooted up onto the pillows beside him. He gave her a glass of champagne before picking up his own.

'Here's to us,' he said, toasting her.

'To us and our deal,' she agreed as they chinked glasses.

Not that the deal was going to be much comfort to him that night, Patrick reflected grimly. It looked like being a very long night.

And it *was* a long night. It was all very well reminding yourself that you were grown up, and far too old to be embarrassed about something so silly, but somehow that didn't help very much when you had to contemplate taking your clothes off and climbing into bed together.

Feeling about sixteen, Lou shut herself in the bathroom to change into the silk nightdress Marisa had given her as a mock wedding present. 'You might as well look good on your honeymoon, even if you are just going to sleep,' she had said.

If only it weren't quite so obviously made for seduction. Lou regarded herself in the bathroom mirror in dismay. The creamy oyster silk was a cool ripple against her skin, with a plunging back held up by whisper-light straps that were just begging for the brush of a man's hand to send them slithering off her shoulders. It felt lovely, it looked lovely, it was perfect for a sophisticated honeymoon. She just wished that it were a high-necked flannelette nightgown like the ones Fenny sometimes wore in winter.

Holding her clothes in front of her to hide as much of it as possible, Lou took a deep breath before walking out of the bathroom with assumed nonchalance. 'The bathroom's all yours,' she said casually over her shoulder, managing not to look at him at all as she put her clothes away.

'Thanks.'

By the time Patrick came out, she was lying on her side in the bed, the duvet pulled primly up under her chin. She had left a lamp burning on his side, but otherwise the room was in darkness, much to Patrick's relief. He always slept naked, so it had never occurred to him to buy pyjamas, but he had done his best to preserve the decencies by keeping his shorts on. Still, he was very glad Lou's eyes weren't on him as he crossed over to the bed. That glimpse of her bare back emerging from oyster silk had done alarming things to his blood pressure.

The mattress shifted as he got into bed and switched off the light. 'Goodnight,' he said gruffly.

'Goodnight.'

Oh, yes, it was all very polite. They were adults. They could deal with this. But it didn't stop Patrick being burningly aware of her, while, a few inches away, Lou could hear him breathing. It was so long since she had shared a bed that she was aware of every move he made as he stretched and settled in a studiedly relaxed way.

Long minutes ticked past. They weren't touching at all, but it was stifling under the duvet. Lou eased it off, kicking her legs free as quietly as she could, and cursing the long silk that kept tangling round her. She was longing to turn over, but she was terrified of brushing against Patrick—not that he would probably notice now. She could tell from the change in his breathing that he had fallen asleep. It was all right for some, she thought sourly.

She was exhausted, but too tense to sleep, and it felt as

if she lay there for hours, willing herself to relax. Then, just as she drifted off, she would jerk awake as Patrick sighed or stirred.

She was cold, too, now, but somehow the duvet had ended up all on Patrick's side. Lou tugged at it as discreetly as she could, and finally managed to get enough to cover herself once more, only to find to her horror that she had roused Patrick from the depths of his slumber. Rolling over, he flung a heavy arm over her and pulled her back into the warmth of his body so that he could nuzzle her neck, and Lou's attempts to wriggle free only made him tighten his grip in instinctive response.

'Patrick!' she said at last, and jabbed him with her elbow.

Waking with a start, Patrick took a moment or two to remember where he was and what he was doing. When he did, he recoiled as if he had found himself cuddling a black mamba. 'Sorry,' he muttered as he rolled hastily back to the other side of bed. 'I must have thought…'

'It's OK,' said Lou, not wanting to know who he had thought that she was. 'Go back to sleep.'

Fat chance of that when he had been pressed against her softness and his face had been buried in her hair and he had breathed in the warm fragrance of her skin! Patrick spent the rest of the night lying grim and rigid on the edge of the mattress, and trying not to remember how it had felt to wake holding her.

They didn't have to share a room again, and that made things much easier. No more lying stiffly on one side of the bed in case he rolled against her inadvertently. No more thinking about how close she was, or how easy it would be to reach out for her, to snuggle up like spoons the way he had before.

And what a mistake *that* would have been, Patrick told himself constantly. That would have been the end of his free and easy lifestyle, the end of beautiful girls, the end of freedom.

So he couldn't get Lou's warm body out of his mind? So he kept thinking about how luminous her skin had seemed in the dim light, and the curve of her shoulder in the darkness? He would get over it as soon as they got home and things went back to normal.

In meantime, they were friends, and that was fine.

Both were heartily glad when their supposed honeymoon was over and they could try and establish a new routine in London. Patrick went back to work with his new PA, and Lou stayed in the big, empty house and tried not to miss him. Things were better when the kids came back from Lawrie's. They loved living with Patrick, and the pool was a huge draw, especially while the summer holidays lasted and the house was always full of their friends, who spent the whole day splashing around and shouting.

There wasn't much for Lou to do, though. 'How are things in the office?' she asked almost wistfully when Patrick came home.

'OK,' he said, but without much enthusiasm. 'Jo's very efficient, but she's not like you.' He looked at Lou, who was cutting back the wisteria that was running rampant over the back of the house. 'It's funny without you there,' he said slowly. 'I miss you.'

Lou kept snipping at the top of her ladder. There was no need to start glowing just because he had said he missed her.

'I miss working with you more than I expected to,' she confessed. 'All those years commuting and longing not to have to work any more, and, now that I don't, I feel at a bit of a loose end. I'm quite glad Theresa's left now. At least I can keep house now. When she was here, I always felt awkward about going into the kitchen.'

Patrick sat down at the table and stretched his long legs out in front of him as he watched Lou cutting back the tendrils that were rioting away from the wires designed to keep the plant flat against the brick wall.

'It's all very quiet,' he said, suddenly realising that the pool lay silent and gleaming in the evening light. 'Where are the kids?'

'They're both on sleepovers with friends,' said Lou as she climbed cautiously down the ladder.

'Odd how empty the house feels without them,' said Patrick.

It was extraordinary, he thought, how quickly he had got used to coming home to noise and what seemed like perpetual motion. There always seemed to be a pack of kids running around, or splashing and shouting in the pool. The television would be going in one room, a CD of strange music Patrick had never heard before blasting from another. It had used to be such a quiet house too, he remembered. Quiet and very dull, now that he came to think about it. No wonder he had spent most evenings out.

Nowadays he found himself coming home earlier and earlier. He could bank on finding Lou in the garden, usually on her knees as she weeded and pruned and watered. Patrick had grown to like the way she looked up at him and smiled a welcome. She would sit back on her heels and brush the hair from her face, leaving a smudge on her forehead.

Most evenings they would sit together on the terrace and talk over a glass of wine. It felt very comfortable being with Lou, Patrick thought, and was glad that they had opted just to be friends. Later they would have supper in the kitchen with Grace and Tom, often with an assortment of other children whose names Patrick never established. The summer holidays were particularly chaotic, but Lou was always serene in the heart of it all. She seemed to know what was going on and who was going where, and after a while Patrick relaxed and left it all to her.

It had all worked out better than he had imagined, he congratulated himself. Now and then he would remember the other life that he had planned for himself, but it was puzzling now to know how that would have worked. He had been going to have a completely detached existence, hadn't he? The idea was to go out with other women with a guilt-free conscience, and to have nothing much to do with Lou and certainly not with her children. Patrick had been so sure then that was what he wanted.

Now…now it was different somehow.

He looked at Lou as she pulled off her gardening gloves and brushed wisteria leaves from her hair. She was wearing a faded shirt and the loose trousers she kept for gardening, and her hands were grubby. For an incongruous moment he remembered his cool, immaculate PA in her neat suits, but it was hard to reconcile her with the warm, slightly dishevelled woman who stood in front of him now.

'It's just us tonight, then?' he said.

'I'm afraid so.' Lou reached for a brush and began to sweep up the wisteria trimmings.

'Why don't we go out to dinner?' Patrick asked her on the spur of the moment, and she sent him a quick glance before bending back to her sweeping.

'You don't need to entertain me,' she said carefully. 'I'm fine on my own. Why don't you take Ariel out instead?'

Ariel? It took Patrick a moment to remember who she was talking about. 'Didn't I tell you? Ariel's gone back to the Maldives.'

Lou looked up from her broom. 'Really?'

'Apparently she met some diving instructor or something while we were there, and now she's decided that she wants to marry him and have babies. Whether he'll be able to keep her in the manner to which she is undoubtedly accustomed is another matter,' said Patrick in a dry voice.

'Are you OK with that?' asked Lou cautiously. He certainly sounded OK, but with Patrick you could never tell.

'Of course,' he said, surprised. 'I was just glad to be spared a horrible emotional scene when we came back. She'd made up her mind even then. To be honest, I'd forgotten all about her until you mentioned her.'

Lou bent to brush the leaves into a dustpan and dumped them in a wheelbarrow. 'Haven't you found anyone else to catch your fancy?' she said, determinedly casual and friendly. It was the kind of thing she would ask Marisa, after all. She and Patrick were friends, and asking how the other's love life was going was part of what friends did.

'No,' said Patrick slowly, realising that it was true. 'No, not yet.'

'Well, I don't mind being taken out until you find a new date,' said Lou, determinedly cheerful. 'I'll need to shower, though.'

'There's no hurry.'

Patrick had to force himself not to imagine Lou in the shower as he flicked through his organiser for the number of a restaurant. There were any number of trendy restaurants where he was pretty sure of getting a table, but it was hard to picture Lou in them. They were the kind of places you took glamorous girls like Ariel who cared about seeing and being seen. Lou wouldn't be bothered with any of that, he just knew.

'We're not going anywhere too smart, are we?' Lou called down the stairs, as if reading his mind.

Patrick went out into the hall and craned his neck to see her hanging over the banister from the landing. Her hair was wet, her shoulders bare above the cream towel she had wrapped around her, and she looked pink and glowing.

And alarmingly desirable. Patrick wondered what it would be like to be able to climb the stairs towards her and tell her how she looked. What would it be like if she smiled at the expression in his eyes and reminded him that they had the house to themselves for once? Would she laugh as he pulled her into the bedroom? Would she fall with him onto the bed? Would she let him unwrap her, unlock her, let his hands drift over her curves as he savoured the texture of her skin, the taste of her, the touch of her?

No, she wouldn't. Patrick reeled his wayward thoughts abruptly back. Of course she wouldn't. That wasn't the kind of thing you did when you were just friends, was it?

'Where would you like to go?' he asked, aware that his voice was hoarser than usual.

'Let's just go to that little Italian round the corner,' said Lou. 'It's always good there and we won't need to book. I'll be down in just a minute,' she assured him, disappearing from view.

Patrick went into the sitting room and sat on one of the sofas, dropping his head into his hands. He had to stop thinking about Lou like that, or one of these days he would forget himself, and that would spoil everything. It was only now that he was realising how important she was to him, and he didn't want to lose her as a friend. He was happy with how things were, and Lou seemed happy too, but that would only last if he stuck to the deal they had agreed.

So stick with it he would. And he would find a new girlfriend, the sooner the better.

'Are you OK, Patrick?'

Patrick jerked his head up to see Lou looking at him in concern from the doorway. She was wearing a pale blue silky skirt and a white top, with a soft little cardigan, and she looked cool and fresh and comfortable.

And just as desirable as she had looked wrapped in that towel.

Patrick swallowed hard and got to his feet. 'I'm fine,' he said brusquely. 'Let's go.'

'Brewer's First are having a big bash to mark their fiftieth anniversary at the end of September,' he told Lou over a bowl of pasta. 'We're both invited.'

'Do you want me to come and do my corporate-wife act?' asked Lou.

'Would you mind?'

'Of course not. I haven't done anything to keep my side of the bargain yet.' She smiled at him. 'I haven't forgotten our deal.'

'Good.' Patrick looked away, but her smile still shimmered behind his eyelids. He cleared his throat. 'Good.'

'Will it be a very posh affair?' Lou asked after a moment, a little puzzled by his silence. 'Should I dress up?'

'It's black tie, so you'll need evening dress, yes. Why don't you buy yourself something new?'

Lou ran a mental eye over her wardrobe. She didn't have anything very exciting, but there were a few basics she could easily glam up. 'I'm sure I can find something suitable at home,' she told him.

'You never buy yourself anything new,' said Patrick abruptly. 'I've noticed. You're still wearing the same clothes you had before we were married.'

'There's nothing wrong with them, is there?'

'It's not that.' He hunched a shoulder, obscurely hurt but not wanting to admit it. 'It's like you don't want to spend any of my money,' he explained as best he could. 'You hardly touch the money I put in your account.'

'I use it for food,' she protested.

'It's your money,' he said irritably. 'You don't need to account to me for what you do with it. Buy whatever you want.'

Lou set her jaw stubbornly. 'I don't feel comfortable about doing that,' she said and Patrick rolled his eyes.

'I thought you married me for my money!'

'I married you for security,' she said evenly. 'For a better life for me and the kids, and you've given us that. You have no idea what it's like living in that beautiful big house after that flat we were in. We don't need your money as well.'

'Try and spend some of it anyway,' said Patrick with an exasperated sigh. 'Buy yourself a new dress for that reception—and don't you dare buy anything cheap because you think it's not your money!' he added with a stern look. 'You'll be there as my wife, and I don't want you to give the impression that I'm tight-fisted!'

Lou rang Marisa the next morning. 'Patrick's practically ordered me to go and squander a fortune on a dress,' she said. 'You'd better come and help me choose.'

'Ooh, he didn't wake you up by waving a credit card in front of your face and telling you that you had shopping to do, did he?' said Marisa enviously. 'That's been my fantasy ever since I saw *Pretty Woman*!'

'No, but it feels a bit as if I'm being bought,' Lou confessed. 'I don't like it.'

'Honestly, Lou, you're his wife, not a hooker! Most women would be falling over themselves to spend his money. It's not like he can't afford to pay a few credit-card bills.'

'That's not the point,' said Lou stubbornly. 'Patrick's already been more than generous. We live for free in this fantastic house—the children even get to have their own pool!—and we don't do anything for him in return. It would be different if we were properly married.'

'Hey, I was your witness, remember?' said Marisa, unimpressed. 'It looked like a proper wedding to me. And you *can* do something for him now,' she pointed out. 'He's asked you to go and buy a posh frock, so let's go and find one to knock his socks off!'

They found it at the very end of the afternoon, just as Lou was ready to give up and go home.

'This is *it*!' Marisa held up a wonderful shimmering dress in that perfect shade of red between pink and scarlet. A layer of chiffon covered the arms and wafted over a simple silk under-dress. When Lou tried it on, the material slithered tantalisingly over her skin.

'She'll take it,' Marisa said to the sales assistant as soon as Lou stepped out of the changing room.

Lou was scandalised at the price, but Marisa overrode her, bullying her into matching sandals, earrings that glittered and swung tantalisingly, and an eye-catching bag, handmade with feathers and sequins.

'And you'll need a new lipstick too,' she said to Lou. 'I know just the colour.'

She insisted on coming round to supervise Lou's makeup on the night of the reception, too. 'You look fabulous!' she declared, standing back and eyeing her critically.

'You don't think it's a bit…much?' said Lou, who was rapidly losing her nerve. She felt ridiculously nervous, the way she had at sixteen before her first real date.

Which was stupid. This wasn't a date. She was just attending a function with her husband. Nothing to be nervous about in that.

It was just that this dress made her feel very aware of her own body. It made her feel…sexy. Too sexy for a forty-five-year-old who was supposed to be content with just being friends.

Patrick didn't help matters by looking devastatingly attractive in a dinner jacket whose severe black and white accentuated the hard lines of his face and sat easily on his powerful frame. He was waiting for her in the hall and Lou felt the breath leak out of her lungs as she walked down the stairs, very aware of the slippery material shifting suggestively over her body, and wishing that there were just a bit more chiffon to cover her cleavage.

'You look nice,' said Patrick in an odd voice.

Behind her, Lou heard Marisa let out a slow breath of exasperation. 'No, she doesn't look *nice*, Patrick. She looks absolutely gorgeous! Try that again,' she told him bossily, ignoring Lou's attempts to frown her down.

'You look gorgeous,' said Patrick obediently.

A chauffeured limousine was waiting for them outside, but Lou was too consumed by a mixture of disappointment and embarrassment to appreciate the luxury. She had wanted Patrick to think that she was gorgeous without prompting from Marisa, she realised. Now she felt as if she had tried too hard.

Beside her in the back of the car, Patrick was looking distant and preoccupied. Probably terrified that she was about to jump on him. Why on earth had she let Marisa bully her into this dress? Lou wondered desperately. She should have worn her old black silk trousers and cream top and been done with it.

It was a relief to get to the reception at last. It was a glittering affair, and the room seemed full of men looking far more distinguished than they merited in their dinner jackets, and beautiful women in fabulous dresses, many of them a lot more dramatic than Lou's. At least that meant

that she looked less conspicuous. Less like a woman who
had tried too hard to catch her husband's flagging attention.

She was agonisingly conscious of Patrick beside her, of
his warm hand at her elbow as he introduced her, at the
small of her back as he manoeuvred her through the crowd.
Inevitably, they got separated after a while. Lou couldn't
decide whether that made things easier or more difficult.
She was quite capable of talking to people on her own, but
even as she smiled and talked and listened she was acutely
aware of Patrick a few yards away.

No sooner had she been detached from his side than one
girl after another zeroed in on him. She could see them
flirting openly with him, tilting their pretty heads appeal-
ingly, shaking back their blonde manes, laying their perfectly manicured hands on his sleeve, moving closer as they
smiled suggestively.

Lou wanted to march over and slap their hands off him.

But she didn't have the right to do that. She had signed
that away when she'd agreed to their pre-nuptial contract.
She wasn't here to be jealous and possessive. She was only
here to support Patrick and his business, and she had better
not forget that.

Turning deliberately away from him, Lou smiled brilliantly at her companion, a young merchant banker called
Charles who seemed visibly dazzled by her. It was nice to
be appreciated for a change, Lou thought, her ego a little
soothed. Nice to meet a man who didn't necessarily think
that young blondes with long legs were the ultimate female
company.

'I think we should go soon.' Patrick materialised at her
elbow, looking grim.

'What, already?' Lou asked in surprise. They hadn't been
there long.

'We've been here long enough,' he said.

Charles was looking a little daunted by the way Patrick was glaring at him, and Lou introduced the two men awkwardly, stumbling over describing Patrick as her husband.

Given no encouragement whatsoever to linger, Charles took himself off. 'I hope we'll meet again,' he said to Lou.

'I hope so too,' she said to make up for Patrick's rudeness. 'It was lovely to meet you. Really.'

'"*It was lovely to meet you*",' Patrick mimicked furiously as he propelled Lou towards the exit.

'Why were you so rude to him?' she demanded, practically running to keep up.

'I didn't like the way he was ogling you.'

Lou gaped at him. 'Ogling? He wasn't ogling me!'

'Come on, Lou, the guy was halfway down your dress!'

'At least he noticed me.' Lou's temper was simmering as she got into the car that was waiting for them at the bottom of the steps. 'It's more than you did. I might as well not have been there for all the notice you took of me.'

Patrick leant forward, had a word with the driver, and then closed the window between the front and back seats with a snap.

'Of course I noticed,' he said grittily. 'It was hard not to notice the way you were flirting.'

'I was not flirting,' said Lou through her teeth. 'I was being pleasant to your business associates, which is what you asked me to be.'

Patrick knew that. He had been watching her all evening out of the corner of his eye. She hadn't been the youngest woman there, or the best-dressed, or the prettiest, but she had the style and assurance of an older woman and an elusive charm that drew people to her. He just hadn't liked the way other men had looked at her in that dress.

Letting out a sigh, Patrick ran a hand through his hair. 'You're right, I'm sorry,' he said. 'You did a good job tonight. Lots of people told me how charming you were. You're obviously going to be a great asset to me. I'd rather you didn't wear that dress again, though,' he added, trying to sound humorous, but failing.

'Listen, you told me to go and buy a dress,' said Lou angrily. 'So I did. What's wrong with it?'

'There's nothing wrong with it. It's just that it's too…too…'

'Too *what*?'

'It's too disturbing,' Patrick said. 'It's the kind of dress that gives a man the wrong idea.'

And quite suddenly the atmosphere changed. Lou was stunned at how quickly she could go from anger and frustration to an electric awareness. The very air between them seemed to be vibrating as Patrick looked into her eyes, his deep, dark voice caressing her skin.

'It's the kind of dress that makes a man think about unzipping it,' he went on softly. 'It makes him think about what you're wearing underneath, what your skin would feel like…'

There didn't seem to be enough air to breathe properly. Unable to tear her eyes away from his, Lou moistened her lips. 'It wasn't meant to make you think that,' she managed.

'I know, but it does.' Tantalisingly, Patrick brushed the hair away from her face. 'That dress makes me wonder what it would be like to kiss you.'

'You should try wearing it,' said Lou unsteadily, desperately trying to make a joke of it. 'It makes you wonder more than that!'

'Does it now?' Patrick's smile gleamed in the darkness. 'Then maybe we should stop wondering and find out.'

A dim part of Lou's brain was jumping up and down and telling her that this was a bad idea—a *very* bad idea—but it was hard to pay attention to it when every nerve in her body was pointing out that this was what she had been thinking about for months.

She hadn't let herself accept the way her fingers itched to reach out and touch him whenever he sat near her. She hadn't wanted to admit how much she wanted to run her hands up his arms and over his shoulders so that she could feel the powerful flex of his muscles. How much she wanted to bury into his lean, hard body, to crawl all over him, to press her lips to his throat, to kiss the edges of his eyes, the corner of his mouth. How she wanted to feel him smile as she kissed him.

Or how much she wanted him to pull her into him, to roll her beneath him, to make love to her until they forgot everything but the clamour of their bodies.

And now, here, in the dim cocoon of this luxurious car, isolated from the outside world, she had her chance. *Go for it,* her body was yelling. *Don't listen to your brain!*

So Lou closed her mind and gave in to temptation. She didn't even hesitate as Patrick leant slowly towards her. Enveloped in hazy excitement, she lifted her hands to his shoulders and spread them over his back, revelling in the strength of his muscles beneath the dinner jacket, and as his mouth came down on hers she drew a breath of exquisite anticipation.

Giving herself up to the rush of pleasure, to the touch and taste of him, to his scent and his feel, she kissed him back with deep, hungry kisses. It felt wonderful to wrap her arms around his solid strength, to feel his hands slide over her, hot and insistent through the flimsy material of her dress, making her gasp with excitement, and she shivered at the press of his lips against her throat.

Her blood was pounding, her body booming so loudly that it took some time before she even realised that the car had stopped. 'We're home.' Patrick's ragged voice penetrated her swirling mind.

*Home?* Lou struggled to make sense of the word, struggled to remember where she was, what she was doing.

Somehow she found herself out on the gravel. Patrick was leaning through the front window, saying something to the driver, and then the car slid out of the drive and the gates closed silently behind it.

Patrick was still reeling from the rocketing excitement. How long had it been since he had necked in the back of a car like that? If the driver hadn't knocked to indicate that they had arrived just then…!

Smiling, he walked back to Lou, still standing exactly where he had left her and looking as shell-shocked as he felt. Who would have thought that a kiss could spin so quickly out of control?

'Your room or mine?' he said.

'Wait.' Lou put out her hands to ward him off as he reached for her. 'I'm not sure we should be doing this.'

'Not sure?' Patrick couldn't believe it. 'You seemed pretty sure in the back of the car there!'

'I know, I know.' She was trembling with reaction, but the air had cleared her head and she could think properly again.

'Don't try and tell me you don't want me,' he said angrily.

'No, I won't try and do that.' Lou swallowed. 'But you need to make a choice, Patrick. You can have me, or you can have your blondes, but you can't have both. I'm not going to sleep with you now and then accept that you have other girlfriends.'

'Lou…' Patrick raked his hands through his hair. 'Do we have to talk about this now?'

'Yes, we do,' she said. 'I need to know now whether

you want me enough to give up the freedom you said you wanted so much when we were married.'

Patrick stared at her. God, he wanted her. He had wanted her for months, he realised in a sudden moment of clarity. But give up his freedom? Tie himself down to commitment and fidelity, after one kiss? How could he decide that?

His hesitation told Lou everything she needed to know. 'Well, it looks like I've got my answer,' she said, and turned away to walk into the house. Alone.

# CHAPTER NINE

LOU was weeding when Patrick got back from work the next evening. It was the first chance he'd had to talk to her alone since he'd been left standing angry and baffled on the gravel, and he'd been doing some thinking since then.

'I'm sorry about last night, Lou,' he said.

She leant back on her heels and looked at him. 'You don't need to apologise,' she said. 'It was as much my fault as yours. I got a bit carried away by that dress, that was all.'

'You were right to stop me when you did,' Patrick persevered. 'It would have been a mistake.' He hesitated. 'I want us to stay friends.'

'Of course,' she agreed instantly. 'I'd rather keep it that way too. Last night…it was just an itch that we both felt like scratching, but it would have complicated everything. Let's just forget it ever happened, shall we?' She mustered a smile. 'I won't wear the dress again!'

That would help, thought Patrick. He didn't think much of his chances of forgetting that kiss, though. Out loud, he said, 'I was thinking that I should go out more. See other women, the way I planned.'

Lou pulled a straggling weed out of her fork to hide the flash of dismay she felt. 'Good idea,' she said.

It *was* a good idea. She had come too close to getting hurt last night, and she wasn't risking that again. 'Have you got anyone in mind?'

'Well, yes,' said Patrick awkwardly.

He had found the card the young lawyer had slipped him

149

at the reception in his jacket pocket that morning. Fingering it, he remembered her vaguely. Tall, blonde, very attractive, very assured. The card said that her name was Holly. Patrick didn't remember that. All he remembered was how uncomfortable he had felt at her open interest. She must have been able to see his wedding ring. He had only taken the card because it had been less trouble than refusing it.

Holly wasn't quite his usual type, but she was obviously intelligent, beautiful, and ambitious. She hadn't struck him as a woman who would be much bothered with emotional commitment, or the fact that he was married. After a sleepless night trying to convince himself that he had made the right decision in choosing his freedom over Lou, Patrick thought that Holly might be just the kind of woman he needed right then.

'Great.' Lou gave him a brilliant smile, determined to show him that she would be sticking to her side of the deal from now on. 'Is she nice?'

'She seems nice,' said Patrick, but he couldn't help remembering what Lou had said about wanting a relationship with someone prepared to sleep with a married man. 'Her name's Holly,' he blurted out, pushing the memory aside.

'Pretty name,' said Lou, attacking a rogue dandelion.

Her dark head was bent and Patrick watched her, wishing that he knew what she was thinking. 'I thought I'd take her to dinner,' he said. 'Are you OK with that?'

'Of course.' Lou shook back her hair and smiled again as she tossed the dandelion onto the pile of weeds. 'It's what we agreed, isn't it? Don't worry about me. I'm more than happy with the way things have worked out, Patrick. We made a deal and I'm happy to stick to it. You go. Enjoy yourself.'

He didn't, of course. Holly was smart, attractive, successful and clearly up for a no-strings relationship. Exactly the kind of woman Patrick had had in mind when he'd first made his deal with Lou. She had no intention of settling down until she had made a name for herself. Holly was going far, and she couldn't be bothered with emotional entanglements that might slow her down.

He should have dated women like her before, Patrick told himself, but the more Holly talked about her need for independence, the more he caught echoes of things he had said himself in the past, and he shifted uncomfortably. There was a ruthless quality to her, an utter lack of sentiment or any real warmth that appalled him. Was that how *he* seemed to other people?

He took Holly to the latest restaurant, where she picked at the wonderful food and he thought about Lou. She would have eaten with the kids. Patrick wondered how Grace had got on with her maths test while Holly talked about the glittering career she had mapped out for herself. Tom had been playing in a football match that afternoon, he remembered. Lou had gone to watch him. Patrick would have liked to have gone with her.

The evening seemed endless. He drove Holly back to her trendy apartment, but made an excuse when she invited him up for a nightcap. He wanted to go home.

Lou was already in bed when he got in, but she had left some lights on for him. Patrick wandered through the house, noticing how much warmer and more welcoming it was these days. The kitchen table was covered with school books. He picked up Tom's French exercise book and grinned at the excruciating errors. Tom was a mechanic, not a linguist.

There was a jug of flowers on the window sill, and the kitchen smelled appetising. Patrick sniffed. They must have had something cheesy for supper. He wished he had been there instead of eating his way through the elaborate and expensive meal he had shared with Holly.

He walked softly upstairs. Lou's door was closed. Hesitating outside it, Patrick wished that he could go in and sit on the edge of her bed. They could talk the way they had used to talk and he could tell her about his awful evening and the feeling he had that he had got everything very wrong.

But he couldn't do that, not after last night. He had made his choice, and now he would have to stick with it.

'Mum, can we go away at half-term?'

Lou was wrapping sandwiches in cling film and trying not to be too aware of Patrick, reading the *Financial Times* at the end of the kitchen table.

The atmosphere between them had been strained ever since he had started dating Holly. Lou didn't know what he saw in the woman, but the relationship certainly didn't seem to be making him particularly happy. He was brusque and irritable a lot of the time, rather the way he had been when she'd first met him, Lou thought. It made it difficult to maintain the friendship that had been so easy that summer.

It was partly her fault, Lou knew. She was trying to be pleasant about it, but the effort of appearing not to mind that he was seeing another woman had left her tense and the only way she could cope was to withdraw into herself. She was spending a lot of time in the garden these days, but it wasn't having the same restorative effect it used to have. She was snappy with the kids, too, which wasn't fair on them, and the guilt only made her worse.

'I thought we'd go and see Fenny,' she told Grace, packing the sandwiches neatly into their lunchboxes. 'We haven't seen her since the wedding.'

'Oh, Mu-um...' Grace moaned. 'Not Yorkshire *again*!'

'Yes, can't we go somewhere different?' Tom chimed in between mouthfuls of cereal.

Lou kept her voice even with difficulty. 'You love Fenny,' she reminded them.

'Yes, but she could come here, couldn't she?' said Grace. 'We don't have to spend a whole week there. It's so *boring*.'

Lou thought of the green hills and the river, of walking in the wind and the rain and coming in to a roaring fire and Fenny's scones. Of clean air and simple needs and no Patrick twisting her entrails into knots and making it hard to breathe. No trying to convince herself that she had been right to walk away from him that night, that it was better to just be friends. Suddenly she yearned to be there.

'It's not boring, Grace,' she said tightly. 'If you're bored there, that's your problem, not Yorkshire's.'

Grace looked mutinous. 'India's going to Majorca. And Marina's dad says he'll take her to New York!'

'You've got a dad, too,' said Lou with an edge to her voice. She found two apples in the fruit bowl and polished them on her sleeve before wedging them in next to the sandwiches. 'Ask him to take you.'

'I did, and he said it would be better if we went with you.'

That sounded like Lawrie, thought Lou bitterly.

'He said you could afford it more than him now,' Tom offered helpfully.

Lou sucked in her breath and bit back an angry rejoinder. She tried so hard not to criticise Lawrie in front of the children, but when she thought about the money he must have spent on his new sports car, a fraction of which would have enabled him to take Grace and Tom on the holiday they craved, she wanted to scream and shout and hit something.

She vented her fury on the lunchboxes instead, slamming them both shut.

'I'm sorry, but I've already told Fenny we'd go and see her.'

The children immediately set up a chorus of moans. 'It's not *fair!*'

'If you're not careful, we won't go anywhere,' she said, warning in her voice. 'It's not as if you'd miss out on much. You've got your own pool here, for heaven's sake! What else do you need?'

Tom and Grace exchanged martyred looks. 'It's not the same as going away,' Tom said. 'And you *can* afford it, Mum. I mean, that's why you married Patrick, isn't it?'

Sensing that Lou was at the end of her tether, Patrick put down his newspaper. 'That's enough,' he said sternly.

'But, Patrick, you want to go away somewhere, don't you?' Grace tried to cajole him.

'Patrick has a job to do,' said Lou quickly, not wanting him to get any more involved. 'He'll probably be busy at the end of October.'

And there was always Holly to keep him at home now.

'I could probably take some time off,' said Patrick. He glanced at Lou, who was at the sink, the set of her shoulders tense. She hadn't said anything to him about half-term, he realised. Perhaps she didn't want him to go with them?

'Lou?' he said tentatively. 'Maybe we can work something out here.'

She turned, wiping her hands on a tea towel. 'What sort of something?'

'Why don't you go and see Fenny on your own? There's no reason why you shouldn't go next week if you want.

I'll look after the kids. And then perhaps we could all go away together at half-term?'

'Oh, yes! Yes! *Please!*' Grace and Tom were ecstatic, but Patrick held up a hand to check their exuberance.

'I want to know what your mother thinks first.'

Lou was torn. Part of her longed to go away on her own, but there had been nothing in their agreement about Patrick looking after the children. He hadn't wanted anything to do with them at all, but now he was offering, not only to care for them, but also take them away for a week for a holiday she was pretty sure he wouldn't enjoy.

'That seems to be asking a lot of you,' she prevaricated.

'Not really.' He shrugged. 'I'm quite happy to do that. I just don't want to undermine your authority. If you think Grace and Tom should go to Yorkshire with you at half-term, then that's what will happen, and there'll be no more arguing. I was simply suggesting a compromise.'

He was offering her a way out of what would otherwise turn into an entrenched battle of wills, Lou realised. This was not the time to stand on her dignity. That would just make things worse.

'It sounds a good compromise to me,' she said.

Grace and Tom were delighted and immediately set up a clamour of conflicting demands about the holiday.

'OK, here's the deal,' said Patrick, shouting them down at last. 'You two go away and agree on the kind of holiday you want. You choose a country that's within three hours' flying time from London, and what you want to do when you're there, and we'll all go there for a week.'

'We can *choose*?' They couldn't believe their luck.

'Only if you stop hassling your mother,' he warned them, and they nodded eagerly as they scrambled off their chairs and gathered up their school bags.

'OK, Patrick.'

'That was very kind of you,' Lou said quietly when they had gone.

Patrick made a big deal of folding up his newspaper. 'Anything for a quiet life,' he said.

'Still…'

He looked up and their eyes met for what seemed the first time in weeks. 'You look tired,' he said roughly, not liking the drawn look she had.

'I haven't been sleeping well recently,' she admitted. 'I don't know why.'

Although it probably had a lot to do with the fact that he was seeing another woman and she was supposed not to care.

'You could probably do with a break,' said Patrick, and the warm concern in his eyes made her want to cry.

'It sounds wonderful,' she admitted. 'But I don't feel I deserve it. It's not as if I have a hard life here.'

'Go and have a holiday anyway. I expect Fenny would like to see you on your own.'

'But I can't leave the kids,' she said, fighting temptation. 'Someone really has to be here when they get in from school.'

'I can do that for a few days. I've got a computer here. There's plenty I can do from home if I need to.'

'What about meals, though?' Lou fretted and Patrick pushed back his chair.

'I'm not entirely helpless. I can peel a potato and use a microwave. They won't get the kind of meals you cook for them, but it won't kill them for a few days. We'll manage.'

Lou thought Tom and Grace would probably love a week of not being made to eat fresh fruit and vegetables the whole time.

'What about Holly?' she blurted out and Patrick stilled for a moment as he shrugged on his jacket.

He had taken Holly out once more. They had gone to
the opera one night, but the evening hadn't been any more
of a success than the first one, and he had found himself
repelled by her ruthlessness and unconcern about the fact
that he was married. When he had made another excuse to
leave her at her door, she had laughed mockingly.

'Funny, I didn't have you down as the hen-pecked type.
Is she very fierce, your wife?'

Patrick was furious that Holly would dare mention Lou.
'She's worth a thousand of you,' he said coldly.

Holly smiled with calculated allure and stepped closer to
run a suggestive hand down his lapel. 'Then why are you
here?'

Patrick detached her hand with distaste. 'I don't know,'
he said.

Now he looked across at Lou, still sitting at the kitchen
table with tired eyes and a worried expression. She would
look washed out next to Holly today. Holly was cleverer,
smarter, prettier.

And Lou was warmer and kinder and more loving.

'You don't need to worry about Holly,' he told her.

Lou left for Yorkshire two days later. Patrick missed her
horribly. He kept looking for her, expecting to turn round
and see her, dark and warm. He felt restless and uneasy,
forever fidgeting and unable to concentrate on work. It was
as if he were waiting and waiting for something, but he
didn't know what it was.

Whatever it was, he wished it would just hurry up. He
hated feeling like this. Patrick was proud of his ability to
focus. It was the secret of his success, after all. Always he
had been able to identify what he wanted, and go for it.

Now he didn't even know what he wanted.

Unless it was for Lou to come home.

The house was empty without her, even though Grace and Tom were there. They seemed to accept their mother's absence more readily than he did, and were full of plans for the half-term holiday, heatedly arguing over which resort was likely to have the most attractions for them.

Patrick made sure they rang Lou every night. He thought she would want to hear from them, but deep down he knew his reminders were purely selfish. He could always think of an excuse to take the phone when the kids had finished and hear her voice.

She was having a great time, she told him. She and Fenny pottered around the garden, and she had been for some long walks on her own. She felt much better. The weather was beautiful. If it weren't for the kids, she would be tempted to stay for ever.

'I think they'd miss you,' said Patrick. *I'd miss you.*

'They sound absolutely fine,' said Lou, and he could hear the smile in her voice. 'But I supposed I'd better come home and let you get back to work. I'll see you on Friday.'

Patrick couldn't wait. He caught himself looking at the clock and calculating how many hours until he would see her. Pathetic. He rolled his eyes at himself. Anyone would think he was in love with her.

*Anyone would think he was in love with her.*

He rewound mentally and played the same thought over more slowly while the truth of it sank into his mind. Of course anyone would think that. They would think it because it was true. He was in love with Lou.

How had *that* happened?

Falling in love with Lou hadn't been the idea at all. Patrick sat stunned at his own obtuseness. Oh, he could appreciate the irony. After all those years avoiding love, avoiding commitment, running away from the beautiful girls who tried to get too close, it turned out that the only woman he wanted was a middle-aged mother of two.

A middle-aged mother who had insensibly become the centre of his existence, whose dark eyes lit with laughter, and whose presence calmed and consoled him in a way nothing else could.

A middle-aged mother who only wanted to be his friend.

*I'll never fall in love again,* she had said. Lawrie had hurt her too much, she had said. She didn't want to love again. It would take a lot for her to trust enough to love him the way he loved her, Patrick realised, especially given the deal they had made.

So he wouldn't tell her yet. He would try first to get back the easy friendship they had lost since that kiss in the back of the limousine. They had both been trying since then, but it hadn't been the same, and they both knew it. That could change, though. And when they were friends again, he would tell her that he didn't want his precious freedom any more. He only wanted her.

Lou was his wife, after all. Surely he could tell her that?

Together with Grace and Tom, Patrick planned a special meal to welcome Lou back that Friday. Most of it was pre-prepared, it was true, but they had chosen each dish carefully, laid the table and lit candles.

'We even got salad for you, Mum,' said Tom, wanting to make sure that she appreciated the lengths they had gone to for her.

Lou looked at the three of them and her throat felt so tight she was afraid she might cry. 'It all looks lovely. Thank you.'

'We missed you,' Grace said. 'Didn't we, Patrick?'

'Yes, we did.' Patrick was amazed at how calm his voice sounded. Inside he felt like a stammering schoolboy. His chest hurt at the sight of her smile, and he was so pleased to see her again he could hardly speak.

Lou was glad to be home. She had enjoyed her time with Fenny, and was restored by her week away. She had been doing a lot of thinking on her long walks in the hills, and she knew now how close she had come to falling in love with Patrick.

Patrick had never pretended that he loved her, or that there was any chance of him loving her. She had been a fool to forget how much it had hurt when she'd realised that Lawrie didn't love her any more. Her world had fallen apart, and she wasn't going to let herself get hurt like that again. The dull ache she had felt when he had told her about Holly was a mere foretaste of what would be to come, and Lou couldn't face it.

She hadn't fallen too far, she convinced herself. She could stop now, seal off her heart, and not let herself feel any more for him than tepid friendship. It was merely a matter of mind over matter as in the old calypso song that her mother used to play.

And so it was. Lou didn't think it would be easy, but she knew she could do it. Living with Patrick would complicate matters, but she couldn't leave him. Grace and Tom were so happy. They didn't just accept Patrick, they liked him, and he liked them. Lou wouldn't do anything to jeopardise that relationship. Her children had had enough upheaval in their lives.

But she had to protect herself, too, so she would go back and be a friend to Patrick, just as she had promised. No more lying awake when he was out, wondering what he and Holly were doing. No more yearning for the impossible. No more would her heart pound when he walked into the room, Lou vowed to herself. She wouldn't even *think* about touching him, holding him, kissing him.

That way lay heartache, and her heart was scarred enough as it was.

'I'm sorry I was so tense before I went away,' she told Patrick that night after Grace and Tom had gone to bed.

'You seem much more relaxed now,' he commented, thinking how much better the world seemed just because she was there on the other side of the table.

'I am,' she said. 'I've been doing a lot of thinking.'

'What about?'

'About us. About our marriage.'

'Oh?' Patrick's guts knotted in anticipation. Was it possible that she had changed her mind too?

'I've realised how important our friendship is to me,' said Lou. 'I think I was a little jealous of Holly,' she admitted honestly, 'but I know that being friends is worth so much more than a physical relationship. I just wanted you to know that I won't be tense like that again when you go out with her or anyone else for that matter. That side of your life is nothing to do with me, and I want it to stay that way.'

Right, so no change of mind, then. Patrick fought down the disappointment. 'Great,' he said.

Lou got up and smiled at him. 'I don't think I've ever thanked you properly for everything you've done for us, Patrick,' she said. 'You've given us somewhere wonderful to live. The children are happy. Thanks to you, Fenny and I had a lovely week together.' She gestured at the guttering candles. 'And now this lovely meal.'

Sitting heavily in his chair, Patrick closed his eyes and breathed in the scent of her perfume as she bent and kissed him on the cheek, very gently. 'Thank you,' she said softly. 'This is the only way I'll kiss you now, so you don't need to worry about any more emotional hassles. I'm glad we didn't make love that night. It's better to be dear friends, isn't it?'

What could he say? 'Yes,' said Patrick in a curiously colourless voice. 'Much better.'

'So how are things going with you and Patrick?' Marisa asked a few weeks later. She was sitting at the kitchen table, filing her nails while Lou got supper ready. They were going out for an evening together as soon as Patrick got home.

'Fine,' said Lou. 'Great, in fact.'

They *were* great, she thought. Grace and Tom's choice of Minorca for a holiday had been a great success, and Patrick had joined in with everything with good grace. Back home, he didn't seem to be going out very much at all so that they had almost got their old, easy companionship back.

Almost, but not quite. Not once, by a word or a look, did Patrick ever do anything to suggest that he wanted more than quiet friendship either. Sometimes Lou even wondered if she had dreamt that wild, passionate kiss they had shared. In the circumstances, she should have been able to relax completely, but she still didn't seem to be able to do anything about the instinctive tightening of her muscles at the sight of him, or about the subtle shift in the atmosphere when he was in the room.

Mind over matter, Lou reminded herself when she found herself noticing it too much.

'Still on the just-good-friends thing?' asked Marisa, apparently intent on a hangnail.

'Yes.' Lou could hear the faintly defensive note in her voice. 'Why?'

'I just wondered. I saw your face when Patrick came in the other day, that's all.'

'What day was that?'

'You know, Grace's birthday.'

'Oh, then.' Lou rummaged in the fridge to avoid Marisa's sharp eyes. For all her friend only ever seemed to be concerned about her appearance, she missed nothing.

Patrick had come back from work on that wet November evening to find the kitchen full of warmth and light and laughter. Grace had invited her three closest friends round, and they had lobbied to make pancakes in lieu of a more traditional birthday dinner. There had been flour everywhere and stray splatters of pancake batter had decorated the work surfaces.

Lou had been supervising. Marisa, there in her role as Grace's godmother, had been drinking champagne and keeping well out of the range of the pancake tossing, but Tom had been in the thick of it and allowed to have his own go at flipping a pancake in the air.

There had been much giggling when Patrick had walked in.

'Patrick, come and have a go,' Grace insisted, dragging him over to the table.

'Give him a chance to get his coat off, Grace,' Lou protested, but she might as well have saved her breath. Patrick was bullied into discarding his jacket and rolling up his sleeves.

'I've never done this before,' he said as he loosened his tie.

'It's quite difficult,' Tom told him. 'Mum can do it, but the rest of us are useless.'

'I did it,' Grace fired up immediately. 'Sort of. But you show him, Mum,' she added graciously.

So Lou showed Patrick how to pour in the batter and swirl it round, then wait for just the right moment before giving the pan a quick, sharp flip.

She was standing very close to him, close enough to smell the clean, distinctive male scent of him. Close enough to see the texture of his skin, the way his hair grew, and the prickle of stubble on his jaw. Close enough to count the lines starring his eyes. It was hard to breathe there for a minute. Hard to remember that it was merely a matter of mind over matter.

Patrick made a comical face and flipped the pancake over, just catching it back in the pan. He turned with a mock bow to receive the applause of his audience.

'You did it!' The children were all gratifyingly impressed.

'Beginner's luck,' Patrick explained over the excitement and glanced at Lou with a smile. 'And a good teacher!'

He had given Grace shaggy snow boots for her birthday. They were for her to take on the skiing trip she had so longed for and which was now confirmed. Lou remembered how Grace's face had lit up that morning when she'd opened them, the easy way she'd hugged Patrick to thank him.

She watched him laughing with the children as they insisted that he eat the pancake he had tossed so impressively. Grace sprinkled on sugar while Tom leant against Patrick's shoulder, and Lou's heart contracted at the sight of them together.

And of course Marisa had seen.

'How long are you going to keep up this pretence that you don't love him?' said Marisa, holding the back of her hand up to inspect her nails.

There was a tiny pause. 'I don't love him,' said Lou.

Marisa sighed. 'Lou. Look at me.' Reluctantly Lou met her friend's eyes. 'Now say that again.'

'I don't *want* to love him,' Lou said wretchedly, abandoning the supper to slump down at the table opposite her friend. 'I want things to stay as they are. I want us to be friends.' If she said it enough, she would believe it.

'Friends isn't enough when you look at a man the way you look at Patrick,' said Marisa.

'It's better than being hurt.'

'Lou, Patrick isn't Lawrie. I'm sure he's stubborn and pigheaded and unbelievably difficult a lot of the time, but basically he's a good man. And he loves you.'

'He doesn't.'

'Of course he does.' Marisa rolled her eyes. 'God, it's so obvious! Honestly, Lou, I can't believe you two are being so obtuse. The man can't take his eyes off you.'

'Really?' Lou was torn between disbelief and hope.

'Yes, *really*, and it's time you did something about it. You're married to a good man who you love and who loves you. Why are you wasting time like this?'

Lou chewed her thumb. 'I don't want to risk what we've got,' she tried to explain.

'Then you're a fool,' said Marisa roundly. 'Sure, it's good to be friends, but you've got other friends. You could have Patrick as a lover as well. You could have a real marriage.'

She gave an exasperated sigh when Lou still dithered uncertainly. 'You've talked a lot over the years about wanting Grace and Tom to grow up with the example of a loving relationship, Lou. Well, give them one! Don't waste your life being afraid that he'll let you down and hurt you the way Lawrie did. There are no guarantees in any relationship, and I guess you'll have to work at it, but it seems to me that a strong and loving marriage would be worth the effort and the risk.'

It would be. Of course it would be. But only if Patrick wanted it too, and Lou wasn't sure that he did. He had chosen his freedom over her once before.

She tried to explain this to Marisa. 'And I've spent so long insisting that I just want to be friends, I wouldn't know how to tell him that I've changed my mind.'

'You could always try sending the kids to bed early and coming down in stockings, high heels and something lacy,' said Marisa. 'He'd be bound to get the point then.'

'I can't do that!' Lou felt her face grow hot at the very thought. 'It would just embarrass Patrick.'

Marisa grinned. 'It's a long time since you've been with a man, isn't it, Lou? Of *course* he wouldn't be embarrassed. He'd be too busy not being able to believe his luck! And Patrick looks like a stocking man to me. I saw the way he was looking at that suit you wore at the wedding.'

'I'm not prancing around in stockings!'

'Well, then, you're going to have to fall back on the last resort of relationships in crisis.'

'What's that?'

'Talking,' said Marisa. 'I hate to break it to you, Lou, but you're both big people. For heaven's sake, just sit him down and tell him how you feel!'

Easy for Marisa to say, thought Lou the following evening as she waited edgily for the time when she could legitimately send Grace and Tom to bed. By the time she and Patrick were finally alone, she was in such a dither that she could hardly sit still.

'I was, er, wondering if we could have a little chat,' she said and grimaced inwardly as she heard herself. She sounded as if she were inviting the office junior in to talk about unpunctuality.

'Sure.' Patrick looked a little surprised at her formal tone. 'Is this serious?'

'No…well, yes…in a way…' Lou trailed off helplessly.

'Shall we have a drink, then?'

'Good idea.' She certainly needed one.

When Patrick brought her a whisky, she gulped at it for courage. After a moment's hesitation, he sat down at the other end of the cream sofa.

'What is it, Lou?'

Lou cleared her throat. 'Well, I was just wondering…that is…well, no, the thing is…' Oh, God, how *were* you supposed to ask your husband to make love to you?

She was still dithering about how to put it, and beginning to wonder if it might not have been easier to go for the stocking option after all, when the phone rang.

It was the perfect diversion. Lou leapt up to answer it, but as she listened to the voice at the other end the colour drained slowly from her face.

'Lou?' Patrick got up in concern as she put the phone down and he saw her expression. 'What is it?'

'It's Fenny,' she said in a voice that seemed to belong to someone else entirely. 'She's had a stroke.'

# CHAPTER TEN

Lou wanted to set off immediately. 'I've got to get to the hospital,' she said, pacing around the room, desperately trying to work out what needed to be done. 'If I got a taxi to the station, I might still be able to get a train... I'll have to tell the kids... Perhaps I should take them with me, but it's too late to wake them up...'

Chewing her thumb anxiously, she turned to Patrick. 'What do you think?'

'I think you should sit down and drink this,' said Patrick, topping up her glass of whisky. 'You're not going anywhere tonight.'

'But I must see Fenny!' she protested as he pushed her gently back onto the sofa and made sure that her fingers had closed around the glass.

'There's nothing you can do tonight, Lou. Even if you get the last train north, you won't be able to get a connection to Skipton. We'll get up early tomorrow morning and I'll drive you to the hospital. If we leave at five, we could be there by nine.'

'But you've got meetings...'

He shrugged. 'Meetings can be rearranged.'

Lou felt shaky and close to tears. 'What about Grace and Tom?'

'We'll ring Marisa in a minute. She'll come and look after things here.' Patrick sat down next to Lou and nodded at the whisky. 'Drink that. It'll steady you.'

Obediently, Lou took a sip, choking a little as the fiery liquid hit the back of her throat.

168

'Better?'

The peaty warmth was spreading down her throat and settling in her stomach, and Lou felt steadier, just as he had said she would.

'Yes. Sorry. I don't seem to be able to think clearly.'

'You don't need to think about anything right now.' He took her hand. 'I'll sort it out. Now, tell me what Fenny's neighbour said.'

His warm, firm clasp was immensely comforting, but made it harder to be strong. Tears prickled behind Lou's eyes and she blinked them fiercely back.

'She didn't know much. She'd just popped in to see Fenny about flowers for the church, and she found her lying on the kitchen floor. She called an ambulance, and went with them to the hospital because there wasn't anyone else.' Lou drew a shaky breath. 'She told me the doctors said it wasn't looking good.'

She looked at Patrick, her dark eyes stark. 'Fenny's my rock,' she said, trying to keep her voice under control, but it cracked a little all the same. 'I can't bear to lose her. It would be like losing my mother all over again.'

'I know,' he said, and his grip tightened around her hand. 'I know.'

With a huge effort, Lou pulled herself together. She put down her whisky and dabbed her fingers under her eyes to stop any rogue tears from spilling over. 'I mustn't carry on like this,' she said. 'I've got to be strong.'

Patrick let go of her hand and pulled her firmly into his arms. It wasn't the way he had wanted to be holding her, but right now she needed to be held like a child, not a woman, and after a moment's resistance he felt her weaken and turn instinctively into him.

'You don't need to be strong tonight,' he said, resting his cheek against her silky hair. 'I'm here.'

*　　*　　*

Fenny looked very small and very frail in the hospital bed. She had always been so active that Lou had never thought of her as elderly, but she looked old now. Throat tight, Lou sat beside her aunt and held her thin hand, willing her to get better.

But Fenny didn't get better. At one point she opened her eyes and saw Lou sitting desperately beside her.

'...oo,' she slurred.

'Yes, Fenny, it's me, Lou. I'm here.'

Fenny tried to say something else, and Lou leant forward to try and make out the word.

'Patrick?' she guessed, and Fenny managed a tiny nod of assent.

'Patrick's with me. He's just outside. Look, here he is,' she said, turning as she heard the door open behind her.

Patrick moved over to the bed so Fenny could see him. He had been talking to the ward sister who had told him that Fenny was sinking fast. 'Hello, Fenny,' he said, and his voice was so normal, so reassuring, that Lou wanted to cry all over again. Funny how he could make everything seem better just by standing there.

Fenny struggled to say something more, her eyes trying to convey some urgent message as they flicked between him and Lou, and Patrick suddenly realised what it was that she wanted.

He put a hand on Lou's shoulder. 'Don't worry, Fenny,' he said. 'I'll look after Lou. I promise.'

There was no mistaking the relief in Fenny's eyes, and one side of her mouth tried to smile. '-ood,' she said, and visibly relaxed, lapsing back into sleep.

She died just over an hour later, very quietly, with Lou still holding her hand.

Patrick dealt with everything. He talked to the nurses and

made all the arrangements, while Lou sat numbly, unable to take in the fact that Fenny had gone. Then he put his hand under her elbow and guided her out of the hospital, and put her in the car. He didn't try to make her talk. He just made sure the car was warm, and drove her back to Fenny's house, where he lit the fire and made her tea, and then held her when the numbness cracked and she fell apart.

He let her cry until she was too exhausted to cry any more, and then he took her upstairs and put her in a chair while he made the bed up for her. Numb with misery, pig-eyed from crying, Lou sat unresisting as he wiped her face with a flannel and helped her out of her clothes.

For the next couple of days, he was everywhere, dealing with all the practicalities, gently bullying Lou into eating, buttoning her coat and taking her out for a blustery walk, cleaning the fire and laying it so that he could light it for her as soon as she came in.

And gradually, Lou began to feel better, better enough to feel a real pang when Patrick told her that he was going back to London.

'I'll go and get Grace and Tom,' he said. 'They'd want to be here for the funeral. We'll be back tomorrow.' He hesitated, looking at Lou in concern. 'Will you be OK here on your own for a night?'

'Yes, I'll be fine,' said Lou. 'I'm OK now.'

But she missed him horribly when he had gone.

I'm relying on him, she thought, watching the Porsche drive out of sight, and letting her hand fall forlornly to her side. It was so long since she had let herself rely on anyone that it felt strange. Strange and indescribably comforting.

They buried Fenny on a crisp winter day. The trees were stark against a pale blue sky and the bite in the air brought colour to Grace's pale cheeks. Lou held her hand, and

Patrick stood beside her, a comforting hand on Tom's shoulder.

Lou watched desolately as Fenny's coffin was lowered into the ground next to her husband. Fenny had been there for her when her parents died, when Lawrie left her, through all the bad times, and the good. And she had understood what it was like to be on your own. A widow for thirty-five years, she had only been forty-nine when Donald had died.

Not much older than Lou was now. Lou felt sick and giddy at the thought. How would she feel if she lost Patrick? If she had to spend thirty-five years wishing that she had made the most of the time they had together, as Fenny and Donald had done, instead of pretending that she didn't care, that it didn't matter if Patrick didn't love her the way she loved him?

She glanced at Patrick, standing massive and reassuring beside her, offering her son unobtrusive comfort, and she remembered how anxious Fenny had been to see him, how her aunt had relaxed at his promise. *I'll look after Lou,* he had said.

Surely he loved her too? Like Fenny, he had been there when she'd needed him. For the first time, Lou hadn't had to deal with everything by herself. Patrick had done it all. He wouldn't have done that unless he loved her, would he?

The only question was *how* he loved her. Did he love her as a dear friend, or as a wife?

She was going to have to find out, Lou resolved. Not right then, when they were all still so upset about Fenny, but soon. Marisa was right. Their marriage couldn't carry on the way it had been. Being friends wasn't enough, and Lou was just going to have to do something about it.

Patrick drove Grace and Tom back to London the next day. Lou was going to stay on for a few more days to sort out Fenny's things and see her solicitor about settling her affairs, but the children needed to go back to school, and Patrick had some urgent meetings he couldn't put off any longer.

'I'll come and get you next weekend,' he said to Lou as he closed the boot of the car. She had kissed Grace and Tom goodbye, and stood waiting to wave them off, hugging her arms against the cold.

'You know, there's no need for you to drive up and down the country like this,' she tried. 'I could get the train back.'

Patrick opened the driver's door. 'I'll be back on Friday night,' he said as if she hadn't spoken.

As she had known he would. She was getting used to being looked after, Lou thought guiltily. But it was a nice feeling.

'Thank you for everything, Patrick,' she said.

He hesitated, then came back and kissed her on the cheek. 'Take care,' he said.

A peck on the cheek, was it? That was going to change.

'Drive carefully,' said Lou, and gave him a friendly hug in return. She could do friends. For now.

What she needed was a plan of action. Lou waved until the car was out of sight, and then turned back to go into the cottage. Inside, the fire was swept and laid ready for her to light it. Patrick must have done that this morning while she was having a bath.

She searched for the matches on the mantelpiece. Crouching in front of the fire, she struck a match and held it out to a piece of paper, watching as the flame caught, flickered and then grew, spreading under the kindling.

Like her feelings for Patrick, really. It was hard to remember now how completely uninterested she had been in him when she had first met him. Three months working with him, and not once had she noticed his mouth or his hands or the way his eyes lit when he smiled. Not a flicker.

Then there had been that night in Newcastle. That had been a spark.

And then that kiss in the back of the car. That had been a definite flicker.

Now Lou wanted a blaze.

Patrick had been so kind over the last few days. She thought about that first night when they had come back from the hospital to find the cottage empty. His kindness and gentleness had been what she'd needed that night, but she didn't need that any more. She wanted him to take her to bed again, and this time she wanted him to treat her like a woman, not a friend. She wanted him to be demanding, not gentle, hot, not warm, but he wouldn't be as long as they stuck to their agreement to be just friends.

Their marriage was just like the fire that Patrick had made for her so carefully that morning, thought Lou. It had everything necessary to burn but right now it was cold, still perfectly laid, needing only a match to get it going.

And she would light it when Patrick came back.

Patrick parked the car outside the cottage. It was late, but he hadn't wanted to wait another day before seeing Lou. The lights were on in the house, glowing and welcoming through the dark and the rain.

The next moment the front door opened and Lou appeared, silhouetted in a rectangle of yellow light. Patrick felt the tension inside him release at the sight of her. It had been a wet and windy drive, with endless hold-ups on the motorway as the heavy traffic crept along nose to tail, but it was worth it to think that he would be walking into the warm house and she would be there, smiling.

He was going to tell her how he felt. Patrick had decided

that on the way up in the car. He wasn't that sure if this was the right time—it wasn't that long since Fenny had died, after all—but he wasn't going to ask anything of Lou or make any demands. He would give her all the time she wanted. He just needed to say that he loved her, that was all.

Pulling his mac over his head, he grabbed his overnight bag and ran through the rain for the door.

'Hello.' Lou stepped back to let him into the warm, and Patrick was seized by an inexplicable shyness as he shook the raindrops from his coat. What was going on? He had never been shy in his life. It was just Lou. His wife.

She looked so beautiful, though, with her dark eyes and her dark hair. She was wearing a soft red jumper and a straight skirt that stopped at her knees and reminded him irresistibly of those little suits she had worn when she was his PA, the ones that she might or might not have been wearing stockings with. Just looking at her made Patrick's chest hurt.

But there was a constraint about her that made him hesitate. It wasn't shyness, he realised. It was fear that she might not want him the way he so desperately wanted her. He would have to be very careful.

'Let me take that for you.' Lou took his coat and hung it up on a hook.

She was nervous. She had thought it all through, and now she had a plan. Even if they hadn't been interrupted by that awful phone call from Fenny's neighbour, Lou knew that she would have made a mess of sitting down and talking to him. It had been too difficult to find the right words.

So now she was going to try Marisa's first suggestion. She was going to seduce her own husband.

All she needed to do, Lou had decided, was to build up

some sexual tension, the kind that had fizzled so unexpectedly across the restaurant table in Newcastle. Then it would be a question of not spooking him. She needed to be sexy, but subtle. She had already created an intimate atmosphere in the sitting room, with the sofa pulled up in front of the fire, and a single table lamp adding a soft glow to the flickering firelight.

The only problem was her outfit. She didn't have anything remotely sexy in the clothes department with her. Understandably, it had been the last thing on her mind when she had thrown a few things into a case that night she had heard about Fenny's stroke. This jumper and skirt were the best she could do. Not exactly the slinky, shimmery little number that would slide off her shoulders at the mere brush of his fingers.

Still, slinky, silky dresses weren't ideal for opening the door on a night like this, or for hanging around in cold Dales kitchens, and she would probably have ruined the whole effect by putting a cardigan on whenever she left the warmth of the fire.

Once there, though, it would be fine. She would sit next to him on the sofa and inch gradually closer. She would run her fingers through her hair, make a lot of eye contact, moisten her lips a lot. She had seen it on television and it always worked then.

And then—Lou was a bit hazy about how this would happen exactly—they would kiss, and whoosh! The match would start the fire.

It was a good plan, but her desired image as a sultry, mysterious seductress was immediately thrown off balance when Patrick filled the hall, his nearness making her woozy, making it hard to remember her careful plan, urging her instead just to jump him and tell him she'd die if he didn't make love to her, right there, up against the coats hanging in the narrow hall.

And that wasn't likely to go down very well when he had been driving for five hours through the rush-hour traffic and the rain and the dark, was it? Lou took a steadying breath. No, let him come in, sit down, relax a bit. Then she could put her plan into action.

'Do you want a cup of tea?' she asked instead, backing away in case she brushed against him and ended up jumping him after all. 'Or something stronger?'

'Tea would be good,' said Patrick, rubbing a hand wearily over his face, and her heart clenched.

'Go and sit by the fire. I'll bring you a cup.'

Lou concentrated on breathing calmly as she waited for the kettle to boil. 'I can do this,' she told herself. 'I just need to be that match.'

When she carried the tea through into the sitting room Patrick was sitting on the sofa, his head dropped back and his eyes closed, but he stirred as she set the tray down on the stone hearth.

Lou had a moment's compunction. Maybe he was too tired for seduction? But tomorrow they were going back to London, and it would be so much harder once they were back in the usual routine with kids and homework and long days at the office.

She poured the tea and gave Patrick a mug, before sitting next to him with her own and gazing into the fire, taking courage from its merry blaze. Her relationship with Patrick could be that hot, if only she could find a way to convince him of that as well.

'How are the kids?' she asked. Pretty lame on the seduction front, but she had to start the conversation somewhere.

'They're fine,' he said. 'They'll be glad to have you back, though, and get back to normal.'

Lou sipped her tea. 'Funny, it's hard to remember what normal is now,' she said carefully. Perhaps this would be a good way to start the ball rolling?

'Our lives have changed so much this year,' she went on. 'It wasn't so long ago that normal was living in that cramped flat and taking the tube to work every morning. Since I've married you, there's been a whole new kind of normal. Not that you can really call our marriage normal, can you?'

'No, you can't.' It was too good an opening to miss, and Patrick decided to take the plunge. 'I guess most couples don't have the deal we do,' he said, equally cautious. 'And talking of that, Lou, there's something I think you should know.'

Lou went cold at the ominous phrase. He was going to tell her about some new girlfriend. Her cue was obvious. *What's that?* she was supposed to say, and then he would tell her about some long-legged blonde who had taken his fancy.

Unable to face hearing the words just yet, she rushed into speech. 'Actually, there's something you should know too,' she said. 'Something amazing, really.'

'Oh?' said Patrick, accepting his cue more readily than she had done.

'I went to see Fenny's solicitor yesterday,' Lou told him. 'Patrick, Fenny left me everything!'

'Surely you expected that?' he said gently.

'I knew she wanted to leave me the cottage, but I didn't think that there would be anything else,' said Lou. 'Fenny lived so frugally that I always assumed that she had to be careful with her pension. So much so that I can remember hoping that I would be able to afford to keep the cottage when the time came. I knew I would hate to sell it.'

She looked around the cosy sitting room, remembering the times she had sat there with her aunt. 'This is the closest I've got to a home.'

You've got a home with me, Patrick wanted to say, but didn't. Perhaps it didn't feel like home to Lou? The thought gave him a pang.

'Did she have some money put by, then?' he asked instead.

'A bit.' Lou's mouth twisted at the understatement, remembering how unprepared she had been when the solicitor had folded his hands and looked over his glasses at her.

'Your aunt was a very wealthy woman, Mrs Farr,' he said. 'I tried many times to get her to realise some of her assets to make her life more comfortable, but she always insisted that she had everything she wanted. She said that she couldn't be bothered to deal with it, and told me to invest it on your behalf. I naturally obeyed her instructions.'

The solicitor smiled a thin smile of restrained satisfaction. 'I have to tell you that you inherit a substantial amount of money, Mrs Farr.'

'I was flabbergasted,' Lou said, recounting the story to Patrick, who was listening with a sinking heart. 'I didn't have a clue that Fenny had any investments at all, and when he told me how much it was, I nearly passed out!'

Patrick put down his mug very carefully. 'It's a lot of money,' he said in a colourless voice.

'I know. He was full of advice about re-investing it, and thinking it through before I made any decisions. I think he thought that I was going to rush out and squander it all.'

'You should listen to him,' said Patrick. 'Think about what you really want and don't make any decisions in a hurry.'

'Well, I won't, but it's not as if anything's going to change, is it?' said Lou.

'Isn't it?' said Patrick flatly. 'I would have thought that everything was changed now.'

She stared at him. 'What do you mean?'

'You won't want to stay married to me any more, for a start,' he said with a forced smile. 'I know you miss Fenny badly, but if you'd known that this was going to happen, you wouldn't have made a deal like the one we made, would you?'

'No,' said Lou slowly.

She didn't like the way this conversation was going. She had only told him about the money to distract him from whatever he had been going to say, and now it looked as if she had given him another perfect opening. 'No, I wouldn't.'

'From what you've told me, you've got all the financial security you could ever want now,' said Patrick, trying to be fair, trying to be pleased for her, but all he could think was that she didn't need him any more.

Lou hadn't thought of it like that before. She hadn't really absorbed much beyond the fact that Fenny had been richer than she had ever imagined. Typical of her, really. She could have bought herself a new dress occasionally, or had a new range put in the kitchen, but Fenny had never bothered about things like that. As long as she could stay in the cottage and have her beloved garden, that was all she'd wanted.

'Yes, I suppose I have,' she said without enthusiasm.

Patrick took a deep breath. It wasn't fair on Lou to confuse the issue with emotions until she had absorbed all the implications of having financial independence of her own. She needed some time alone to think everything through.

'I'll quite understand if you want to reconsider the deal we made,' he said. 'I wouldn't contest a divorce.'

Lou couldn't believe that he was calmly sitting there, offering her a divorce, for all the world as if he didn't care one way or another. As if that was what he wanted.

*Was* that what he wanted?

She felt sick.

'What about you?' she said tightly. 'You wanted something from our deal too,' she reminded him.

Patrick avoided her eyes. 'Things have changed now. I don't want to make you stick to an agreement that doesn't make sense for you any more. We always agreed that we could divorce without any hard feelings.'

He might not have any hard feelings, but she certainly did. Lou was suddenly, gloriously, angry. If Patrick wanted out of their marriage, he could say so. She wasn't having him using her inheritance from Fenny as a convenient excuse to back out of an agreement that no longer suited him.

'Is reconsidering our deal what you wanted to talk about?' she asked him.

Patrick shifted uncomfortably. He didn't want to lie to her, but this obviously wasn't the time to tell her how he felt. 'Yes, in a way,' he said reluctantly.

'What's your problem with it?'

'I don't really want to talk about this now,' he said, cornered. Lou might not think that inheriting over two million pounds changed anything, but of course it did.

'Well, I do!' said Lou angrily. 'I think this is exactly the right time to talk about it. Tell me what you don't like about the deal we've got now.'

'It's too…constricting.'

'How? Have I ever made a fuss about you seeing anyone else?'

'No.'

'So you're just tired of the deal?'

'Yes,' Patrick admitted. At least he could be honest about that. 'I came here planning to ask you if you'd consider tearing up the pre-nuptial contract we both signed. And now that you're a wealthy woman in your own right, it's even more in your interests to think about doing just that.'

Lou had been gripping her mug of tea, but now she put it down on the tray and turned on the sofa so that one leg was tucked up beneath her.

'I want you to be honest with me,' she said, keeping her voice steady with an effort. 'Have you met someone else?'

'No.'

'So you don't want to marry anyone else?'

'God, no,' said Patrick, appalled.

'OK.' Lou tried to think of another reason why he might want to end the marriage, as it sounded as if he did. 'Do you just not want to be married?'

'*No!*' he protested, goaded into the truth at last. 'I like being married. I like being married to *you*,' he amended. 'I like coming home and finding you there. I like Grace and Tom. I like the way the house feels like a home. I like the mess and the noise and the fact that you've unpicked everything I paid that garden designer a fortune to do. I'm used to you,' he told her. 'I miss you when you're not there,' he said almost accusingly.

Lou's anger began to evaporate. She could feel it fizzling out of her as a tiny glimmer of hope uncurled deep inside. 'So what's wrong?'

'The deal's wrong.' Patrick ran a hand despairingly through his hair. 'I hate it that I can't touch you. I hate that when I come in you don't kiss me. I hate having separate rooms. Of *course* there isn't anyone else! I don't *want* anyone else. I just want you,' he finished, sounding defeated.

'I love you,' he said simply as Lou sat there, stunned. 'I

thought about you all the way up the motorway tonight. I planned what I was going to say. I was going to tell you how I felt and ask you if you would forget that stupid deal, if we could be married like normal people, arguing sometimes, and getting in a muddle but talking about it and getting through it, and loving each other... And now you tell me don't need me any more.'

Surprise helped Lou find her tongue. 'When did I say that?'

'Just now. Fenny's bequest has left you financially independent.'

'That's true,' she said, marvelling that he could be so dense. 'I don't need your money,' she agreed. 'But I need other things, Patrick. I need you to make me tea when I'm tired. I need you to help me deal with the kids. I need you to drive me up and down the country and be there for me the way you've been there for the last few weeks.

'But most of all, I need to see you. I need to know that you'll come home to me. I need to be able to reach out and touch you whenever I want.'

A smile hovered around her mouth. 'And what I need absolutely most of all is for you to kiss me.'

Patrick was staring at her, as if unable to believe what he was hearing.

'Now,' she prompted in case he had misunderstood, and a smile that started deep in his eyes spread over his face.

'If you insist,' he said, and Lou leant to meet him halfway, and then they were kissing, deep, sweet kisses that went on and on as they shifted to get closer, wriggling to touch, to press against each other, to feel each other. Patrick's hands were sliding under her jumper, hot against her skin, exploring her, unlocking her until she sighed with pleasure.

'I need you to love me,' she whispered between kisses. 'Do you think you can do that?'

Patrick pulled her down so that she slid underneath him. 'Yes, I can do that,' he said, kissing her throat, his lips warm and possessive, and she shivered luxuriously.

'Only me? Nobody else?'

He paused and lifted his head. 'What, not Grace and Tom?'

'No, I don't mind you loving them,' she conceded, pulling his shirt free of his trousers.

'What about my mother?' he teased her.

'Nobody young and beautiful that you're not related to,' said Lou, trying to sound stern, but it was hard when his hand was curved over her breast and his smile was warm against her skin.

'No, I won't love anyone like that,' he promised. 'I'll just love you…and my car. You don't mind that, do you?'

Lou smiled and wound her arms around his neck. 'I can live with that,' she said and sank back into his kisses.

'You're the only woman I've ever loved like this,' Patrick told her shakily a little later. 'You're the only one I've ever wanted like this. I haven't been able to think about another woman since that night in Newcastle.'

'Ha, and I suppose you were just playing tiddly-winks with Ariel in the Maldives!'

His lips twitched. 'I only took her to prove to myself that I wasn't obsessed with you, and it didn't work.'

'I don't believe you were obsessed with me at all!'

'I was. Utterly. I have been ever since I looked over that table and wondered whether you were wearing stockings or not. After that I couldn't *stop* wondering. I used to fantasise about you all the time.' He looked down into Lou's dark eyes. 'You can tell me now. Were you wearing stockings under all those little suits?'

Lou smiled and put his hand on her knee. 'Why don't you find out?' she whispered.

Patrick's hand slid under her skirt, feeling the warmth of her thigh beneath its sheer covering, drifting upwards until he caught his breath as his fingers found the top of the stocking, the clip on the suspender belt.

'If we weren't already married, I would ask you to marry me,' he said, his voice ragged with desire.

'And I'd say yes,' said Lou, no steadier.

'Would you? Would you marry me, not my money?'

'If you'd promise to love me for ever and not even look at a blonde again.'

'I promise,' he said seriously.

'It looks as if we won't be needing that divorce after all, then,' she said. 'You're stuck with me.'

Patrick laughed and pulled her closer. 'You're the only one I want to be stuck with!' he said as he kissed her again.

'You know, I had a plan to seduce you this evening,' said Lou breathlessly, long delicious minutes later. She wriggled on top of him so that her hair swung down and tickled his face and began to unbutton his shirt, kissing his chest as she went.

'That's the trouble with you middle-aged women,' Patrick pretended to grumble. 'You're only interested in sex. You haven't even told me that you love me!'

Lou kissed her way back up his throat. 'I love you,' she said, dropping soft kisses on his mouth between each promise. 'I love you, I love you, I love you.'

Patrick smiled against her kisses. 'It looks like you're going to get lucky, then,' he said, and rolled her over so that they slid off the sofa onto the hearthrug. His hands were warm on her thigh, fingering the top of her stocking, and Lou forgot about the need for a match. Their very own fire was already blazing high, and nothing could stop it now.

*Jessica Hart brings you more out-of-hours romance in*
Honeymoon with the Boss,
*available in June from Mills & Boon® Romance.*

# THE BOSS'S
# MISTRESS

**KATHRYN ROSS**

**Kathryn Ross** was born in Zambia, where her parents happened to live at that time. Educated in Ireland and England, she now lives in a village near Blackpool, Lancashire. Kathryn is a professional beauty therapist, but writing is her first love. As a child she wrote adventure stories, and at thirteen was editor of her school magazine. Happily, ten writing years later, *Designed with Love* was accepted by Mills & Boon. A romantic Sagittarian, she loves travelling to exotic locations.

# CHAPTER ONE

THE October day was drawing in early. It was only four-thirty and already a dark mist was settling over the River Liffey and the lights of Dublin twinkled in the dusky glow of the approaching evening.

Laura turned her car down the street that led to her office. She had just been out to the McClusky residence and was feeling pleased with herself. Clara McClusky was a very satisfied client and, though she said it herself, Laura had made a very good job of the interior design for her house. It looked stunning.

She smiled. All she had to do now was type up a report and add the photographs she had taken, then she could get home for the evening—perhaps take the children out for a pizza to celebrate the successful conclusion to a major contract. Hopefully, it *was* something to celebrate and she would still have a job next week. The unbidden thought made a cloud of concern settle over her.

The company she worked for was being taken over next week and she would have a new boss. It seemed strange to think that James Design was no longer going to be a family concern. She had been working for Robert James since her husband died four years ago. The job had been a godsend, coming at a time when she'd been most in need, with two children to take care of and a mountain of debt which her husband had left behind.

Robert had been so sweet to her and had overlooked the fact that she had little practical experience in the workplace, owing to the fact that marriage and children had taken her away from her career. Instead he had con-

5

centrated on the fact that she was a very well-qualified interior designer.

Laura hadn't let him down. She had worked hard and had more than proved herself in her job, so much so that she was subsequently made senior design consultant. Now, suddenly, Laura had this awful feeling that she was going to have to prove herself all over again. She very much wanted to make a good impression with the new owner, and prayed the McClusky account would swing it for her. She really needed this job.

Robert was nearly seventy, but she had hoped that when he decided to retire he would hand over the reins of the business to his stepson, Paul, and that the company would continue to run in the same time-honoured tradition that had made the James name synonymous with quality and distinctive furnishings in Ireland.

It had come as a severe shock when Robert had announced that the company was being taken over by a big multinational corporation. Powers PLC sounded big and impersonal and, by the sound of things, the man in control was ruthless and ambitious. Laura tried to console herself that Paul was still going to be on the board of directors so there would still be some of the old family's involvement...but somehow she couldn't see Paul standing up to a multinational firm if they decided on radical changes.

Robert had mooted to her that things would probably remain the same and not to worry about her job, but that was easier said than done. Whispers about redundancies and closure had been rife for a while now in the office.

This morning the rumours had escalated with the circulation of a memo to all members of staff, telling them that the new managing director would be interviewing each of them during the coming weeks. To help matters they were asked to fill in details about themselves on the accompanying forms.

'That's it,' Laura's secretary, Sandra, had muttered woefully. 'He's going to start weeding out the staff.'

'Not necessarily,' Laura had said, trying her best to be optimistic. 'Why would he do that when James is so successful? He probably just wants to get a clearer picture of his new staff.'

'Huh! Have you seen some of the questions on here?' Sandra had flapped the form in disgust. 'The only thing it doesn't ask is how many times you visit the bathroom in a day. Mark my words, our new boss isn't a kindly, approachable gentleman like Mr James—this man is only concerned with profit margins.

'If I were you, Laura, I wouldn't bother to answer some of the questions on his form. I certainly wouldn't tell him you're a single mother—it will probably go against you. He'll think you need to take time off for the children and kick you out.'

'He couldn't do that.' Laura had been appalled by the suggestion.

'He could if he had a good enough excuse.' Sandra had been unrepentant. 'Apparently, he's ruthless.'

Scaremongering rubbish, Laura told herself again now. It had come almost as a relief to get out of the office today, away from the gloomy mood which had descended.

Her thoughts were abruptly interrupted by a black cat, darting out into the road from between parked cars. Although she wasn't going fast she knew there was no way she could stop in time as it was too close so she reacted instinctively and swerved to avoid it. The next moment there was a sickening sound of metal scratching against metal as she scraped against the side of a car which had been in the process of overtaking her.

She slammed on the brakes a sinking feeling in the pit of her stomach. The other car continued for a moment and stopped just ahead of her. She noticed with horror that it was a brand-new, shiny, black BMW. Her hand shook as she reached for her doorhandle and stepped out into the road.

A bitter wind caught her long dark hair, swirling it across her face and obscuring her view of the tall man who climbed out of the driver's side of the other car.

'I'm really sorry—' She started to apologise in a low tone but he cut across her abruptly.

'You were driving like a damn maniac.'

She noticed his American accent. It was husky and, despite the angry note, quite sexy. She swept a hand over her face to hold her hair back so that she could look at him properly.

She would have estimated him to be about five years her senior, putting him at around thirty-seven, and he was very good-looking in an autocratic, overpowering kind of way. He had dark eyes in a lean, square-jawed face. 'I am sorry,' she said again, a trifle breathlessly. She glanced at the door of his car and tried to console herself that the damage wasn't too bad, just a long, ugly scratch.

'What the hell were you playing at?' he demanded.

'A cat ran out in front of me and I didn't want to hit it.' She shrugged helplessly. 'I didn't know what else to do.'

He looked at her as if he couldn't quite believe what she had just said. For a moment his eyes raked over her, taking in the gentle light in her wide green eyes and the generous curve of her soft lips. He could smell the warm tones of her perfume on the frosty air. She smelt of summer, honeysuckle and roses. He frowned. 'I didn't see a cat.' His voice had lost some of its abrasiveness.

'Well there *was* one, I assure you,' she told him crisply. She shivered. It was too cold to stand out here arguing. 'Anyway, you needn't worry, I am insured.'

'Damn good job. I've just taken delivery of my car today,' he muttered. 'Couldn't you just have slammed on your brakes?'

She opened her handbag, searching for a pen and paper with impatient fingers. 'Believe me, I would have if I could,' she said with annoyance. 'This is going to cost me dear—I'll lose my no-claims bonus. But let's keep things in perspective. At least it was just a piece of metal that got damaged and not a living creature.'

'It's a BMW, not a piece of metal.'

She flashed him a scathing look, and unexpectedly he grinned. 'Yours is the piece of metal.'

She had to admit that her car had seen better days but it was all she could afford and she took exception to the remark. 'There's nothing wrong with Doris,' she told him loftily. 'She has never let me down yet.'

One dark eyebrow lifted and he looked more amused than ever.

There was something extremely attractive about his smile and the gleam of his eyes in the darkness. It made him appear rakish, devilishly handsome. The notion and the feeling that suddenly stirred inside her made her feel awkward.

'Doris?' he drawled wryly. 'You call your car Doris?'

She felt herself flushing to the roots of her hair as she realised what she had said. He must think her completely crazy. She had used the car's name without thinking. Her children had named it Doris and the name had kind of stuck. It was her mother's influence. Laura's mother, Cora, had always named her cars.

'Yes. Doris.' She tried to sound matter-of-fact, as if everyone gave their car a name and it wasn't just one of her family's idiosyncrasies.

Thinking about her mother made her forget her embarrassment. She glanced at her watch. She didn't want to be late home. Cora looked after the children from the time they came home from school until Laura got in from work. It was a very satisfactory arrangement. Cora loved her grandchildren's company and Laura could re-

lax, knowing they were with someone she could wholeheartedly trust.

Her mother lived in the house next door so it didn't
really matter if she was home a little late but, even so,
Laura never overstepped the mark and always tried to
be home on time. Now she was behind schedule and she
still had to go into the office.

She scribbled down her details for him. 'Look, I've
got to go. Give me a ring tomorrow and tell me how
much the damage will cost. If it's not too high I might
not claim on my insurance.' She swept a hand through
her hair, her thoughts running to her financial situation.

He glanced at the piece of paper, before pushing it
into the deep pockets of his dark overcoat. 'OK, I'll
speak to you tomorrow.'

As Laura went back to her car she saw the black cat
on a garden wall, watching her, his green eyes luminous
in the glare of a passing car's headlights.

'Be more careful in future,' she told him sternly.
'You've just used up one of your nine lives.'

'Don't tell me you talk to Doris as well,' the man said
in a droll tone as he opened the door of his car.

'I was talking to the cat.' Laura nodded towards the
wall and the man followed her gaze, but the cat had
gone.

He shook his head and muttered something under his
breath, something she couldn't hear. Maybe it was just
as well, she thought as she started her car up again. It
would probably have been derisive.

She overtook him with a cursory nod of farewell.

'Where the heck have you been?' Sandra asked as she
walked into her office a couple of minutes later. 'Everyone has been looking for you. Mr James wanted a word,
and someone's been in to ask for your completed form
three times now.'

'What form?' Laura asked distractedly as she took off
her heavy overcoat and sat down behind her desk.

'The one for the profit-hungry new boss.' Sandra grinned.

'I'll fill that in over the weekend and hand it in on Monday morning,' Laura said decisively.

'It's up to you, but everyone else has handed theirs in,' Sandra said, before adding nonchalantly, 'And, apparently, the new boss is upstairs with Mr James as we speak.'

'What's he like?' Sandra had her full attention now.

'Haven't a clue. All I know is that Rosie, Mr James's secretary, was sent out for cherry buns, ready for his arrival, at four-thirty.'

Laura sighed. That was so typical of Robert James—he was so delightfully old-school and thoughtful. Things just wouldn't be the same around here without him.

'The days of cherry buns and coffee with the boss are well and truly in the past for us now.' Sandra sighed as well, and for a moment looked as if she wanted to cry.

'Look on the bright side. It will make it a lot easier for us to stick to a diet in future.' Laura smiled.

Sandra laughed and shook her head as she rose to leave. 'That's what I love about you, Laura. You always look on the positive side of things.'

The door closed behind her but Laura could still see her, walking down the corridor. The glass walls gave the feeling that one was sitting in a giant glass jardinière. Large plants broke up the modern geometric design of the place but there was little in the way of privacy. Except, of course, if you were the boss. He had a suite of offices upstairs.

She reached across and put on her desk lamp, then glanced at her watch. She hoped the new boss's sudden appearance today wouldn't delay her getting away tonight. Maybe she should take the children for pizza tomorrow night instead. Saturday was probably better than Friday night and she wanted to do some reading with Matthew before bedtime anyway.

Her eyes alighted on the photograph of her children on the desk. Joanne was so pretty, with straight blonde hair and blue eyes. She was almost thirteen now and the image of her late father. Matthew was more like Laura, dark hair and green-eyed. He was seven and a bundle of mischief.

Like most working mothers, Laura wished she could spend more time with her children. They were the most important thing in the world to her. But it was a catch twenty-two situation because she needed to work to pay the bills. The fact that she enjoyed her career made things a lot easier. She was good at her job. In fact, Robert James had come to rely on her more and more over these last few months.

The door of her office opened, for once catching her off guard. She glanced up, expecting to see Sandra again. She nearly fell off her chair as her eyes collided with those of the tall, handsome stranger whose car she had pranged earlier.

'What on earth are you doing here?' She felt her breath catch with a mixture of nerves and annoyance. Had he followed her to check up on her in case she didn't cough up for the damage to his car? The last thing she needed was a scene here in the office, with the new managing director prowling about. 'Look, this is not a good time for me. Please go away and we'll discuss the damage to your car tomorrow.'

One dark eyebrow lifted sardonically. 'But I want to talk to you now,' he said calmly.

She frowned, and out of the corner of her eye she saw Robert, walking down the corridor with another man following him who looked to be in his late fifties—obviously the new owner of the business. Her heart thumped unsteadily. 'Please,' she implored. 'I'm under a lot of pressure. I've got a new ogre of a boss about to breathe down my neck. You have my word I'll make it right with you about your car.'

'But how do I know you'll keep your word?' he drawled lazily.

'What?' Laura pulled her eyes away from her approaching boss as he passed the office next door and seemed to be heading straight for her. 'Look, just go...please. You've got my details and there's nothing more I can do right now about your precious car.'

'Ah, there you are, Laura.' Robert James walked into the room. He was a sprightly man, still handsome despite his advancing years. He smiled warmly at her. 'You've met the new managing director of James, Mr Rogan Powers?'

'No.' Laura rose from her desk and smiled at the grey-haired man who had come into the room behind him.

'Yes.' It wasn't the grey-haired man who spoke but the American stranger she had been hissing at a few seconds earlier. He stepped forward and held out his hand. 'We bumped into each other a little while ago, but we haven't yet been formally introduced,' he said with an amused smile.

Laura stared at him in shocked dismay. 'You're my new boss?'

He inclined his head. 'The ogre himself. Come to breathe down your neck with impunity.'

Her heart seemed to drop into her stomach and bounce back up again in a crazy lurch. Realising that he was still holding out his hand to her, she tried to pull herself together and limit the damage. 'Pleased to meet you, Mr Powers.' She extended her hand. 'I wish you had introduced yourself earlier.'

'I'm sure you do.' He didn't try to make her feel better—his tone was dry—but there was a gleam of amusement in his eyes as they met hers. 'By the way, everyone calls me Rogan.'

His handshake was firm, confident, as was his whole demeanour. He was very much in control of the situation. Laura felt completely out of her depth.

Her hand seemed to tingle long after he had released it from his grip. 'This is my accountant, Roland Cooper.' He indicated the man she had mistaken for him earlier.

The man smiled and nodded at her.

'Laura Taylor is one of my top interior design consultants,' Robert said with a smile. 'She knows this business inside out. A very talented woman.'

'Really.' Rogan Powers reached over to the desk and picked up some drawings she had left lying there. He leafed through them idly, yet Laura sensed that beneath the insouciant manner there was a sharp, perceptive mind at work.

He was very young to be managing director of such a large company. She wondered how he had achieved that at such a young age? Possibly Powers PLC had been a family-run company and his father and grandfather before him had built up the business.

'Have you got the photographs you took of the McClusky residence, Laura?' Robert asked now.

She nodded and got up to get her handbag from the desk behind her.

'All the soft furnishings used were from James Design, of course,' Robert continued.

She was aware that Rogan Powers was watching her, that his eyes were slipping over her slender figure and weighing her up, almost as if he could see through the fine linen material of her blue trouser suit to the silk of her underwear.

The idea made her hand a little unsteady as she closed her bag again and took the photographs out of the envelope. He took them from her and gave them a cursory look. They were interrupted by the appearance of a woman in the doorway. She was a very attractive blonde, probably a year or two older than Laura.

'Sorry, I'm a bit late, Rogan. I got held up at the office.' She also had an American accent, which was warm and almost honeyed as she spoke to Rogan.

'That's OK,' Rogan said nonchalantly. 'Karen White, meet Laura Taylor.' The two women nodded at each other. 'Karen is my private secretary.'

'These look good,' Rogan said slowly, returning his attention to the photographs, 'but, really, they don't mean a lot to me at the moment. I'm still feeling my way into the world of design.'

'Well, if you need to know anything Laura is your woman,' Robert said firmly. 'She's got a good business sense as well as an artistic eye.'

Robert was really building her up. Laura felt grateful to him, yet a little embarrassed as she met Rogan's dark eyes.

'I'll bear that in mind, Robert,' he murmured.

Laura wondered if he was being facetious. It was hard to tell just what was going on behind those dark, enigmatic eyes.

'Well, now that the team is all here, shall we adjourn upstairs?' Robert James suggested.

'By all means. Lead the way,' Rogan said easily.

One by one they filed out of Laura's office. Rogan was last. He paused in the doorway as the others walked down the corridor towards the lifts.

'I'll speak to you on Monday, Laura, about my… precious car.'

She tried not to blush. 'Yes, fine.' It was all she could think of to say.

He smiled. 'Let's hope Robert is right, and you design better than you drive.'

The door closed behind him and she flopped back into her chair, her legs feeling weak. So much for wanting to make a good impression on her new boss.

# CHAPTER TWO

'ISN'T Mr Powers absolutely gorgeous?' Sandra murmured dreamily as she came into the office to put some mail on Laura's desk. 'I think I'm in love.'

Laura grinned. 'Is this the same woman who was calling him a profit-hungry ogre last week?'

'Be fair, I hadn't seen him last week.' Sandra laughed.

'He is very good-looking,' Laura had to admit.

'Mind you, Carmel in Accounts says that he has a reputation with the women—breaks their hearts.'

'With respect, Sandra, how would Carmel know that? She does tend to like gossip and she doesn't always get things right.'

'Oh, Carmel's pretty reliable. Her cousin knows someone who knows him. He's got Irish roots on his mother's side. He's thirty-seven and still single.' Sandra's eyes sparkled with excitement.

'Imagine—all that wealth and those good looks and he's unattached! Apparently he made his fortune in computers—designed games or some kind of software. He founded Powers PLC and has diversified into lots of different businesses. The company is based in New York, and they own a big department store on Fifth Avenue.'

'Really.' Laura flicked through the diary on her desk and tried not to be interested. It never ceased to amaze her how comprehensive the gossipmongering was in these offices. Someone could come in as a complete stranger and half an hour later the whole block would know their seed, creed and generation. It irritated Laura because she liked her privacy and thought it was something everyone was entitled to.

16

'What's this?' Laura changed the subject and pointed to her diary.

Sandra bent over to peer at it. 'Lord Fitzroy changed the time of his appointment to four this afternoon. I took the call a little while ago.'

'Oh, no!' Laura shook her head in dismay. 'That means I'll be late getting home.'

'You shouldn't be. It's just a first consultation—'

'Sandra. He's the guy with the castle—remember? I know it's about three years ago now since we did a few rooms for him, but he does stick in the memory. A one-hour consultation lasted all day.'

Sandra giggled suddenly. 'Not the one you went to with Mr James's son?'

Laura nodded. 'One and the same.'

'I do remember him now.' Sandra laughed again. 'He didn't like Paul and insisted on you doing everything.'

'Who didn't like me?'

Both women looked up as Paul James strode into the room. He was in his early thirties and a good-looking man with thick blond hair and vivid blue eyes.

'Lord Fitzroy.' Laura smiled at the horrified expression on his handsome face at the mention of that name.

'You're not going to see him again?' he asked.

'Afraid so. Four o'clock this afternoon.'

'All I can say is I'm glad I'm just a director in the company now and not a designer.' Paul sauntered over and put a playful arm around her shoulder. 'You have my deepest sympathy, Laura, darling.'

Laura laughed. 'Sympathy is no help at all. You should be coming with me. I need moral support. Or do directors not venture out into the field?' she asked playfully.

'Certainly not. They drink coffee and attend only high-level meetings,' Paul said teasingly as he patted the thick file he had put on her desk. 'I'm here in an advisory capacity only. Got a meeting with Rogan in ten

minutes. I just popped in to ask you if you'd like to go
to the cinema tomorrow?'

'I can't, Paul. My mum goes out on a Tuesday night
and I've no one to babysit,' she said briskly. She was
used to Paul asking her out. There was no romance between them—they were just good friends and very often
when one or other was without a date, or at a loose end,
they would team up and go out.

'Maybe another night, then?' Paul said easily. He
broke off as he saw Rogan Powers, strolling down the
corridor towards the office. 'Here comes the great man
himself.'

Rogan stopped by the door and looked in. 'Good
morning.' Although the tone was jovial, the eyes that
swept over them were sharply assessing. With one
glance he took in the way Paul was standing so close to
Laura and the arm which still rested lightly around her
shoulder. 'You seem deep in conversation,' he remarked.

'Trying to cheer Laura up.' Paul grinned.

Rogan sent a questioning look at Laura. His eyes were
compelling, and she felt a tremor of awareness flow
through her body. It was an effort to think straight.
Rogan Powers was far too good-looking, she thought
with panic. The dark suit sat stylishly on his broad shoulders, and his chiselled features and penetrating eyes
added up to a tremendous sexy magnetism.

Mentally Laura shook herself and switched her
thoughts to business. 'I'm to go up to Lord Fitzroy today. He's thinking of having a few rooms in the castle
restored. The problem is he has changed the time of his
appointment to four o'clock this afternoon,' she explained. 'It means I'll probably finish late.'

'Does he live far away?'

'A bit of a drive, all right—back of the Wicklow
mountains. But it's not that. He tends to take up a lot of
time.'

'He lives in a castle so I suppose he would.' Rogan's

eyes rested on Laura for a few moments. The autumn sunshine slanted through the windows and caught her hair, showing the fiery red lights in the deep mahogany strands. Her skin was very pale and soft, in total contrast to the darkness of her hair.

'In fairness to Laura, it's not the work but Fitzroy himself that takes the time,' Paul said with a laugh.

'The Wicklow mountains,' Rogan said thoughtfully, without glancing at Paul. 'Wouldn't mind a drive up there myself. I think I'll come with you.' Laura felt a tremor of unease at the suggestion. 'Come with me?' she said, trying very hard to think of some excuse why he shouldn't. 'I'll be several hours, you know. I have a lot of rooms and plans to discuss.'

'That's OK. I'll enjoy watching you in action. It will give me some idea of how you operate.'

'Fine.' She tried to sound nonchalant, as if the whole idea didn't make her as nervous as hell. What could she say? She could hardly tell her boss that she was far too attracted to him and therefore would feel safer if he just kept his distance.

His eyes flicked over her slender figure in the smart blue trouser suit. 'What time should I pick you up?'

Heavens, he made it sound like a date! 'In about two hours?'

'Fine, see you then.' Rogan glanced at Paul. 'If you are ready, we'll go over that file now.'

Paul moved to pick up the paperwork. 'I'll ring you, Laura, and we'll arrange another time for the cinema—OK?' he asked casually.

She nodded, for some reason very aware of the way Rogan was watching them and listening to them.

Sandra sighed enviously as they were left alone again. 'You lucky devil, wish I was going out for the afternoon with Rogan Powers.'

Laura didn't feel lucky, just apprehensive. Rogan Powers made her feel on edge—very aware of herself as a woman first and an employee second. It was most disconcerting.

As Sandra left to go back to her own office Laura reached for the phone to tell her mother she might be late home.

As good as his word, Rogan arrived at her office door exactly two hours later.

They strolled out into the car park together. The sky was a clear baby blue and a chill breeze was ruffling the waters of the Liffey and stirring the trees so that the red and gold leaves fluttered to the ground, where they crackled underfoot.

'Where is your BMW?' Laura asked as she noticed he was leading her to a red estate car.

'It's being resprayed today. I hired this to be going on with,' Rogan answered as he put her briefcase in the boot.

Laura was horrified. 'But you should have given me the bill or at least an estimate for my insurance company.'

He laughed. 'Laura, I decided you were right and it's just a piece of metal. Forget about it.'

She frowned. 'I don't want to forget about it. I did the damage and I should pay for it.'

'Well, we'll come to some agreement,' Rogan said offhandedly as he opened the passenger door for her.

'Some agreement?' Laura said, as he took his own seat, and frowned. She felt a bit dubious about that remark. 'What do you mean?'

He flicked her an amused look as he started the car. 'I mean I want your body in part repayment. What do you think I mean?'

Her cheeks flared with heat at the outrageously sarcastic statement. 'I don't know, otherwise I wouldn't have asked,' she muttered crossly.

'You really think I would want your body as payment

towards the respraying of my BMW?' He roared with laughter. And the more he laughed the more foolish Laura felt.

'It's not that funny,' she said. 'No, I didn't think that. I guess I'm just very independent and I didn't like feeling…under an obligation to anyone, that's all.'

He glanced across at her, taking in the vulnerable light in her wide eyes. 'I was thinking more in terms of some work that I want doing,' he said gently. 'I've just bought a house here and the lounge and some of the bedrooms could do with an overhaul. I'd very much like it if you would have a look and give me your professional opinion on what should be done. I know you are very busy at the moment but if you could fit me into any spare time you have I'd be grateful.'

'Oh… Well, I can manage that.' She smiled at him.

She had a beautiful smile, fresh, exhilarating and utterly sincere.

Every now and then there was something about Laura that took him by surprise. It was a weird sensation for just a smile, a glance, or the way she held her head captivated him.

Her dark hair was slightly wild, as if she had hurriedly tried to tame it with some expensive product before she came out but it had failed to respond totally, giving the luxuriant waves a glossy wayward bounce which was somehow tremendously endearing.

She had incredible eyes, wide and an unusual shade of green, fringed with thick, dark lashes. A guy could just sink into those green depths and be very happy, he found himself thinking.

He wanted Laura Taylor. He had known it yesterday when he had watched her in her office, her eyes flashing with anger and then dismay, every emotion so clear and vividly intense. He had been surprised at the intensity of the desire she had stirred in him. He wanted to take her to bed…wanted that right now.

He raked a hand through his hair and told himself he was being completely crazy.

Women flowed through his life. He enjoyed being with them and respected them, but the relationships were never serious. That had only happened once and once had been enough. Now he preferred to take things at a more relaxed level. For all his dalliances he had two strict rules—no married women and never mix business with pleasure.

Although Laura didn't wear a wedding ring, she did work for him. He reminded himself of this now and looked away from her. 'Better give me directions to this castle,' he told her briskly.

She leaned forward as he drove out of the car park. 'First left,' she murmured, then looked down at the notes she held on her knee. 'Then right at the next traffic lights.'

He could smell her perfume—honeysuckle and roses. It reminded him of something in his childhood.

'So, what do you think of the transition at James?' he asked.

'A bit early to say yet.' Laura was truthful. 'I have to admit everyone has been a bit apprehensive about the safety of their jobs.'

'If they are doing their work well they have nothing to worry about,' Rogan said, 'but I can understand their concerns. I shall be calling a meeting in a few weeks after I've had a chance to see the place in operation. I'll put everyone in the picture as to what to expect then.'

The steely note under his jovial tone told Laura a lot. Rogan was a businessman—a man who was probably very astute, very sharp. Certainly no pushover.

'Is that why you've come along with me today—to see how well I can do my job?' she asked directly. 'Is it a case of ''Big Brother'' is watching me?'

'I hope I'm not in the least like Big Brother,' he said

with some amusement. 'No, I'm just interested to see how the business runs on a day-to-day level.'

'But, nevertheless, I had better be on my best behaviour.' She smiled.

He glanced across at her for a second. 'I can't imagine you being anything other than yourself. You are very natural.'

'I'm not sure how to take that.'

'Take it as a compliment,' he said with a smile. 'I like the way you say what you think. So many people tiptoe around me in the workplace. It gets very monotonous.'

'So I can say what I like to you, then?' she asked, a mischievous light in her green eyes. 'That's a dangerous licence you are handing me. I do tend to be very forthright sometimes.'

'Now you're scaring me,' he said with a grin.

She laughed at the idea of Rogan Powers being scared of anything.

They stopped at traffic lights. 'You're very beautiful, Laura. How come you've escaped the marriage net?' he asked suddenly, looking across at her. 'You're what? Twenty-seven?'

'I'm thirty-two.' She smiled. 'Don't you know it's bad form to ask a lady her age?'

'Well, as I'm your boss, we'll call it professional interest,' he said with a teasing gleam in his dark eyes. 'Actually, I have to admit that I had all the employees' files out last night, looking for yours. I was most disappointed when I discovered that the only details I had were your name and address.'

Laura tried not to be flattered by the way he was looking at her and by that underlying husky quality to his voice. 'Robert James didn't go in much for forms and questionnaires,' she said with a shrug.

'Well, I do.' Rogan grinned. 'I did circulate some last week, but you don't appear to have filled yours in.'

Laura felt her skin grow a little hot at that. 'Haven't

I?' she said airily, knowing full well that the form in question was still in the top drawer of her desk.

'No,' Rogan said, 'so you'll have to tell me all about yourself.'

'There's not much to tell.'

The low burr of Rogan's mobile phone cut across their conversation and Rogan reached to answer it. Laura was glad of the distraction. She didn't want the conversation to drift onto personal ground.

'Hi,' he said warmly. 'How are things?' He laughed at whatever had been the reply. 'I enjoyed it, too. We must do it again some time. I'll ring you, how's that? Fine. Got to go, I'm in heavy traffic. Great. See you.' He put the phone down again.

That had to be a woman, Laura thought. She remembered the gossip Sandra had been repeating this afternoon about him being a womaniser and a heart-breaker.

It was probably true. He was single and he was attractive so he could have his pick of women. And flirting would be as natural to him as eating. She shouldn't be flattered by his manner or the way he looked at her from time to time. It would mean nothing to a man like Rogan Powers.

'So, where were we?' Rogan asked. 'Oh, yes, you were telling me why you never married.'

'I did marry,' she said quietly. 'John died four years ago in a car crash.'

'I'm sorry.' His voice changed, the light teasing quality gone.

The genuine sympathy in his dark eyes made her heart contract sharply. 'It's OK, I've come to terms with it now,' she said simply. She took a deep breath and changed the subject. 'What do you think of Dublin?'

For a moment he hesitated, then he went along with her. 'I think it's a lovely city.' They were passing Trinity College with its green railings and serene lawns.

'I live just on the outskirts, but I love it here,' Laura said honestly. 'I can't imagine living anywhere else.'

'Who's that?' Rogan pointed to a bronze statue of a woman, wheeling a barrow, at the end of Grafton Street.

'Molly Mallone, of course.' Laura laughed. 'Or, as the wags like to call her, "the tart with the cart".'

Rogan laughed at that. It was a warm sound. She found herself staring at him and taking in everything about him—the fine crinkle of lines at the sides of his eyes, the sensual curve of his lips and the firm jawline that spoke of strength and determination.

He slanted a look at her and caught her watching him, and immediately she felt embarrassed.

'I suppose I'd better brief you about the client we are visiting today,' she said briskly, trying to pretend that the only thing on her mind was business.

'Maybe you'd better,' Rogan agreed, with a glint in his eye.

Did he know she was attracted to him? Laura wondered. She hoped sincerely that he didn't—it would make working with him too uncomfortable.

'What's his Lordship like?'

'A bit eccentric.' Laura started to feel better as the conversation centred on the work ahead. 'He likes to talk... I think in all honesty the poor man is a bit lonely. Although I sympathise, I feel I should warn you it might be best if we tell him we have another appointment today or we'll be stuck there for hours.'

'Got a hot date tonight, I take it?' Rogan asked with a smile.

She was about to tell him that she was rushing home to her children, but decided it was really none of his business. It was ridiculous but she was a bit nervous about mentioning the children after Sandra's crack in the office the other day. She wasn't sure what kind of man Rogan Powers was so she said instead, 'I've got plans for this evening.'

'With Paul James?'

'No, not with Paul.'

'I thought from the way he was speaking to you today that maybe you two are an item.'

'We do go out together on occasions, but it's nothing deeper than friendship.'

Rogan's eyebrows lifted at that. 'I've always maintained that it's not possible for a man and a woman to go out together and be just friends.'

'Well, we are,' Laura said firmly. 'I've known Paul for years.'

Rogan shook his head. 'I've always found that the sex issue clouds a relationship like that. Unless, of course, you have the passionate affair first—get it out of the way—then it's easier to drift into friendship.'

Laura felt her cheeks burning at those words. It was ridiculous the way he was able to embarrass her so easily. Her body reacted to him in a way that baffled her. 'I don't know how we got onto this subject,' she said with a nervous laugh, 'but I think we should leave it.'

'Why?'

'Because you are embarrassing me,' she said simply.

'Am I?' He slanted an amused look at her.

They were heading out into the country now and Laura paused to give Rogan more detailed directions on how to get to their destination, glad of the opportunity to change the subject.

The light mist which had risen as they left the city was becoming thicker the further up into the mountains they got. As they left the main roads for narrow winding ones it swirled in heavy, clammy swathes over the road ahead, making it necessary to drive very slowly.

'The castle is around here somewhere,' Laura said, her eyes straining to see through the mist. Suddenly dark wrought-iron gates loomed ahead. 'There!'

They drove through the gates and on for another few miles before the castle came into view. It was a spec-

tacular sight, tall with round towers that soared like
spears into the mist.

'Looks old,' Rogan remarked, as he parked the car
near the enormous brass-studded door.

'According to Lord Fitzroy, it is reputed to have been
the home of one of the Kings of Ireland. Though it looks
ancient enough to be true, I sincerely doubt a lot of the
tales and legends associated with it,' she said, as they
left the warmth of the car.

It was bitterly cold and they stood for what felt like
ages on the front step, waiting for someone to answer
the bell. Then there was a sudden commotion from inside—the slither of claws on a stone floor and the deep
barking of some ferocious-sounding dogs.

'Don't forget to play along with me when I tell him
we have another appointment,' she reminded Rogan as
she heard the bolts on the door being drawn back, 'otherwise we'll never get away.'

'Making sure you get home for that date?' Rogan enquired with an amused grin.

'Of course.'

Maybe it would be best to keep up the pretence of
another man in her life so she could distance herself
from him, she thought wryly. There was no need to tell
him that she was rushing home to her children.

The door swung open and two Irish wolfhounds leapt
out to run past them, nearly knocking Laura over in the
process. Rogan reached to put an arm around her shoulders to steady her.

'Thanks,' Laura said breathlessly.

'You're welcome.' He didn't release her immediately
and for a moment she found his closeness most disconcerting.

'Ah, it's you, Laura.' Lord Fitzroy's friendly voice
pulled Laura from her reverie. 'Come on in. It's a terrible filthy day, isn't it?'

'Dreadful,' Laura agreed, stepping inside and shaking him by the hand. 'Good to see you again.'

It wasn't much warmer inside the hallway. The floor was slabbed stone with tapestry rugs thrown down in an attempt to stop the cold striking upwards, to little avail.

'This is my boss, Lord Fitzroy. Mr Rogan Powers.'

Rogan held out his hand and the two men shook hands.

Laura noticed how Rogan seemed to tower over Lord Fitzroy, who was slightly built, with thinning grey hair. He was dressed in an odd assortment of clothes, brown breeches, a grey jumper and a red jacket. It was as if he had just taken out the first things he'd come across in his wardrobe that morning and put them on, without looking at them.

'Just call me Fitzroy,' he said to Rogan. 'I can't be doing with all that Lord stuff. Now, come on in and we'll have a drop of the crater to get us warmed before we start.'

'Whiskey,' Laura mouthed quietly to Rogan as she saw him looking slightly puzzled.

Lord Fitzroy led the way into an enormous sitting room. There was a huge stone fireplace at one end with a roaring turf fire. Both Laura and Rogan moved towards it gratefully.

The wing chairs at either side of the fire were occupied. In one a grey cat was curled up fast asleep and in the other a large grey wolfhound was snoring.

Rogan moved the pile of magazines off the settee so he could sit next to Laura.

'No whiskey for me, thank you, Fitzroy,' Laura said quickly, as the man started to pour amber liquid into three Waterford tumblers.

'Ah, just the one to blow the cobwebs away,' he insisted, holding the glasses out to each of them.

'Your good health,' Rogan said, as he sipped the drink politely.

'*Slainte.*' Lord Fitzroy finished his with relish in one swallow and put the glass on the mantelpiece.

'I believe you want us to look at the first floor of the castle?' Laura launched straight in.

'Yes, I should have had it done when you were here last time, but even people who live in castles have to watch the pennies.' Lord Fitzroy laughed. He looked from Laura to Rogan. 'You're not the man who came last time.'

'No, I've only recently come into the company,' Rogan told him.

The man nodded. 'American,' he observed. 'That's a fine country. Met my wife there.'

Laura sipped her drink and tried not to choke on the fiery liquid. It was obviously the best Malt whiskey, but Laura didn't really drink—a glass of wine was about her limit. She put the glass on the table next to her.

Lord Fitzroy was showing Rogan a picture of his wife from the sideboard. 'That was Maeve when she was just twenty, God rest her soul.'

'She was very beautiful,' Rogan said.

'Laura has a look of her, don't you think?' Lord Fitzroy said conversationally. 'A fiery, passionate look.'

Laura cleared her throat and tried not to look at Rogan, who was studying her and then the picture. She knew he was amused by her embarrassment. 'Yes, I know what you mean,' he agreed.

'Have you any specific ideas for the first floor, Fitzroy?' she asked, hoping her skin hadn't gone too wild a shade of beetroot.

'Not really.' Fitzroy refilled his glass and went to replenish Laura's. 'You haven't touched your drink.'

'I don't drink much. I'll just sip it slowly as we work.' Laura said politely. She opened up her briefcase and pulled out a large brown envelope. 'I've brought the plans we had drawn up last time.'

'There's time enough for that.' Fitzroy waved a hand

dismissively and started to tell Rogan about the castle's history instead.

Laura stood up decisively. 'If you'll excuse me, gentlemen, I think I'll just go upstairs and take a look around. Get a feel for what needs doing.'

She left the two men talking and went to get on with her work.

When she came back some time later, her notebook filled with details of each room on the first floor, Lord Fitzroy was still talking.

He smiled at her. 'Now, you'll stay to dinner, won't you?' he said.

'Oh, no, we couldn't possibly,' Laura glanced at her watch, appalled to see how late it was getting. 'But thank you for the offer, it's very kind.'

'Oh, but you must stay. I had it planned that you would.' Fitzroy looked wounded. 'You can't come all this way, without having a bite to eat.'

'Dinner would be lovely,' Rogan said suddenly from beside her.

Laura turned to look at him, her eyes wide. She tried to remind him of their earlier agreement a note of desperation in her voice. 'But we've got another client, remember?'

'I forgot to tell you, Laura.' He shook his head, a wry gleam of amusement playing around the firm line of his lips. 'That client cancelled earlier this morning.'

When Lord Fitzroy went off gleefully to inform his housekeeper that there would be two extra for dinner. Laura looked at Rogan in agitation.

'What on earth did you say that for? Now we'll be here for hours!'

'It seemed a shame not to humour him.' Rogan shrugged. 'He's a very pleasant man. Besides,' he added, a gleam in his eye, 'I fancied having dinner with you.'

Laura tried hard not to be flattered by the way he was looking at her. 'I had other plans,' she murmured, thinking about the children. She liked to read with Matthew each night and at this rate he'd be in bed by the time she got back. 'Anyway, haven't you a girlfriend or a wife waiting?'

'No, no one,' Rogan said calmly. He reached into the pocket of his jacket, which was draped over the arm of the settee, brought out his mobile phone and handed it across to her. 'I think you should cancel your plans.'

Laura glared at him, her green eyes shimmering. It was very apparent that Rogan was used to getting exactly what he wanted. She wasn't so sure she liked his high-handed manner.

'Laura, this is a very big account and I expect my employees to give of their utmost when so much work is at stake,' he said to her in a steely tone that told her in no uncertain terms that he was the boss.

'Pulling rank now?' Laura asked with a lift of one eyebrow, but she took the phone from his outstretched hand. 'OK, you're right,' she agreed. 'It is a big account. We should stay.'

He grinned at her. 'I'll have to remember in future that pulling rank with you works.'

Laura noticed that now he'd got what he wanted the easy charm had reappeared, like the sun from behind a cloud. She hated to admit that all he had to do was look at her like that and it would be dangerously easy to give Rogan Powers anything he wanted.

'You're the boss.' She forced herself to sound businesslike and turned to go through to the hallway to phone her mother.

'Need your privacy?' Rogan remarked as she walked away from him. 'This boyfriend must be quite some guy.'

'I wouldn't bother with him if he wasn't,' she couldn't resist answering with a grin.

It was a good job that her mother was so understanding, Laura thought a few hours later when they were still seated at the end of the large banqueting table in the dining hall.

It was dark outside now, and elaborate silver candelabra lit the length of the table. A huge fire crackled in the stone grate beside them.

Cora had told her not to worry what time she got back, that she would stay overnight. Just as well, Laura thought as she listened to Lord Fitzroy, telling them about the ghost who roamed about the rooms of his castle in the early hours of the morning. It was starting to feel as if it would *be* the early hours of the morning before she got away from here, she thought dryly.

'A woman it is, all dressed in black.'

'I don't know if I believe in ghosts,' Rogan said.

'Oh, she's here all right. If you listen in the still of the night you can hear the rustle of her gown as she moves along the top corridor. She's looking for her long-lost love, the scoundrel who jilted her and broke her heart.' Fitzroy grinned. He was enjoying his guests' interest. 'Sometimes when the place is silent you can hear her sobs, echoing through the towers.'

'That's the risk you take when you make a promise to a woman,' Rogan said wryly. 'They'll haunt you, even from beyond the grave.'

Lord Fitzroy seemed to find that remark highly amusing. Laura wasn't so entertained. 'We are no longer in the Dark Ages, Rogan,' she murmured. 'These are modern times. Women aren't that bothered about getting married any more. In fact, some of them would run a mile at the very first hint of marriage.'

'Would they?' Rogan met her eyes across the table. He looked highly amused by her words.

'Yes, they would.' Maybe he was teasing her but, even so, the touch of arrogance in his voice irritated her intensely. 'It's more likely to be the women who seduce the men nowadays and leave them, sobbing in the attic.'

Rogan laughed. 'Maybe you're right,' he said slowly.

He was watching the way the candlelight flickered over her features, highlighting the bright sparkle of her eyes. It was as if the flame were burning inside Laura, a passionate, lively flame he was drawn to almost against his will.

The housekeeper opened the door. 'Phone call for you, Fitzroy,' she announced bluntly.

With a sigh Lord Fitzroy got to his feet. 'Excuse me. I won't be a minute.'

'The way he can talk he'll be at least two hours,' Laura said with a smile once they were left alone. She glanced at her watch. 'Do you think we can steer him onto the subject of work as soon as he comes back?'

'I'll see what I can do.' Rogan sat back in his chair and watched her.

Silence stretched between them. Laura glanced over and met his eyes then promptly wished she hadn't. All evening she had been acutely aware of Rogan's every glance, every smile, in her direction. Now it was just the two of them she felt unaccountably shy.

'I should be apologising for ruining your date this evening,' he said slowly.

'It doesn't really matter.' Her long slender fingers played with the stem of her wine glass.

'Good.' He smiled, a teasing, warm light in the darkness of his eyes. 'Because I'm not really sorry.'

'Work has to come first,' she said lightly, deliberately misunderstanding the husky undertone. She felt at a complete loss to know how to handle Rogan Powers. He attracted her and she knew that attraction spelt danger. She also knew he was practised in the art of seduction. She could hear the smoothness in his voice, in his eyes. She was old enough and wise enough not to be flattered…or so she kept trying to tell herself.

'I wasn't referring to work.'

'You should be,' Laura said swiftly. 'We should be concentrating very seriously on it.'

'You're right.' He smiled. It was a smile that did very strange things to Laura's pulses. 'I've been trying to tell myself that all evening. Trouble is, all I want to concentrate on is you.'

'You're very smooth, Mr Powers.'

'Rogan.' He corrected her swiftly.

'Rogan.' She assented. 'I don't think you should flirt with me. It feels wrong somehow.'

'Why?' He shrugged. 'You're not married.' Even as he spoke he was telling himself she had a point. This was against all his own rules. He'd have to stop.

'You're my boss.' She gave a small smile and from somewhere she found the humour to hide behind. 'And I'm Irish and we like to do things correctly, you know.'

He laughed at that. 'In that case, I'll try to behave myself.'

Lord Fitzroy returned to the room. 'Have you seen the weather out there?' he asked with a shake of his head. 'It's appalling.' He picked up the decanter to try and top up Rogan's glass.

'No, I'm driving, Fitzroy,' Rogan said firmly, putting his hand over the top. 'I can't have another drink.'

Lord Fitzroy pursed his lips and shook his head. 'I don't think you'll be driving anywhere, by the looks of things outside. Ah, sure, you may as well stay the night and relax. There is plenty of room here for you.'

'Oh, we couldn't possibly,' Laura said swiftly. She got up to go and look out of the window as the housekeeper came in to clear the table.

Laura pushed back the heavy curtains and was surprised to see that the fog was a lot thicker than it had been. 'We'll be all right,' she said hesitantly. 'It will be better once we hit the lower roads.'

Rogan came to stand beside her. 'I'm not so sure,' he murmured.

'Rogan!' Laura turned to look up at him, her eyes wide. 'Of course you can drive.'

'Have another drink,' Lord Fitzroy said from behind them. 'I'll go and tell the staff to make ready the accommodation.'

'That's very kind of you, Fitzroy,' Rogan said easily.

Before Laura could dissent the door closed behind the old man as he hurried to inform the staff.

Laura glared at Rogan. 'Now you are going too far. Dinner was one thing but this is ridiculous!'

'Laura, the weather is extremely bad.'

She shook her head. 'I'll drive,' she said firmly.

'Are you serious? I've seen your driving, remember?' He laughed as her eyes glittered with a fiery anger.

'No, we'd better stay. Besides, have you seen the time? It's nearly midnight—it will be four in the morning before we have all our business concluded,' Rogan decided sensibly. 'Far better to turn in, get up early and finish things with Fitzroy in the morning. His Lordship's head might be a lot clearer then, anyway. We can't, in all honesty, expect the man to sign any contracts after the amount of whiskey he's consumed.'

Laura stared at him uncertainly. What he was saying made a certain amount of sense but she felt as if she was treading in dangerous territory.

'It's up to you,' Rogan said nonchalantly. 'If you really want, we can brave the fog, just make another appointment with his Lordship and go over it all again another day.'

That swayed it. 'No, all right, we'll stay,' she muttered, then held out her hand. 'Perhaps you'd lend me your phone again.'

'Your boyfriend isn't still expecting you at this hour, is he?' Rogan frowned.

'Is it against company rules?' Laura asked, a gleam of devilment in her eyes. She was damned if she was going to tell him she was ringing her mother.

Rogan handed her the phone and watched as she went

out into the hallway once again to make her call in private.

Lord Fitzroy came back into the room. 'All fixed.' His mood was jovial. 'Una is preparing a room in the west wing.'

'That's very good of you, Fitzroy,' Rogan said absently, wondering what exactly the state of play was between Laura and this guy she kept phoning.

'All organised?' Rogan asked Laura when she returned.

'Yes, thank you.' She picked up her briefcase and started to take her files out. Thank heavens for a wonderfully supportive mother, she thought. Cora had been reading in bed and had just been amused to hear of her predicament.

'He wasn't too devastated?' Rogan asked her, a dry note to his voice.

'He'll survive,' she said briskly. 'Now, Fitzroy, would you like to look at some of these pictures?' Laura was determined that she would at least get her job done.

Lord Fitzroy filled her glass. He had been topping it up all evening, and although she had only taken a few sips from it she had lost track completely of how much she had consumed.

He peered at pictures and the samples of material for a few moments, then started to tell a story about his wife wanting to decorate their bedroom on their first anniversary.

Laura reached for her drink and finished it in one swallow. It was an instinctive reaction but a second later she wished she hadn't done it because she could feel the effects of the alcohol, invading her brain like a blanket of cotton wool.

'Maybe we should turn in for the night,' Rogan suggested soothingly, as soon as there was a lull in the conversation.

'Perhaps you are right,' she said, and started to pack

away her work. There seemed little point in continuing and she suddenly felt extremely tired.

'What about a nightcap?' Lord Fitzroy asked earnestly.

Laura shook her head, but she had to smile. She was sure, given half a word of encouragement, Lord Fitzroy would be up all night, drinking and talking.

Rogan was the first to go upstairs. 'Left-hand side of the stairs,' Fitzroy directed him. 'It's the room right at the end of the corridor.'

Rogan nodded and was going to wait for Laura but she waved him ahead. 'I'll see you in the morning,' she said. 'I'm going to see if I can get a glass of water from the kitchen.'

When she returned to the dining room Lord Fitzroy had gone. The housekeeper showed her up to her room. Laura was very grateful. She could hardly keep her eyes open and she felt a little light-headed.

She made a mental note on the way up the wide staircase to suggest to Fitzroy that he change the light fittings. It was very shadowy along the corridors and a bit eerie. The housekeeper left her outside her bedroom and went on up another flight of stars to her own quarters.

When Laura opened her door she was pleased to find there was a fire blazing in the hearth. It sent warm orange shadows flickering invitingly over a very large four-poster bed.

She didn't bother to switch any other lights on, just undressed quickly and slipped between the cool cotton sheets of the bed. Bliss, she thought dreamily.

As she drifted to sleep she was completely unaware that a few centimetres from her naked body Rogan Powers was also sleeping.

# CHAPTER THREE

ROGAN turned over. The bed was warm and very comfortable. The crackle of the fire was a deeply relaxing sound. There was a scent almost like honeysuckle from the warmth of the sheets—it was deliciously familiar.

A soft sigh, barely audible yet sweetly erotic, stole through his subconscious as he lay midway between sleep and wakefulness. For a moment his lips curved in a smile.

Then he opened his eyes.

He was stunned to see Laura's face a little way from his on the same pillow. The early light of morning touched her features gently.

She looked peaceful, her long lashes sooty dark against the creamy quality of her skin. There was a faint flush to her cheeks and her lips were a rose petal shade, the soft Cupid curve full and very inviting.

He wondered if he were dreaming. How had this happened? The last thing he remembered was getting into bed and falling straight to sleep. He had been on his own then—he knew that. He hadn't been drunk. In fact, he'd managed to avoid most of the alcohol Fitzroy had been pressing on him last night. Perhaps he was still a bit jet-lagged from his flight from the States a few days ago, but he must have been in a hell of a deep sleep, he thought with agitation, as he watched Laura.

She smiled in her sleep and gently stretched the arm that was resting on the outside of the covers. The movement lifted the sheets for a moment, giving him a tantalising glimpse of breasts which were full and uptilted with perfect rosy pink nipples.

Her hand came down and rested on his shoulder.

For a second Rogan hardly dared to breathe. He was extremely aroused, and thought if she moved one fraction nearer he would have to kiss her, explore the delights of that wonderfully curvaceous body.

He was just stealing himself to do the gentlemanly thing and move away from her when she snuggled closer. Her lips were now just a breath away from his.

Then she opened her eyes.

Rogan had never seen such wide, vivid, green eyes. They were misty with sleep, like an emerald sea on a summer morning. There was a bewitching glimpse of desire for one fleeting second as her eyes focused on his. Then incredulity and shock sharply replaced it.

'What on earth…?' Laura moved back from him, her hair flowing over her naked shoulders in a wild tumble of dark curls as she propped herself up and held the sheet against her body like a battle shield. 'What the hell are you doing in my bed?'

'I was about to ask you the same question,' he drawled.

'What do you mean? What are you doing in here?' She was appalled and confused.

'I was sleeping…with you, as it's turned out.' His lips curved in a smile of total amusement. 'This has to be a first. I'm in bed with a gorgeous woman and I've hardly touched her.'

'What do you mean, "hardly"?' Her eyes widened. 'If you've laid one hand on me, Rogan Powers, so help me I'll…I'll…' Her voice trailed off in trembling fury as she searched desperately to think of something bad enough to do to him.

'You were the one who laid a hand on me, if we want to be pedantically precise,' he said, and grinned as he saw the heat rising under the pallor of her skin. 'As this is the era when women seduce men and leave them, sobbing in attics, maybe I should be the one to be thinking of some suitable punishment for you.'

'This isn't funny.' She was as far away from him in the bed as she could get. She noticed that she had pulled the sheets from him so that they now rested low on his abdomen.

He had a fabulous body, broad-shouldered with a powerful chest covered generously in dark swirls of hair. Before she could stop herself her eyes slipped further down to the hard, flat stomach, and then lower. She wondered if he was wearing anything at all. The thought that they had both been lying naked next to each other all night made her temperature rise wildly.

'Do you like what you see?' Rogan asked with a grin. 'I know I do.'

Quickly she lay down again and glared at him from the other pillow. 'The joke's gone far enough, Rogan. I want you out of my bed,' she told him frostily.

'As I was here first, strictly speaking, you're in my bed.' He made no move at all. 'You must have come to the wrong bedroom last night...or maybe the right one, depending on how you want to look at it.'

'If you are trying to say that I deliberately came to your bed then you couldn't be more mistaken—or more conceited.' She was very angry now. She would have jumped out of the bed herself except for the fact that she had absolutely nothing on. The knowledge made her cling all the more tightly to the sheet.

He rolled over and leaned on his elbow to look at her, wry humour in his dark eyes. 'Are you sure?' He whispered the words in a seductive tone.

He was too close, his mouth just inches from hers. She found herself moistening her lips, her breathing uneven and her eyes captivated by his.

'Of course I'm sure. Look, this is all a ghastly mistake. If you would be good enough to get out of the bed and go, I'd be very grateful.' With an effort she tried to be calm.

'Seeing as you put it so nicely.' She thought he was moving to go but, in fact, he was a little closer now. 'How grateful…enough for one kiss?'

Her heart thundered in her ears. She wanted him to kiss her. As she wrestled with this sudden awareness he leaned closer and their lips collided with a kind of wanton passion that completely wiped every thought out of her brain.

The caress of his lips against hers was sensational, erotic. She had never experienced a more explosive feeling.

For one wild moment Laura's hand moved to his chest, not to push him away but in a gesture almost of submission. The warmth of his skin and the feel of the strength of his muscles made her stomach contract with a surge of pure longing.

Rogan had intended just to kiss her and move away but when he tasted her passionate response, feeling the heat of her body as she moved closer, his good intentions deserted him completely. His hands reached and curved around her waist, drawing her nearer. She made no sound of protest—indeed, she gave a husky little moan of pleasure.

The sound ignited his passion further. His hands stroked the smooth curves of her body, finding her satin smooth, so sexy, so enticing.

His lips moved from hers to rove across her face and down the long column of her neck. Then with a groan he rolled over so that his body was suddenly pressing against hers.

Shock waves of pleasure rippled through Laura. The sensation of his body pressed so close was powerfully erotic. Heat lashed through her body. She was oblivious of everything except the bliss of his love-making, the skilled way he held her and caressed her to a fever pitch of arousal.

She felt his hands stroke the soft swell of her breasts, and felt his lips travel downwards to kiss the rosy peaks.

Her hands moved to caress his broad shoulders then up through the dark thickness of his hair. She moaned feverishly.

'Laura...?' He pulled back and looked at her with a raised eyebrow.

They stared into each other's eyes, and in the ensuing moment's silence good sense came rushing back.

Horrified by how she had just responded to him, how her naked body was pressing so close against his, she used her hand as a lever to push him away.

'What the hell are we doing?' Her voice was a whisper of anguished disbelief at how she had been so easily carried away by his caresses.

He moved away from her and sat up. He pushed a hand through his hair and gave her a slightly bemused glance. 'I think it's called making love,' he said wryly.

'I think it's called insanity.'

She was probably right, Rogan acknowledged. He certainly hadn't meant things to get so out of hand. His eyes moved to the soft curves of her figure. She was simply gorgeous.

She snatched the sheet up to cover herself, trembling with indignation. He smiled. 'The modest maiden act is very endearing,' he told her huskily. He reached out, intending to gently brush back a stray curl from her face with a tender hand, but she shrank from him as if afraid.

'Don't...don't touch me.' Her temper blazed, her green eyes burning into his.

He looked amused now. 'That's not what your lips were saying a moment ago.'

'How dare you?' she said fiercely, both to him and to the feeling he had created inside her with such nonchalant ease.

'I...I know about your reputation with the ladies, Rogan Powers. Don't think for one moment that I would be charmed or seduced by the likes of you. I'm not one of your conquests.'

He shrugged and smiled at her. 'I hate to point this out, Laura, but you wanted me. You responded to me—passionately.'

'In your dreams. You just caught me off guard, that's all.' She glared at him fiercely. 'I wasn't even properly awake.'

He laughed at that and she felt herself blushing, knowing full well that her excuses were weak in the extreme. She had enjoyed his kisses, was still very aroused by his closeness. The knowledge was very distressing.

'I'll remind you that you're my boss.' Her voice was not at all steady. 'And I expect a professional, polite distance to be maintained.'

His gaze moved to the bed between them with sardonic amusement. 'A bit late for that, don't you think?'

'We have to work together, for heaven's sake!'

'You're right. We shouldn't have allowed ourselves to get so carried away,' he agreed lazily. 'But it was only a few kisses. We are both consenting adults. I don't think it will affect our working relationship.'

It was affecting *her,* Laura thought with real panic.

'The last thing, the absolute last thing I would want would be any involvement with my boss,' she found herself babbling. 'My job is too important to me.'

'Not to mention your boyfriend,' he said calmly.

She glared at him with fury and he laughed.

'I'm glad we have the embarrassing situation in hand,' he said smoothly. 'Now, if you don't want to be shocked any further, I suggest you avert your eyes while I get up.'

He didn't wait for her to turn away and Laura had a fleeting glimpse of his strong back and lithe hips as he swung away from her before she hastily closed her eyes.

A second later she heard the sound of a shower being switched on at full blast. She glared at the door. Obviously he had just gone straight through to the *en suite* bathroom. The nerve of the man.

She sat back against the pillows, not knowing what to do.

Then she heard the shower snap off and he stepped back into the room.

Their eyes collided and he smiled nonchalantly as if they spent every morning in such an intimate way.

Rogan was only wearing a towel, strung loosely around his waist. The hair on his powerful chest glistened with droplets of water and his hair was slicked back from his face. For a second all Laura could do was look at him. He had such a fabulous body.

'Won't be a moment.' He smiled as if he was well aware of the effect he was having on her then he moved to the chair to pick up his clothes. Laura was mortified when she noticed he had to take them from beneath hers.

He flicked her a grin. 'The proof of the pudding,' he murmured, dropping her lace bra and panties on the velvet covers. 'Told you I was here first.'

He laughed as he saw the expression on her face. 'Don't worry. It will be our little secret.'

The way he lowered his voice to that husky tone made her temperature rise dramatically.

'This is ridiculous,' she said furiously. She turned on her side, away from him, hoping that turning her back on him would help to lower the tense, intimate atmosphere which had sprung between them.

He disappeared into the bathroom again, and when he returned he was fully dressed. The transformation made her heart start to thud unevenly again. He was now the smoothly handsome businessman in a dark suit, white shirt and tie.

'Don't be too long, Laura,' he said briskly as he met

her eyes. 'I've a meeting at nine-thirty at the office and we still have business to discuss with Fitzroy.'

The swift metamorphosis from teasing seducer to brisk businessman made her blink. Rogan Powers was obviously unembarrassed and unaffected by this incident. Maybe he was used to waking up with a different woman on the opposite pillow every morning!

Laura's breath escaped in a shuddering sigh of relief as he left the room. She lay there, staring up at the ceiling. She should be equally unperturbed, she told herself, but the fact remained that her heart was still racing and her body still tingled from the warmth of his caress.

Hurriedly she went through to the bathroom and turned on the water. Her eyes moved to the wash-basin. Rogan had left his watch behind, a slender gold Cartier.

Something made her pick it up. There was an inscription on the back. It read, 'All my love, Sophie.'

She put it down as if it had burnt her.

Who was Sophie? she wondered.

She tried not to think about it, and opened the bathroom cabinet instead to see what was there. She was very relieved to see some new toothbrushes, still in their Cellophane wrappings, toothpaste and scented soap.

When Laura went downstairs a little later she felt calmer and more rational about the situation. The housekeeper had made a mistake about which room she had showed her to last night. It hadn't been her fault, and it hadn't been Rogan's. Obviously neither of them had been thinking clearly this morning and it was best to forget the whole embarrassing incident.

The fog of last night had melted away into a mellow morning. Lord Fitzroy and Rogan were seated in the breakfast room. The French doors open wide onto vast sweeping lawns, allowing the dogs to amble in and out from the early misty sunshine.

Both men rose as she joined them and Rogan held a chair out for her to sit down. His arm brushed against hers as she did so and, uninvited, the memory of the way he had kissed her this morning returned with vivid intensity. Stricken, she pushed it all from her mind.

'Good morning, Fitzroy,' she said with bright, breezy cheerfulness.

'Good morning, my dear. Did you sleep well?'

Laura avoided catching Rogan's eye. 'Very well, thank you.'

'I was just telling Rogan here that I've decided to leave the decor of the rooms entirely in your hands.'

'Oh? Good.' Laura nodded and reached for the pot of tea the housekeeper had brought for her. 'I'll get my files out and we can decide what you want—'

'No, Laura. I mean I want you to decide. I was thinking of a budget of…' Lord Fitzroy pursed his lips, before naming a vast sum that made Laura nearly drop the delicate china teapot.

'Would that be all right with you?'

'Fine. But it's a very large order. Wouldn't you be happier to discuss the plans before I order the—?'

'Laura, I trust you implicitly,' Fitzroy cut across her briskly. 'You did a wonderful job last time. Just do what you think is best.'

Across the table Laura caught the gleam of laughter in Rogan's eyes. Obviously, like her, he was thinking that if Fitzroy had said this last night they could have been home early and not had to stay the night.

Laura drank her tea and tried to console herself that at least they had the order. 'I'll just have a walk around the rooms again,' she said, standing up. 'Would you like to come up with me, Fitzroy, just so I have some idea of your thoughts?'

'If I must.' The man sighed.

Fitzroy wandered through a few of the rooms with her, before getting heartily tired of the subject and wandering away.

There was no sign of Rogan or Fitzroy when Laura returned downstairs.

She noticed Rogan had left his mobile phone by her briefcase and she glanced at her watch. It was seven-thirty. The children would be just getting up. It would be an ideal time to phone and make sure everything was all right.

She was pleased when her daughter answered almost immediately. 'Hi, Mum,' Joanne said brightly. 'How are things?'

'Fine. What about you? No raving and misbehaving while I was away?' Laura asked teasingly.

'What, with Grandma?' her daughter spluttered. 'I had to go to bed at nine o clock.'

Laura laughed. In the background she could hear the usual morning chaos of her house. Matthew was singing at the top of his voice and the radio was playing. She was filled with an absurd rush of homesickness. Completely crazy—she had only been away one night.

'Matthew wants to speak to you.' Joanne handed the phone over to her brother.

'Hi, Mum. Will you bring some sweets home with you?'

Laura laughed. 'If that's what you want.'

'I do. Can we have lemonade and chocolate tonight when you get home?'

'Sounds like our very own private party. I'll look forward to it.' Laura turned slightly and saw Rogan, leaning indolently against the open doorway, listening, and he didn't look one bit pleased.

'Listen, honey, I've got to go,' Laura said nervously. 'See you later.'

She put down the receiver and looked over at her boss.

'Boyfriend again?' he asked drolly. 'Must be a pretty heavy relationship—you're never off the phone to him. Did you tell him about last night?'

'There's nothing to tell,' Laura said crisply, trying not to blush at the remark.

'Well, you could have told him that you got what you wanted,' Rogan remarked, and then watched the tide of colour rise under her delicate skin.

'I beg your pardon?'

'I was talking about Fitzroy's contract.' He smiled. 'What did you think I meant?'

He was teasing her, she realised, enjoying her discomfiture.

'Yes, I got what I wanted. By the way, you've left your watch in the bathroom.' She decided to play him at his own game so that maybe he'd stop teasing her. 'Sophie wouldn't be too pleased that her present meant so little.'

'I've just retrieved it.' He sounded coolly indifferent to her remark and he didn't try to explain who Sophie was. None of her business, she thought.

It was half an hour before they finally set off back to town, a signed contract tucked safely in Laura's briefcase.

The sun's brief, tantalising appearance that morning had not delivered the golden day it had promised. The sky was dark, the clouds low over the country road.

There was silence for a while before Laura asked softly, 'Would you mind dropping me off at my house? I want to change, before going into the office. I'll get a taxi in.'

Rogan flicked a glance at her. 'What's the matter—want to rush home for your private party?'

'No, I want to get changed. You were listening to my phone conversation,' she said accusingly, furious at the connotation he had put on something so totally innocent.

'It was a bit hard not to,' he muttered. 'So, who were you arranging your private party with?'

'None of your business Rogan,' she said. 'Just as Sophie is none of my business.'

'Maybe we had better talk.' Rogan pulled the car to a halt by the side of the road.

'Talk about what?' she asked apprehensively.

'About what happened between us this morning,' he said calmly, turning to look at her.

It started to rain, a sudden wild squall which bent the twisted branches of the trees that lined the deserted road.

'Nothing happened so I think we should just forget about it.' She tried very hard to sound as composed and cool as he did.

He smiled. 'My grandmother…who, incidentally, was Irish…once said to me that the Irish temperament was as capricious as its climate.'

'Very profound,' Laura murmured sardonically, but she had to smile. 'But I don't know what that has to do with what happened between us this morning.'

'It has to do with the fact that this morning in bed there was a lot of passion between us. If I hadn't pulled back from you we would have made love.'

'That's not true!' Even as she denied his words she knew she was lying, but she was too scared to admit he was right.

Rain ran in rivulets down the windows of the car, obscuring the countryside in a murky mix of greys and greens and enclosing them in a cocoon, shutting out the outside world.

'It is true, Laura. I don't think we should pretend it didn't happen. There is an attraction between us and you know it.'

She closed her eyes.

'Are you in love with your boyfriend?' Rogan asked suddenly.

Laura opened her eyes and looked at him. 'That's a very nosy question.'

'I'm curious to know more about you—especially now we've spent the night together.'

Something about the deep, rasping quality of his voice

made a shiver race through her body. 'We didn't spend the night together...not in the way you make it sound.'

'We shared a bed.' He grinned across at her.

'Stop saying that,' she muttered, more disturbed than ever about the effect his words were having on her body. 'It's crazy.'

'I'll tell you what's really crazy, Laura. I'm eaten up with curiosity about your love life.'

Her heart felt as if it skipped then faltered against her chest. 'Completely crazy,' she said, but her voice wasn't entirely steady.

'I'm your boss. I'm not supposed to be interested in what you do in your free time—right?'

'Right.' Her body felt as if it were on fire suddenly.

'But I am.'

Her gaze was held by his. He had the most gorgeous eyes, she thought hazily. Deep, profoundly intense. She moistened her lips nervously.

'Rogan, we can't get involved.' She was desperately trying to be sensible, but at the back of her mind she was wondering if she was using the fact that they worked together as an excuse, a barrier to hide much deeper, more serious reasons for not getting involved with him. This man could hurt her, she could sense the danger. Her body's traitorous surrender every time he came close told her very clearly that she could lose her heart here. The last person to make her feel like this had been her husband, and John had hurt her badly. She couldn't risk her emotions like that again.

'I agree that our working relationship makes for complications. I have always had a strict rule of conduct that business and pleasure should be kept separate.'

'A rule that everyone else has to keep except you?' Laura asked lightly.

He smiled at that. 'Well, no, actually. Up until now I've always stuck to it.'

He leaned closer. Then he touched her face. The sensation of his hand against her skin set up a whole chain of reactions inside her, dulling her thoughts and fading everything except his closeness into insignificance.

She was acutely aware of everything about him in those few seconds, such as the way his eyes were flecked with a sherry brown and the faint dark shadow on the masculine strength of his jawline.

Then he lowered his head and kissed her.

His lips were skilfully seductive. They moved over hers with a tender, teasing slowness at first until she pressed herself closer and the kiss deepened. Then his lips were demanding, ravaging her mouth. She responded totally, hungry for much more.

She gave a small moan of pleasure deep in her throat as she felt his hands range down over her body, drawing her closer.

Then the only sound was the drumming of the rain on the car and the sound of their breathing. Laura wanted the moment to go on and on.

They pulled apart only when they became aware of another sound outside—that of a hooter behind them. Rogan glanced in the driving mirror. A large tractor was sitting behind them, unable to get past them on the narrow road.

'We'd better go.' He started the car again and then looked over at her. 'Will you have dinner with me tonight so we can...take this further?'

Laura's breathing felt restricted. She felt totally at a loss. 'I can't,' she said finally. Having spent one night away from the children already, she needed to spend time with them tonight.

Rogan frowned. 'We can't just leave things as they are.'

'Rogan, I think you should just give me some space to think about this.' Somehow she managed to sound calm and in control, but it was light years away from how she felt.

'If that's what you want.' He put the car in gear. 'I haven't time to drop you home, by the way.' Once more his tone was businesslike. 'I've got to get to that meeting.'

# CHAPTER FOUR

LAURA leaned back and tried to relax in the silken, steaming waters of her bath. From along the corridor the sound of Joanne's music blared loudly.

'Yeah, yeah, I want you,' some rock star screamed through the house. What a day, Laura thought wearily as she closed her eyes and tried to ignore the noise.

The memory of Rogan's kiss penetrated sharply through the mists of her thoughts.

She had been out on quite a few dates since her husband's death, but it had been a long time since a man had made her feel like that. In fact, if she was totally honest she couldn't remember ever feeling so out of control—as if her mind had no hold whatsoever over her body. It scared her.

Her husband had been a charmer, smooth and wonderfully sexy. She had trusted John, loved him. It was only after his death that she had discovered that her handsome husband hadn't been all she had thought.

She shied away from those thoughts now. She wasn't going to start thinking about John. All that was behind her. She was getting on with her life. Her children, her mother, her job—they were her priorities.

She groaned and felt like sliding beneath the water as she remembered drawing up outside the office this morning in Rogan's car. They had arrived at the same time as Carmel Murphy. And that woman missed nothing.

Laura got out of the water and reached for a towel.

Now wasn't the time to dwell on the embarrassment of that scene. People at work might speculate but most likely it would die away and be forgotten.

She put on a long white towelling robe and went out into the corridor.

'Joanne, turn down that music, please,' she said, pausing for a moment at her daughter's bedroom door.

Obligingly the volume went down...but only by a few decibels.

Laura went downstairs to check on dinner. Then she put her head around the lounge door.

Matthew was playing with his game of Connects, pieces of it spread all over the coffee-table and the floor. Laura smiled to herself at the look of intense concentration on her son's face.

The shrill ring of the doorbell startled both her and him.

Captain, their red setter, sprang from his slumber by the fire to dash inquisitively into the hallway.

'Stay where you are, Matthew,' Laura said as her son started to get up. She closed the lounge door behind her and went to glance out through the window.

It was a wild night. The wind was howling around the terrace cottage, bending the trees and sending dark clouds scudding over the full moon.

As the moon came out Laura saw Rogan on the doorstep. He was wearing a long, dark overcoat and his head was bent against the wind.

She stepped back as he looked directly at the window.

What on earth was Rogan Powers doing here? she wondered in panic.

He rang the doorbell again. 'Laura, open the door. I'm freezing out here.'

With a sigh she went to the door and undid the bolts.

'What took you so long?' he said, stepping into the hall and pushing the door closed behind him.

Captain jumped up at him, his tail wagging with delight as Rogan immediately bent to pat him. 'Hello, it's nice to see you, too,' he said in a friendly tone

He straightened and looked directly at her. His eyes

moved over Laura's white robe and the way her hair was up in a ponytail. She was suddenly acutely conscious of the fact that she was in a state of undress and wasn't wearing a scrap of make-up. Still, it wasn't as bad as this morning when she had been wearing nothing at all, a little voice inside reminded her.

From above them the sound of Joanne's music boomed insistently. The sound of it increased Laura's tension. Obviously Joanne hadn't heard the doorbell, but the odds of her coming downstairs and meeting Rogan were enormously high. Either that or Matthew would come out to see who was here. It was almost a foregone conclusion that Rogan was going to meet her children. It made her heart skip and bounce.

'Getting ready for your date?' Rogan asked nonchalantly.

'I am pretty busy.' She tried desperately not to be flustered by the way he was looking at her...by that attractive husky note in his voice.

'Nice place you've got here,' he commented, looking around the hallway. The cottage was quaint and Laura had decorated it with a skill which was a credit to the James designs and her talents.

'Thank you.' She was quite proud of her home. It was small but she loved its cosy atmosphere, its warm floral chintz tones.

He smiled. 'I've come to apologise for this morning. For placing you in an embarrassing situation.'

She wasn't sure if he was talking about the bedroom or arriving at work together. 'Let's just forget about it,' she mumbled.

'Hello.' The small voice, coming from behind them, made them both turn with a start.

Matthew was standing in the doorway, watching them, an earnest expression on his face. He looked cute in his denim jeans and Aran jumper, very like Laura with the same dark hair and pale skin. He had a sprinkling of freckles over his nose and a gleam of devilment in his eyes.

'Who are you?' he asked Rogan with the directness only a seven-year-old could manage, without sounding very rude.

'Rogan Powers. I work with…Laura.' Rogan looked from the child to Laura as if unsure of the connection.

'Oh, OK,' Matthew said easily. 'Mum, can I have my sweets now?'

'Not until after dinner—' Her sentence was cut off by the overhead light being switched on. Laura looked up and saw Joanne on the staircase.

'Oh… Hi.' Joanne frowned, her eyes moving from her mother to the tall stranger in the hall. 'I thought I could hear voices.'

Laura felt momentarily lost for something to say. Then she shrugged helplessly. It was just as well that Rogan should know that she had children, she told herself sternly. 'Jo, this is my boss, Mr Powers.' Her voice sounded high and unnatural even to her own ears.

'Really!' Joanne looked at Rogan with renewed interest.

Rogan frowned and swivelled his gaze from the jeans-clad girl to Laura.

'This is my daughter, Joanne,' she enlightened him, trying to sound matter-of-fact. 'And my son, Matthew.'

'Anyone want coffee?' Joanne asked with a grin as Rogan continued to stare at Laura.

'Mr Powers is just going…' Laura's voice trailed off as Rogan interrupted her.

'Coffee would be great,' he drawled.

'I'll go and put the kettle on,' Joanne said cheerfully, taking Matthew's hand and disappearing into the kitchen.

'Any more going to appear from the heavens?' Rogan asked, looking towards the stairs.

'Any more?' Laura stared at him blankly.

'Children,' he said, a sardonic expression in his dark eyes. 'How many of them do you have hidden away?'

'Just the two, and they weren't hidden away.'

'No?' His lips twisted in a wry smile. 'Then why didn't you tell me about them?'

'You never asked.' She shrugged.

He glared at her. There was something very autocratic about him when he was annoyed...also something vaguely intimidating.

'The fact that I have children won't affect my work, Rogan,' she said succinctly. 'I am still able to give the company my undivided attention during working hours.'

He looked incredulous. 'Is that why you didn't tell me you had children—because you thought it would be detrimental to your career?'

'Well...' Laura shrugged helplessly. 'I didn't think that it would exactly help me to get on within the new company...' She trailed off as her eyes met his.

He raked an impatient hand through his hair, then lowered his voice to a husky undertone. 'How desperate are you to get on within the company? Desperate enough to come to the MD's bedroom last night? Kiss him very passionately and then bat those beautiful oh-so-innocent eyes?'

'The bedroom was a mistake!' Her skin was on fire now. 'You have no right to talk to me like that.' Her voice shook with fury. 'You were the one who initiated that...that episode in bed this morning and the...kiss in the car.'

'As I recall, you kissed me back,' Rogan reminded her, but his voice softened. He noticed the fierce gleam in her eyes, the defensive way she had angled her chin so she could meet his gaze directly. He shook his head. 'No, of course you didn't come to my room on purpose.'

The notion had been brief and fleeting. Hell, sometimes he could be so cynical. Just because one woman had ruthlessly pursued him for money and power didn't

mean every woman was like that. He hated himself for
the thought. Especially now as he saw the vulnerable
glitter in Laura's eyes and the proud way she stood, angry yet somehow so...defenceless.

'I'm sorry,' he said gently. 'I guess I was just shocked
that you hadn't mentioned your children to me.
Especially as we have spent the night together.' The
warm, teasing light was back in his eyes.

'We may have accidentally shared a bed, but you
don't know me,' she said slowly.

'No—but I'd like to.' His eyes narrowed. 'Who did
look after the children last night, anyway?'

'My mother.'

'Oh!' He smiled at her. 'You know, the fact that you
have children has no bearing whatsoever on your career
within the company. The only thing I'm bothered about
is performance at work—nothing else.'

'I guess I knew deep down that the fear was crazy,'
she admitted, 'but there have been lots of nervous rum-
blings since the take-over. I couldn't help feeling just a
little bit apprehensive.'

His lips quirked. 'Laura, my financial director back in
the States is a single mother with four children.'

'In that case, perhaps I should fill in that questionnaire
you gave me tomorrow,' she said with a grin. 'Maybe
I'll get a promotion. What is it, kids make bonus points?'

'You need two more to catch up with Tanya in New
York.' He grinned back.

For a moment there was silence between them as their
eyes met. Laura felt tension and heat escalate wildly inside her.

The atmosphere was broken by the sound of the
kitchen door opening. 'Mum, there's a burning smell
coming from the oven,' Joanne called urgently.

With a shriek of alarm Laura hurried to investigate.
She didn't realise that Rogan had followed her until

he reached to help her as she struggled to lift the deep tray of lasagne from the oven shelf.

She allowed him to take over and he set it safely on top of the stove.

They all peered at it. 'Doesn't look too bad,' Laura said. 'I think it's just caught at the edges.'

'It looks good to me,' Rogan said.

'I made you your coffee, Mr Powers,' Joanne said, lifting it up to hand it to him.

'Thanks.' Rogan grinned at her. 'And my name is Rogan.'

Laura was amused to notice Joanne's cheeks flushing faintly and the spark in her bright eyes. Heavens, she thought wryly, Rogan could even set the pulses of a twelve-year-old a-flutter.

'How old are you?' Rogan asked her in a friendly tone.

'Twelve. I'll be thirteen in a few weeks, though.'

'Your mother must have been a child bride,' Rogan remarked, slanting an amused look at Laura.

'Mum got married when she was eighteen,' Joanne informed him.

'And how old are you?' Rogan asked Matthew, who was hanging back reservedly, watching Rogan as if he hadn't made up his mind about him.

'Seven.'

'You're tall for seven,' Rogan said with a smile.

'My daddy was tall.' Matthew looked over at Laura for confirmation of this. 'Wasn't he, Mum?'

'Yes darling, he was,' Laura agreed gently.

'You must take after him,' Rogan remarked easily.

'Rogan, are you going to stay and have dinner with us?' Joanne asked suddenly, her eyes also moving to Laura—only where Matthew's were wary and uncertain Joanne's were wide and imploring.

'Maybe your mother is expecting company this evening,' Rogan said as Laura hesitated.

'No...no, I'm not expecting anyone.'

Their eyes met. 'Then, if you're inviting me, I'd love to stay,' he murmured huskily.

Immediately she could feel her pulses starting to race.

'I'll just go and get changed before I serve the meal, then.' It was an effort to sound relaxed and casual.

As soon as she was upstairs in her bedroom she started to panic about this new development. Somehow, letting Rogan stay to dinner seemed to be taking their involvement a massive step forward when she wasn't sure it was the right thing to do.

The more she was around Rogan the more she felt herself drawn to him. It was crazy, she had to work for the guy.

Laura took her hair out of the ponytail and brushed it vehemently so that it fell in long, shiny waves over her shoulders.

Then she grabbed her jeans and a jumper from the wardrobe and dressed hurriedly.

When she got back downstairs she found Rogan was serving dinner, with a little assistance from Joanne. And the table was laid.

It seemed so strange to have a man in her kitchen, organising things. She stopped in the doorway and watched for a moment before any of them noticed her presence.

Joanne was chatting to Rogan as if she had known him all her life. Rogan was now pouring Matthew a glass of Coke.

'How's that? OK?' he asked, as he only half filled the beaker.

Matthew nodded solemnly.

Laura had the strangest sensation in the pit of her stomach, as if someone had pushed her headlong into something for which she was totally unprepared. She didn't understand the mixture of emotions she was feeling. The apprehension...the longing.

'Gran comes around here every afternoon so that we won't be coming home to an empty house,' Joanne was telling him.

'You're lucky,' Rogan said. 'I used to come home to an empty house when I was your age.'

'Did your mother have to work?' Joanne asked curiously.

'My father brought me up on his own.' Rogan looked up and caught Laura watching him.

'You've managed to suss out the complexities of my kitchen, I see?' From somewhere she managed to gather her senses and walk in to join them.

'With a little help from your family.' He smiled over at her. 'If you'd like to take your seat, dinner is served.'

Laura found herself sitting opposite Rogan at the kitchen table. Joanne was still talking animatedly. In a way her conversation was a relief as it gave Laura time to sort her feelings out a little.

It seemed strange to think that this morning she had woken up with Rogan, had kissed him and now here they were, seated around the dinner table like a family. The last time her day had started and ended like that was when John had been alive.

'What part of America are you from, Rogan?' Joanne asked.

'Baltimore originally, but I have an apartment in New York now...it's convenient for business. I suppose you could say that's my base.'

'You don't live in Ireland, then?'

'I have a house here, but it's a second home.'

'Which do you prefer, Ireland or America?'

'Joanne, will you stop with the questions,' Laura said to her daughter with a smile, 'and eat some dinner.'

She glanced over at Rogan, an apologetic light in her eyes.

'I don't mind,' he said, 'but I don't know if I can

answer that last one, Jo. Both places have their own unique charm…and attractions.'

He smiled at Laura. As their eyes met she felt a shiver of awareness suddenly shoot through her. There was something about him that profoundly disturbed her senses—made her heart jump, her skin prickle with heat. She looked away from him.

'My daddy was an airline pilot,' Matthew told Rogan suddenly. 'He flew to America a lot.'

'Did he?' Rogan smiled at the boy. 'He must have been very clever to be able to fly a plane.'

'He was.' Matthew nodded. 'I'm going to be a pilot when I grow up, just like Daddy.'

'What sort of planes did he fly?' Rogan asked.

Matthew launched into a list. He knew all the names and a little bit about each.

It was a long time since Matthew had talked so much about his father. Laura listened quietly as he told Rogan that his dad had been the best in the world.

Her heart contracted painfully. John was just a shadowy memory for Matthew now, but Laura did try to keep that memory alive. She thought it was important that the children had a sense of their identity and the knowledge that their dad had loved them.

She had never once let anything slip about the problems that had existed in her marriage. The fact that John had been seeing another woman was a secret Laura had buried with him.

'He must have been a very special person,' Rogan said, listening attentively to Matthew. 'You obviously miss him a great deal.'

'Mum misses him, too,' Matthew said, looking over at his mother. 'Don't you, Mum?'

Laura smiled at her son, a great wealth of sadness in her eyes. 'Yes, Matt, we all miss Dad.'

She met Rogan's steady gaze across the table. 'How's

dinner?' she asked him, trying to lighten the suddenly tense atmosphere. 'Not too burnt, I hope.'

'It's great.' He smiled at her. 'It's a long time since I had a home-cooked meal. No doubt my sister will try to remedy that when I fly back to New York next week.'

'Are you going back on business?' Laura's heart missed a beat.

He nodded. 'Only for a couple of days.'

It was strange to feel such a sense of relief at those words. For one panicky moment she had thought he would be gone for some considerable time—she thought it best not to analyse those feelings.

The conversation moved to Joanne's favourite pop group and for a while they all relaxed and laughed. Rogan seemed to know all the latest gossip and records.

'You're very up with the music scene,' Laura remarked when finally she got up to clear the table. 'I'm very impressed. I couldn't tell you who was who these days.'

'Mum is a bit square,' Joanne told Rogan with a grin.

'Is she?' Rogan looked over at Laura. His eyes slipped over her slender figure in the tight-fitting jeans. 'She looks anything but square from where I'm sitting.'

The seductive flattery was hidden behind a teasing drawl. The children didn't notice, but Laura did.

She pretended she hadn't and pushed the last of the dishes into the dishwasher. 'OK, we'll have lemonade and sweets in the lounge before bedtime.'

Laura met Rogan's eyes over Matthew's head. 'Would you like to stay for a coffee?' she asked gently.

'Sounds wonderful.'

'Go through, then, and I'll bring the drinks.' Laura tried not to notice the warm light in his eyes. She turned briskly to put the kettle on as Joanne and Matthew went into the lounge with Rogan.

When Laura followed them with the drinks a little

while later there was a lot of laughter coming from the room.

Joanne was sitting on the floor next to the coffee-table, looking up at Rogan with intense concentration. Captain was beside her, his head resting on Rogan's knee. Matthew was sitting next to Rogan on the settee. It was a cosy scene. If she had been a stranger, looking in, she would have assumed that Rogan belonged there.

She put the tray on the table and sat opposite, listening in to the conversation for a while.

'Rogan had a dog just like Captain when he was a boy,' Matthew told her.

'Did he?' Laura's eyes lingered on the handsome face.

She liked the way he talked to her children as if they interested him, entertained him. She liked the way he was stroking Captain's head with gentle, soothing strokes.

He looked over at her.

She tried very hard to pull her thoughts away from the dangerous cliff-edge towards which they had been heading. They should talk about work, make it quite clear to the children that that was the extent of their involvement. She cleared her throat. 'We'll have to discuss what you want me to do at your house, Rogan.'

'Yes, we will, won't we?' The way he looked at her made her heart jump unevenly. It was as if he was deliberately misinterpreting what she was saying. 'You'll have to come out and have a look—perhaps tomorrow night.'

Matthew picked up his Connects to show Rogan what he had been building.

'Wow!' Rogan's eyes widened. 'Did you do this all yourself?'

Matthew nodded, looking pleased with himself, and got up to get the box so he could show it to him.

'I can't come tomorrow night. I've no one to babysit,'

Laura said. 'My mother goes out several times a week and I don't like to ask her on those nights—'

'That's OK, Laura,' Rogan broke in with a grin. 'Bring the children.'

'Yes!' Both Matthew and Joanne were quick to take up the invitation. Their eyes were shining with excitement.

'Oh, no, we can't do that,' Laura said. 'It's a school night. You've got homework.'

'Oh, Mum!' Joanne glared at her reproachfully.

'Tell you what,' Rogan said easily, 'you finish early tomorrow, Laura, and collect the children. Then you can bring them out to my house straight after school.'

'Yes, but—'

'I'll help them with their homework while you have a look at the house. And then we'll all have dinner together.'

Laura frowned, unsure. 'That's very good of you, Rogan, but I hate to impose and—'

'It's no imposition.' Rogan grinned at the children. 'But, I warn you, my cooking isn't that great.'

'Can we have sausages and chips?' Matthew asked seriously. 'That's my favourite.'

Rogan laughed and his eyes met Laura's. 'I don't think that will be a problem.'

The phone rang and Joanne jumped up to go into the hall to answer it. It was obviously one of her school-friends because after a moment Laura could hear her chatting and laughing with someone.

'The phone calls are always for Joanne,' Matthew told Rogan.

'Really?' Rogan smiled. 'But sometimes your mum calls to speak to you, doesn't she? She called you last night and again this morning.'

Matthew thought about that for a moment and then nodded.

Rogan looked over at Laura. 'And the party was lemonade and sweets before bedtime...?'

She shrugged. 'What can I say?' She tried to keep her voice light. 'You've found me out.'

Matthew reached to help himself to more sweets from the packet on the table. 'No more now, Matthew,' she said. 'It's time for brushing teeth and going to bed.'

'Ah, Mum! Not yet.'

'Yes, *now*.' Laura was firm. 'You have school tomorrow.'

Matthew's face fell.

'Say goodnight to Rogan,' Laura said briskly, 'and I'll be up in a moment to see you.'

Obediently the boy stood up. 'Night, Rogan.'

'Goodnight, Matthew. See you tomorrow.'

'Why did you do that?' Laura asked quietly as the door closed behind her son.

'What?'

'Invite my children to your house.'

He smiled. 'Because I wanted to.'

The lounge door opened, interrupting their conversation. 'Mum, I'm going to bed,' Joanne said cheerily. 'See you in the morning.' She smiled at Rogan. 'Bye, Rogan. See you tomorrow.'

Laura glanced at her watch as the door closed again. It was very unusual for Joanne to volunteer to go to bed, especially at the same time as Matthew.

'You have lovely children,' Rogan remarked. 'They are a credit to you. It can't have been easy, bringing them up on your own.'

'No, it hasn't, but I've had a lot of help from my mother.'

'So Joanne was telling me.' Rogan grinned. 'She lives next door, she's a widow like you and she thinks you don't go out enough.' He counted on his fingers as he reeled off the points he had been told.

Laura smiled ruefully. 'Honestly, kids! You can't have many secrets with them.'

'Some escape, I'm sure.'

'Not many.'

'Mum.' Matthew's voice drifted downstairs. 'Are you going to tuck me in?'

Laura rose and Rogan also got to his feet.

'Are you going?' She looked over at him.

'I suppose I should, but I do feel that you and I have some unfinished business.'

He moved closer to her and suddenly she felt very unsure.

'And what is that?' she whispered unsteadily.

He reached for her and took her into his arms. 'Something we started this morning.' He murmured the words gently. 'Something that has been eating away at me ever since.'

His lips touched hers, gently at first, and then as she responded he kissed her with a fierce hunger that tore into her very soul.

'Unquenched passion,' he whispered, kissing her neck then her face before finding her lips again.

Her body was out of control now and her mind knew it. Her body ached for him.

Instead, he stepped back from her.

For a moment or two their eyes met in powerful communication which left her in no doubt that he knew very well she was well and truly aroused. She tried to be sensible.

Rogan Powers was probably a master of seduction, a philanderer. A kiss—a night of passionate love-making—wouldn't cause him a second thought. It would mean nothing.

Laura's cheeks flared with colour at the mere thought of spending a night, making love with him. She tried to move away and found that her limbs wouldn't respond.

'I think it would be best if...if you just went, and we

forget this ever happened.' From somewhere she found some sanity.

'Nothing has happened—yet,' Rogan remarked, a gleam in his eyes. 'Of course, you could invite me to your room and we could remedy that.' His voice was a seductive, teasing whisper that made her skin prickle with awareness.

Laura forced herself to laugh at that remark. The fact that, in reality, there was a large part of her which was tempted by his outrageous suggestion made her feel more vulnerable than she had ever felt in her life before.

'I'll take that as a no, shall I?' he enquired with a hint of laughter.

'I think you should,' she agreed. 'For one thing, I hardly know you.'

One dark eyebrow lifted. 'What better way to remedy that?' he drawled.

She shook her head, glad that he wasn't touching her, kissing her. If he had been, she didn't think she could keep up her resolve.

'Rogan, I don't want a casual affair with you.' Her voice was clear and steady. 'I've got my children to think about. I need my job. My life is organised and I'm happy. I don't want anything to rock that stability.'

Rogan stared at her for a moment. No one had ever turned him down like that before—so coolly, so rationally. 'But you will come out to my house tomorrow for dinner?' he enquired with a good-humoured smile. 'Sausage and chips is my speciality.'

She had to laugh at that. 'Who could resist such a temptation?'

She was drawn to him against all her inner warnings. But this was just work, she told herself firmly. The fact that it made the children happy was an added bonus. It was just one outing, full stop.

# CHAPTER FIVE

'ARE we nearly there, Mum?' Matthew asked impatiently from the back seat.

'Nearly,' Laura said distractedly. The narrow country road hugged the coastline, all the houses hidden from view behind trees and rich vegetation. She had to drive slowly, looking for Rogan's house.

She found the gate and turned her car up the gravel drive. It seemed to wind for ever, through trees whose leaves had turned a vivid scarlet and gold. The afternoon light was starting to fade. The last of the autumn sunshine lit everything in a rich red light as the house came into view.

Laura let out her breath in a sigh. The house was a Georgian property of considerable charm. Large and rambling, it was three stories in a warm red brick. Flame-red Virginia creeper encircled the dark green front door and the windows.

She pulled the car to a halt next to Rogan's BMW and climbed out hesitantly into the watery afternoon sunlight.

'Wow, this is fabulous,' Joanne murmured in awe. 'Do you think Rogan lives here all alone?'

'It's Mr Powers to you, Joanne,' Laura reminded her daughter gently.

'He told us to call him Rogan,' Joanne said mutinously. 'Don't you remember?'

'Yes.' Laura did remember but she was anxious to put this visit on a correct, businesslike footing. She was very nervous about bringing her children here. Why, she couldn't have said. Perhaps the fact that both Joanne and

69

Matthew had done nothing but rave with excitement about this outing at breakfast this morning, and again all the way here this afternoon, had something to do with it.

Or maybe it was the fact that she knew she wasn't immune to Rogan Powers—that he turned her on, excited her.

She switched her mind from those disturbing thoughts. She was here to work, to repay Rogan for the mess she had made of his car. It was as simple as that.

'I just think it would be more respectful to call him Mr Powers. He *is* my boss,' she reminded the children softly. 'And you will remember to be on your best behaviour,' she added as they walked up towards the house.

They didn't answer her, just nodded. They both looked very smart in their navy blue school uniforms. In contrast, Laura had gone home once she'd left the office this afternoon and had changed from her suit into more casual clothes—jeans and a pretty blue jumper and blazer.

Their shoes crunched on the gravel as they crossed to the front door. The air was crisp and there was a faint smell of smoke in the air as if someone was burning leaves somewhere.

'Good afternoon.'

All three of them whirled around at the sound of Rogan's voice. Laura was surprised to see that he was gardening in one of the large flower-beds that encircled the sweep of a perfectly manicured lawn.

He left the spade with which he had been digging stuck in the soil and strolled across towards them. He was wearing a faded pair of Levis and a blue denim shirt. The casual attire took her by surprise. She had only had a brief glimpse of him today in the office because he had left work very early, but as usual he had been wearing a dark business suit. Maybe, like her, he was more at home in casual clothes. He certainly looked good in them.

'Hi, Rogan.' Both children greeted him enthusiastically, forgetting Laura's words about what they should call him. Matthew even ran across to him to take his hand.

'How was school?' he asked them, ruffling Matthew's hair with an affectionate hand.

'It was OK.' Joanne wrinkled her nose and Rogan laughed.

'As good as that, eh?' He glanced across at Laura and she felt her whole system go into overdrive as their eyes met.

'Guess what, Rogan?' Matthew tugged at Rogan's hand, taking his attention from Laura.

'I've got to go to the dentist on Saturday and have a tooth out.'

'Really?' Rogan looked down at him.

'It's a baby tooth and the dentist says I might need some gas.' There was a tremor of apprehension hidden beneath Matthew's words.

'Well, that will mean that you won't feel a thing. It will be completely painless and all over when you wake up,' Rogan said gently.

'Do you think so?' Matthew asked him, his eyes wide as he sought reassurance.

'I know so,' Rogan said confidently.

Matthew grinned. 'And then the tooth fairy will come,' he said in a happier voice.

'She will, indeed.' Rogan grinned at Laura. 'Come on in and we'll have a drink.' He led the way up to the house, but instead of going in through the front door he led them around and in the kitchen door which was open.

'Would you like coffee?'

Laura dragged her eyes away from the pristine white kitchen, which was large and ultra-modern. 'That would be nice, thanks.'

'And what about you?' He turned his attention to Joanne and Matthew. 'I've got Coke, if you'd like?'

Joanne was looking out of the back window. There were some slides and a swing at the bottom of the garden. 'Can we go and explore outside for a little while?' she asked.

'I don't see why not,' Rogan said, looking enquiringly over at Laura.

She nodded. 'Don't get muddy, and don't be too long. You've got homework, remember.'

They both nodded solemnly then hurried out of the back door.

Laura smiled as she watched them race across the lawns towards the swings. 'Thanks for reassuring Matthew. He's been worrying about this trip to the dentist.'

'He'll be fine. Are you going with him?'

She nodded and turned towards him. 'How come a confirmed bachelor has a children's playground in his garden?' she asked with a laugh.

'We can thank the previous owners. This was very much a family home.' He flicked the switch on a coffee-making machine and then turned to look at her.

She was wearing that same perfume, honeysuckle and roses, he noted. Its warm tones were gentle, evoking a feeling of beauty and tranquillity.

He had been going to talk about business but for a moment he couldn't think about anything except how lovely she was. 'How was work today?'

'It was OK. I made a start on the designs for Fitzroy.'

'Good.' His eyes swept over her. She looked good in jeans. She had a fabulously curvy figure, very sexy. He found himself remembering the morning he had woken up with her...the softness of her skin, the perfect tilt of her breasts.

'You have a beautiful house.' There was a light of shyness in her eyes now, as if she had noticed how closely he was watching her and it made her self-conscious. 'It doesn't look as if it needs much doing to it.'

He made a determined effort not to think about how desirable she was. 'I like the kitchen. The problem lies in the fact that the people who owned the property before me have tried to modernise it. Fireplaces have been ripped out and newer ones put in, totally out of keeping with the character of the place. I'd like you to restore it to its former glory—that goes for the furniture and soft furnishing as well. Some of the stuff that's in here at the moment is too modern.'

'Well, I am very much a traditionalist.' She smiled.

'I noticed that when I looked around your house,' he said with a smile. 'Come on, I'll give you the tour before coffee.' He kicked off his shoes, before leading the way out into the hallway. Laura could understand why when she saw the pale-coloured carpets.

There were two reception rooms on either side of the hallway, with magnificent views down to the sea.

Everything was so neat, ornaments and flowers were positioned strategically for perfect effect. She supposed when you were a wealthy bachelor it was easy to have perfection.

He had been right. The fireplaces were wrong, as was the modern furniture.

He led the way upstairs. There were six bedrooms, most furnished basically. Rogan's room was the largest and had the most magnificent views of Dublin bay. It was a very masculine-looking room, with polished wood floors and blue rugs. The bed was enormous.

Laura didn't walk in, but stood inside the doorway, trying to concentrate in a purely professional manner. She couldn't help but notice the silver-framed photograph next to his bed. It looked as if it was a picture of two small children, but she couldn't see properly and she was loath to walk towards the bed.

It suddenly struck her that Rogan Powers might have children. Although she had been told he wasn't married, he could have a partner... She didn't really know much about him.

'Are they your children?' she asked casually, nodding in the direction of the photograph.

'Heavens, no!' They are my sister's children.' His eyes met hers. 'I suppose you could say that I'm not big in the commitment stakes.' He suddenly felt impelled to make that clear to her. As his personal battle to keep his hands off her faltered he felt he needed to make it plain that he wasn't looking for a long-term relationship.

She had two lovely children. He didn't want to hurt her—or them—so it was important to be honest with her. He also sensed a certain vulnerability in her. He couldn't quite say what exactly it was, but something about the way she looked at him sometimes with those gorgeous wide eyes brought out a tremendous feeling of protectiveness in him. It was a long time since a woman had made him feel like that.

'I have no desire to start a family at all,' he said firmly.

'Then why have you bought a family home?' As soon as the question was out she regretted it.

He seemed unconcerned. 'I wanted a base for when I'm here on business. And I think it will be a good investment.'

'I suppose it will be.' Her eyes swept around the room again. 'So, what do you want me to do in here?'

As soon as she'd asked that question she felt the colour steal up underneath her skin. Her eyes met his and he laughed.

'Now that,' he said huskily, 'is what I'd call a leading question.'

'You know what I mean.' She tried to be brisk and gloss over the moment. 'Do you want me to completely—?'

'Yes, I want you completely,' he cut across her, his tone gentle and amused. He reached out and touched her face. It was just a gentle caress but her skin seemed to ignite.

His eyes lingered for a moment on her lips.

She remembered the heat of his kisses, the need he had stirred up in her. She felt a spiral of desire curling up from the very depths of her soul, a deep yearning ache. The feeling took her body by storm and it was a shock.

She felt almost mesmerised by his eyes and his voice. The sexual chemistry between them in that instant was electric.

She dragged her eyes from his.

The children's voices drifted up to them. 'We'd better go and see what they are doing,' she said, pulling away from him.

Rogan closed the bedroom door as they left.

Joanne and Matthew had come inside and were in the lounge.

They had taken all the CDs out of the rack and were riffling through them, arguing about which one they wanted to listen to.

Laura's body had been in turmoil to start with, but this scene did little to calm her. 'I told you two to behave yourselves!'

'It's OK, Laura.' Rogan, in contrast to her, was calm and unconcerned.

He came over and bent down beside the children. 'We'll listen to these another time,' he said gently. 'Now it's time for homework.'

The argument ceased instantly and they helped him to tidy up the mess they had made.

'Sorry, Mr Powers,' Joanne said earnestly. 'We didn't mean to make a mess.'

'It's OK, Joanne.' Rogan grinned at her. 'And what's with the ''Mr Powers''? I told you, call me Rogan.'

'Mum said we should be more respectful,' Matthew chirped, 'Cos you're her boss.'

Rogan looked over at Laura with a raised eyebrow, before turning back to the children. 'I'd be happier if you would call me Rogan,' he said. 'We're friends, aren't we?'

Both children nodded.

'That's settled, then.' Rogan glanced back over at Laura.

'OK?'

The shrill ringing of the phone cut the suddenly tense silence between them. 'Excuse me.' He got to his feet and went over to the table behind them to answer it.

'This is a nice surprise.' His voice was warm. Whoever was calling was obviously somebody close to him. 'No, you didn't wake me.' He laughed. 'It's afternoon here.'

It was somebody in America, Laura concluded.

'Come on, Matthew, Jo.' She indicated that they should leave the room to give Rogan some privacy.

'I'm not exactly sure what date I'll be back in the States,' Rogan said. 'No, I won't be back then.' He laughed. 'Don't start with the dinner dates again...'

Laura was trying not to listen, trying not to wonder what he meant about dinner dates, as she shepherded the children out and closed the door.

She sat them at the kitchen table so that they could start their homework.

'Sorry about that,' Rogan said as he came through. 'That was my sister, inviting me for dinner next month.' He laughed suddenly.

'She's always trying to matchmake me with one or other of her friends. Even having the Atlantic between us doesn't deter her. She phoned to tell me she has an uneven number seated at her table and could I possibly save the day. I know what that means.' Rogan grinned at her. 'It means one of her friends is without a man.'

Laura laughed with him, feeling absurdly relieved that it hadn't been a girlfriend. 'I know how you feel. My mother used to do the same kind of thing to me.'

'Did she?' Rogan looked across at her and smiled. His warm look made her feel incredibly hot.

Matthew interrupted them with his reading book. 'Who can I read to?'

'Me,' Rogan said easily, 'while your mum takes the measurements for the house.'

It was strange how they all felt at home with Rogan, Laura thought a little while later when all the work was done and they sat around his kitchen table, eating and talking about their day. It was hard to believe that this was her high-powered boss, she thought dazedly.

She couldn't quite work him out. He was a successful businessman, a man who didn't want ties or commitments. Why was he bothering to be so nice…so good with her children? Was it just to get her into his bed? Surely not. Rogan could have his pick of women—he didn't need to go to those lengths.

He looked across and met her eyes.

Whatever it was it was working, she thought with panic. She found herself liking him more and more.

'Have you had enough to eat?' Rogan asked her.

'It was lovely, thank you.'

'Hardly exciting, though.' He grinned. 'How about us going out for Sunday lunch together? I'll treat you to something a bit better than sausages and chips.'

'That's really nice of you, Rogan, but—'

'Afterwards we can visit Mystic. I'd like to introduce the children to her.'

'Mystic?' She was intrigued.

'A racehorse I impulsively purchased a few weeks ago. She's stabled not far from here.'

'Wow, you've got a horse!' Matthew's eyes shone with excitement. 'Can we go, Mum? Please?'

'We'll see.' Laura fell back on the standby she always used when she wasn't sure about making a promise.

'Please, Mum.' Joanne said intensely.

'I've said we'll see,' Laura said gently. 'Now we should go. You've got school tomorrow and it's getting late. I think you should gather up your belongings and thank Rogan for a lovely dinner.'

Dutifully Matthew and Joanne got up. Laura also rose and started to load the dishwasher for Rogan.

'Leave that, Laura.' He came across and took one of the plates from her hand. 'I'll do it later.'

'I don't want to leave you with all this,' she said quickly. 'You were good enough to cook tea for us.'

'Laura.' He caught hold of her arm and turned her to face him. 'Leave it,' he said gently.

The kitchen door closed behind the children as they went to get their coats from the other room.

'I get the feeling you'd rather I hadn't invited you out on Sunday,' he said.

The light touch of his hand against her arm was sending a burning sensation right the way through her. 'It…it isn't that I don't want to go,' she murmured.

'So what's the problem?'

What *was* the problem? she asked herself. The children seemed to like him. She liked him. And it wasn't as if he was asking her out on a real date—this was just an invitation to the children.

'Is there someone else?' Rogan asked quietly. 'I thought when Matthew said it was them you were phoning the other night—'

'It *was* the children,' she interrupted. 'There's no one else.'

'Then why are you being so hesitant? I know you told me you don't want a casual affair, and I can respect that. Can't we go out as friends?'

'Weren't you the one who told me that men and women can't be friends?' she said with wry amusement.

'What was it you said—that the sex issue always clouds the relationship?'

'Unless you have the passionate affair first—get it out of the way.' He grinned. 'I do believe I might have uttered something to that effect. Come on, Laura, I'd really like to take you all out. And the children seem keen on the idea. It will give Matthew something to look forward to after he's had his tooth out.'

She felt herself weakening.

'I'll behave myself, I promise,' he added.

Laura smiled. 'No doubt Joanne and Matt will go on and on about wanting to go, anyway, and wear me down until I feel like the meanest monster in all the world.'

'I'll take that as a yes, shall I?' he murmured huskily.

She looked up into his dark eyes. She wanted him to kiss her, touch her—the craving was intense. 'I think you should,' she said gently.

The kitchen door opened, breaking the mood.

'Have you got everything?' She moved away from Rogan with difficulty and forced herself to speak normally as she went to help Matthew on with his coat.

'Yes.' Matthew smiled and looked over at Rogan and there was a mischievous gleam in the depths of his eyes. 'Thank you for a lovely dinner, Rogan.'

'You're welcome.' Rogan walked outside with them to their car. It was very cold now, and a light frost covered the ground. It sparkled in the bright gleam of Laura's headlights as the car turned away down the drive.

Rogan stood and watched until the taillights of Laura's car had disappeared, then he returned to the warmth of the house.

It was strange but it suddenly felt very empty. A house certainly felt like a home, with the sound of children's voices echoing through it. The notion gave rise to a hint of sadness which unsettled the confident certainties of the life he had drawn up for himself. It made him remember a time when he had dreamed of having children, and had planned them with Melony. That had been before he'd realised that the only serious thing on her mind had been his money.

Since then he had closed his mind to the idea of having a family. And it was for the best, he told himself, yet that reassurance felt extremely hollow for just a moment.

He switched off the lights in the kitchen and went through to the lounge. In the centre of the table, neatly and prominently stacked, were a pile of school books.

He went across to have a closer look. They belonged to Matthew.

Laura was in the process of tucking Matthew into bed when he mentioned he had left his books at Rogan's.

'What, all of them?' Laura was astounded.

Matthew nodded. 'Will you ring Rogan and ask him to bring them? And can you tell him that we really want to go with him on Sunday to see his horse?'

'Matthew, is this an excuse so that you can get me to phone Rogan?' Laura asked sternly.

She watched as her son's face flared a bright guilty red.

'Oh, Matt!' she groaned.

'It was Jo's idea,' he said defensively. 'She said if I left the books Rogan would bring them back and he might persuade you to change your mind about us going out together.'

'That's so naughty.' Laura shook her head. If she hadn't known Joanne was fast asleep she would have gone into her room to have words about it.

The sound of the front doorbell cut through the silence of the house.

Laura looked sternly down at her son. 'You're in trouble now.'

She left him to run down the stairs and open the door.

'Special delivery.' Rogan grinned as he stepped into the warmth of the hall and deposited the pile of books on the hall table.

'I'm really sorry,' Laura said sincerely. 'I can't believe that he did that.'

'Well, it's easy to forget things. Good job I don't live too far away.'

'Mum, is that Rogan?' Matthew called downstairs anxiously. Can I see him? I want to tell him something.'

'Go to sleep,' Laura called back.

Humour gleamed in Rogan's eyes.

'You know he did this on purpose,' Laura said in a low tone. 'It was a ploy to get you out here so you could talk me into going out with you on Sunday.'

Rogan laughed. 'Didn't you tell him I had already done that?'

'No... I'm wondering if as a punishment for this I should tell him we're not going,' she said.

'Who are you trying to punish—the children or me?' Rogan enquired drolly. 'Don't do that, Laura.' Her heart seemed to skip crazily at those words.

'Mum,' Matthew called again.

'Let's see what he wants,' Rogan said with a smile.

Laura found herself leading the way upstairs. Her son's room was directly opposite her own. The door was open and he was in bed.

Rogan smiled as his eyes moved over the child in his red pyjamas, his teddy bear snuggled close to him on the pillow.

'What is it, Matt?' he asked gently.

'I just wanted to say sorry.'

'I should think so.' Laura moved to tuck the blankets around him more securely.

Matthew looked over towards Rogan, who was standing at the foot of his bed. 'Can we still come and see your horse?' he asked, his eyes wide and questioning.

'You can,' Rogan agreed cheerfully.

His eyes flicked around the room and took in the model aeroplanes that hung from the ceiling and the framed photograph of a man in his pilot's uniform beside the bed, before resting for a moment on the tender way Laura brushed back a stray lock of dark hair from the child's forehead.

'Now get some sleep.' Laura pressed a kiss against the child's cheek, before turning off the lamp. 'Goodnight, Matthew.'

'Night, Mum. Night, Rogan.'

As they closed the door on him, Rogan smiled at her. 'He seems happy now, anyway.'

'Now he's got his own way, you mean?' Laura grinned.

'He's a true man in the making,' Rogan agreed with an indulgent gleam in his eye.

He looked across the corridor towards Laura's bedroom. The door was open and the bedside lamp was on. It sent a soft light over the white daisy covers on the bed, then caught the jewellery that sat on a stand on the pine dressing-table.

'Do you have a photograph of your late husband beside your bed?' Rogan asked her suddenly.

The question took her by surprise. 'No… I put that away a long time ago,' she answered hesitantly.

Their eyes met and Laura could hear her heart beating wildly in the silence between them. She made to turn away from him but he reached out and pulled her gently towards him.

'I've been wanting to kiss you all evening,' he said in a low velvety tone.

She found herself staring up at him with a feeling of helplessness. She wanted him to kiss her. He touched his fingers against her lips. The feeling was erotic.

'I'd like to take you to bed and kiss every little part of you.' His voice was so low that she could barely hear him.

She couldn't speak, could hardly think.

He moved closer and his lips touched where his fingers had rested, carefully caressing the warmth of her lips.

She responded, kissing him with a passion that was suddenly wild and demanding. Maybe she could handle an affair, her body cried out. His hands touched her, lightly caressing, not assertive, just gentle, tender... exquisitely tormenting.

'I should go.' He was the one to move back from her. 'If I don't I'm going to want to take this further.' He reached out and touched her face. 'Much further.'

Laura watched him walk away from her down the stairs and it took all her strength not to call out for him to come back. He stopped at the foot and looked up at her.

'What are you doing Thursday night?' he asked suddenly.

'Thursday?' Laura hesitated, surprised by the question.

'I don't want to wait until Sunday, before seeing you again socially.'

The husky admission made Laura's mind fly into a whirl of confusion. 'It's Hallowe'en,' she recalled. 'The children are both going out to parties. Matthew is sleeping over at his friend's house.'

'I wasn't inviting the children,' Rogan said smoothly, 'just you. I'd like to take you to dinner.'

'Oh.' She looked down at him and her heart seemed to beat so loudly that it was like a drum, beating overtime.

'How about it?'

She smiled, her resistance melting. 'I'll look forward to it.'

# CHAPTER SIX

THE house was unusually silent, so quiet, in fact, that the sound of the clock in the hall seemed far too loud. Its ticking reminded Laura that Rogan's arrival was imminent.

A couple of hours ago the house had been in chaos as Matthew and Joanne had raced around, getting ready for their fancy-dress parties. There had been a good deal of laughter and frivolity and it had helped to take Laura's mind off the fact that tonight it would just be her and Rogan.

Now she stood before the mirror in a plain black jersey dress and tried to stifle the butterflies which seemed to have emerged from nowhere.

She hadn't spoken to Rogan on a personal level since the other night when he'd brought back Matthew's books, but today in the office his eyes had caught hers and the feeling of sexual magnetism had been so overpowering that Laura had felt weak. Just remembering the throbbing sensation of heat made her heart thump unevenly in her chest.

This was definitely a mistake. She was too attracted to him.

The sound of the doorbell made her whole body go into a state of alarm. She glanced at her reflection and tried to reassure herself. It was just a date, she would keep him at arm's length and they would probably spend the evening talking about work.

The reassurance she gained from telling herself this flew out of her mind once she had opened the front door to him. Rogan was wearing a dark suit and a black cashmere overcoat which seemed to emphasise the power of his build and the darkness of his hair and eyes. He looked spectacular.

'Hi.' He smiled at her, a smile that tied her emotions into knots.

'Hi.' It was all she could think of to say. She stepped back and allowed him to enter.

'You look nice,' he said nonchalantly, yet the male gleam of appreciation in the darkness of his eyes was anything but casual.

'Thank you.' She reached for her coat and tried to ignore the flutter of awareness that accompanied just the merest brush of his fingers as he helped her to put it on.

'Listen, I—'

'I thought—'

They both started to speak at the same time.

'You first.' He grinned at her.

She found herself grinning back at him. She said with a husky honesty, 'This is kind of crazy, isn't it? I don't know about you, but I feel very unsure about us, going out together on a date.'

One eyebrow lifted at that, but before he could say anything she rushed on. 'You said yourself that you have a strict rule against mixing business with pleasure. I can't help feeling that it is a very sensible rule.'

'It is,' he agreed softly, then he reached to touch her face. 'But I don't seem to be able to play by the rules where you are concerned. Believe me, I've been trying to.'

The caress of his fingers made her heart almost stop, then jerk crazily into double time. She had to force herself to move back from him.

'Perhaps we should try a bit harder,' she said, her voice not entirely steady. 'I meant what I said about not wanting complications in my life, Rogan. I...I just want to make it clear to you that I haven't changed my mind.

I'm having dinner with you tonight as a friend… It isn't anything deeper.'

'I won't get my hopes up, then,' he said. There was a mischievous glint in his eye as he spoke, one which made her laugh.

'I'm sorry. I'm rambling on needlessly, aren't I?' She shrugged. 'You were probably thinking the same thing.'

'In theory, maybe,' he admitted with a grin. 'You'll have to help me out and slap me back if I get out of control.'

She smiled at the light-hearted words, but deep down she knew that she, too, had difficulty in keeping control of her senses around him.

The night air was laced with the smoke from bonfires, which hung, like a stage effect, around the glow of the streetlights. Three children dressed as witches darted across the gateway with their cloaks flying out behind them, the fleeting snatch of their laughter the only sound on the quiet road.

'There is some black magic cooking tonight, by the sound of it,' Rogan said with some amusement. 'What did Joanne and Matthew dress up as?'

Laura smiled. 'Matthew is Spiderman and Joanne is a black cat. We had fun getting the make-up and the clothes just right, I can tell you.'

'I bet you did.' Rogan laughed. He unlocked the car. 'Bearing in mind that you have to be home for when Joanne gets in, I booked a table at a local restaurant.'

'Oh… That was thoughtful of you.' Laura hesitated. She remembered she had told him that Matthew was sleeping over at his friend's house tonight, but since then Joanne's plans had changed and she had also arranged to sleep over with a friend.

For some reason she shied away from enlightening him that she had the house to herself tonight, instead changing the subject. 'So, which restaurant did you book?'

'Shelley's.'

'Heavens!' Laura's eyebrows rose slightly. He had chosen one of the trendiest, most expensive of restaurants.

'What's the matter? Is the food no good?'

'I don't know, I've never eaten there. Apparently, the prices are out of this world.'

'Let's hope the food is as well,' Rogan said.

The food was excellent, as was the ambience of their surroundings. Polished wood floors reflected the glow of candlelight, and the tables were set in secluded wooden booths so that diners had maximum privacy.

Laura really enjoyed the evening, but most of all she enjoyed Rogan's company. He was an amusing and fascinating man. They were halfway through their main course when it dawned on her that they hadn't discussed work once and that she didn't want to.

'What's it like, living in Manhattan?' she asked as he leaned over to pour her a glass of wine.

'Well, people tend to live life at full speed. They don't just have one business lunch—they have two within the hour.'

Laura laughed. 'At least there's no time to get bored.'

'No time for anything.' He poured himself a mineral water. 'I spend my days running between meetings and deals.'

'You must enjoy it, otherwise you wouldn't do it, would you?'

'Once you get on the treadmill it's hard to get off.' He smiled. 'But, yes, I suppose I still get a kick out of a successful deal.'

'You sound as if business takes up much of your life.'

'It does,' he acknowledged. 'I suppose it's a price you pay if you want to be successful. Relationships seem to have taken a back seat.'

'Even Sophie?' She tried to sound casual as she asked him that question but, in fact, she had been eaten up

with curiosity about who Sophie was since she'd read
the inscription on his watch.

'Sophie is very much past history,' he said firmly.

When he didn't enlighten her any further she just
shrugged and said lightly, 'Well, it's no wonder you
aren't looking for heavy relationships. It seems Powers
PLC is a demanding mistress.'

'Not exactly.' He smiled. 'There is still room in my
life for a demanding mistress.' His eyes met and held
hers across the table. She felt her skin tingle with an
awareness of him which was purely sexual.

'I've embarrassed you now.'

'No. I know you are only joking.' She hoped her skin
wasn't as hot-looking as it felt.

'Am I?' he murmured softly. 'To be honest with you,
Laura, it isn't my work that holds me back from having
a serious relationship with a woman. I've seen too many
marriages crumbling around me, my own parents' marriage amongst them. Nowadays, I feel an allergic reaction coming on whenever anyone even mentions the
word 'commitment.''

Although there was a gleam of humour in his eyes
she sensed that beneath it he was very serious.

'How old were you when your parents split up?' she
asked curiously.

'Ten. It was a very unhappy period of my life. My
parents argued like crazy and then one day, out of the
blue, my mother left. She took my sister with her…oh,
and the dog.' He smiled, a mocking kind of smile. 'She
left me with my father because she said it would be cruel
to leave Dad all alone and us "men" would be good
company for each other.'

Laura stared at him, saddened by the story, her heart
going out to him. 'How awful for you.'

'I adjusted, and my father was a good man.' He shook
his head. 'I don't know why I just told you that.' He

sounded uncomfortable. 'It's years since I talked about my parents' divorce.'

'I'm glad you told me,' she said softly.

Their eyes met and held for a few moments before she looked away, confused by the emotions he stirred up in her.

'It makes me realise you are not quite the tough guy you pretend to be.' She tried to lighten her tone to break the feeling of intimacy. 'And I don't blame you for being wary of marriage,' she said candidly. 'It's not for the faint-hearted.'

He frowned. 'But it's not all like that. You were happy, weren't you?'

She hesitated, her mind dissecting his question. She had been happy, but she had been living a lie. John hadn't loved her. 'Yes, I was happy.' Some things were too painful to discuss, she decided.

His eyes moved over her, noting the sudden shadows in the vivid green eyes. 'But you're afraid of being hurt again,' he suggested gently.

'What makes you think that?' She was taken aback by his perception. He was right—she was afraid of opening her heart, of being betrayed and hurt again. But how could he possibly know?

He smiled. 'I can see it in your eyes. You have a vulnerable, almost "little girl lost" look about you sometimes.'

'And I hoped I looked like a confident career-woman.' She had been startled by his observation. It made her feel exposed, as if her protective barriers had been ripped away, leaving her wide open to him.

'You do.' He nodded. 'Just every now and then I catch a glimpse of what is beneath.' He reached out and covered her hand with his.

The warmth of his touch did very strange things to Laura's emotions. She felt as if he had brought her to the edge of some precipice and now she was holding onto her balance by a thread. She forced herself to pull her hand from his.

'Have there been any serious relationships in your life since your husband died?' Rogan asked suddenly.

'I've been out on some dates,' Laura answered hesitantly, 'but I've got to be careful. I've got the children to consider. They have to come first.'

Rogan nodded. 'And I suppose the pain of losing someone you loved must be very hard to get over,' he said gently.

He thought her reluctance to get involved with a man again was due to grief. It was something of a relief to know he hadn't guessed how much more complex her feelings were. The shock of her husband's infidelity had torn away her confidence. She found it hard to trust men now.

The waiter interrupted them, and Rogan asked if she would like dessert and coffee.

'Nothing more for me, thank you. It was a lovely meal,' Laura said sincerely.

As they were left alone again Laura's eyes moved thoughtfully over Rogan's handsome features. He was very suave and sophisticated yet she had seen another side of him tonight. Behind that veneer there was a gentleness, a warmth, that made Laura like him all the more. 'You're welcome to come back to my house for coffee,' she offered impulsively.

'That would be nice.' He smiled confidently, a smile that told her Rogan was well used to melting woman's hearts. She wondered if inviting him back had been a mistake.

It seemed colder than ever outside. There was a freezing fog and the road surfaces were slick and icy. It was a relief to get into the car and turn on the engine.

'How's Joanne getting home?' Rogan asked as he swung the car out of the car park. 'Would you like me to pick her up on the way?'

His concern for her daughter touched her. 'No, thanks, Rogan, there's no need. She decided she wanted to sleep over at her friend's house.'

'Really?' He said no more until he had negotiated the traffic and was pulling into her road. 'So you've got the place to yourself tonight.'

'Yes, very unusual.' Her jovial reply was tinged with uncertainty. The butterflies were back.

He pulled the car to a halt by her front door and they hurried in from the cold.

The house was still warm from the central heating but Laura asked Rogan if he wouldn't mind lighting the fire while she made the coffee.

When she returned to the lounge with their drinks the turf fire was blazing and Captain had moved himself from his slumber by the radiator to lie in front of it.

'That's the life, isn't it?' Laura said with a smile as she looked with affection at the sleeping dog.

She sat on the settee next to Rogan and reached to pour his coffee. The soft crackle of the fire was the only sound in the house.

The silence between them lengthened. It wasn't an uncomfortable silence but it was loaded with tension, a sensual tension which had been increasing all night every time their eyes met, every time he brushed against her. The knowledge that they were sexually attracted to each other lay like a trap, waiting to be sprung, waiting to compromise both of them. It was too dangerous an attraction to acknowledge.

'I've got a meeting with the design team tomorrow to discuss the renovations for the castle.' She resorted to work in an attempt to lighten the atmosphere. 'I've put some preliminary ideas on the computer already and—'

'Laura.' He cut across her. 'Let's talk about that tomorrow.' His voice was firm, as was the hand that reached out, took the coffee-cup from her and placed it back on the table. 'Work belongs in the office,' he said huskily.

'I...I thought we had agreed we were playing things by the rules...' Her voice trailed off as he reached out to touch a strand of her hair with a tender, stroking caress.

'I know what we said.' His lips slanted in a self-derisory smile. 'Believe me, I keep kicking myself, trying to remind myself of it, but I'm fighting a losing battle because I just can't resist you.'

His lips were inches from hers. If she swayed against him she would be in his arms. The temptation was overwhelming.

'You know I read...somewhere...that some firms in America have outlawed office romances.' She tried desperately to think straight. 'Apparently, they are bad for production.'

'Really?' Rogan's lips curved in a mischievous grin. 'Well, I think that's a mistake. I've come to the conclusion that nothing is more enticing than forbidden fruit.'

His lips touched hers. The sensation was overwhelmingly sensual. His caress was gentle, yet had all the power of a hurricane on her senses. She put one hand on his shoulder and he moved closer and kissed her again.

'This is probably a big mistake,' she murmured, but her words were fevered with passion.

'A big mistake,' he echoed. His hand moved to hold her close against his body.

Laura held onto him tightly, loving the feel of his caresses. She revelled in them, lapping them up, greedy for so much more.

For a long while they just kissed, the softness of his lips and the wildness of his passion setting Laura's body on fire. She felt his hands on the zip at the back of her dress and she didn't try to stop him as he gently slipped it down. She wanted the touch of his hands against her skin.

She was wearing a black lacy bra under her dress, and he stroked the lace aside and kissed her breast with an unreserved hunger that made her groan with pleasure.

Laura pressed herself closer to him. The soft material of his suit against her naked skin felt incredibly erotic.

'Laura, I want to make love to you.' He whispered the words against her ear in a low husky tone.

The demanding yet sensual note in his voice made her emotions boil.

'I don't know, Rogan. I'm not sure.' Her voice came out in a rush of panic as his hand moved to the buckle on the belt of his trousers.

He stopped and looked at her. 'Hell, maybe you're right.' He pushed a hand through his hair, as if willing himself to get his thoughts in order and his passion back under control.

He looked down at her, noting the way she was now holding her dress in front of her body in a defensive way.

'I think I should go,' he said quickly.

'Yes.' It took all her control to agree with him. He stood and reached for his coat. Then quietly, without another word—without even looking back at her—he let himself out of the front door.

For a while Rogan sat in his car. Even the cold night air didn't help to cool his ardour, but he was glad he had pulled back from her. She seemed too vulnerable for a casual affair and it was all he could offer.

He needed to call a stop to this, he told himself firmly.

# CHAPTER SEVEN

LAURA stared unseeingly at the work in front of her. All that played in front of her eyes was the scene on her settee last night. Over and over it went, mocking her, tormenting her.

She had wanted Rogan so badly. The thought of lying upstairs in her bed with him had been a temptation her body had craved.

Her office door opened and her nerves jangled violently as for a second she thought it might be Rogan. She didn't know if she was relieved or disappointed when she looked up to find that it was her secretary.

'I'm collecting for Robert James's leaving present.' Sandra waved a large jar in Laura's direction.

'What are we buying him?' Laura reached to get her purse.

'Some Waterford crystal. We'll present it at the leaving party next week.'

Laura pushed a note into the jar.

'It should be a really good party, you know. Rogan is helping to organise it.'

'Is he?' Laura was surprised.

'He's such a nice guy.' Sandra sighed dreamily. 'I'm just hoping that he will have one dance with me.'

Did the whole world have a crush on Rogan Powers? Laura wondered dryly.

'By the way, Shay O'Leary has been on the phone,' Sandra went on in a more serious tone. 'He has the fireplaces you ordered for Rogan's house and he can deliver tonight after six.'

Laura nodded. 'Have you checked the time is OK?'

'No. Rogan's been in a meeting all morning. I told Shay we'd phone him back and confirm.'

The knowledge that Rogan had been tied up all morning was vaguely reassuring. At least he hadn't been deliberately avoiding her.

Sandra glanced at her watch. 'I'll check with his secretary now. He should be finished.'

'No. Don't bother.' Laura said impulsively. 'I'll go up and see him. There are a few details I want to discuss about his house, anyway.'

It was an ideal excuse, she told herself as she reached to get his file. She desperately wanted to know how he felt about the way things had gone between them last night, and it was better to do it under the guise of work—see how he reacted to her.

As the lift doors closed and whisked her smoothly to the top floor Laura felt her heart pounding with anticipation. The thought of being alone with Rogan for even five minutes acted on her like an aphrodisiac.

Was she out of her mind? she berated herself sharply.

Wasn't it crazy in the extreme to lower her defences around a man who seemed irresistible to women? She really had to get a grip.

The lift doors swished open and she walked slowly towards his office.

She'd go in there and tell him that last night had been a mistake and would never be repeated, she told herself sternly. Then she found herself wondering if Rogan would say the same thing to her.

Rogan's secretary, Karen White, looked up as she entered the room.

'I'd like to speak to Mr Powers for a few minutes, if I may?' Laura requested politely.

The woman pursed her lips and shook her head. 'Have you an appointment?'

'No—'

'Then, I'm sorry, you can't see him.'

At that moment the door to the inner office opened and Rogan came out with another man. 'Thanks, Len, I'll look into it before the next meeting,' Rogan said in a friendly tone.

He glanced over towards Laura as the man left. 'Hello, Laura,' he said. 'What can I do for you?'

Although his tone was businesslike, she noticed the way his gaze lingered for a fraction of a second on her long legs and shapely figure. She was glad she had worn her pale vanilla suit. She knew she looked good in it and she needed the boost to her confidence.

All her sensible thoughts seemed to be deserting her. All she could think about was how wonderful it had felt to be in Rogan's arms.

'Just wanted to have a word about the decor for your house.' Somehow she managed to sound brisk.

He smiled and she wondered if he realised that she was just using an excuse to see him.

'OK, give me a moment. I've got to make a phone call first. Take a seat.' He indicated the comfortable seats behind her.

'If you are too busy it doesn't matter,' she said quickly. 'I've got an appointment in a little while, anyway…'

'Laura, it's fine. I won't be long.' He returned to his office and the door closed.

Laura met Karen's cool, glittering gaze. She had the distinct impression that the attractive secretary did not like her or the fact that she was to be granted an appointment when she had turned Laura away.

Karen returned her attention to her keyboard. The sound of her fingers hitting the keys punctuated the frosty atmosphere.

Laura sat. Her eyes moved from the secretary to the pictures on the walls. Some were of the New York office and some of what looked like a large department store.

The phone rang on Karen's desk and she snatched it up.

'Rogan Powers's office. Hold the line one moment, please,' she said in a lilting tone, before flicking the switch on the intercom. 'Rogan, sorry to interrupt but your wife is on line two. Do you want me to put her through? OK, will do.'

The shock was immense. For a moment Laura wondered if she had misheard. Rogan Powers—married?

'Yes, Mrs Powers, putting you through in one moment,' Karen was saying smoothly.

Laura hadn't misheard.

The lies, the deceit, made Laura feel sick as for one awful moment memories of her own husband's infidelity came flooding back.

She rose and Karen looked over at her.

'It sounds like Rogan will be a while,' she said quickly. 'Tell him I'll speak to him later.'

Was that her voice—so cool, so controlled? Inside she felt like hitting Rogan, fiercely smacking that smugly handsome face.

She didn't remember getting back to her office. She sat behind her desk, fizzing with fury—and with pain.

How could she have been so taken in? Allowed herself to believe his lies? All that talk about being frightened of commitment... Hell, he had even evoked tenderness and empathy within her when he had spoken of his parents' divorce. He had seemed so genuine.

And all along he had been cheating on his wife.

Her office door opened and she looked up as Robert's stepson, Paul, came in.

'Hello, gorgeous, how are things?' He grinned at her in his usual good-natured, teasing way.

'Not so bad.' With a supreme effort Laura forced herself to sound relaxed. 'What are you doing here?'

'Meeting with Rogan Powers,' he said. 'I tried to ring you on Tuesday night but there was no answer. I thought you said you couldn't go out because you'd no one to babysit?'

'I took the children out for something to eat.' The memory of that trip to Rogan's house taunted her. That wonderful way he had with her children. Maybe he had children of his own—if he'd lied about one thing he could lie about the other. Hurriedly she put a stop to those thoughts.

'Sorry, Paul, was there something in particular you wanted?' She focused her attention on him with difficulty.

'I was wondering if you'd like to accompany me to this party for Robert next week.'

Laura hesitated.

'Oh, go on, Laura. Say you'll come with me. It will make my night.'

Laura glanced up and saw Rogan Powers, walking down the corridor towards her office. She felt a frisson of absolute loathing for him. He looked sensational in his dark suit, his tall, well-built body drawing female eyes to him the way flowers attracted butterflies.

'So, what do you say, have we got a date?' Paul pulled her attention away from her boss.

'Yes, Paul. It's a date,' she found herself saying firmly.

'Great!'

The door of the office opened and Rogan strolled in. Paul smiled a greeting at the other man. 'Hello, Rogan, good to see you.'

The two men shook hands. 'I was a few minutes early for our appointment so I thought I'd have a few words with Laura.'

Rogan's eyes moved over towards her. 'I wanted a few words myself,' he drawled. 'Perhaps you'd go on up to my office, Paul. I won't be a moment.'

'Fine.' Paul smiled at Laura. 'I'll ring you later.'

She nodded.

'What was all that about?' Rogan asked as the door closed behind the other man.

'It was personal.' Laura was so mad with him she couldn't bring herself to look him in the eye.

There was a brief pause and she could feel the tension coiling between them.

John had cheated on her, lied to her. Rogan was doing the same to his wife and she wouldn't be a part of it.

She suddenly remembered the outing they had arranged for Sunday. Of course, that was now out of the question. The knowledge that Joanne and Matthew would be bitterly disappointed added to her fury.

'It certainly looked personal,' Rogan remarked calmly, 'but you're right. It's none of my business.'

She looked up at him and her eyes shimmered a vivid intense green.

'You rushed off, without seeing me. I wondered why,' he said nonchalantly.

'I didn't have time to wait around for you.' Her voice was overly bright as she tried to force herself to concentrate on business. 'I only wanted to know if there would be anyone in your house after six. I've found the correct Georgian fireplace for you and the guy wants to deliver.'

He shook his head. 'I won't be home until late. Can you reschedule, perhaps for tomorrow morning?'

'Yes, I'll do it now,' she murmured, raking through her files in an efficient way to find the phone number. She didn't dare to look at Rogan again or say anything personal because she was only just holding onto her temper. If she told him what she thought about him she might well be out of a job tomorrow.

'Laura.' His calm voice cut across her thoughts and she was forced to look up at him.

He smiled. 'You have very eloquent eyes, do you know that?' he murmured, a hint of teasing warmth in his gaze. 'Sometimes they seem to speak volumes.'

'Do they?' Her voice was flat. 'And what are they saying now?'

His lips twisted. 'They are calling me a rat. They are telling me that I have a wife and that you don't want anything more to do with me because I'm a cheat.'

'Sounds like you've got a guilty conscience,' Laura said, leaning back in her chair and trying to appear relaxed. Inside she was simmering.

Rogan shook his head and smiled at her. 'That's one thing I don't have.'

'Well, maybe you should.' Laura couldn't resist the gibe and her voice was laced with fury.

'Ah!' A flicker of amusement lit his dark eyes and it made Laura's blood pressure rise dramatically. 'Perhaps I should explain. It was my *ex*-wife who was on the phone earlier. I'm divorced.'

'Your ex-wife?' Laura stared at him and felt the colour return to her skin in one almighty rush. She shook her head. The relief was immense. 'I thought—'

'I know what you thought,' Rogan interrupted smoothly. 'I could see all too clearly what was going through your mind.'

'Well, it's not really any of my business.' Laura tried to sound indifferent.

'No?' Rogan looked at her with a wry lift of one eyebrow. 'So you wouldn't care if I was married?'

'Of course I'd care,' she blurted out furiously. 'I'd never…get involved with a married man.'

He smiled as he saw the colour rise even further beneath her cheeks. 'Last night was fabulous, by the way,' he said in a very low, very husky tone. 'You were probably right to call a halt to things when you did… maybe things are happening a little too quickly between us.'

'Maybe we should just call a halt to the whole thing—'

'I don't want to,' he cut across her quickly, then

frowned. 'I want to continue seeing you, Laura,' he admitted huskily.

Laura's heart thudded unsteadily in her chest. She had been going to say that last night had been a mistake and that it wouldn't happen again, but she couldn't think straight.

He glanced at his watch. 'Look, I can't keep Paul waiting any longer.'

The swift transition from personal conversation to business made her frown.

'Are we still on for Sunday?' he asked her, one hand on the doorhandle.

'Is your wife called Sophie?' she asked, with total disregard for his question or the fact that Paul was waiting for him. She felt she needed to know more before she committed herself to going out with him again. She wasn't sure at all about what had happened between them last night. The fact that he hadn't mentioned that he had been married stung. She felt as if she were now stepping out into totally uncharted territory.

He shook his head. 'Her name is Melony and she's my ex-wife. Sophie is my ex-girlfriend.'

'You seem to have been through a lot of women,' Laura said wryly.

'I did make it clear that I don't go in for serious relationships.' His tone was serious.

She shrugged, but inside her emotions were bobbing up and down. 'Of course you did. And I told you I don't want complications in my life. Which makes me think that both of us nearly took leave of our senses last night.'

'A very pleasurable leave.' He smiled slightly.

'It shouldn't have happened.' She forced herself to say the words. 'I'm glad I called a halt to things because, believe it or not, I don't go in for casual sex.'

The buzzer on her desk broke the tense silence that fell between them. 'That will probably be Karen, looking for me,' Rogan remarked. 'Look, we can't really discuss this here, but I do want you to know that I respect your feelings, Laura.'

Laura stared at him and felt her heart pumping painfully. It was hard to keep a distance between them when he was behaving like the perfect gentleman. 'Can we find some space to discuss this further on Sunday?' he continued gently.

She continued to stare at him.

'You do still want to go out with me on Sunday?' he asked with a frown when she didn't answer him immediately.

For some reason the note of uncertainty in his voice made her throw away caution. 'Yes,' she admitted huskily. 'I do.'

He smiled back. 'I'll pick you and the children up at midday.'

The buzzer rang again. 'I'm sorry, Laura, but I have to go.' He shook his head regretfully. 'Tell Karen I'm on my way, will you?'

He made to open the door, then suddenly stopped and looked back at her. 'By the way, have you mentioned to anyone that we are seeing each other socially?'

'No.'

'Good,' he said. 'Maybe we had better leave it that way. Our private lives are our own business.'

'Fine.' She shrugged and then watched as he walked away from her towards the lifts. She didn't blame him for wanting to keep his private life separate from work and, anyway, she didn't want to be labelled as the boss's mistress. The very thought made her freeze. If she continued on this track it was only a matter of time before he did make her his mistress.

It was all very well for Rogan to tell her that he respected her feelings about casual love-making, but he had also made it clear once again that he didn't want anything deeper than an affair. So where on earth could they go from here?

Laura returned her attention to the drawings on her desk. She should have told him that she didn't want to go out with him on Sunday. That was the only logical thing to do. But she didn't want to be logical.

Deep down warning bells were ringing.

A roaring fire warmed the dining room of the local inn. The place had character, with a low-beamed ceiling and small windows that overlooked the blue Irish Sea.

Sunday lunch had been very pleasant and they had lingered over it. The children were in their element, both vying for Rogan's attention. Matthew told Rogan about his trip to the dentist, and was full of bravado now it was over. Joanne talked about a school trip she wanted to go on.

Laura glanced across and met Rogan's eyes. He had been watching her for the last few minutes, she realised suddenly, as if he was deep in thought.

'Shall we go?' He smiled, making her wonder if she had imagined the intense gaze.

She nodded and he got up from the table to go and pay their bill, with Matthew following.

Laura watched them. Her son looked so small next to Rogan's tall frame. She noticed that he was copying Rogan, standing just as he was, with legs slightly apart and one hand on the top of his back pocket as if he were getting his wallet out.

'Rogan's really nice, isn't he, Mum?' Joanne asked her suddenly. 'I think he's the best boyfriend you've ever gone out with.'

'He's just a friend, Jo,' Laura said firmly, but even as she spoke she was wondering how much longer she could hold on to the pretence of that. Every little glance, ever warm word, made an impact on her.

'Do you think Rogan likes living in that big house of his all alone?' Jo continued, regardless of her mother's statement. 'I mean, he must get lonely, don't you think?'

Laura flicked an amused glance at her daughter. 'No, I think that's the way Rogan wants it. Some people like their space.' She stood to go and get their coats.

It was cold outside, one of those brilliantly blue clear days where the ground was frosty and the air sharp. Laura was glad of her warm cords and suede jacket.

'Are we going to see your horse now?' Matthew asked Rogan as they walked through the little rose garden outside the inn.

'Yes, I thought, if we were all in agreement, we could walk.' He nodded towards a path that led from the car park around the headland. 'The stables are on the other side. It's about two miles.'

'Great.' Matthew was the first to run to the path, his red coat flapping open.

'Zip your coat up,' Laura called after him.

He paid no attention. Maybe he couldn't hear. 'One word from me and he does as he likes,' she said jokingly to Rogan.

'I'll tell him.' Joanne hurried after her brother.

'You don't mind walking?' Rogan asked Laura as they were left alone.

'Not at all.' She glanced up at him. 'Thanks for lunch, it was lovely.'

He didn't answer her and he seemed to be deep in thought again. For a while they walked in silence, watching the children up ahead.

'What are you thinking about?' she asked him suddenly.

'Nothing.' He frowned. That was a lie. He had been thinking about the fact that he had told himself he mustn't see her again yet he seemed incapable of sticking to the resolution.

Yesterday an attractive woman he had taken out once had phoned him and invited him to dinner. Without even the slightest of hesitations, he had politely refused. Even when her voice had been filled with husky inducement he hadn't been in the slightest bit tempted.

All he could think about was Laura...and, worse still, he had found himself worrying about Matthew yesterday, wondering how he had got on at the dentist. He'd had to ring Laura to find out.

He raked an impatient hand through his hair. Laura was getting under his skin. That was definitely against his rules. He'd have to have a wild affair with her and get her out of his system, he decided forcefully.

'Why didn't you tell me you'd been married?' Laura asked him suddenly, breaking into his thoughts.

'It's something I like to forget.' Rogan shrugged.

'Was it that bad?'

'I never want to repeat the experience, put it that way.' His voice was heavy for a second, his eyes distant.

'What happened?'

He flicked a sardonically amused glance down at her. 'She didn't understand me.'

'You mean she didn't understand your affairs?' Laura retorted, irritated by the flippant reply.

'I didn't have affairs,' he said quietly, 'but she left me anyway.'

'I'm sorry.' She took a deep breath. 'I shouldn't have said that.'

He grinned. 'You have a quick Celtic temper, don't you? Your eyes were certainly flashing fire on Friday when you thought I was married.'

'It's little wonder I was annoyed. You should remind your secretary that you no longer have a wife—that she's now your ex-wife.

'Karen is extremely efficient, but that is one mistake she has made many times,' he drawled with lazy amusement.

'It's one way of seeing off unwanted girlfriends, I suppose,' Laura said stiffly. She was still upset by the episode...hurt that Rogan hadn't told her about his past.

'I can do my own, "seeing off", as you call it,' he assured her briskly, 'and I have spoken to Karen about her error.'

'If you'd told me you were divorced it wouldn't have been an issue.'

'It was hardly an issue. It was a small misunderstanding.'

Remembering the shock and the pain she had felt, Laura felt a dart of annoyance. 'Hardly small. Your secrecy left me thinking I'd been consorting with a married man, and that's something I'd never do.' Her voice was low and laced with fury. 'I even started to wonder if you had children tucked away somewhere.'

'I told you I had no children.' He seemed unconcerned.

'You told me you were wary of marriage because your own parents had been through a bitter divorce,' she snapped. 'You forgot to mention you'd been through one yourself.'

He stopped suddenly and turned her to look at him. 'Laura, you're blowing the whole thing out of proportion. I've been married. It's over. It's not a secret, just something I don't like to talk about. Some things are too painful to rake over.'

Laura stared up at him. She could understand that, could even empathise, especially with that momentary raw note in his voice. She looked up at him and her heart melted.

Their breath merged in the frosty air.

'You asked me what I was thinking about earlier,' he murmured in a low tone. 'I was thinking how you are driving me out of my mind,' he admitted softly.

'My Celtic temper is getting to you?' she asked in a mock-playful tone, but deep down she knew exactly what he meant.

'Your curvaceous body, your eyes, your mouth, yes,

even that fiery Celtic temper—everything is getting to me,' he whispered huskily. 'I want you like crazy.'

Her heart pounded. She wanted him, too.

The children's voices, calling them, penetrated hazily through the mist of desire. She pulled away from him. 'We had better keep an eye on them,' she said unsteadily.

Rogan fell into step beside her as she walked on. For a while they walked in silence. The path was close to the sea and the waves were rippling in over the stony shore in a tranquil way, making a soft sucking sound on the pebbles as they withdrew.

'Do you want me, Laura?' he asked gently after a while.

'I'm not sure how I feel.' She took a deep breath and admitted softly, 'The last man I went to bed with was my husband.'

'And you think that giving yourself to me would be disloyal to his memory?'

She smiled at that. 'No...' Nothing could be further from the truth. 'I told you, I just don't go in for casual relationships. I'm a single parent, Rogan. My children are my main priority in life.'

Up ahead Joanne and Matthew were jumping over the rock pools with squeals of laughter.

'I can understand you wanting to protect them—'

'Can you?' She glanced up at him.

He nodded. 'But I think you're hiding behind them now.'

'I'm not.' She was indignant. 'It's very hard, you know, bringing up two children on your own. And they've been through such a lot, with losing their father. I do my best for them but sometimes I wonder if it's enough.' She hesitated for a moment, deep in thought.

'Especially for Matt. There's no doubt that he would have been his father's boy. He loves to talk about sport or cars and planes...' She shook her head. 'I try to keep up an interest in them, but I'm afraid Jo and I are more into the latest fashions.'

Rogan laughed at that and took hold of her hand. 'I think you do a wonderful job,' he said warmly.

The words and the touch of his hand made her heart contract.

'Thanks, but you don't really know me.' She tried to sound sensible.

'I think I do. I think you are scared as hell of giving yourself to me because you don't want to be hurt.' He grinned and admitted huskily, 'And I'm scared as hell of hurting you. That's the main reason I rushed so quickly from your house the other night.'

When she didn't say anything he continued, 'I admit my intentions aren't strictly honourable. I want you as my mistress...not my wife. But I do care about you.'

She smiled at that. 'You're so honest,' she said wryly. Then she looked up at him directly. 'I'll think about it.'

He stared at her. Usually women fell over themselves for him. Laura was so different...so adorable...so maddening.

The children were calling again, and Laura picked up her pace. 'Come on,' she called back to Rogan. 'I'll race you to the end of the path.'

Suddenly they were running after the children and then laughing helplessly with them as they chased them along the shore.

They were all breathless when they finally reached the stables. Laura sat on a fence while Rogan went to organise a ride around the paddock for the children.

Mystic was the most gorgeous thoroughbred, her coat the colour of gold and her mane pure white. Matthew and Joanne fell instantly in love.

'This day is going to be discussed again and again for the next year,' Laura told Rogan when he joined her.

They watched Matthew slide from the horse's back so that the stable girl could help Joanne mount. 'I hope you know you've started something. Matt is now going to add horses to his cars, planes and boats list.'

Rogan laughed. 'I shall take it as a compliment if he does.'

Laura looked across at him. Something about the way he said those words made her heart melt.

'I've got something to ask you,' Rogan said suddenly, his tone serious. 'I probably should wait to discuss this in the office but as we are together…' He shrugged.

She looked at him with a frown.

'I want you to come to New York with me next week.'

Her eyes widened. 'Why?'

'Work, of course.' He grinned, then conceded, 'Although we don't have to rule out having fun.'

'I don't know, Rogan…' Immediately she was wary.

'Before you answer I have to tell you it's a serious business trip. I'm going to include a section on James Home Design in one of the New York stores—soft furnishings with a Celtic theme. I think it will go down well in the American market.'

'And where do I fit in?' Laura was slightly bemused to be talking about big business in such a relaxed way.

'It will be an opportunity for you to meet my other staff, and I'd very much like your input into the designs for the showcase.'

She looked over at him. 'Where would I stay?'

He hesitated. 'Depends on you,' he said huskily. 'You can stay at my apartment or, if you prefer, I'll organise a hotel for you.'

Still she didn't say anything. 'It will be three days, Laura. I think it would be good for you to see how we operate Stateside. It would give a boost to your career.'

'Oh, yes?' She turned to him with eyes that were half smiling, half cautious. 'Are you trying to induce me with bribery, Mr Powers?'

'I think I'd rather induce you with promises of untold pleasures.' He grinned. 'But I assure you this is work.'

'I'll have to check that my mother is free to take care of the children,' she said slowly.

'Fine.' He nodded.

'Then there is the party we are throwing for Robert next Friday. I really should be there.'

'We'll be back for that. It's three days, Tuesday and Wednesday, arriving back Thursday. Laura, I do want you to do this. It's a serious project and I think it could be the link that will strengthen business between Dublin and New York.'

# CHAPTER EIGHT

As THE Power company jet banked, ready for descent at JFK airport, Laura felt suddenly very apprehensive.

They had worked throughout the long flight and the paperwork had taken her mind off the more personal side of this trip. But now as she looked across at Rogan she wondered what on earth she was doing here with him.

Rogan packed away the mountain of paperwork he had been working on since take-off from Dublin.

'A bit late, but it was a good flight,' he said nonchalantly as he met Laura's eye.

She nodded, struck afresh by how relaxed he sounded. He had been like this throughout the long flight. Friendly, yet not overly familiar, as if this was all really business and he had no designs on her body.

She should be pleased that they had only discussed work and that the flight had been nothing but paperwork, interspersed with a few meals and polite conversation.

As the noise of the engines increased and the plane descended towards the runway Laura turned to look out of the window. Her first trip to New York. She wished the children were with her.

The thought made her remember their smiling faces when she had told them she was accompanying Rogan on a business trip. They had been so excited for her. Come to that, so had her mother. Cora had instantly volunteered to look after the children.

'You seem to be getting on very well with your new boss,' she had remarked cheerfully.

'I enjoy his company.'

'That means a lot. And the children seem very fond

111

of him, don't they? Do you think Rogan intends to live full time in Ireland?'

'I don't think so, Mum.'

The conversation had been casual but Laura had known that hidden behind her mother's words was a voice urging caution. A relationship with Rogan could lead nowhere, she knew that, so it was best not to get too involved.

The wheels of the plane touched down smoothly on the runway, jolting Laura from her thoughts. The seat-belt sign went off and Rogan rose to get their belongings together.

'It looks cold out there,' she said, looking out.

'Yes, the snow seems to have come early this year, and the weather forecast is for more of the same.'

Rogan helped her on with her coat, the touch of his hand against her arm sending a wave of desire racing through her.

She watched as he put on the long, dark, Armani coat over his dark business suit.

Hell, he was gorgeous, she thought suddenly. The smart suit, the dark hair with just a few strands of grey at the temple, the dark eyes and square jaw just seemed to scream sensuality.

He looked over at her and smiled and her heart seemed to go into overdrive.

It astonished her that she should have to fight so hard for control every time Rogan so much as glanced at her or touched her. It frightened her.

'Did you book a hotel room for me?' she asked him suddenly. She tried to sound casual but her apprehension showed in her voice.

He smiled. 'I will if you want me to, Laura. Or there's a spare room at my apartment. We'll talk about the sleeping arrangements later, shall we?'

He was so cool.

'If you want.' She tried to match his urbane indifference, but her voice wasn't entirely convincing.

There was a gleam in his eye, as if he found her endearing.

He knew, she thought suddenly. He knew that she was weakening towards him...that there was a part of her that wanted to throw caution away.

All she needed to do was say that she wanted him, and he would take her back to his apartment and make love to her... She had no doubts about that.

Of course, it would mean nothing...but it would, in all certainty, feel wonderful. Just to be held close in his arms, to be stroked tenderly and kissed...

She turned from him.

The doors of the plane were opened and they stepped into the wintry New York morning.

She felt both excitement and apprehension as they cleared immigration. She wondered suddenly if Rogan had got her here under false pretences, if there was no work involved at all?

The thought was very disquieting. Then she remembered they had been doing costings all the way from Dublin airport. Of course this was business. She felt foolish for a moment. Rogan was charming and seductive, but he was a straightforward businessman. And he had never lied to her.

He had made it clear that he wanted to sleep with her, but it was up to her. And he hadn't tried to pretend to her that he was looking for serious involvement.

A limousine met them at the airport and they sat in silence for a while as it whisked them towards Manhattan.

'Are you all right, Laura?' Rogan asked, as he opened his briefcase to read through some files.

'Yes, of course.'

His eyes moved over her gently, as if noticing the strain in her eyes and the tense way she was sitting so far from him on the long seat. 'I'll be finished with this paperwork soon. The more I can get done while we're travelling the more free time I can grab later.'

Free time for what? The question blazed through her. 'That's fine,' she answered, trying to sound indifferent.

She turned her head and looked out at the New York skyline. It was spectacular. Buildings towered into the ice-blue sky and glass shimmered in the early morning sunlight. A light covering of snow was on the pavements. People were well wrapped up against the weather in fur coats and woollen hats. She noticed the food stalls and the wafts of steam that seemed to rise mysteriously from the road.

They drove along Fifth Avenue and she leaned forward, craning her neck to look at the shop windows.

They passed Tiffany's, Trump Tower. She was truly in New York and it was just as she had imagined it—better, in fact.

The limousine slowed as they reached Central Park.

'Almost home,' Rogan said with a smile as he started to put his work back in his briefcase.

'Home?' She looked at him with a frown.

'Yes, I thought we would call at my apartment first and freshen up, before going in to the office. You can check in at your hotel later if you want.'

Home for Rogan Powers was an enormous penthouse on the top floor of a twenty-storey building.

Wooden floors and white walls added to the feeling of space. It was all very ultra-modern and uncluttered. Modern expressionist and abstract paintings hung on the walls, and occasional furniture was in glass and chrome. The only colour to be seen, apart from the paintings, was the green of large plants and the beige and tan of leather upholstery.

Laura couldn't help comparing it with her home. Suddenly she had the feeling that she wouldn't fit very easily into Rogan's high-flying, sophisticated world. She liked chintz and warm floral tones. Rogan was the extreme opposite.

'You don't need me to design the decor for this place,' she said in admiration. 'It's lovely.'

'In keeping with the surroundings, I suppose,' he said.

'Who looks after it for you?' she asked as he opened the door to a kitchen that was whiter than white with tubular steel stools and chrome pans.

'I have a housekeeper who comes in daily.' Rogan went across to put some coffee on. 'Are you hungry?'

'No, thanks. I ate enough on the plane.' Laura's attention was taken by a bowl of red tulips on the kitchen counter. There was a note propped up against it. She could read it, without picking it up. It said, 'Welcome Home, Love Sarah.'

Immediately Laura felt a thrust of jealousy. Whoever had written the note must be pretty close to Rogan—and must have a key to his apartment.

'Your housekeeper has left you a love note,' she said lightly.

He looked at the flowers and came across to pick up the note. He smiled. 'It's not from my housekeeper,' he said quietly.

Laura fought with herself not to ask, and when he didn't immediately volunteer the information she felt slightly annoyed.

'Did...did you say there was somewhere I could freshen up?' she asked him, wanting to get away from his disturbing presence for a while.

He smiled. 'Sure.' He led the way back out into the corridor and picked up her suitcase to carry it towards a room at the far end.

'And the flowers, by the way, are from my sister. She only lives a few blocks away.'

'You didn't need to explain.' Now that he had she was perversely pretending to be indifferent. But the truth was that she felt tremendously relieved. She really hadn't liked the idea of any other woman having the run of Rogan's apartment. It smacked too much of permanency. She didn't analyse her feelings...she didn't dare.

'Maybe I can meet your sister while we are here,' she ventured cautiously.

'I don't know if we will have time.'

'So it's going to be all work, then?'

'With a little time left over for getting to know each other better,' he said as he opened the door into a large bedroom.

Picture windows looked out over Manhattan. The bed was enormous with an ornate wrought-iron frame.

Was this where he wanted to get to know her? The thought tumbled into her mind from nowhere.

'You've got fabulous views,' Laura said, for want of something better to say.

'They are even better at night.'

'I'll take your word for it,' Laura said, 'but I'll probably be at a hotel...won't I?'

Their eyes met and he grinned as if she thoroughly amused him. He put her suitcase down and opened the door to an *en suite* bathroom. 'There will be plenty of hot water so feel free to take a shower. That way we can go straight on to the office.'

The shrill tone of the phone interrupted them. 'Make yourself at home,' he said as he left her.

She opened her luggage and found a trouser suit in soft cream, which she put on a hanger in the bathroom so that the steam of her shower would help eliminate any creases.

Once she was dressed she inspected her appearance in the mirror, before going back out to Rogan.

She looked stylish. Her hair was sitting perfectly and her make-up was light, yet gave her a healthy glow.

No one looking at her would have guessed that she was a woman who had just made a transatlantic flight.

She walked back through the apartment and found

Rogan at the dining-room table, looking out over the skyscrapers and the distant green of Central Park.

He got to his feet as she joined him. 'I've made coffee. Would you like some?'

'Thank you.' She sat and looked out at the view. 'Wow, this city is even more fantastic than I had imagined.'

'If we've got any spare time I'll show you around.'

Laura looked back at him and their eyes held for a moment. She'd like that, she realised, but she would have preferred to have met his sister. Obviously he hadn't been keen on that idea. Maybe it smacked too much of intimacy for him.

It didn't matter, she told herself firmly. She was here on business.


Rogan's offices were in the financial quarter of the city. They were much bigger and more impressive than the offices in Dublin, Laura thought as they walked into the marble foyer and then went straight up to the fortieth floor.

She took off her coat and hat as the heat started to thaw her out. She was very glad she was wearing a smart suit. Rogan's staff were all very stylishly dressed.

Rogan got someone to show Laura around while he went into a private meeting with two of his chief accountants. When she came back to his office they all rose politely.

'Gentlemen, I'd like to introduce Laura Taylor,' Rogan said smoothly. 'She's going to be lending her expertise to the Celtic range for our store on Fifth Avenue.'

They shook hands with her then settled back into the leather chairs as the girl who had shown Laura around poured them all coffee.

Laura took in the stylish decor and a view of Manhattan which was truly magnificent.

However, there was little time to admire the view. Rogan launched straight into an in-depth discussion on the project, a discussion that lasted two hours and was so intense that Laura's head was swimming with details when it had finished.

After that she was whisked away to the department store to look around the space available for their display. Rogan didn't come with her. He said he'd see her at the offices at the Fifth Avenue store a little later.

It was seven-thirty when she had finished. The light had faded outside, leaving the lights of the skyscrapers twinkling against the dark velvet of the sky.

She didn't realise how late it was until Rogan put his head around the door of the office she was using. 'How's it going?' he asked gently.

Laura smiled. She was really excited about this assignment. It had been great, working with so many different talented designers. 'Your timing is impeccable. I've just finished.'

'Really?' He crossed the room and stood behind her to read the figures she had scribbled down and the preliminary sketches.

'You've done well,' he said, and she could hear by his tone of voice that he was impressed. She smiled, feeling pleased with herself.

'At least I'm on target now. I should finish here tomorrow.'

'Good.' He reached across and switched off the desk light. 'So how about joining me for dinner?'

She turned in her chair and looked up at him. The semi-darkness of the room lent an intimate atmosphere.

'I don't know, Rogan. I have to check into my hotel.'

'We'll have dinner first, then back to my apartment to pick up your luggage.'

'You sound as if you've got it all worked out.'

'I have.' He reached out and took hold of her hand.

'And I've got a wonderful restaurant in mind for you. The perfect place to unwind.'

The touch of his hand against hers set off all kinds of tremors inside her, but she allowed him to pull her to her feet.

'It sounds good.' They were standing very close, perhaps too close, but she felt incapable of moving away.

He smiled and reached for her coat.

They took a yellow cab outside the offices and it slipped into the grid of traffic.

Despite her busy day and all the travel, Laura didn't feel tired but exuberant and alive. New York seemed to be vibrating with excitement and she was happy to be a part of it.

When they reached their destination and got out into the cool night air Laura shivered. Immediately Rogan put an arm around her.

She liked the feeling. She liked being close to him, and found herself remembering the way they had woken up together at Fitzroy's, the immediate feeling of sensuality…and belonging. The way he had kissed her.

The idea of waking up with him again, but this time making love, was so urgent that there was a part of her that wanted to say, Hey, let's forget dinner.

She looked up at him and he smiled. And Laura knew she was falling in love with Rogan Powers. The truth was so startling that she almost caught her breath.

When had that happened? She shook her head, feeling dazed. Had it been when they had been alone together at the castle? Or when she had watched him talking to her children and had felt as if some circle had been completed—as if the four of them were like a family.

Yes…possibly then. She shivered and he drew her even closer against his body. 'Cold?'

She nodded and allowed him to hold her. But she wasn't cold, she was afraid. Afraid of where this was leading.

She couldn't fall in love with Rogan. He would be horrified. If he even suspected that she felt like this he would end things with her here and now.

No, she'd have to forget her feelings, bury them back where they had come from, because they would lead to nothing but heartache.

# CHAPTER NINE

THE restaurant was excellent. Not only was the food good but the setting was breathtaking. Yet afterwards, when Laura thought about it, all she could remember was Rogan. She wouldn't have been able to tell anyone what she had eaten.

They sat at a window seat, and the views down towards the street, where the traffic flowed in long straight lines of yellow and red lights, made her feel dizzy.

A dance floor was lit by the glitter of subdued lighting and a small band was playing for the few couples dancing.

Most of the way through the meal Laura managed to keep the conversation on the work she had done that day.

Then Rogan sighed and leaned back in his chair. 'I think we have talked enough about that project for one day. If I'm honest, I never wanted to talk about it tonight in the first place.'

Her heart thudded rapidly as she looked across at him. 'What do you want to talk about?'

'You.'

'That's not such an exciting subject,' she said with a small smile.

'It is to me.'

For a moment his eyes moved over the porcelain paleness of her skin and the wide beauty of her eyes.

'Why don't we talk about you instead?' she asked lightly. 'You never did tell me about your ex-wife.'

'Now there's a subject to dampen the proceedings.'

She toyed with the wine glass in front of her. 'Was the marriage that bad?'

'It started out all right. I don't know, I guess I just got married too young. I was twenty-three. A very ambitious twenty-three. If the truth be told, I had an eye on achievements and not on my marriage.'

'So what happened?' she asked gently.

'The old story. I was out, making money, and she was home, making out. With a guy who called himself my friend.' Rogan shrugged. 'But I suppose it takes two to make a lousy marriage, and I did neglect her. I had a computer programming company at the time and it consumed a lot of my time and energy. I thought she was as dedicated to making a success of things as I was. But I was wrong. She was interested in the money and the lifestyle, but nothing else.'

She heard the pain in his voice and her heart ached with sympathy for him. 'Do you still love her?'

He shook his head. 'No…I got over that a long time ago. At least we didn't have children. It's one thing to mess up your own life but I wouldn't want to have pulled children through the trauma. But I've learnt from my mistakes—I'd never go through that again.'

'Never get married again?'

As soon as she spoke the words she regretted them. He looked across at her and grinned. 'I guess I've got used to being on my own. I was married five years, and I've been divorced eight.'

'Somehow I thought it was more recent than that.' Laura frowned. 'How come your ex-wife still phones you?'

'I gave her shares in the company as part of our divorce settlement. I'm now in a position to buy them back.' Rogan spread his hands. 'I'm in the middle of heavy negotiations with her at the moment.'

Laura noticed the serious look in his eyes now, the note of determination in his voice. 'You are still the ambitious person with an eye to achievements?' she said with a smile.

'I suppose I must be. The company is all-important to me—' He broke off. 'We're talking about business again!'

'Sorry.' She smiled at him. 'It's my fault. I was curious.'

'Talking about being curious, what was Paul James talking to you about in the office the other day? I've noticed that every time he comes into the office he heads straight for you.'

'We were just discussing Robert's retirement party.' Laura suddenly remembered the invitation Paul had issued to her to accompany him to that party. She frowned at the memory.

She wouldn't mention the planned date, she decided swiftly. In fact, maybe she would ring Paul and have a quiet word to see if he would mind if she didn't accompany him on the night of the party. She was sure he wouldn't—they didn't have that kind of relationship.

'Paul went with you to the Fitzroy castle the first time, didn't he?' Rogan recalled.

She nodded. 'We were kept late...but not as late as you and I.' She met his eyes across the table.

'He didn't get to wake up with you,' Rogan said huskily. 'Poor Paul. Now I feel sorry for him. You look very beautiful first thing in the morning, Laura Taylor.'

She tried not to feel embarrassed by the compliment. 'I'm sure I looked no such thing, but you really do know all the right things to say,' she murmured.

'Perhaps the time for talking is past...'

For a second her heart missed a beat as she wondered what he was leading up to, then he grinned teasingly. 'So how about having a dance with me instead?'

Laura hesitated. The band was playing a Nat King Cole number, 'Unforgettable.'

He stood and held out his hand.

Slowly she got up and allowed him to lead her out to the dance floor.

A tremor raced through her body as he took her into his arms. One hand rested against the soft material of her blouse, and she could feel it burning through to the soft skin beneath.

As a saxophone played they swayed together. Laura rested her head against his jacket. She imagined she could hear the steady thud of his heart.

His hand stroked her gently, a whisper-soft caress that heightened her awareness of him, bringing it to an unbearable ache of sweet yearning.

He bent his head towards hers. 'Sweet Laura.' His voice was a mere husky murmur against her ear. 'I'd like to have a million nights like this one.'

She closed her eyes, breathing in his closeness and his words and storing them away to be treasured, to be remembered, for ever.

As the music finished Rogan released her from the warm circle of his arms and she felt bereft suddenly. She had never wanted anyone the way she wanted Rogan.

'How are you feeling?' Rogan asked as they went back to their table. 'Are you tired?'

'Not too bad, considering I should have jet lag,' she said with a smile.

'Maybe we should go.' Rogan's voice was thick with desire.

Laura knew that hidden beneath the words was the invitation to his bed. Should they go back to his apartment and make love? She felt her heart miss a beat... and knew that was what she wanted.

She met his eyes, so incredibly wonderful. Gentle, passionate. She couldn't find her voice. Anyway, she was scared that if she spoke he would hear the desire that was eating through her so she simply nodded.

They didn't speak at all on the cab ride back to Rogan's apartment. Rogan's arm rested lightly around her shoulders but to Laura it was like a band of possession.

She needed to think sensibly about this, she tried to tell herself sternly. She needed to be sure that she was doing the right thing.

But how could anyone be sure? She had dated John for six months and had thought she knew him.

What would she have to lose by sleeping with Rogan? a small treacherous voice inside asked.

She was a grown woman. Surely she could handle her emotions, keep them in check. She could handle an affair—take whatever Rogan had to offer her.

By the time they reached the front door of Rogan's apartment her emotions were torn apart with doubt... with need.

Rogan flicked a switch and a few lamps lit the room with an intimate glow. 'Would you like a drink?'

'I don't know... Perhaps I should just collect my case and go...'

'Is that what you want?'

She met his dark eyes. 'No...' Her heart was thudding so unevenly against her chest that it was painful.

He pulled her to him and found her lips. His mouth was gentle, persuasive, against hers. 'I want you so much, Laura, but I don't want to hurry things between us, not if you're not ready. I know you like to do things correctly...' He trailed off, a teasing note in his voice.

She smiled, a gentle, reflective smile. 'I just thought we should get to know each other better before we took things any further,' she whispered.

He smiled. 'I've got a bottle of champagne in the fridge. Shall we start getting to know each other a little better over a glass of Moët?'

'What about my hotel room?' She hoped she didn't sound as breathless as she felt.

'We can get to know each other back there if you

want.' He grinned teasingly as he saw the heat racing into her cheeks.

'That's not what I meant—'

'I know.' He placed a soothing finger against her lips for a moment. 'I know what you meant, but I don't want you to go to a hotel. If you really feel you must, you can have the spare bedroom, Laura. I'm not going to force you into anything you don't want.'

She liked the fact that he wasn't going to hurry anything. She felt as if he was allowing her to dictate the pace of the way things went, and it eased her doubts.

'What I want to do...and what I ought to do seem to be two entirely different things,' she said in a low tone. 'Let's have that champagne and talk about it.'

She took off her coat and moved towards the windows to admire the night view of Manhattan. Then turned as she heard Rogan coming back into the room with the champagne, and as she did she noticed there was a red light on his telephone. Immediately she thought about the children.

'Someone has left a message on your answerphone.'

'Yes, I noticed.' He uncorked the bottle of champagne and poured it into two crystal flutes.

'Aren't you going to see who it is? It could be important. It could be my mother.'

'If it's important they'll phone back,' he said, handing her drink across. 'And it won't be your mother.'

'How do you know?' She frowned.

'Because I didn't give you my home number for her. I gave you my work number.' He held up a hand as she made a noise of protest. 'That's not as terrible as it sounds,' he assured her quickly. 'I have a member of staff on my switchboard twenty-four hours a day. And I have a pager with me at all times. That means no matter where we are—out having dinner, even in a taxi—the children can reach us. It made sense to give her that number rather than this one.'

'Oh.' She sat on one of the leather settees. Thinking about the children had brought some sense of responsibility back to her mind.

He sat next to her. 'Now you are thinking about Joanne and Matthew, aren't you? Worrying about them.'

'No, I know they are in safe hands and I rang earlier.' She smiled, then there was a moment's silence before she admitted, 'Well, maybe I am a little worried. You know, it's hard to switch off from the responsibility of children. When they aren't with you it's like some string is pulling you back, making you constantly think about them.' She was quiet for a moment, thinking about her life.

'It's right that your children should be at the top of your list of priorities but you have needs, too, Laura. You shouldn't overlook them.'

She met his eyes and her lips curved in a tremulous smile.

'Is that a purely unselfish remark?'

'No,' he said, 'but at least I'm honest. I told you I'd never knowingly hurt you Laura. On the other hand, I would never make promises I couldn't keep.'

'You mean, if you were to take me to bed it's not because you love me but because you desire me.' Her voice was flat. 'I think I've figured that out by now, Rogan.'

'If it means anything, I am crazy about you...'

She shook her head. 'I wouldn't fool myself that that means anything at all.'

He tipped her chin so that he could look into her eyes. The strange half-light seemed to illuminate the glitter in his eyes and his strong bone structure.

She shivered as his finger moved down to her neck.

'I'm not so sure. I've never wanted any woman the way I want you.'

Her breathing felt restricted. He was so close and she felt so much for him. He leaned closer and kissed her.

She returned his kiss, her heart now slamming furiously. Did he mean it...?

He took her champagne from her hand and placed it on the table.

'Now, where was I?' Rogan murmured huskily as he reached once more to take her in his arms. Laura closed her eyes as his head lowered towards hers again. Her whole body felt alive with longing.

When their lips met again the feeling was electric. This time the gentleness was replaced with a fierce, bitter-sweet longing. Laura felt his hands move around her and draw her closer. His hand stroked her back then moved upwards to sweep the heaviness of her hair back from her face as he kissed her neck.

'I want you so much, Laura,' he murmured against her ear.

She felt her defences crumbling...felt the heat of desire start to take over. Her whole body was alive with a vibrant, passionate need.

'I want you, too,' she murmured, the words almost incoherent.

Only when Rogan pulled away from her slightly to look down into her eyes did she become aware that she had spoken aloud the words that were drumming throughout her entire body.

'Do you mean it?'

Trembling, she nodded her head, not trusting herself to speak. He put a hand under her chin and tipped her head up so that he could look into her eyes, then he smiled as if what he saw pleased him more than the words she had spoken. Softly, he kissed her lips.

As he did so she felt him unbuttoning her blouse. She wasn't wearing a bra and, feeling suddenly shy, she put up a hand to stop the silky material from falling.

He kissed her neck, then her ear, his hands stroking her naked back. Then gently he uncurled her fingers, allowing the material to slither downwards.

She shivered, and snuggled closer against the warmth of his body. She wasn't cold—the fire that was blazing through her was much much too strong. Her shivers were a mixture of desire and apprehension. It had been so long since she'd trusted a man, so long since she had wanted unreservedly to give herself like this.

His hands stroked the narrow curve of her waist and he made no attempt to move her away from him. He just held her.

'You're not nervous, are you?' he whispered against her neck, sending delicious little shivers of desire shuddering through her.

'A little,' she acknowledged softly. 'It's been a long time.'

'I won't hurt you...I promise.'

Laura knew that Rogan would be a skilled and sensitive lover—she had no doubts about that. It was her emotions that she worried about. She cuddled closer, hearing the steady beat of his heart against her ear.

It was delicious to be held like this. She felt cherished...loved. The words rang inside her and even as she acknowledged how foolish they were the feeling refused to die. She had never felt like this before. She felt protected inside the warm circle of his arms.

Then he picked her up and carried her through to the bedroom. He didn't turn on a light. The city lights lit the room in a kaleidoscope of colour against the stark white of the sheets on his bed.

He placed her on the bed, then his hands moved to take the rest of her clothing off.

'Let me look at you,' he said, his voice a husky rasp as he caressed her naked skin.

Her long, dark hair lay in a swathe across the perfect smoothness of her skin. Her figure was curvaceous, with high, full breasts above a taut ribcage, small waist and gently curved hips.

'You're so beautiful.' He breathed the words in a se-

ductive whisper. Reaching out, he stroked her breast.
The nipples were hard and erect with desire and she
shuddered with pleasure. Slowly, he bent his head to
touch his lips to her breast.

'Laura, I'm too impatient for you.' She felt his hands
against the silk of her underwear, pulling them down. 'I
want you now.'

The feeling was mutual. Laura felt that if he didn't
make love to her straight away she would go crazy with
desire. She watched as he took off his tie, then started
to unbutton his shirt. She reached out to curl her fingers
through the dark hair on his chest, then slid her hand
lower to rest on his flat, tightly muscled stomach.

She felt his muscles contract at her gentle touch and
she smiled, filled suddenly with a tremendous sense of
power that she could turn him on so easily. She bent and
pressed her lips where her hands had been, breathing in
the clean, musky scent of him.

Rogan gave a low growl of desire deep in his throat
and bent to kiss her lips with fervent passion, his hands
caressing her breasts—teasing her nipples until they
were so hard she felt she would burst.

He took off the rest of his clothing and then his legs
straddled her hips as he knelt over her. She arched her
back in longing, aching for the full force of him to touch
her.

'Patience,' he growled teasingly, then kissed each of
her breasts, sucking at them and licking at them until
she cried out for him in desperate anguish.

'Not yet,' he murmured silkily as he kissed her stomach. Then his fingers moved to stroke the soft, wet core
of her womanhood.

Every part of her throbbed with the most piercing desire. She wanted him, she needed him. If he didn't enter
her soon she was going to explode without him. She
raked her hand through her hair, pulling it back from her
scalp in a kind of frenzied frustration. The action lifted

her breasts even higher and he lent to lick at them with the tip of his tongue.

'Rogan, I can't wait any longer, I just can't.' Her voice trembled with urgency.

As she spoke he reached toward the bedside table for something. Seconds later he was inside her. Great shudders of pleasure ripped through her entire body.

He sat above her and watched the way she writhed under him. He pushed deeper and deeper, stroking her body in a way that sent her almost wild.

Just when she thought she couldn't take any more he controlled the moment, leaving her frantic with longing. Then he built the momentum again as she cried out his name in gasps of yearning. This time there was no holding back. He thrust into her, allowing their passion full rein, as they rocked together in spasm after spasm of complete fulfilment.

## CHAPTER TEN

THE noise of traffic twenty floors below them filtered through the double-glazed windows. Laura lay, listening to the distant hum. She saw the sun strengthening from weak red-gold to blazing yellow across the white walls and carpets.

She stretched luxuriously in the enormous bed and turned to look at Rogan. He was lying on his side, facing her, still in a deep sleep.

It was no wonder he was tired, she thought, a smile curving the softness of her lips. They had been very...very energetic last night. And it had been wonderful, she thought dreamily...perfect.

The sheets were low on his waist. He looked very tanned against their whiteness, the hair on his chest extremely dark.

Impulsively she reached out to stroke that coarse hair, remembering how it had felt against the softness of her breasts last night.

He opened his eyes and looked directly into hers. 'Laura?' His voice was a gruff, seductive sound.

Her heart lurched crazily, tipping and tilting as if she were on some kind of fairground ride.

'Last night was fabulous.'

'Yes,' she agreed, and leaned closer to kiss his lips. They were warm against hers, and inviting.

'Mmm.' He made a guttural sound deep in his throat which seemed to inflame her all over again.

Her breath caught, and she rolled closer. She could feel her whole body pressing against his, could feel the muscular strength of him. He smiled and caught her in powerful arms to roll her on top of him.

She could feel his arousal and she smiled, feeling shy...pleased...overwhelmed by him. 'Do you think it's possible to have too much of a good thing?'

He reached up and raked his fingers through the thick glossy fall of her hair. 'I can never have too much of you...never.'

The sound of the telephone was an unwelcome intrusion. Its shrill ring filled the silence between their raging heartbeats and their desire.

'Damn it all!'

'Don't answer it,' Laura said, and bent to kiss his cheek, then his chin, working her way around to his lips.

'I'll have to.' He reached to snatch up the receiver.

Much as she was disappointed that he had picked up the receiver, she had to smile at the note in his voice. She had caused that growl, that tremor in his voice. He had wanted her as much as she wanted him.

'No, it's all right. I'll see you later.' He slammed down the phone.

'Who was it?'

'The damn office. I'll have to go in straight away.' He turned his head to look at the clock, then sighed. 'It's still very early, I'm sorry, Laura, this has messed up our morning.'

'It's OK. Another ten minutes and we'll both go.'

'No point you coming in this early.' His eyes darkened and his hands curved around her breast. 'Besides, I think you had better lie here for a while and regain your strength. You might need it later.'

'I have got a busy day ahead of me.' Laura grinned.

'I wasn't thinking about work,' Rogan assured her. 'I was thinking about ravishing your body again as soon as is decently possible. Even if that means making love to you on my desk.'

'Rogan!' She was half amused, half shocked.

He smiled. 'I love the way you can sound so prim and proper and act like a wildcat in bed,' he murmured teasingly. 'It really turns me on.'

Laura felt her skin heat up at those words and he laughed then kissed her forcefully and possessively on the lips, before rolling her away from him and getting out of bed.

He disappeared into the bathroom and she heard the sound of the shower. She couldn't help feeling disappointed. She had hoped that they would have a few hours together before work encroached.

When he came back into the bedroom he was wearing just a towel around his waist. For a moment she was reminded of that morning at the castle when he had walked into the bedroom like this. In a way she wished their affair had started back then. She wanted to know so much about Rogan, wanted to melt into his life.

'I'll leave the address of the office on the dressing-table,' he said nonchalantly, 'then you can follow me down at your leisure. Get a cab.'

She watched as he dressed in a smart dark grey suit. He came to sit on the edge of the bed to look down at her. 'Will you be all right? You know you have to keep alert in New York—'

'I am not a country bumpkin,' she said forcefully.

'I know you are an intelligent woman. I'm just reminding you to be careful.' He bent and kissed her lips tenderly.

A flare of longing, so piercing and acute, took her breath away.

'Now, you do know where you are?' he asked as he straightened.

'Yes, I'm in your bed…' she reached up and touched the side of his face '…where I wish you were.'

He smiled, a tender indulgent smile, as he took in the beauty of her features—the way her eyes seemed suddenly too large for her face, the softness of her lips, the blush of colour on her high cheek-bones. 'I wish I was staying there with you,' he assured her, bending to kiss her once more. 'But I can't,' he finished regretfully as he stood up.

Laura's mouth tingled from the touch of his lips, and her body cried out for him.

He opened the bedside table and bent to search through some papers. 'Here we are.' He took something out and put it next to the phone. 'A map and the address and phone number of my office. Now, have you got enough money?'

'Rogan!' Her voice rose in sharp annoyance. 'If you are going to go, just go.'

'I'm going.' He held up his hands in mock surrender. 'Just be careful.'

'It's a bit late for that, isn't it?' She couldn't help the words as she remembered last night.

He grinned. 'You've got nothing to worry about. I always practise safe sex.'

Before she could say anything to that he had gone. She supposed she had asked for that comment, she thought angrily. She shouldn't have made such a flippant remark.

She lay, staring up at the ceiling. Why should those few little words upset her so? After all, it had just been a statement of fact—nothing derogatory, nothing to suggest he regretted what had happened between them. Even so, the mere word 'practise' irritated her intensely. He made it sound as if he were playing with her until the real thing came along. Then there was the word 'sex'. Why couldn't he have said 'love-making'?

She rolled on her side and closed her eyes but she couldn't relax. She was wide awake now. She got up and went through to have a shower, then she dressed in a long, dark skirt and a silk fitted top in cream, before going through to the lounge.

The champagne glasses were where they had left them

last night, the bottle of champagne still almost full. She went across to pick them up and as she passed she noticed that the red light was no longer on the answer-machine.

Had Rogan listened to his message? She hadn't heard him.

Something made her pause by the phone. She looked down at it, hesitated and then, before she could think better of her action, she pressed the play button.

A woman's voice filled the room, tearful, accusing, pleading. 'Rogan, it's Sophie. I know you are home. Why don't you return my calls? Please, Rogan... I love you.'

The tape switched off and rewound, the whirring, mechanical noises the machine made as it reset itself resounding in the silence of the apartment.

Laura stood where she was for several long moments. She felt shocked at the anguish she could hear in the woman's voice—shocked and, to some degree, sympathetic. She turned, picked up her bag and her coat and left the apartment.

She went straight to work. She didn't know what else to do with herself and it seemed safer to bury her mind in the designs for the Celtic range rather than go over and over the chilling memory of Sophie's voice.

When Rogan heard that she was in he came across to her office.

'I thought you wouldn't be in until at least ten o'clock.'

'I've got a lot to do before we leave for Dublin tomorrow.' She barely looked up at him. She couldn't bring herself to meet his eyes.

'Is everything all right?' He came closer, the warmth of concern in his voice making her emotions cloud with confusion.

'Yes.' Her voice was sharper than she'd intended. 'Of course. I've just got a lot of work to get through.' She forced herself to regain control and soften her tone. 'And I'd like to gain some time to look around the shops later. I want to buy the children something.'

'OK.' He seemed to think this was perfectly reasonable. 'I'll catch up with you later. I've got to go, Laura. I'm in the middle of a meeting.'

'Yes, fine.'

He hesitated for a moment then he closed the door behind him. Laura let out her breath in a long, shuddering sigh. Then she turned her attention to the papers in front of her and tried to blank everything else out of her mind.

As far as work was concerned, the day went smoothly. Maybe because Laura was so determined not to let her mind wander from her job she finished it with a single-minded attempt at perfection. The designs and the costings were printed out and checked by three-thirty, leaving Laura free to leave the building.

Rogan had been astounded when she had walked in and put it on his desk. 'You've finished!'

'That's right.' Laura had been brisk. 'I'm going to wander along Fifth Avenue now and do some shopping, if that's all right with you.'

'Yes.' He looked up at her, his eyes moving over the slender lines of her body, and she knew that he was wishing they were alone, that the team of accountants in his office could be melted away.

Laura didn't know how she felt. In one way she was glad that he hadn't had a chance to talk to her in that seductive tone of his. In another way, like him, she just wanted everyone to go away.

He glanced at his watch. 'If you'd like, I'll meet you at the Rockefeller Centre for coffee. I should be finished here soon...so, say five o'clock.'

'OK.' She turned and left the office, but was surprised when he followed her out.

'Laura.'

She looked around at him.

'Do you have that map that I gave you this morning?'

'Yes.' She was acutely conscious of his two secretaries, watching them with interest from their desks. She
wondered bleakly how many of Rogan's women had
passed through this way. His secretaries probably had to
screen calls from girlfriends he was no longer interested
in.

'See you later.' Not giving him a chance to say anything else, she left the office.

Even after work, the freezing cold air and a walk around
some of the busiest shops in the world Laura still hadn't
got that phone call out of her mind.

She sat, drinking coffee and watching the people at
the Rockefeller Centre, and tried not to think any more
about it, but somehow she couldn't get it out of her
mind.

She put her hands around her coffee-cup in a vain
attempt to warm herself up.

She should forget about Sophie, she told herself
crossly. It was none of her business—she should never
have listened to that tape. Lord alone knew what had
possessed her to turn it on.

What had Rogan said about Sophie? She racked her
memory to remember. Nothing much, just that she was
an ex-girlfriend. She had presumed that the woman had
been way back in his past but now she remembered that
he still wore the gift she had given him—the gold Cartier
watch.

Maybe the affair had been recent and Rogan had only
just dropped her when he'd gone to Ireland.

Sophie was probably someone like her, someone who
had given herself to Rogan in the hope that he might
feel something for her. Laura swallowed hard. She
would never, ever, beg Rogan to get in contact with her,
she told herself fiercely. Never. When he moved on to

his next conquest she would melt quietly into the background. She had her pride.

'You found your way around all right.' Rogan's hand pressed warmly on her shoulder as he walked up behind her. He bent to kiss her cheek and she forced herself not to pull away.

'Of course I found my way around. Did you ever doubt it?' She tried to sound light-hearted, as if she hadn't a care in the world.

'No…never.' He picked his way around the mound of shopping bags at her feet and pulled out a chair opposite her.

'I see you've bought out New York, single-handed,' he observed with a grin.

'I can flex my plastic with the best.' She tried not to think about how handsome he looked. He was wearing his heavy overcoat over his suit and a lock of his dark hair was resting on his forehead. She longed to reach across and brush it back with tender fingers, but clamped her hands tighter around her cup.

'Did you buy anything for yourself?'

'I got some things for the house.' Laura shrugged. 'There are presents for Joanne and Matthew and my mother…'

'I thought so.'

Should she ask him about Sophie? The answer was immediate and vehement. No, definitely not. He would only think her possessive and jealous. Rogan would be the type to panic at possessiveness. She knew that as surely as she knew how much she loved him.

'That's why I decided to buy you a present.'

She watched as he reached into the inside pocket of his overcoat, took out a long box and handed it across to her.

'"Tiffany's".' She read the lettering in a flat, unemotional voice as she took it from him.

He watched as she opened it.

Inside a diamond necklace glittered as the cold sunlight hit it. It was, without a doubt, the most beautiful piece of jewellery Laura had ever seen, and it must have cost a fortune. She stared at it for a long moment, not knowing what to say.

'Do you like it?' he asked. 'If not, we can go back and change it for something else.'

'It's beautiful.'

'No, you are beautiful.' He stretched out a hand and lifted her chin, forcing her to look up and meet his eyes across the table. 'Exquisite, in fact,' he murmured huskily.

'What is it for?'

He frowned as he heard the brittle note creep into her voice. 'It's for you...'

'As a thank-you or a goodbye?'

He stared at her in perplexity for a moment, taking in the shadows in her eyes and the way she held her head, proud and yet at the same time defenceless. 'It's neither.' He shook his head. 'What's got into you, Laura? It's a present from me to you. No strings, no hidden agenda—just a present.'

She swallowed hard. 'No strings, no hidden agenda,' she repeated, and then closed the box with a snap. 'Of course. I didn't expect strings. I know you don't like them. Do you, Rogan?'

'Do you want to tell me what this is about?' he asked, his voice lower and suddenly very serious, 'because I feel as if I've missed something.'

'You missed a phone call.' All Laura's good intentions were suddenly tossed aside. She never had been one for holding in her feelings, she thought despairingly. If she had something to say she had to say it.

'A phone call?'

'Sophie,' she enlightened him, her voice heavy.

The name hung between them for a second. Then Rogan shrugged. 'So?'

'So you led me to believe that she was in your past?'

'She is, she's an ex-girlfriend.'

'She doesn't seem to know that she's an ex.'

'Look, Laura, Sophie has nothing to do with you and me. My relationship with her ended ages ago.'

'She sounded upset.'

'What do you want me to do—go round and comfort her?'

She flinched at his cool sarcasm. What she wanted was to know that she herself meant something to him, that she wouldn't be discarded like Sophie. It was a forlorn hope and she was being ridiculous, she knew that. She also knew that the longer she pursued this particular line of conversation the sooner he would tire of her.

'You have no need to be jealous of Sophie, Laura. I can assure you of that.' He touched her face in a gentle, persuasive and compelling caress.

'I'm not jealous.' She pulled away from him.

'So what's this about, then?' he asked patiently.

She met his eyes, so dark, so seductive. This was about being in love with someone who didn't return her feelings, she thought with a sigh. It was her problem, not his. He had promised her nothing and she would have to accept the status quo or else walk away from the relationship. Walking away seemed an unendurable option. She wanted so much to be part of his life.

'Nothing,' she said in a low voice. Then she shrugged. 'It's just that she sounded so upset on the phone, and you're still wearing her watch. The affair must have been serious once.'

'It's a nice watch.' He shrugged. 'Yes, I'm not saying I wasn't fond of Sophie. We had some good times together. But then she changed and became obsessively possessive.'

'Cardinal sin,' Laura drawled sardonically.

'To be perfectly honest, I started to worry about her, Laura. I never led her on, but she refused to believe me when I told her that I didn't feel the same way she did. The affair got very claustrophobic. In the end I had to be cruel to be kind and I made a clean break with her. I really thought I was doing her a favour and that she'd be happy with someone else by now. 'I feel sorry for her, Laura, but I have moved on. She's part of my past and she's going to stay there. I never go back.'

Her eyes moved over his strong, handsome features. 'Am I part of your future?'

'You're part of my present,' he said firmly.

She smiled at that, but it was a trembling shadow of a smile. 'You don't make promises, do you, Rogan?'

His eyes moved tenderly over the porcelain paleness of her skin and the soft curve of her lips. 'Only ones I am absolutely sure I'll be able to keep.'

'And you are not absolutely sure about me?'

'I'm absolutely sure that I want you in my bed.' He smiled at her. 'I've been wanting you all day.'

She wanted him as well. But it wasn't enough. The ache inside her wouldn't be satisfied just with having his body—she wanted him totally. She almost laughed aloud at her own foolishness.

He reached out and covered her hand with his. 'OK?'

She said nothing but she knew it would have to be—for now.

'Shall we go back to the apartment?' His voice was husky and her body heated instantly. She hated herself for the weakness he could stir up inside her with no effort at all.

'Shouldn't you see your sister before you go back to Dublin?' she asked him, forcing herself to ignore the demands of her body.

'I called her from the office. We're not going to have time.'

'Fine.' Laura forced herself to sound unconcerned, but the fact that he hadn't introduced her to his sister seemed to speak volumes. It proved that he wasn't serious about her.

She slid the box with the necklace in it back across the table towards him. 'I can't accept such an expensive gift, Rogan, but thank you anyway.'

'Why?' He stared at her. 'I want you to have it.'

She shook her head. 'It would just make me feel beholden to you.'

'I don't mind,' he assured her with a return of that amused tone in his voice.

'I do.' She kept her voice calm and rational. 'If I took it I would only feel guilty.'

'Guilty about what?'

'Seeing someone else, of course.'

'What the hell are you talking about?' He sounded really irritated now and a few people at surrounding tables glanced over at them.

Laura suppressed a smile. Maybe she was being childish, but she wanted him to feel as uncertain about her as he made her feel about him. Perhaps if she played him at his own game, kept herself slightly aloof, she would have more chance of pulling him closer than if she were to turn possessive. It was worth a try—anything was worth trying.

'We may as well be adult about this.' She reached out and touched his hand in the same way he had hers a few moments ago. 'You are not the only one who doesn't want to make commitments—who wants a no-strings affair,' she said simply. 'And I just don't feel right about accepting such an expensive gift. OK?'

He stared at her. It was clear that he was used to calling the shots in a relationship and this turn-about frankly astonished him. 'You are one unpredictable woman, Laura Taylor,' he said, with a shake of his head. 'Obstreperous, too.'

'I'll take that as a compliment, shall I?'

'Take it any way you want.' He put the box with the

necklace back in his pocket. 'Shall we go back to my apartment?' He looked at her with a raised eyebrow.

The seductive gleam in his eye reminded her sharply that she wasn't as in control as she had tried to sound. 'If you want.' She tried very hard to appear indifferent.

'I do want, very much.' The come-hither tone made her last vestige of self-control melt.

She looked across and met his eyes. 'Shall we call a cab?'

# CHAPTER ELEVEN

ROGAN was alone in bed when he woke up the next morning. He stretched and sat up, wondering where Laura was.

Then the bedroom door opened and she came in. He was surprised to see she was fully dressed. She looked well groomed and confident in a black trouser suit and white silk blouse. Her hair, softly shining, was gathered back from her face and fastened with a silver clasp.

'What time is it?' he asked with a frown.

'Seven o'clock.' She put a cup of tea on his bedside table for him.

'You had me worried. For a moment I thought it was later. How come you are up and dressed so early?'

'This is my usual time for getting up.' She was going around the bedroom, picking up items that belonged to her—a pair of shoes from beside the bed, a dressing-gown on the chair. 'I thought I may as well pack and be ready to leave.'

'But we don't have to go for a good few hours.' He stretched out and caught her arm as she passed close by him. 'We have plenty of time to play before we pack.'

The note of desire in his voice nearly tempted her to sit next to him on the bed. It was only with a supreme effort that she made herself pull away from him. 'I think we've had our play time,' she said briskly. 'I want to run my eye over those designs and phone through to your office, make sure Helen and I are in complete agreement with the final plans.'

'Helen?' He frowned. 'Who—?'

'Your chief window-dresser at the store on Fifth.'
Laura turned and left the room.

With a sigh Rogan got out of bed. He didn't want to
talk about business, he wanted Laura back in bed, but
as she seemed to have other plans he would have to go
along with it.

Laura threw the last of her belongings in her case and
stared out of the window at the Manhattan skyline. It
had taken every scrap of her will-power to walk out of
that bedroom, but she sensed that if she were to have
any kind of relationship with Rogan she'd have to try
much harder to be something she wasn't. Controlled,
casual. Act like her affair with him was secondary to her
work.

She heard the hiss of the shower in the bathroom.
Rogan would be out in a little while and she would take
it from there.

She walked across to the telephone and called the office on Fifth.

She was still talking about the plans for the Celtic
designs when Rogan emerged from the bedroom, fully
dressed.

'You think so?' Laura was saying. 'OK, well, I'll fax
the details to you when I get back to the Dublin office.'
She smiled indifferently at Rogan, as if he were someone
who had just walked into her office and was waiting for
an appointment.

'OK, thanks, Helen. I'll speak to you later.' She put
down the phone and turned to Rogan. 'Listen, I've had
a wonderful idea,' she said brightly. 'Why don't we use
pictures of the Fitzroy castle to publicise the Celtic
range?'

Rogan nodded, his eyes moving over her slowly. She
looked gorgeous. Her eyes were shining with enthusiasm, her hand on her hip pushing her jacket back slightly
to reveal the soft curves of her figure. He felt a longing
well up inside.

'Rogan, are you listening to me?' she asked with a tinge of impatience.

'Sure, sounds like a good idea.' He reached out and pulled her into his arms.

For a while she allowed him to kiss her. The warmth of his lips almost made her forget what she was doing. The heady sensuality that flowed between them too strong to pull away from.

It was with a supreme effort that she put a hand against his chest and gently levered herself away from him.

'So shall I put the plan into action when we get back to Dublin? The castle is a very dramatic, romantic image. I'm sure Lord Fitzroy would be thrilled.'

She felt a little surge of pleasure at the momentary gleam of annoyance that lit Rogan's dark eyes. 'Can't we talk about this later, on the plane? We've got two hours to spare before we have to leave. I thought we could use it for pleasure.'

She felt herself weakening. 'If that's what you want...'

The ringing of the phone interrupted them. Laura pulled away from him. 'That will be Helen. She said she'd phone me back.'

Rogan stretched across her and lifted the receiver. 'I'll deal with this,' he said firmly.

A second later the tone of his voice changed, became softer and more indulgent. 'Don't worry. As it turns out, I do have some time. I'll come over and see what I can do.'

'Problems?' Laura asked as he put the phone down.

Rogan grinned at her. 'A crisis at my sister's house. Her washing-machine has packed in and the repair man can't come until tomorrow.'

'Now that is a crisis,' Laura agreed with a smile.

'I guess pleasure will have to wait.' Rogan pulled her towards him and kissed her gently on the lips. 'I'll have to go around and see if I can do anything. Would you like to come?'

She laughed. 'You know very well that I would.'

Sarah lived in a large brownstone family home not far from Rogan's apartment.

Laura liked her immediately. She also liked the warm, friendly atmosphere in the house. Totally unlike the sterile atmosphere of Rogan's apartment, it was filled with books and children's toys and vases of fresh flowers. The lounge with its squashy sofas looked lived-in and slightly untidy.

'Rogan, thanks for coming over,' Sarah murmured as she embraced her brother. 'And, Laura, I'm very pleased to meet you,' she said sincerely. 'Sorry to get you over here under these circumstances, but I can't cope without that machine.'

Rogan laughed. 'I know. I'll go down to the basement and see what I can do.'

'Can you stay for lunch?'

'No time, Sarah. We can only have a quick coffee now,' Rogan said.

Sarah rolled her eyes. 'You never have any time,' she complained with a smile.

Rogan was waylaid on the way downstairs by Sarah's twins, two four-year-old girls who flung themselves on him with squeals of delight.

'Come through to the kitchen, Laura.'

Following Sarah further through the house and into the kitchen, Laura was struck by how like her brother she was. She had the same dark hair and dark eyes but, whereas Rogan was tall and broad, she was petite and very feminine.

'Rogan's good with children, isn't he?' Laura remarked casually as the laughter increased in the hallway and Rogan's teasing voice drifted through.

'Yes, he is. It's a pity he hasn't had any of his own.'

Sarah sighed. 'But, then, you probably know my feelings on that score.'

'Rogan has mentioned you keep trying to marry him off.'

'In a subtle way,' Sarah said.

The women's eyes met and they both laughed.

'Rogan hates it whenever I even mention the M word.' Sarah put some china beakers on a tray.

'I suppose he's had a bad experience of marriage and doesn't want to make another mistake.'

For a moment Sarah regarded her steadily. 'You're right. He did have a particularly tough time of it with Melony. She never loved him. All she was interested in was his money.'

'Poor Rogan,' Laura murmured. 'He hasn't really talked a lot about his ex-wife. It's no wonder.'

'Her affair came as a terrible blow for him. Rogan thought he was building the business up so that they could have a good standard of living, I think he was even keen on starting a family. Then he discovered that Mel was only interested in the almighty dollar…and had no intention of starting a family at all. The only thing she was interested in starting was an affair with Rogan's so-called best friend. She's a very mercenary, very cool customer.'

'It's no wonder that he's wary of commitment,' Laura said sadly.

'The fact that our parents divorced when we were both young hasn't helped.' Sarah pulled a face as she heard her brother's footsteps, coming towards them from the hall. 'For heaven's sake, don't tell Rogan I've been discussing him like this. He'll be mad with me. He thinks I dabble too much in his personal matters as it is.' She smiled at Laura. 'But we women have these things to do, don't we?'

'Certainly,' Laura agreed wryly.

'And, anyway, you've filled me with new hope,'

Sarah said suddenly. 'You are the only girlfriend Rogan has talked to me about in a long time—without my having to twist his arm, that is. He's told me about your daughter who's nearly thirteen and your son... Matthew?'

'That's right.' Laura felt a jolt of surprise and pleasure at this revelation.

'He thinks they are wonderful children.'

'They are but, then, of course, I am biased.'

The door opened and Rogan joined them. He had a little girl tucked under each arm. 'I think I'll have to leave these two in here with you,' he said with a grin, 'otherwise this machine will never be repaired.'

Sarah reached to take the children. 'By the way,' she said, giving him a wide, innocent smile, 'I'm planning a dinner for Thanksgiving. Do you think you and Laura might be able to come? You could bring Laura's children.'

'Sarah, I don't think there is any way we will make Thanksgiving dinner, but thanks, anyway. You are forgetting one little thing. Laura and the children live a continent away.'

Sarah shrugged. 'I've never been one to let little things stand in my way.'


The darkened streets of Dublin glistened from an earlier downpour, the streetlights reflecting in orange pools of light in the puddles. Laura couldn't help thinking how small everything looked after New York, how provincial.

Rogan turned the car away from the city and drove out towards her cottage. The only sound was the swish of the tyres on the wet surface of the road.

The flight home had seemed longer and more arduous than the one going out, perhaps because they were both tired.

Rogan had worked almost continuously throughout

the flight and she had helped out with some of the papers, before finally drifting into a deep uncomfortable sleep for the last hour of the journey.

She felt tired now, but she was excited at the prospect of seeing the children—of wrapping her arms around them and hearing their excited chatter. She'd missed them. Glancing at her watch, she noticed it was past their bedtime, but with a bit of luck Cora would have let them stay up and wait for her.

For a moment she remembered her pleasure at hearing Sarah tell her that Rogan had spoken about her children, a pleasure which had been quickly swept away at Rogan's curt yet practical reminder later that they lived a continent apart.

Of course they did. Rogan's home was that apartment in New York and her place was here. She had allowed herself to forget that stark truth. All her plans for playing things cool and her hopes for drawing Rogan closer were quite absurd. Rogan was American and she was Irish. The fact that he had a house here didn't mean that much. Hadn't he said himself that it was a second home, that his main business and his life lay in America?

It started to rain again as he turned the car into her driveway. The headlights lit the tangled, overgrown garden, highlighting the silver drops of rain which seemed to hang in suspended animation from the tangled chaos of jasmine and ivy.

The front door opened as soon as they pulled to a halt.

Laura's emotions soared as she saw Joanne and Matthew silhouetted against the warm light from within.

She reached for the doorhandle and dashed through the rain towards the cottage, taking them both into her arms and holding them close.

'Did you have a good time? Was it wonderful?' Joanne asked excitedly.

Before she had a chance to answer Rogan came in behind her with her suitcase.

'Rogan! Rogan!' Matthew ran to him and the next moment he was being lifted and swung in strong arms.

'Good to see you,' Rogan said, as he put him down and ruffled the dark hair.

Joanne also went over to greet him.

The strength of the welcome the children gave Rogan startled Laura.

Cora came out into the hall. 'How was New York?' she asked, kissing Laura on the cheek.

'We didn't have much time for sightseeing, but it's a great city.'

'Even less time, with my sister dragging us around to her house,' Rogan said, a hint of amusement in his tone as he looked over at Laura.

'Come on in and get warmed by the fire. I've just boiled the kettle,' Cora said, leading the way into the lounge.

For a while they sat, talking about the trip. Laura was asked about the flight, the type of plane, the shops and Rogan's apartment. There were shouts of delight as she got out the gifts she had bought.

Then Cora got up to go home. 'Thank you so much, Mum,' Laura said, walking with her to the front door. 'Were the children good?'

'Of course they were good.' Cora grinned. 'We've enjoyed ourselves. By the way—' she dropped her voice to a low whisper '—I didn't have a chance to tell you before you went away, but I think Rogan is gorgeous.'

'So do I.' Laura smiled. 'But the relationship isn't going anywhere, Mum, so don't start dropping hints, will you?'

'You are such a spoilsport.' Cora's eyes were teasing. 'I'm free to babysit for you tomorrow night before you ask.'

'Tomorrow?'

'Robert's leaving party, isn't it?' Cora reminded her.

'Oh, yes.' Laura nodded. 'Are you sure?'

'Course I'm sure. Goodnight, darling.'

As Laura returned to the lounge she remembered she was supposed to be attending that party with Paul. She wondered if Rogan would want to take her.

Matthew was sitting next to Rogan on the settee. Laura noticed he was listening with an enraptured expression on his young face as Rogan answered more questions from Joanne about New York.

'Are you going to marry my mum?' he asked suddenly and very solemnly when there was a gap in the conversation.

Joanne's face went red with embarrassment. Laura nearly fell over the dog. Only Rogan seemed unfazed. 'Your mother and I are very good friends,' he answered, without the slightest flicker of awkwardness. 'Is that all right?'

Matthew nodded. 'It would be all right if you got married, too. I wouldn't mind, neither would Joanne. We talked about it yesterday.'

'Matthew!' Joanne wailed, her cheeks going even redder.

Rogan laughed.

'Now, come on, you two, enough of this nonsense.' Laura cut across the proceedings quickly, her voice brisk. 'It's time for bed.'

They both rose immediately, Joanne looking as if she would be glad to get out of the room and Matthew innocently unabashed.

Laura could hear them arguing as they went up the stairs. 'I told you not to ask him that,' Joanne was saying in a low, angry tone.

'Sorry about that,' Laura said looking over at Rogan.

'That's OK.' He seemed amused.

There was a moment's silence, filled only by the soft crackle of the fire.

'I suppose you are tired and you'll want to get home,' she said.

'I'm ready for bed, but I don't know about the second part of that question,' he drawled. 'I was hoping you might ask me to stay, and we could make up for the time we missed together in New York.'

She felt the heat of longing steal through her body, surreptitiously countering her questions and doubts about where this relationship could lead.

'You know, I've never had a casual affair before,' she said hesitantly. 'I'm not sure of the ground rules.'

'I'm making the rules up as I go along, as far as you and I are concerned. Hadn't you noticed?' he said teasingly.

'I'm not sure if I should let you stay here,' she said quietly.

One eyebrow rose at that. 'Why not?'

'Because it might confuse the children. They already seem to be thinking along the wrong lines. I don't want them to be hurt.' She put into words the niggle of fear she had felt since seeing how delighted the children had been to welcome Rogan back.

He frowned and seemed to be seriously considering her words. 'Maybe you're right,' he said slowly. 'The last thing I want is to upset the children.'

'Mum.' Matthew's voice drifted downstairs. 'Mum, are you going to tuck me in?'

'Coming.' Laura looked over at Rogan. 'I won't be a moment.'

By the time Laura had tucked Matthew in and kissed him, he was already asleep. Obviously the excitement and the late night was taking its toll. Laura switched off his lamp and closed the door of his room quietly, before going down to the end of the corridor to check if Joanne was all right.

She was surprised to see that she, too, was fast asleep, her long hair spread over the pink covers in a mane of

gold and her cheeks faintly flushed with healthy colour.
Laura kissed her and switched off the light.

When she went back downstairs Rogan was standing
in the lounge.

'Are they OK?'

She nodded. 'They are both fast asleep. Would you
like another drink?' There was a part of her that didn't
want him to go, couldn't bear to say goodbye. To sleep
alone in her bed, after the warmth of sharing a bed with
him, was a very unwelcome thought.

Rogan seemed to think about the invitation.

'If you're tired—' she began.

'Surprisingly enough, I'm not tired,' he interrupted. 'I
was trying to be sensible, but I find that's very difficult
around you. I understand what you said about the children and giving them the wrong idea, but I find myself
thinking that if they are asleep do they need to know
that I've stayed?'

Laura didn't answer him immediately and he came
over to her and kissed her.

'I'll leave very early before they wake up,' he whispered against her ear, before kissing her again.

The heat of his kiss melted her resistance and her
heart.

She found herself wrapping her arms around his neck
as he picked her up to carry her upstairs.

Rogan lay, staring up at the ceiling and listening to the
heavy lashing of the early morning rain. They had come
to bed in such a hurry last night that the curtains weren't
properly drawn. As the dawn light stole into the room
he could see a triangle of light on the ceiling. The reflection of the water, running down the window-panes
in seemingly never-ending rivulets, gave the effect of
tears over the white ceiling.

He could hear Laura's steady breathing next to him
and feel the warmth and the softness of her skin.

He wanted her again. He never seemed to be able to get enough of her. But he was thinking about what she had said about the children and remembering Matthew's words and the way the little boy had greeted him with such unreserved pleasure last night.

Rogan had meant it when he had said that the very last thing he wanted was to hurt the children. He was very fond of them—in fact, he was surprised by the strength of his feelings for them in such a short space of time. Maybe it was because he sensed a certain vulnerability in them. They both missed a father figure in their life. Matthew, especially, seemed to look at him with a kind of expectancy—a kind of hope—that tore at him. He knew what it was like to miss a parent.

Laura was right. They shouldn't give them false expectations. He rolled over and looked at the clock on the bedside table. Then his eyes moved to Laura's sleeping form. She was beautiful.

She opened her eyes as if she sensed him watching her. He leaned over and kissed her gently on the lips.

'What time is it?' she murmured sleepily, moving a little closer to him.

For a moment he allowed his hand to curve around her waist and stroke her silky skin. Then he pressed a kiss against her cheek. 'Time I was going.'

She rolled over and watched as he pulled back the covers and swung out of bed.

'Rogan?'

'Mmm?' He didn't glance at her. He was busy buttoning up his shirt.

'It's the leaving party for Robert tonight.' She sat up and pushed a hand through her hair.

'Yes, I know.'

She waited to see if he would say he'd pick her up or even ask if she would accompany him. He said nothing more.

'Paul asked if I'd go with him. I was wondering—'

'Good idea.' He cut across her briskly. 'We can't very well turn up together at a business party. It would set people talking. Far better if we turn up separately.'

'So, if Paul accompanies me who will you go with?'

'A partner isn't a problem, Laura.'

Laura felt as if he had just hit her.

He was now dressed and obviously anxious to leave without further discussion. He picked up his jacket from the chair. 'See you at the office.' He bent to kiss her and she had to force herself not to turn away.

'See you at the office,' she murmured as the door closed behind him.

# CHAPTER TWELVE

LAURA stood at the bedroom window of her cottage that evening. Heavy rain battered the pane of glass, almost obliterating the path which was lit by the outdoor light.

The wind was getting up. It howled and whooshed over the small house in an eerie way. It wasn't a night for going out but a night for curling up in front of the fire...preferably with Rogan.

She sighed and turned to look at her reflection in the cheval mirror. There was no chance of staying in, and certainly not with Rogan.

She was going to Robert's party tonight with Paul. And Rogan would probably be there with another woman.

Thinking about that made her heart thud unevenly. Was it only this morning that he had been in her bed, holding her and kissing her? She had tried not to be angry about his suggestion that they should attend tonight's function with different partners but inside she was still raw about it.

She supposed he was right. If they arrived together and left together people would talk.

Things would be a lot simpler if she wasn't in love with him, Laura decided, if she could just enjoy having an affair with him without the intensity of emotions which were tearing her apart.

But that wasn't her style. She didn't seem capable of giving her body without giving her heart. She ran a smoothing hand down over the figure-hugging red dress.

She heard a car pull up outside and picked up her wrap and her handbag to go downstairs.

The children were in the lounge, and Cora had gone to open the front door. Laura could hear her voice warm with welcome as she talked to Paul.

She went into the hall to join them. Paul looked very suave in a dark dinner suit, his blond hair groomed neatly into place with the aid of styling gel.

'Laura, you look lovely,' he said, his eyes sweeping admiringly over her slender figure.

'Thank you, Paul,' she said, averting her cheek as he bent to kiss her. She turned and saw Matthew and Joanne, watching them from the doorway of the lounge.

She was aware that the children were not pleased that she wasn't going to the party with Rogan. Both had expressed dismay and then annoyance when Laura had tried to explain, by saying very simply that Rogan was just a friend and her boss. She had tried to act as if there had never been any question that they would be attending the party as a couple.

'You remember Joanne and Matt, don't you, Paul?' she said in an attempt to draw the children out of the sullen way they were regarding them both.

'Yes, of course I do. Hi, there, kids,' Paul said in a bright but rather insincere tone. 'Haven't seen you for a while.'

'Hello.' The reply from both children was flat.

'How's school?' Paul made a more determined effort to get a response.

'OK.' Joanne was the only one to answer, her curt reply filled with hostility. Then they both turned and went back into the lounge.

'I won't be a minute, Paul,' Laura said, and followed the children, closing the door behind her and leaving her mother to entertain the visitor for a moment.

'OK, you two, you were a bit abrupt with poor old Paul, you know,' she said gently. 'He didn't deserve such a welcome.' She sat next to Matthew on the couch. 'What's the matter?'

'You know what the matter is,' Matthew mumbled. 'You should be going to the party with Rogan.'

'You are being very silly, you know.' Laura strove to find the right things to say to make them feel better. The trouble was she felt low herself. It wasn't what she wanted either.

'It's all Matthew's fault,' Joanne said crossly. 'If he hadn't said what he did Rogan would be here now. Matt scared him away with that marriage talk.'

'Oh, that's rubbish, Jo, and you know it.' Laura put her arm around Matthew and pulled him close to give him a cuddle.

'Rogan and I are still very good friends and nothing you have said or done has influenced anything... honestly.'

Laura looked over at her daughter. 'Come and give me a hug and tell me you love me and let's forget this silliness.'

Joanne didn't move immediately, then she got up grudgingly. 'I'm a bit old for giving hugs,' she murmured, then grinned as she caught the look of horror on her mother's face.

'You're never too old to hug.' Laura put her arm around both children and drew them close against her, drawing strength from their love. 'You know, we have got each other and that's what really counts. Now, how about us going to the theatre tomorrow night? I think *Riverdance* is on. What do you say?'

'Is Rogan going to come?' Matthew asked.

'No, just the three of us. The three musketeers.'

'The three musketeers were men,' Joanne muttered.

'What do you say? Shall I try and get tickets?'

'OK.' Joanne shrugged.

'That's not the response I want.' Laura tickled them both so that they started to giggle. 'I want shrieks of excited enthusiasm.' She kept tickling them until they rolled to the floor with laughter.

'Great, great,' Joanne gasped. 'The theatre will be wonderful.'

'That's better. Now, come out and say goodnight to Paul and behave like the kind-hearted and polite children I know you really are.'

Jewels blazed at the throats of fashionably dressed women and the men all wore dark dinner suits. A band played and the dance floor was almost as packed as the sides of the room.

Laura took a glass of orange juice from the tray of a passing waiter, and as she did so she saw Rogan. His height and bearing made him stand out from every other man. There was something about him, something that exuded power and confidence and magnetic attraction.

He was surrounded by people, one of them a glamorous blonde. Her hair was piled on top of her head in a sleek style and her curvaceous figure was shown to its best advantage in a glittering gown of gold which was low and plunging at the back—and the front.

Rogan threw back his head and laughed at something she had said.

Laura's body responded with a violent thrust of emotion. She wanted Rogan so much. It was like a form of torture, seeing him with someone else.

She was going to have to pull herself together, she told herself. It had been difficult enough to cope with the children's disappointment without this emotional turmoil, tearing her apart. She needed to compose herself.

She sipped at her drink, looked around in the opposite direction from her boss and tried to concentrate on Paul's conversation.

She saw Robert James, making his way across the room towards them.

'Laura, how nice to see you.' His face was wreathed in a smile of pleasure.

'How are things, Robert?' she asked, kissing him on the cheek. 'Are you enjoying your retirement?'

'Oh, I'm getting by.' Although there was humour in his tone, Laura thought she detected a certain sadness as well.

'You've certainly got a good turn-out tonight,' she said brightly. 'It's a tremendous accolade to your business achievements.'

'Yes, I suppose it is.' He nodded. 'It's nice to see everyone again. Tell me, how are things going at the office?'

They talked for a while about business and then, when someone else claimed his attention, Paul asked if she would like to dance. They made their way to the crowded dance floor.

'Robert hasn't quite reconciled himself to retirement,' Paul said, taking her into his arms and bending to speak in a low tone against her ear.

'It will take a while, I suppose. James Design has been such a large part of his life.'

As they turned in time to the slow music she saw Rogan.

He was standing at the other side of the room, still surrounded by the same crowd of people, with the same woman by his side.

He looked directly over at her and she looked hurriedly away, but she was aware of his eyes, resting contemplatively on her.

She smiled up at Paul. 'How are things with you, anyway? It seems ages since we went out together.'

'It is ages.' Paul sounded glum.

Something about his tone made her frown. 'Are you all right, Paul? You sound...I don't know...different somehow.'

Paul shrugged. 'If I'm honest, I suppose I'm jealous.'

'Jealous?'

'You and Rogan Powers. Your mother mentioned that

you were in New York with him when I phoned you this week.'

'It was just business.' Laura looked away from him, feeling uncomfortable about lying. 'Anyway, you and I have always just been friends, Paul. You've had your girlfriends, and I've been out with other men—'

'I know, but somehow I feel Rogan is different. It made me start to think about things between you and me.' He put a hand under her chin, forcing her to look up into his eyes. 'Laura, I want you,' he said softly. 'Listen, how about you and I going out for something to eat tomorrow night?'

'I hate to interrupt such a touching scene but I wondered if I might have this dance?'

Rogan's deep voice from behind them sent Laura's emotions into a spin. Somehow she forced herself to turn and meet his eyes with cool composure.

'Good evening, Rogan.' She managed a smile and was quite proud of herself.

His eyes moved over her figure. Her dress was simple yet elegant, the soft silk emphasising her womanly curves and the dramatic colour a vibrant contrast to the darkness of her hair and pale smoothness of her skin.

Then Rogan's gaze moved to Paul in a swift assessing look, taking in the possessive arm that he still had around Laura's waist.

'You don't mind, Paul?' he asked.

'Well…no…' Paul didn't look too pleased as Rogan reached out to take Laura by the hand.

Laura felt torn. She wanted to be with Rogan but she hated to think Paul was upset. She didn't want to hurt him, though she'd been quite shocked by his words.

Paul made the decision for her, turning quickly to leave them.

Her heart felt as if it was pumping overtime as she stepped into Rogan's arms.

The scent of his cologne and the way he held her close

to his body reminded her of that night in New York when they had dined together and then made love afterwards.

She tried to close her mind to those memories. She felt hurt that he had brought another woman with him tonight. She supposed dully that, like Paul, she was jealous. It was an emotion alien to her and she didn't like it one little bit.

She angled her chin and met his eyes. 'Aren't you afraid that people might talk if they see us dancing together?' she asked him coolly. 'It could cause quite a scandal, I'm sure.'

'I've decided to weather the storm.'

His dry amusement angered her. OK, he probably had a point. If they had come here tonight as a couple there would have been gossip. She tried to reason with herself so that she wouldn't say anything she might regret.

'Very brave of you.' She gave a small laugh. She didn't feel like laughing. Strangely, she sounded as if she couldn't care less.

'You seem to have been enjoying yourself with Paul,' Rogan remarked.

'He's a terrific guy.' She looked up at him and felt a sense of exhilaration when she saw the flicker of annoyance in his dark eyes. 'But, then, I've always had a soft spot for Paul.'

'Is that so? I thought you said he was just a friend and nothing more.'

'Like you and I.' She smiled airily. Let him make what he wanted of that, she thought. 'Actually, he was just asking me out to dinner when you interrupted us.'

'Was he, indeed?' Now Rogan sounded totally unconcerned. 'By all means, don't let me stand in your way if you want to accept.'

Her small sense of power, of wanting to hurt him the way he had hurt her, was extinguished like a candle by a fire extinguisher.

'You don't mind, then?' She tilted her chin to look at him again.

'I have no real right to mind, do I?' he drawled. 'Not when I told you that you should come here with him tonight.'

'I suppose not.' She looked away from his eyes.

'Who is the woman with you?' She hated herself for asking. She didn't want him to guess at the depth of the jealousy she felt.

'Which woman?'

Laura felt a stab of annoyance. 'The one with the blonde hair and gold dress.'

'Jennifer Kelly. She's the daughter of a business associate.'

'She's beautiful.'

'She's only eighteen.'

Old enough for an affair, Laura thought dryly. 'Well, you know what they say—variety is the spice of life,' she said lightly.

She looked up at him, and suddenly found herself saying something she hadn't planned at all. 'You know, Rogan, I think I will accept Paul's invitation to dinner. I hope you won't be too cross with me but I think we should call a halt to our…association. I've got the children to think of and, really, if I'm going to get involved with anyone for any length of time it's got to be a steady, reliable relationship.'

The music came to an end and she took the opportunity to pull away from him. 'Thanks for the dance, Rogan.' She smiled up at him, her manner very cool yet dignified at the same time.

He didn't answer her. He was stunned, and yet she had only done what he himself had been thinking of doing since their return from New York.

As she walked away from him his hands tightened into clenched fists at his side. He wanted to run after her, run after her and say… What the hell would he say?

he asked himself, and raked an impatient hand through his hair. Instead, he moved across to where Jennifer stood patiently, waiting for him.

Robert James stopped him on the way across. 'Lovely girl, isn't she?' he said to Rogan with a nod in Laura's direction.

'Yes...lovely.' Rogan agreed. He found he wasn't much in the mood for small talk.

'I'm hoping that Paul will have the good sense to propose to her,' Robert said idly. 'I've always thought Laura would make the perfect daughter-in-law.'

Rogan frowned and looked at Robert, as if seeing him for the first time.

The music was dying down and someone was getting onto the stage at the far end of the room, calling for Robert to come up and speak to everyone.

Thunderous applause filled the ballroom. It seemed to echo hollowly through Rogan's very soul. Everyone's eyes were on Robert as he went up to the front of the room, but Rogan's attention was firmly centred on where Laura stood with Paul.

# CHAPTER THIRTEEN

LAURA closed the front door quietly. She was relieved to be home, away from the noise and the cheerful atmosphere of the party. She didn't feel cheerful. She felt like crying.

Paul had been disappointed not to be asked in and despondent when he couldn't change her mind about going out with him. She'd noticed when she'd told him she was going to the theatre tomorrow night with the children that he hadn't asked if he could come with them. Rogan would have done.

The thought was unwelcome. It was over between her and Rogan. She leaned against the door and tried to gather her thoughts, before going through to her mother.

She hadn't intended to call everything off with Rogan, but it had been the right thing to do. She had been naïve in the extreme to think she could handle an affair with him. Just seeing him talking to another woman had cut her in two.

Taking a deep breath, Laura went into the lounge.

The television was on, with the volume turned low. Her mother was sitting in the chair next to the fire, with Captain asleep at her feet.

'Had a nice time?'

'It was pleasant,' Laura lied. 'Were the children good?'

'A bit subdued,' Cora admitted, 'but they were all right by bedtime.'

Laura looked over at her mother. She was struck by how lovely she looked. Her hair was a very light blonde, its short layers framing a face that had classical features.

'So, what's the problem between you and Rogan Powers?' she asked gently.

'Did the children say something about him?'

'They didn't have to. You all look as if you've lost your best friend.'

Laura had to smile at that. Her mother had always been there for her in good times and bad. She was nothing if not perceptive. 'I'm in love with him,' she admitted huskily.

'Good.' Her mother smiled. 'It's about time you risked giving your heart again. You are too young to be shut away from life.'

'I'm not shut away from life, Mum,' Laura said patiently.

'You are afraid of getting hurt again,' Cora said decisively. 'I don't blame you, Laura, you've been through a tough time. But that's in the past. You should enjoy yourself now.'

'I agree with you and I might just be tempted to throw caution away and have a fling with Rogan except that I've got to consider the children.' She sighed. 'They are getting far too fond of him, Mum. If I allow him into their lives any further they'll be devastated when the relationship ends. I can't risk that. They've been through enough, losing their father.'

There was silence for a moment. 'They do like him a lot.'

Laura nodded. 'I've done the only thing I can do. I've told Rogan we can't see each other socially again.'

Cora frowned. 'But isn't that running away? You don't know the relationship would have ended—'

'I do,' Laura said firmly. 'I've got to be realistic. Rogan isn't one for long-term commitments. Then there's the problem that he lives in the States...' She shook her head. 'I've done the right thing.' The words sounded as empty as she felt.

'He seemed to really like the children, though,' Cora said with a shake of her head.

'He's out tonight with another woman,' Laura said flatly.

'Pity, I was starting to think you might get married again.'

'Married?' Laura looked at her mother, shocked.

'Isn't that what you wanted?' Cora asked calmly.

'No.' Laura's eyes widened. 'I'll never get married again. I...just wanted a steady relationship.'

'In my day that was called marriage,' Cora said dryly.

Laura had waited all Monday morning for a glimpse of Rogan, but she didn't see him. Her disappointment was acute. She didn't know what she had expected today, but it wasn't his silence.

It was Paul who strolled into Laura's office early in the afternoon.

'Hello.' Laura looked up at him in surprise. 'I thought you were supposed to be taking things easy now that you're a director here.' Her voice was light and jovial.

'I can't keep away from you,' Paul murmured, but there was a return of the teasing glint in his eye and his good-natured grin. 'I'm not going to give up, you know, not until you tell me you'll come out for dinner.'

'Paul, I explained on Friday night—'

'Is this a meeting-house or a place of work?' The sarcastic voice cut across Laura's words, taking both of them by surprise.

Laura looked up and her temperature soared as she met Rogan's eyes. Of all the times for him to choose to come and see her... Why did he have to come now?

'Sorry, Rogan.' Paul turned, his manner one of easy charm. 'I was on my way up to Accounts with those figures we discussed the other day and I got waylaid. I just had to have a minute with Laura.'

'Really.' Rogan's tone was flat. 'Don't let me detain

you with those figures, then.' He nodded at the file Paul
had put down.

'No...right.' Paul flashed a rather puzzled look at
Laura. 'We'll arrange dinner later,' he said firmly, before
heading for the door.

Laura couldn't wait for Paul to go. She felt as if
Rogan's eyes were cutting into her. As the door closed,
the atmosphere in the office was electric.

'What can I do for you, Rogan?' she asked, her manner businesslike. She glanced down at the work on her
desk, pretending an indifference to him she just didn't
feel.

He didn't answer, and when the silence grew longer
she was forced to look up at him. He looked great, she
thought, her heart twisting. He was wearing a dark blue
suit, the white of his shirt contrasting with the darkness
of his hair and eyes. She was so much in love with him
that it hurt.

She looked away again at the drawing board in front
of her. She wondered if he had started an affair with that
woman he'd brought to the party on Friday night. All
weekend that notion had tormented her.

'Will you come and have lunch with me?' Rogan
asked suddenly.

She shook her head. 'I'm busy.' It took all her will-
power to turn down the invitation, all her stamina to be
able to look up at him again. 'Besides, we don't have
anything to say to each other, do we?'

His eyes moved contemplatively over her. 'You are
not in love with Paul James,' he told her decisively.

'What would you know about love?' Laura was stung
to retort sharply.

'Not much,' Rogan admitted, his tone suddenly gentle. 'I do know that marrying the wrong person can make
your life hell.'

'Who's talking about marriage?' Laura frowned.

'Robert James seems to have the idea that Paul is serious about you…that it will lead to marriage.'

'Really?' Laura's eyes widened at that. Then she shrugged. 'My mother had the same idea about us.'

She watched the look of surprise on his face and her lips twitched. 'Yes, the idea shocked me as well. Robert was wrong about Paul and I…and my mother certainly got it wrong. I have no interest in getting married again.'

The silence between them was very strained for a moment. Then Laura added, 'I will continue to see Paul, though.'

'But you won't continue your relationship with me,' Rogan said suddenly in a grating voice, raking a hand through his hair. 'Hell, Laura, I don't understand you. I mean, up to a few nights ago you were making love with me.'

'I beg your pardon?' She glared up at him.

'You heard what I said. You are running away.'

She shook her head. 'Now that's something you *do* know about.' Her voice dripped with sarcasm. 'You are so frightened of commitment that you almost run backwards when you hear the word. You talk about claustrophobic relationships when someone gets too close. Of no-strings affairs and casual sex.' All pretence at civility was thrown aside as her temper suddenly flared.

'I've never talked about casual sex,' he muttered furiously.

'No, you've just "practised" that one.' Laura's tone shook with anger. 'Well, I'm not like you, Rogan. I understand you, I even sympathise with the fact that you are determined not to get hurt again.' She started to gather up the papers on her desk. 'But you don't have a monopoly on being hurt.' She swept the papers into her briefcase. 'My husband was unfaithful to me. It caused me a lot of pain…but I haven't given up on relationships because of one bad experience.'

He stared at her and frowned. 'You never told me that before.'

'Some things are too painful to discuss. I was devastated, Rogan, when I found out. Apparently, he had been lying and cheating on me for years and, naïve fool that I was, I never guessed a thing. An experience like that makes you very, very careful about who you choose to give your heart to.'

For the first time in Rogan's life he was totally at a loss.

She stood. 'Now, if you'll excuse me, I've got an appointment with a client.'

'No, I won't excuse you.' He caught her arm as she made to walk past him. 'I want you to answer my question. Are you in love with Paul?'

Laura stared down at the hand on her arm. 'I'd be careful, Rogan. People will talk,' she murmured. 'Remember, people who work in glass towers shouldn't have affairs.'

'I don't give a toss who talks about what,' Rogan murmured huskily, all control gone. He pulled her closer.

The next moment she was in his arms.

'Stop it, Rogan.' Her heartbeat was out of control as she looked up at him.

'No.' He smiled suddenly as if everything in his mind was suddenly clear. 'I'm going to give this office block, this town, something to really talk about.'

She shook her head and put her hand on his shoulder to push him away.

Then he kissed her. The feeling was electric. Laura wanted to melt into his arms and never let go. Her lips met his with passion—and love.

When he let go of her she felt dazed, yet at the same time her body felt as if it were on fire.

'I don't want you to see Paul again,' Rogan murmured as he let go of her. 'I want you in my life, Laura.'

Laura stepped back from him. Her eyes moved from him through the glass walls to the rest of the office. She felt colour rising in her cheeks as she saw that everyone was watching them. As she watched, everyone stood up and started to clap. She couldn't hear it. It was like a mime—a charade, she thought angrily.

'Well, you've certainly succeeded in gaining everyone's attention,' she murmured unsteadily. Rogan looked around at the sea of faces and then grinned at her, unconcerned.

'You haven't answered me,' he said calmly.

'Well, it's quite simple. You have no right to tell me who I can and cannot see so your little piece of play-acting is of no consequence.'

'Come on, Laura, you don't really want to continue seeing Paul,' he said. 'You did it to make me jealous and it's worked. I want us to go back to the way we were—'

'I never go back.' Laura was furious now. Rogan's arrogant statement had incensed her…but she was even more angry with herself because she wanted him to kiss her again. 'Isn't that what you said to me in New York?'

'Yes but I wasn't talking about us. I—'

'You want me back because I'm the one who ended things between us, not because you're jealous,' Laura told him calmly.

For a moment he just stared at her. 'That's not true.'

'Yes, it is, hence this charade.' She gestured to indicate the office. 'You think you just have to click your fingers and you can have me back. But you can't, Rogan. I'm not playing games with you. I'm serious.'

'So am I,' Rogan said quietly.

'No, you're not,' she told him with barely concealed fury, 'otherwise you wouldn't have told me to go to that party on Friday with Paul, and you wouldn't have turned up with that…that bimbo.'

'What bimbo?' He shook his head.

'Jennifer something.'

'Oh, her! That was nothing.'

'Typical.' Laura nearly spat the word. 'The girl has my sympathy.'

The phone on the desk stared to ring but both of them ignored it. They were facing each other intently, oblivious to anything or anyone else.

'Laura, you don't understand—'

'I understand all too well. I ended our relationship on Friday night, Rogan, and I meant it.' Even as she said the words they caused a pain so deep it was almost unbearable.

The door opened and Sandra put her head around. 'I'm sorry,' she murmured apologetically as both protagonists glared at her, 'but there's an important phone call for you, Laura. It's the headmistress of the children's school.'

'What?' Laura immediately felt a wave of concern. 'Thank you, Sandra.'

She moved swiftly to pick up the receiver.

'Mrs Taylor?' The headmistress was brief. 'I'm sure it's nothing to be unduly alarmed about but I have to inform you that neither Matthew nor Joanne have returned from their lunch-break.'

'Where are they?' Laura didn't waste time on social niceties as panic rose. 'They've never skipped school before.'

'I've questioned a couple of their classmates and they said they saw the pair of them get onto a bus across the road from the school.'

Laura frowned. 'Do they know where they were going?'

'They don't seem to. I've still got them in my office and I shall question them further, but I thought you should know straight away.'

'Yes, thank you, Mrs Buckley. I'll come down to the school and see if I can find out what's happened.'

'What's wrong?' Rogan asked as she put the phone down.

She was silent for a moment as she tried to think, to get herself together. 'The children have gone missing.'

She met Rogan's eyes and was surprised and touched to see that he looked as worried as she felt.

'I'll have to go down to the school.' Her voice trembled a little. Suddenly all their arguments—everything—paled into insignificance in the worry of where the children could be.

'I'll drive you.'

For a moment Laura was going to refuse as she looked over at him.

'You're in no fit state to drive,' he said gently. 'Please let me take you.'

She nodded. She wanted him with her, she realised. She needed him.

## CHAPTER FOURTEEN

THE traffic was dense. Laura was grateful that Rogan was driving. She could never have negotiated this in the state she was in.

Her mind was in turmoil as she strove to think where her children could be.

'Calm down.' Rogan's gentle voice was soothing. 'We'll find them.' He sounded quietly confident. His strength made her feel better—added calm to the chaotic jumble of her mind.

'Do you think they might have gone to your mother?' he asked.

She shook her head. 'Mum was going into town to-day.'

'Was there anything upsetting the children...worrying them?'

Laura hesitated.

Rogan stopped the car at a set of traffic lights and looked over at her. 'Whatever it was, tell me,' he urged. 'It might be something important.'

'They were upset,' she admitted huskily.

Rogan reached across and took hold of her hand, squeezing it gently. 'What about?'

She took a deep breath. 'They were upset on Friday because I went to that party with Paul instead of you.'

Rogan swore under his breath.

'I...I thought I'd cheer them up and I took them to the theatre on Saturday, but they were both very quiet...dejected.'

'Didn't they like Paul?'

'Paul didn't come.' Laura shook her head impatiently.

'It was just the three of us—the three musketeers,' she murmured, tears shimmering in her eyes. 'God, if anything happens to them I'll never forgive myself, Rogan.'

'It isn't your fault.' Rogan squeezed her hand. 'If anyone is to blame I am.'

Laura heard the note of bitter self-recrimination in his voice and turned to look at him. 'It's not your fault,' she said. 'I tried to tell them that we were just friends...tried to explain.'

'What, that I'm a fool and I don't know happiness when it hits me in the face?' Rogan said bitterly. 'How can you explain the stupidity of an adult to the simplistic, innocent mind a child has?'

Laura's heart thundered in her chest. 'They couldn't understand why we weren't together on Friday. It was such a shock to them. I couldn't understand their anger. I mean, it's not as if we'd been dating for years.'

'They sensed the magic,' Rogan said simply.

Laura looked at him with a puzzled frown.

'Come on, Laura. We both felt it. The moment my eyes met yours it was there. I was in denial, but the children recognised it for what it was.'

Laura was silent, her mind racing.

'They say that children are more attuned than adults— that they have almost a sixth sense, you know.' Rogan looked across at her. 'They knew it was right...that feeling when the four of us were together.'

Still Laura said nothing.

'I felt it—didn't you?' he persisted. 'A feeling that this was right?'

Laura tried to think rationally. 'And that's why you brought Jennifer—whatever she was called—to the party on—'

'Laura, I was wrong. I knew when I was doing it that I was wrong. The children knew—'

'Rogan, the only thing I'm interested in right now is

getting my children back,' she said abruptly. 'If anything has happened—'

'Nothing is going to happen,' he said, his voice steady and confident. 'I want you to think about your conversation with them on Friday. Was there any hint of what they might be doing now in what they said?'

'No...' Laura shook her head. She could hardly think straight she was so worried. All she knew was that she loved her children and she didn't want them to be worried or unhappy about anything. 'Oh, Lord, what will I do if?'

'Laura.' Rogan's voice, cool and steady, cut across hers.

'Think about what they said—think.'

'They didn't say much.' She shook her head. 'Except...'

'Yes?'

'Well...' Laura hesitated. 'Joanne blamed Matthew for scaring you away.' She shrugged. 'It was ridiculous and I told them so. But both children had it in their heads that Matt's words to you when we returned from New York had scared you off.' Laura looked across at him. 'I told them it wasn't true.'

'Not in so many words.' Rogan's voice was grim. 'But I was scared of hurting them. I sensed...' He trailed off. 'Laura, I have an idea,' he said suddenly.

She looked over at him, hope flaring.

'It may be nothing but...'

Suddenly Rogan was changing lanes. He drove steadily and took a left turning.

'Where are we going? I—'

'It's a chance.' He glanced over at her. 'But we are close enough to check, without losing too much time.'

'Check what?' Her voice faded as she saw that they were now on the road towards his house. 'You think they might have decided they wanted to speak to you?'

'It's a long shot, but I feel we should check. They do know where my house is.'

She nodded.

'Maybe they just wanted to clear the air. See me and put their minds at rest.'

Laura's heart thudded unsteadily. She hoped and prayed he was right.

There was silence for a while as Rogan negotiated the narrow, winding coast roads. Laura's heart felt as if it might explode as they reached the turning for his drive. She prayed harder than she had ever prayed before.

As the drive turned she had a clear view of the Georgian house, bathed in the misty, mellow tones of the afternoon sunlight.

Nothing. The house seemed quiet. No child waited on the front step.

Rogan let his breath out in a sigh. 'I was nearly sure...'

Laura felt sick with disappointment.

He turned the car on the gravel drive and stopped. 'Let's just check,' he said quietly.

Together they got out of the car. As they walked around the side of the house they heard low voices.

Laura's heart leapt, then she wondered if she was imagining things because she wanted so much to find the children.

'It was your fault so you should tell him first,' a girl's voice was saying.

They rounded the corner and there, sitting on the back doorstep, were the children.

'Rogan!' They both stood up in surprise. Obviously they had been so busy arguing they hadn't heard the car.

'We weren't expecting you for a while...' Joanne's voice faltered as they saw their mother.

'I don't know whether to kill you or hug you to death,' Laura said shakily. Suddenly she was crying. 'How dare you worry me like this?'

'Oh, Mum!' They both ran to her when they saw her crying. 'We didn't mean to upset you…honestly. We thought we'd get the bus out here and talk to Rogan and he would drive us home before it got too dark. We were going to tell you and Grandma that we were delayed with detention—'

'Never…never do anything like this again. I was so worried…so worried.'

'We're sorry, we're really sorry,' Joanne said in a small, miserable voice when her mother wouldn't stop crying. She looked up at Rogan. 'We just wanted to see you. We didn't mean any harm.'

'I know.' Rogan nodded. 'But you've worried us both sick.' His voice was grim. 'Promise me you'll never do anything like this again.'

'We promise.' Matthew and Joanne spoke in unison, distressed by their mother's tears and Rogan's grave expression.

'OK.' Rogan reached to hug them both.

For a while all four of them stood in a group hug on the back doorstep. Then Rogan straightened.

'Now, then, Matt, Joanne, I think I know what you were going to say to me.'

They both looked up at him expectantly, their eyes shimmering with tears.

'Would you do me the honour of giving me and your mother a few minutes' privacy so we can talk?' he asked seriously.

They nodded and Rogan put an arm around Laura's shoulder. 'I just want one moment…please?' he said to her.

Laura looked up at him. She was so relieved she couldn't stop the tears that were flowing down her cheeks in silent witness of the horrors that had gone through her mind.

'Perhaps we can step inside,' Rogan said, getting out

a key to open the back door. 'Apart from anything else, you should ring the headmistress.'

Joanne and Matthew waited outside. They sat on the step, smiling shyly at Rogan as if they trusted him to put the whole matter back together.

It seemed a million years ago since Laura had been in that kitchen. She took deep breaths and tried to steady herself to make the call to Mrs Buckley.

'Laura.' Rogan's voice stopped her as she looked towards the telephone on the counter-top.

She looked at him questioningly.

'Before you make that call I want to talk to you.'

'Yes, but I should really—'

Rogan caught her hand. 'Laura, this won't wait another minute.'

She was turned to face him.

'I want to tell you something.'

She stared up at him silently.

'I love you,' he said simply.

For a moment she thought she was hearing things.

'I love you, and I've been a complete fool,' Rogan said again. 'Everything you said to me in the office was right. Since the break-up of my marriage I've been afraid of commitment—determined not to be hurt again—but you're right. I can't hide from my feelings and I can't give up on love. I never realised that before. I've never felt this depth of feeling before. I adore you, Laura... I need you.'

Laura swallowed the tears that wanted to flow afresh down her cheeks. She could hardly believe what she was hearing.

'The children were right in a way. I was alarmed by Matthew's statement the other day... I'm ashamed to admit it.' He shook his head. 'I was terrified that I'd hurt them. I sensed their vulnerability—your vulnerability. The sense of responsibility that assailed me took me completely by surprise. I'd never felt so seriously, so intensely, about anyone before—let alone one woman and two children.'

Laura's eyes misted.

'I couldn't believe it when you refused to see me again on Friday night at that party.' Rogan shook his head and took hold of her arms. 'Then when Robert intimated that you and Paul might be an item, might get married, his words had a profound effect. I wanted to grab you and march you out of there. I still don't know how I stopped myself.'

'Maybe something to do with that blonde bombshell you were with?' Laura ventured. 'She was extremely beautiful and, I'm sure, deeply comforting.' She couldn't help the note of sarcasm in her voice. The images she had been conjuring up all weekend of Rogan with that woman still hurt.

'Laura, I couldn't tell you the first thing about her except that her father was a business associate. I didn't arrive with her...and I didn't leave with her.'

'I don't believe you.' Laura stared at him.

'Have I ever lied to you?' he asked her calmly.

She didn't answer him for a moment, then admitted huskily, 'No.'

'Laura, I love you.' Rogan stared down at her. 'And I don't want to lose you. Everything you said to me today was true, except that I only want you because you called the whole thing off. That isn't true. What happened on Friday night just helped to focus my mind. I've never met anyone I've wanted to make a commitment to—until now.'

Laura stared at him. 'Don't say it if you don't mean it,' she said breathlessly.

'I do mean it, Laura.' Rogan touched her face, a kind of wonderment in his dark eyes. 'I love you. I think I have since I first set eyes on you. I tried to fight it, tried to tell myself you were not the wonderful person I kept thinking you were. I was almost actively looking for excuses to walk away.' He paused. 'But you are wonderful,' he said softly.

'Don't, Rogan.' She found herself crying again.

'Laura, please forgive the cavalier way I've carried on.' Rogan pulled her closer. 'I want you. I can't imagine life without you now.'

Laura let out her breath in a shuddering sigh. 'I love you, too. I think I have done since the first moment I saw you.'

For a while there was silence as they kissed. Laura poured her heart and soul into the sweetly passionate caress.

'And you aren't going to see Paul again?' Rogan asked as he pulled away from her.

'Oh, Rogan, there was never anything between Paul and I—you know that,' she said with a small laugh.

'No...I wasn't sure. Every damn time he comes to the office he goes straight to you. I wasn't having it today. I told the receptionists to tell me the moment he entered the building.'

Laura's lips curved in a smile of pure astonishment.

'So, what about it?' Rogan asked.

She looked up at him in dazed surprise.

'Will you marry me?' he asked huskily.

'Rogan!' She stared at him. 'I don't think I want to get married again.'

One dark eyebrow lifted at that. Then he smiled. 'We are both very similar, aren't we?' he said teasingly. 'Both scared to death of that great institution.'

Laura gave a tremulous smile. 'Wasn't it Mae West who said she wasn't ready for an institution just yet?'

'Please, Laura.' He said pleadingly. 'I love you, I love the children. I'll do my best for you all, I promise.'

Laura stared up at him. 'I don't know what to say,' she whispered, completely overwhelmed.

'Say yes.'

'Your sister isn't going to believe this.' She took a

deep, shuddering breath. 'Rogan, we are from different worlds. You live in America, I live here—'

'What's the small matter of a continent when you're in love?' Rogan grinned and pulled her into his arms.

For a while there was no conversation, just kisses so sweet that they both felt breathless. Then Rogan looked at her. 'When you told me today about your husband I felt I truly understood the shy uncertainty, the sweet vulnerability, I've seen so many times in your eyes. I knew and understood the feelings you generate in me. I'll try never to hurt you, Laura,' he said seriously. 'That's a promise. I only ever want to protect you.'

She smiled gently. 'That goes both ways,' she said shakily.

She looked into his eyes. 'I love you so much. I don't deserve to be this happy.'

'Believe me, you do.' He smiled. 'Now, what do you say? Shall we get married?'

'It's enough that you've asked me.' She shook her head. 'Now that I know you want me, that you love me, it's all I want.'

'But it's not all that I want.' Rogan tipped her face up so that her eyes met his. 'I want everything,' he said quietly. 'I want you, me and the children to be a real family.'

Her heart melted at those words. 'I want that, too,' she whispered...and outside the children moved away from the window and smiled at each other.

\* \* \*

*Kathryn Ross brings you boardroom seduction and unexpected pregnancy in* Kept by Her Greek Boss, *available next month in Mills & Boon® Modern˝.*

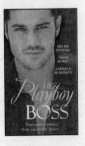

## THE ROYAL HOUSE OF KAREDES

*Two crowns, two islands, one legacy*

*Volume One*
**BILLIONAIRE PRINCE, PREGNANT MISTRESS**
by Sandra Marton

### Wanted for her body – and her baby!

Aspiring New York jewellery designer Maria Santo has come to Aristo to win a royal commission.

Cold, calculating and ruthless, Prince Xander Karedes beds Maria, thinking she's only sleeping with him to save her business.

So when Xander discovers Maria's pregnant, he assumes it's on purpose. What will it take for this billionaire prince to realise he's falling in love with his pregnant mistress…?

## Available 17th April 2009